PREACHER'S
INFERNO

THE FIRST MOUNTAIN MAN
PREACHER'S INFERNO

WILLIAM W. JOHNSTONE
AND J.A. JOHNSTONE

PINNACLE BOOKS
Kensington Publishing Corp.
www.kensingtonbooks.com

PINNACLE BOOKS are published by

Kensington Publishing Corp.
119 West 40th Street
New York, NY 10018

Copyright © 2022 by J. A. Johnstone

PUBLISHER'S NOTE
Following the death of William W. Johnstone, the Johnstone family is working with a carefully selected writer to organize and complete Mr. Johnstone's outlines and many unfinished manuscripts to create additional novels in all of his series like The Last Gunfighter, Mountain Man, and Eagles, among others. This novel was inspired by Mr. Johnstone's superb storytelling.

All Kensington titles, imprints, and distributed lines are available at special quantity discounts for bulk purchases for sales promotion, premiums, fund-raising, educational, or institutional use.

Special book excerpts or customized printings can also be created to fit specific needs. For details, write or phone the office of the Kensington Sales Manager: Attn.: Sales Department. Kensington Publishing Corp., 119 West 40th Street, New York, NY 10018. Phone: 1-800-221-2647.

PINNACLE BOOKS, the Pinnacle logo, and the WWJ steer head logo are Reg. U.S. Pat. & TM Off.

First Printing: January 2022
ISBN-13: 978-0-7860-4878-6
ISBN-13: 978-0-7860-4879-3 (eBook)

10 9 8 7 6 5 4 3 2 1

Printed in the United States of America

THE JENSEN FAMILY

FIRST FAMILY
OF THE AMERICAN FRONTIER

Smoke Jensen—*The Mountain Man.*
The youngest of three children and orphaned as a young boy, Smoke Jensen is considered one of the fastest draws in the West. His quest to tame the lawless West has become the stuff of legend. Smoke owns the Sugarloaf Ranch in Colorado. Married to Sally Jensen, father to Denise *"Denny,"* and Louis.

Preacher—*The First Mountain Man.*
Though not a blood relative, grizzled frontiersman Preacher became a father figure to the young Smoke Jensen, teaching him how to survive in the brutal, often deadly Rocky Mountains. Preacher fought the battles that forged his destiny. Armed with a long gun, he is as fierce as the land itself.

Matt Jensen—*The Last Mountain Man.*
Orphaned but taken in by Smoke Jensen, Matt Jensen has become like a younger brother to Smoke, and even took the Jensen name. And like Smoke, Matt has carved out his destiny on the American frontier. He lives by the gun and surrenders to no man.

Luke Jensen—*Bounty Hunter.*
Mountain Man Smoke Jensen's long-lost brother, Luke Jensen is scarred by war and a dead shot—the right skills to be a bounty hunter. And he's cunning and fierce enough to bring down the deadliest outlaws of his day.

Ace Jensen and Chance Jensen—*Those Jensen Boys!*
The untold story of Smoke Jensen's long-lost nephews, Ace and Chance, a pair of young-gun twins as reckless and wild as the frontier itself . . . Their father is Luke Jensen, thought killed in the Civil War. Their uncle Smoke Jensen is one of the fiercest gunfighters the West has ever known. It's no surprise that the inseparable Ace and Chance Jensen have a knack for taking risks—even if they have to blast their way out of them.

Denise "Denny" Jensen, and Louis Jensen—*The Jensen Brand.*
Denny and Louis are the adult children of Smoke and Sally Jensen. Denny is the wildcard tomboy, kept in line by the more level-headed Louis. The twins grew up mostly abroad, but never lost their love of the Sugarloaf Ranch, or lost sight of what it means to be a Jensen.

CHAPTER 1

For the moment, Preacher lay on his stomach in the brush without moving. That steady-as-a-rock motionlessness was the way he always prepared himself for a kill shot. He breathed slow and easy and stayed focused on his quarry. On this hillside looking down, he was just one more predator in the foothills of the Gros Ventre Range.

Gros Ventre was what the French called the Atsina Indians who lived in this region with the Shoshone, Crow, Bannock, and Blackfeet. French explorers had gotten the name wrong in the translation of the sign language they shared. The translation from French to English was *big belly*. Or maybe the French mapmakers had chosen the name deliberately because the Grand Tetons, north and west of the Gros Ventre Range, called *Les Trois Tétons*, translated into "the three nipples." And seeing them, especially from a distance, certainly brought those womanly attributes to a man's mind.

A small group of pronghorns fed among a copse of pine trees farther down the slope. The trees stood mostly straight and tall, angled back toward the foothills so the tips would find the morning sun, and they were dense enough that if a man didn't know what to look for, or how to look for it, he might miss the pronghorns grazing in the trees.

The spring and early summer had been good to the pronghorns. Water was still plentiful, and the grass was green and thick. In the winter, when the snow came, things wouldn't be so fine for them. The numbers they'd built up during the good months would work against them then. If herds carried too many members, they'd run the risk of starving when grass got hard to come by.

But for now, they were sleek and sassy and had plenty of meat on them. Pronghorn didn't think much past the here and now of things. A man who could hunt could eat well off a herd like that, and Preacher was one of the finest hunters to ever walk the mountains.

With their heads held high and proud, their round eyes watchful, and their ears pricked, the pronghorn bucks circled the herd, kept the does and the young clustered, and remained wary to potential threats. They kept their eyes moving and flicked their ears to track even the smallest sounds.

A small flock of white trumpeter swans flew over the trees, probably headed for the nearby Snake River. The adults had six-foot wingspans and made a lot of noise in passing. The pronghorns shied a little at the racket, and Preacher worried he was going to miss his opportunity if the herd bolted. The swans continued on their way, though, and after a moment, the pronghorns returned to grazing.

All their coats, brown from neck to hindquarters and white bellies and haunches, shined in the dappled sunlight that slid through the gently waving branches. The bucks had tall, thick antlers that hooked on the ends.

A man on foot without a firearm would have a hard

time handling a lone pronghorn. The bucks weighed more than a hundred pounds, and a few of them looked like they'd go as much as a hundred and fifty pounds. And there wasn't much quit in one of them when defending the herd.

Watching the beautiful creatures made Preacher's heart sing, though he wouldn't have told many people that, and never anyone who wasn't a mountain man like him. Only a true man who made his life under the wide-open sky could have understood what stirred his soul while he studied the pronghorns.

It wasn't just the prospect of good meat that put a smile on Preacher's rugged, bearded face. Mostly, he was just grateful to be back home in the mountains. It was where he belonged, and of late he'd been traipsing far from his customary neck of the woods. His travels had taken him away from the mountains for months.

He studied the herd like a man reading a menu in a fancy restaurant in New Orleans. He wanted a buck that was strong and healthy, one that had plenty of meat on it.

The mountain man wasn't planning on just eating good himself today. He was going to pack out meat to friends that he was looking forward to seeing again. When visiting, he wasn't a man to come to the table empty-handed. By this time tomorrow, he planned on being at the mountain man rendezvous near Jackson's Hole.

Anticipation filled him at the thought of seeing old acquaintances. He hadn't seen some of them in years, and he was sure there would be sad news of those who had died during the time he'd been gone. A mountain man's life was hard and filled with the dangers of Indians, bears, snakes, catamounts, bad falls, and loose rock during the spring melts.

And that was if the winter didn't take a man with the

freezing cold or sickness. He hadn't been to a rendezvous yet where someone hadn't been lost to one thing or another.

Lord help him, Preacher looked forward to being back in the mountains for winter with snowdrifts so high they covered anything that would have looked fetching to a civilized person.

He liked seeing new things every now and again, which was one of the reasons he enjoyed his trips to St. Louis to sell his furs. He got to see some of that burgeoning civilization that was casting greedy eyes out West. He usually didn't like what he saw, all those people planning on rolling on west to the Pacific Coast and the free land there. He'd taken note of the goings-on so he could be wary of those people, most of them with their own agendas, and he'd realized again why he loved the mountains so.

While he was in St. Louis, he could sit in Red Mike's and meet with other men like himself who lived by their wits, the strength of their backs, and the keenness of their eyes. They could swap lies in fun and jest, and they could tell stories about the things they'd seen and done that might interest a curious man or a fiddlefooted one.

Preacher knew himself to be guilty on both counts.

Those stories that got exchanged, though, were important because they painted oral maps of places, people, and things a mountain man would find useful while exploring new places. Or even places he hadn't visited in a while.

Things were changing in the mountains and it was all Preacher could do to keep up with it.

St. Louis was a hardscrabble city that was showing growth pains, and Preacher's latest trip there, after a nasty bit of business, had taken him south along the great river. New Orleans had proven cold, secretive, and downright deceitful if Preacher had to be blunt about it. He'd sailed as a prisoner on a pirate ship before making his escape and arranging his return to the city to wreak vengeance on those who had wronged him.

Even Texas and Nuevo Mexico, which he'd only just returned from, were getting too neighborly with civilized ways, and a large slice of treachery. At least out in the mountains a man knew mostly what he could expect from others whose trails crossed his own. Most folks, peaceable and those who would take advantage of others, stayed out of the high country. Places down south were a confluence of opposing forces that changed sides quickly.

Preacher had longed for the mountains and the solitude.

"Lord, I have missed this place," Preacher whispered out loud and surprised himself. As a hunter, he knew better than to go talking to himself while he was hunting.

The pronghorns continued their grazing, never knowing he was only a short distance away.

Dog shifted a little next to the mountain man. The big cur looked like a gray wolf and had often been mistaken for one. His wise eyes were focused solely on the pronghorns. His pink tongue lolled, and his ears twitched. He shifted his attention to Preacher and whined a little.

"Easy, boy," Preacher said softly to his trail companion. "I can taste them steaks, too. We'll have all we want right shortly."

Deftly, Preacher eased up his rifle from his side, pulled the butt to his shoulder all while keeping the barrel low in the grass and making no disturbance. He laid his sights over a proud buck eighty yards away.

The pronghorn was full grown, muscular, and wary. The shot would be an easy one to make even at the distance, but Preacher wanted to be sure of the kill. Tracking a wounded animal would be simple enough for him even in the ragged tree line that ran though the foothills, but he didn't want the pronghorn to suffer.

Preacher aimed a few inches behind the buck's front leg, where the heart would be, and gently eared back the rifle's hammer. The click of the flintlock didn't travel far, and the distance would put the sound late to the pronghorns' ears if it did reach them because he didn't plan on wasting any time.

Totally focused, Preacher slid his finger over the trigger, let out half a breath, and squeezed the trigger just as the pronghorn's head came up sharply and its ears flicked toward the mountain man.

The rifle bucked against Preacher's shoulder. The ball caught the pronghorn right where he'd aimed, and the buck stutter-stepped and went down in a loose sprawl on the other side of the spreading, gray cloud of powder smoke unleashed by the rifle.

With the sharp report of the rifle echoing around them, the pronghorn herd broke cover and ran for the high and uncut in a rippling, bounding mass. The other bucks circled them and headed them to safety farther down the foothills.

When Preacher thought about the way the pronghorn buck had gazed in his direction, an uneasy feeling touched him. He was certain any sound he might have made had gone unheard—until he'd fired the rifle.

That meant the buck had *seen* something that caught his attention, and that something was *behind* Preacher. An itch dawned between Preacher's shoulder blades, and he recognized that feeling.

He wasn't alone on the hillside.

Dog growled and his hackles grew stiff. His big, wedge-shaped head swung to the left, away from Preacher. At the same time, the rustle of someone moving in the brush in that direction reached Preacher's ears.

"You ain't been payin' proper attention, old son," Preacher said to himself.

Despite his focus on the pronghorns, the mountain man knew he wasn't an easy individual to sneak up on. Whoever was out there was good. Dog hadn't marked them, either, and the big cur was canny in the mountains.

Preacher let the rifle lay because he had no time to reload it. He reached for one of the flintlock pistols he carried tucked into his belt at his back. By the time he worked the weapon free, Dog nipped his arm hard enough to pinch even through Preacher's buckskin shirt sleeve.

Taking the big cur's warning, the mountain man rolled to his left, and Dog darted through the brush on his belly and stayed low. Two arrows fletched with turkey feathers thudded into the ground where Preacher had been. Judging from the angle, they'd come from farther up in the foothills. Preacher had approached downwind of the pronghorns, so he hadn't smelled whoever was hunting him because whoever it was had been downwind from him.

Another arrow cut the air over the mountain man's head.

On his back a few feet from his original position but still somewhat covered by brush, Preacher looked farther up the foothills and spotted movement. At least three Indians converged on the mountain man's position from sixty feet away. All of them wore paint and buckskins that allowed them to blend somewhat with the trees around them.

When they saw that he was aware of them, they discarded any notion of slipping up on him quiet-like and came faster down the slope. They stayed behind cover where they could find it, and there was plenty of it.

Preacher rolled to his feet and came up with the pistol in his hand. He cocked the weapon and aimed at the closest warrior, then squeezed the trigger as the man darted out from behind a tree. Packed with a double-shotted load, two .45-caliber balls instead of one, the pistol kicked in Preacher's hand and powder smoke obscured the tree line.

Struck by the pistol balls, his chest bleeding from two wounds that stained his buckskin shirt, the warrior cried out in pain and dropped in mid-run.

Preacher thought the Indians were probably Blackfoot warriors. Those bands traipsed through the mountains, too, and attacked wagon trains headed toward the Pacific coastline. They considered mountain men to be their mortal enemies . . . and they had a deep and abiding hatred for the one called Preacher.

Unwilling to leave the rifle, especially now that he knew who he was up against, and where at least some of his attackers were, Preacher ran back for it. The pistols were good out to fifty feet, sometimes more, but a rifle made a man who could use one a whole lot more dangerous because of the increased range.

Of course, range wasn't going to remain a factor for long. Buckskin-clad shadows darted through the trees toward him and loosed arrows as they came.

A half-dozen more shafts pierced the air around Preacher.

When he reached the rifle, he bent down briefly without breaking stride to pluck it from the ground and headed for a thick spruce. The low-hanging branches would offer some defense from arrows, but they would also limit his view. A battle always involved trade-offs.

Especially one where he was outnumbered.

"Dog," Preacher called.

The big cur sprang out of the brush and ran at the mountain man's heels. When they reached the tree, Dog moved impatiently, darted from side to side around the tree, and checked on all fronts for enemies. The hair on the back of his neck stood up, and a deep growl came from his throat. He was eager to rip some throats out.

"Watch," Preacher ordered. "Stay with me."

Dog answered with a soft, impatient bark.

"Things have already gotten a mite interestin', and we're gonna step up the tune those braves called."

Preacher had seen three Indians. He'd shot one of them, maybe even killed him, but until he saw the body himself and knew the Indian was dead, he wasn't going to count him out. The mountain man didn't know how many more Blackfeet were out there, but if the number of arrows that had whipped through the air was any indication, it was more than three.

He had another flintlock pistol loaded and ready behind his belt, and he wore two of the Colt Paterson revolvers he'd been given by the rangers he'd run into while down in the Republic of Texas. The Patersons rode in holsters made for them. He had two more of the new ree-volving pistols in his saddlebags, but his saddlebags were with Horse and his pack animals, all of them too far away to help now.

Calmly and coolly, because that was the only way to deal with the situation he was in, Preacher dropped the rifle butt-first on the ground and took a cartridge from his possibles bag. He tore the cartridge open with his teeth, poured the powder into the barrel, and dropped a .45-caliber ball in afterward. He freed the ramrod from the rings under the barrel, shoved the ramrod into the muzzle to set the ball properly, and put it back under the barrel.

He kept an eye on Dog because the cur's ears were sharper than his own. He poured powder from his horn into the rifle's lock and eared the hammer back. Working quickly, he loaded the empty pistol, too, and tucked it back behind his belt.

The Colt Patersons held five rounds each and he carried them with the hammers resting safely between cylinders to prevent an accidental discharge. He had extra loaded cylinders for the Patersons in his possibles bag, but it would take time to swap them out. That was time he was sure the Blackfeet swarming around him wouldn't give him.

He saved the revolvers for the moment because the .36-caliber balls loaded in those were smaller than the .45-caliber loads in the flintlock pistols, especially since they were double-shotted. The Patersons had less knockdown power, but that was an acceptable trade-off considering their other capabilities.

Thirteen rounds and he'd be down to the tomahawk and big hunting knife he carried. Preacher intended on making as many of those rounds count as he could.

"Ghost Killer!" a deep-voiced man bellowed in the Blackfoot tongue. "I see you!"

Ghost Killer was a name the Blackfoot tribes had given Preacher. For a time, he'd declared war on them and made a habit of slipping into their camps in the dead of night and slaying warriors with his knife or tomahawk. There was no love lost between Preacher and the Blackfeet, and there never would be.

"You're lyin'," the mountain man bellowed back. "You want to know how I know?"

There was no answer.

Dog shifted at Preacher's feet and his attention was torn on both sides of the tree.

"I know you're lyin' about seein' me," Preacher said, "because if you could see me, *I* could see *you* and you'd be dead."

An arrow skimmed off the tree and shredded bark that fell over Preacher. Another thudded into the tree and stood out like a marker tracking back to the archer. Two more arrows missed the tree, hit the ground, and skidded through the brush.

Marking the direction of the embedded arrow and trusting it to be a signpost, Preacher whirled around the tree and tucked the rifle to his shoulder. He studied the woods over the rifle's sights, spotted a Blackfoot warrior nocking a fresh arrow to his bow at the side of a tree seventy feet away in the shadow of a towering pine, and centered his aim in the middle of his opponent's face. He squeezed the trigger.

When the ball struck the archer, he dropped his bow and fell backward, then the powder smoke haze blocked Preacher's vision and marked his position under the spruce.

CHAPTER 2

Knowing he needed to take the fight to his attackers because staying in one place would allow them to surround him, the mountain man slung the rifle over his shoulder and drew his two flintlock pistols. He'd reload the rifle if he got the chance, but for now he had to get moving. The powder smoke would draw his attackers. Hunkering down in one place wasn't going to work. With him moving, the warriors hunting him would have to move, and that would reveal them to him.

"Dog," Preacher growled and set himself, "hunt!"

The big cur launched himself from hiding around the other side of the tree. Dog hunted by smell, and he'd warred against the Blackfeet enough to know their scent. Even upwind of the Indians, the cur had probably sniffed them out and been alerted to their presence. That was what he'd warned Preacher about.

Pistols in his hands, Preacher followed a half-step behind his trail companion. Running hard, the mountain man stayed bent over to offer a smaller target for his enemies.

Arrows whipped through the branches overhead and pierced the brush around Preacher. He drove himself forward with the pistols in his hands and his arms raised to protect his face from the branches that clawed at him.

Two Blackfoot warriors stepped out from behind a lightning-blasted lodgepole pine. One of them had a rifle and the other raised his bow with an arrow nocked back. He released the bowstring, and his companion eared back the rifle's hammer.

Preacher twisted and dodged, and the turkey feather arrow fletching brushed his right cheek and ear as the shaft sped by. The warrior with the rifle stood a little behind and to the side of the archer. He stood steady and pulled the rifle to his shoulder.

Raising the pistol in his right hand, Preacher shot the Indian with the rifle in the chest before the warrior pulled the rifle trigger. The stricken Blackfoot fell backward and took the unfired rifle with him. Preacher trusted Dog to take the other warrior.

Without a sound, Dog covered the distance to the Indians in the blink of an eye. The cur sprang up and sank his fangs into the archer's groin. The Blackfoot warrior cried out fearfully and in pain. Heavy and muscled, and traveling at nearly full speed, Dog took the man down and landed on top of him.

Trusting his old friend to deal with the Blackfoot warrior he'd knocked down, and knowing other Indians would come running, Preacher quickly knelt beside the warrior he'd shot, laid his pistols on the ground, and picked up the rifle the man had dropped.

The weapon was clean and looked new. Most rifles captured by Indians weren't as well-cared-for as this one. He tapped the butt against the ground to make sure the ball in the muzzle was still more or less in place, then he brought the weapon up to his shoulder and scoured the trees.

A Blackfoot warrior slipped out around a white-barked aspen less than thirty feet away and bent his bow. He kept a low profile so not much of him showed.

Preacher aimed on the fly, squeezed the trigger, and hoped the rifle's sights were fairly true. The ball shattered the bow and deflected off-center, but still tore out the Indian's throat in passing. He dropped his ruined bow and grabbed for his neck. Blood gushed between his fingers as he stumbled away. The arrow struck the ground well short of Preacher.

Only a short distance away, Dog tore at the Indian's groin he'd chomped his jaws on. The Blackfoot wailed in agony and tried to hammer the cur with his fists. He finally thought to grab the knife sheathed at his waist. As he drew the blade, Dog released his hold on the man's groin and lunged up his prey's body to sink his fangs into the Blackfoot's throat. Before the Indian could thrust his knife home, the cur ripped his throat out, then caught the wrist of the arm wielding the knife.

In the time that took, Preacher barely had time to drop the spent rifle and pick up his pistols. Muzzle dripping red with the blood of his vanquished foe, Dog looked up at the mountain man.

"Good job, old son," Preacher said, "but we ain't out of the woods yet. There's more of 'em here. Let's get this finished quick before they get a chance to regroup. Hunt!"

Dog scented the air and loped off.

Preacher thrust his spent pistol behind his back and drew one of the Colt Patersons. On the move, trailing only a few feet after the cur, the mountain man eared back the revolver's hammer. He doubted any of the Blackfeet in the forest with him had seen a repeating pistol.

"Ghost Killer!" the first Blackfoot warrior called again. "Are you going to continue to hide from me?"

Preacher tracked the voice. It came from deeper in the woods ahead of him.

"Dog," the mountain man called softly. "Heel."

The big cur joined Preacher and together they headed farther up the incline. Having the high ground would give him an edge, but it also took away valuable running room if he had to retreat. The Blackfoot warriors could surround and corral him.

The trees and brush were tightly packed. With a practiced eye, Preacher cut through the wilderness and fetched up against a large wedge of rock sticking out of the hillside. He listened intently and reloaded the rifle and pistol.

He considered his options. Horse and the pack animals lay in the other direction, away from where the Blackfeet had settled in. They'd probably cut his trail from the south and come on expecting to catch only a couple of white men. He might be able to reach Horse and ride off, but that would leave the Blackfeet trailing him.

He didn't much care for the idea of leaving enemies behind him, and he wasn't one to cut and run on a fight, either. Especially a fight he didn't start.

He grinned despite the situation. He was more at home here fighting Blackfeet in the mountains than he'd been battling pirates at sea or even Comanche warriors in Texas. He was home, and fighting for his life was just part of that.

Weapons ready once more, Preacher put his back to the rock and looked down the incline. In the distance, the Snake River glimmered silver where it threaded through the trees.

"Preacher!" a man called out hoarsely. "Get yourself gone! I'm done for! You can't help me!"

The voice was familiar, but before Preacher had the chance to run it through his mind again, an agonized scream echoed through the trees.

The mountain man took an even breath and kept his mind clear. Going off half-cocked wasn't going to do anyone any good.

"Come down here and face me, Ghost Killer," the Blackfoot warrior commanded in his tongue. "Do it or this man will die."

"He's gonna die anyway," Preacher replied in English, because he figured that would aggravate the Indian doing all the talking, and an aggravated man didn't always think straight.

"If you don't come out, I will kill him slowly. You will listen to his screams. I can let a man live in pain for hours. I have done it before."

Preacher hoisted himself up onto the rock, clambered over to the left, and looked for a spot where he could see through the trees. He continued shifting his position slowly. Dog trailed at his heels.

"He's a white man. If you don't come out, I will kill him slowly. You will listen to his screams."

"I've heard men die screamin' before," Preacher said. "Fact is, you're liable to die screamin' yourself. I'm a tolerable man most days, but you've dealt yourself into this, and I'm not lettin' go. I'm gonna kill you."

The prisoner laughed. "You tell him, Preacher! I told ol' Silent Owl this wouldn't go like he thought! I told him these twelve braves he has ridin' with him wouldn't be enough to get the job done!"

The man screamed again.

"Open your mouth again," the Blackfoot warrior promised, "and I will kill you."

"Go ahead an' kill me," the man urged. "It's my own damn fault I was hungover an' you snuck up on me this mornin'. I'd have been sober—"

He yelled in pain once more.

Preacher grinned coldly. If the prisoner lived through the situation, the mountain man silently promised he'd stand the man to a drink as soon as they found some whiskey. Thanks to the man's words, he now knew how many Blackfeet he was up against. He and Dog had killed four Indians. That left eight, plus the man leading the war party.

"Ghost Killer, I am going to cut this man's nose off, then his ears," Silent Owl threatened. "Then I will feed them to you before I kill you."

"I don't know you, Silent Owl," Preacher said.

"You killed my wife's father. He was named Runs with Fox."

"I don't recollect meetin' him." Over his years in the mountains, Preacher had killed a lot of Blackfeet, and other Indians, too, when he had no other choice. "Don't have much time for swappin' how-do-you-dos in the middle of a fracas. If you hadn't been introduced to me, likely I wouldn't know your name before I killed you, either."

When he reached a spot that allowed him a narrow view of the small clearing where the Blackfeet had camped overnight, Preacher paused and studied the layout. He counted six of the Indians scattered around the site, so the others were likely in the brush.

That could be a problem. If they found him, and they

would because he'd been talking, he'd have to kill them, and that might prod Silent Owl into carrying out his threats against his prisoner.

All the Blackfeet had bows and spears, but some of them carried rifles, too. Preacher suspected the firearms were bounty taken from other white men the warriors had met and killed. With the rendezvous on, mountain men would be drawn to Jackson's Hole, and they would be traveling in small groups.

Or by themselves like the man Silent Owl and his warriors had captured.

The prisoner knelt on the ground with his hands bound behind him. His broad, bearded face was bloody and bruised. He wore buckskins and well-worn knee-high moccasins. His reddish-gray hair was long and shaggy and matched the beard that hung to his chest.

Either Silent Owl planned on taking the hapless man back to meet with other Blackfoot bands for sport, or he'd figured on providing entertainment later for his own warriors.

One of the Blackfeet was tall and lean. His thick black hair hung past his shoulders and sported three eagle feathers. His buckskins showed dirt and old blood and wear. His youthful features looked arrogant and cruel. Sometime in the past, an enemy had taken a swipe at him with a blade and left a scar from his left temple to his jaw.

He drew a long knife from his hip and strode toward the prisoner. "I've waited too long, Ghost Killer! I'll hamstring this man and come up into the woods to get you!"

"Gonna stick me again?" the prisoner demanded. "If I

wasn't tied up, I'd rip your arm off an' beat you to death with it."

For a moment Preacher had the Indian in his sights. The distance wasn't much more than a hundred feet. It would be an easy shot—unless the gentle wind that stirred the trees shoved a branch in front of the ball and deflected it. That would scatter the Blackfeet and they could dog the mountain man all the way to the rendezvous.

On top of that, leaving them alive would mean not dressing out the pronghorn Preacher had shot. He didn't like the idea of letting all that good meat go to waste, and he didn't cotton to the idea of letting the prisoner die, either.

"Hold up!" Preacher yelled. "I'm coming down!"

Silent Owl, if that was his name, froze in his tracks with the knife a few inches from the prisoner's face.

"Preacher!" the bloody man bellowed. "You stay outta this! This ain't none of your business! This here's between him an' me!"

"I wouldn't begrudge a man a fight," Preacher said, "but looks to me like you've got enough to go around."

Despite his desperate circumstance, the prisoner grinned.

Silent Owl peered around. He pointed to one of his warriors and the Indian quickly took up a position behind the prisoner. The warrior wrapped his left arm around the prisoner's head and bent it back to expose his throat, then he laid the keen edge of a hunting knife against the prisoner's skin hard enough to draw blood.

"Come face me, Ghost Killer!" Silent Owl entreated. "If you do not, my warrior will kill this man!"

Preacher didn't take any chances. He stepped down the hillside without making a sound and circled around the clearing so he could see part of what was behind the

Blackfeet. According to his count, three of the Indians were still in the brush.

Dog moved as silent as a shadow behind him. The cur's hackles were lifted, and the mountain man slid a hand over his trail partner's head.

"Wait," Preacher whispered.

The Blackfeet left their ponies tied in a loose circle to the east of the clearing. With the morning sun just peeping through the trees, the light would be against the Indians and in his favor.

A young Blackfoot warrior knelt with his bow across his thighs and an arrow nocked to his string. He kept watch over the horses, but the events unfolding in the clearing in front of him held most of his attention. He never saw Preacher come up behind him.

Quiet as the fuzz on a dandelion blowing free, the mountain man slipped the rifle over his shoulder and drew his smaller knife from a sheath inside his high-topped right moccasin. He eased up behind the Indian, drove the blade into his head at the base of his skull, and caught the dead man's slack weight before it hit the ground or startled the horses. They nickered gently but continued grazing.

Preacher laid the corpse on the ground, pulled his knife free, and wiped the blade on the dead Indian's buckskins. He returned the knife to his moccasin and drew the flint-lock pistols from behind his belt.

He told Dog, "Stay," and stepped into the clearing.

"Ghost Killer!" Silent Owl yelled. He faced the direction from which Preacher had spoken to him.

The mountain man's senses sharpened, and he readied himself for whatever might happen. He trained both the pistols on Silent Owl and wondered again if he shouldn't just kill the Indian and be done with it.

That would get the prisoner killed, though, more than likely, and the mountain man hated to see a man with sand go down without a chance. No matter how slim it was.

"I'm here," Preacher said in the Blackfoot tongue. He watched the Indian holding the prisoner.

Silent Owl turned quickly. Surprise widened his eyes. Things hadn't gone the way he'd thought they would. He almost brought up the rifle he held, then he took stock of the two pistols pointed at him. The muzzles never wavered. He raised his free hand and held his braves in check.

"Stay," he commanded.

They stayed, but they shifted and moved around so they would have an open shot at the mountain man with their bows and rifles. Twenty feet separated Preacher from the Blackfoot warriors. He was cutting things mighty close. Maybe too close. But it was too late. He'd already jumped in with both feet.

"I will have the prisoner killed," Silent Owl threatened.

"If you kill that prisoner," Preacher said, "the deal's off. I'll kill you where you stand. You'll never get to avenge your wife's father."

"Preacher," the prisoner roared, "I never heard no stories about you bein' a damn fool!"

The mountain man grinned, but he kept watching the Blackfoot warriors in front of him. "Well, then, you probably ain't heard all the stories."

"I've heard more'n a few."

"Maybe you'll get to tell one yourself." Preacher looked at Silent Owl. "How about it, Silent Owl? Do you want a shot at killin' me for killin' Runs with Fox? Me and you? Winner take all? Or do you like your chances better with your men helpin' you?"

CHAPTER 3

A slow smile spread over Silent Owl's face and pulled at the long scar. "I'm young and strong, Ghost Killer. I have killed several men. You are old, and winter touches your beard and hair. I can kill you."

"Maybe so," Preacher said, "but you ain't killed me yet. Nobody has. I earned this winter in my hair."

"You will die today."

"We'll see." Preacher made his words into a challenge. "Do I have your word that you and I will fight? Nobody else?"

Silent Owl smiled again. "Yes."

"You can't trust an Injun!" the prisoner shouted.

The Blackfoot warrior holding the man slammed his knife hilt against the man's head. The prisoner moaned and slumped forward.

Preacher ignored the man and nodded at Silent Owl. "Tell your warriors that *when* I kill you, they're to let me and this man ride out of here."

Silent Owl considered that for a moment, then he nodded. "It will be as you say." He raised his voice. "This is my fight. I will lift Ghost Killer's hair and hang it from my tipi." He looked at Preacher. "We fight with knife and tomahawk."

"Sure." Preacher marked the positions of the Blackfeet. There were two still unaccounted for, and once he opened the ball, things were going to happen quick.

"Lay your pistols down," Silent Owl ordered.

Moving carefully, Preacher placed the flintlock pistols on the ground.

"And the rifle."

The mountain man removed that as well and laid it beside the pistols.

"He still has pistols," the warrior holding the prisoner warned.

"I do," Preacher said. The air around him seemed a little more pure, fresh, and clean just the way he remembered it. He was home. He'd never felt more sure of that since his return.

"Get rid of them," Silent Owl ordered. "Then we fight."

"You know," Preacher said, "I've been thinking about that. Your prisoner is right. I don't much trust you. I figure as soon as you have me unarmed, you'll likely order your men to kill me."

Silent Owl grinned. "There is no honor in white men. I don't need to show you any honor. And now your hands are empty. You are defenseless. I will avenge my wife's father."

He raised the rifle and pointed it in Preacher's direction.

The mountain man filled his hands with the Colt Patersons and threw himself to the side. He rolled on a shoulder and came up in a kneeling position with the revolvers in his hands. The pistols had no sights, so he aimed and fired by instinct.

His first round from the right-hand pistol smashed into the face of the Indian with his blade to the prisoner's throat. His second round, fired from the pistol in his left hand, split the air where Silent Owl had been. The young warrior proved himself intolerably quick.

Preacher fired the gun in his left hand again and caught Silent Owl in the chest above the rifle he was aiming. The Indian hadn't bothered moving again, probably because he believed the mountain man's weapons were empty. Most likely, none of these Blackfeet had ever seen a revolving pistol. The weapons were seldom seen. Until his trip to Texas, the mountain man had never seen them, either, though he had heard stories about them.

Powder smoke hung thickly in the air. Silent Owl fought to stay on his feet and raise the rifle, but his split heart quit on him, and he toppled to the ground.

Two shots from the pistol in Preacher's right hand accounted for two more Blackfeet archers while they rushed to nock fresh arrows to their bows. The archers were more dangerous than the Indians with rifles because bows could be used again more quickly than a rifle could be reloaded.

A flash of brown fur passed on Preacher's right and he held his shot. Dog sprinted and covered the space between himself and one of the Blackfeet. Faced with Dog, the Indian turned and ran, but the big cur leaped onto the Blackfoot's back. Dog's weight and speed drove the warrior to the ground, and he cried out in mortal terror until Dog's teeth closed on his throat.

Preacher stood and stepped through the gray haze created by the pistols. He eared the hammers back on both Patersons with his thumbs. The last two Indians in the clearing had rifles they'd successfully reloaded. They tried to back away and cock the weapons. The mountain man put one ball into each Indian, in one's face and in the throat of the second, which emptied the pistol in his right hand.

Movement to his left caught his attention. Through the trees on the edge of the clearing, a Blackfoot warrior loosed an arrow at Preacher. The mountain man shifted sideways. The arrow struck his left thigh a glancing blow, but the toughened rawhide turned away the sharp flint point.

Preacher fired the two remaining balls into the archer's chest. He holstered both the Patersons and picked up his flintlock pistols from the ground. He was certain he'd accounted for all the Indians.

Dog let go of the Indian he'd killed and walked over to join Preacher.

"Good Lord," the prisoner rasped hoarsely from where he lay with a corpse draped over him. "Are you through shootin'?"

"I'm all out of varmints to shoot," Preacher answered.

"This ain't but nine of them. Ten, countin' Silent Owl." The man looked around worriedly. "There's three more."

Preacher appreciated that the man had kept his wits about him during the free-for-all. "Got those three earlier. If you didn't miss your count—"

"I didn't."

"—then they're all dead." Preacher shoved his flintlock pistols behind his belt and slung his rifle over his shoulder. "Let's get out of here."

The mountain man drew his small knife from his moccasin. He cut the rope binding the man's wrists. He walked a short distance away and picked up one of the rifles the Indians had dropped. Like the one he'd commandeered earlier, this one looked new.

That was mighty interesting. It was also still loaded.

The thing that caught his attention the most was the small triangle burned into the rifle's buttstock.

The prisoner rubbed fiercely at his wrists, probably to restore feeling to his hands. "I'm mighty obliged, Preacher. Thought I was a goner for sure." The man stuck out a bloody, scraped hand. Rope burns showed around his wrists.

Preacher stepped back and took the man's hand for a moment. He still had a lot of strength in his grip, and that fact cheered the mountain man. The prisoner was a big man, and Preacher hadn't been looking forward to having to pack him out.

"The name's Joe Len Darby." The man knelt and took up one of the rifles dropped by the Indians. He checked the lock, blew dust out of it, and recovered a leather pouch from one of the corpses. After a quick search, he smiled, took out a cartridge, and loaded the weapon. "I've been trappin' around these parts for years. Heard a lot about you. Seems like we passed by an' missed each other ever' now an' then."

The man's name sounded familiar to Preacher, but he couldn't tie any stories to it. He knew a lot of the older trappers, but not all of them. Though many of them knew who he was.

"Can you walk?" Preacher asked.

"Since I was knee-high to a grasshopper." Joe grinned.

"How bad are you hurt?"

"You'll have to tell me. I went to sleep drunk last night an' ain't quite sober yet." Joe rubbed at his injured face. "I probably feel better right now than I should. That Indian plumb went to town on me."

"You ain't leakin' too bad," Preacher said. "Before we

rest, we might want to put some miles in between us and this spot."

"Well, I'm all for that."

"Help me pick up the other rifles these Blackfeet dropped. I ain't one to let a weapon go to waste, and I damn sure don't want to leave 'em for other Indians to pick up. This looks like it was a scoutin' party. Probably be more of 'em along soon enough."

Preacher told Dog to "Watch," and set to gathering the rifles, powder, and shot. The big cur strode into the woods and vanished. If Dog found anyone, he'd come running.

"You look like you're pretty well supplied, Preacher," Joe Len Darby said. "You ain't got any who-hit-John loaded in them panniers on them packhorses, do you?"

"I don't," Preacher replied.

On his return to the mountains, he'd wanted to remain sharp and watchful. To really know the rough country around him, a man had to give respect and stay in it regular. The mountains held a million ways for a man to die.

"Sure could use a drink right about now," Joe lamented. "I think I'm soberin' up too fast. It's been my experience that happens at the worst times. Middle of the night when there's not another drink to be had. In the middle of a fight with a woman, an' that's no place to be sober. An' in the tooth-yanker's chair. Yes, sir, I'd have to say that last one is the worst time to be sober." He shifted in the saddle. "Wounds are nettlin' me something fierce."

Joe took a breath in and let it out. He rode easy in the saddle on his own horse behind the pack animals. He'd claimed his own rifle from those that he and Preacher had picked up from the Indians. The weapon rested across his saddle pommel, and the way it moved around had raised considerable concern in Preacher.

"I'll be fine, though," Joe went on. He sleeved his forehead and worked the cud of tobacco he'd started on. "You don't got to fret none about me. I been through worse than this an' come out whistlin'."

Preacher glanced back at his new companion. The man was a talker and evidently loved the sound of his own voice.

Joe looked right enough, but he was pallid and grimaced some as he rocked along on the horse. Still, the mountains made hard men and the old trapper look like he'd survive.

Preacher rode Horse at the head of their procession. They wound up into the Gros Ventre Range on a winding path that sawed between huge rocks, thick trees, and sharp drop-offs. He used Doubletop Peak as his main landmark and meandered up the steady incline.

Hoofprints from pronghorn and pawprints from wolves and other small creatures marked the way as a game trail. Nearby critters used it to get down to the small streams that eventually fed into the Snake River miles to the north. Rainfall had been good this year, and there were plenty of watering holes. That had helped the pronghorn herd to grow. It would be a race to see if the water drying up or the winter hit the herd hardest.

His two packhorses, attached to Horse's saddle by a lead rope, trailed him. They'd all worked together enough on the trip up from Nuevo Mexico that they were in step, even though the packhorses had never seen the mountains. He'd wanted to get animals that were wise to the highlands, but he'd left most of the finder's fee he'd gotten from Daniel

Eckstrom for Alita Montez and Toby Harper as a wedding dowry. The young woman was one of the bravest Preacher had seen. He'd wanted to see the young couple set off right.

The rearmost packhorse carried the dead pronghorn. Since he hadn't wanted the meat to spoil, he'd tied the animal to a tree branch and bled it out while they sorted through the Indians' gear for salvageable goods.

"I can whistle now if you like," Joe said after a bit. "I know a lot of songs. I can play a gee-tar and a banjo, too. You just call the tune an' if'n I know it, why I'll just liven up our trip with whistlin'. I can do a lot of birdcalls, too."

"Maybe we'll hold off on the whistlin' and birdcalls a mite longer," Preacher suggested. Joe's constant talking was getting on his nerves a little. Horse flicked his ears in irritation. "Leastways until we know we ain't got anybody foggin' our backtrail."

Nose to the ground every so often, Dog ranged ahead of the procession. So far, the big cur hadn't noted anything strange, and Dog was locked and loaded for threats.

Preacher had been attentive to the surrounding woods and the rising mountains and hadn't seen any Indians, but that didn't mean they weren't out there. As the run-in with Silent Owl and his band had proven, the country was ripe for Blackfeet. Something had pulled them into the area. Their presence bothered Preacher because the Blackfeet didn't come anywhere around Jackson's Hole except to rob, raid, and cause misery.

"All right," Joe said, "but when you get ready for whistlin', just you let me know."

"I will."

Instead of whistling, Joe sang softly to himself, but his voice grew steadily louder.

Since Preacher couldn't keep the man quiet, he decided

to ask questions that had been bothering him. "How did the Blackfeet take you?"

"Well, like I said, it was my own fault. I woke up with 'em this mornin' before first light. Ol' Silent Owl prodded me awake with the point of his spear." Joe took off his hat and waved it at an annoying insect. "That come as a shock, I tell you. Go to sleep by yourownself an' wrapped up in the lovin' arms of Mother Whiskey, an' I'm not talkin' about that cheap rotgut stuff you can find around here what's full of whiskey made from raw alcohol, chewin' to-bakky, an' burned sugar. Not no Tarantula Juice, Red Eye, or Coffin Varnish, neither. No sir. You can keep all that. I'm talkin' about gin-u-wine sippin' whiskey shipped all the way from Scotland."

"I've had some of that," Preacher said. "Mighty fine stuff when you can get it. But I ain't never seen any of it west of St. Louis."

"I first got some out Califorry way," Joe said. "Developed a taste for it. An' there's a United States Army captain by the name of Diller at Fort Pierre Chouteau who favors that whiskey. Has some shipped in regular when he's over-seein' the soldiers who get stationed at the fort. I was scoutin' for the Army for a time, until me an' Captain Diller had a disagreement an' parted ways."

"What kind of disagreement?"

"He was bein' a damn fool with the scouts. Sendin' us out into dangerous places that I knowed held plenty of Injuns. I think he's scoutin' out land for when some of these immigrants passin' through decide this part of the country is good enough for a man to build a farm or a ranch on. Might be plannin' on gettin' himself a few packets of land to settle into or sell off. He's a man who likes his money."

That thought bothered Preacher. He liked the mountains as they were: fierce and free. He didn't want towns, even little ones, popping up like toadstools and hampering a wandering man's ability to go whenever and wherever he wanted to.

"I wasn't the onliest one that was gettin' done with riskin' my neck like that," Joe went on. "O' course, I tried to be polite about not agreein' with the cap'n. Then one night I had me a skinful of whiskey after damn near gettin' my hair lifted earlier that day, an' I took umbrage with him."

The man stumbled over the unfamiliar word, but he got it out.

"Cap'n Diller, he cut my pay an' sent me packin'," Joe said. "That's how come I ended up with his whiskey before I left the fort." He spat a blob of tobacco and knocked a mosquito looking to light on his arm out of the air. The man grinned and wiped his lips with the back of his hand. "Did you see that? What I done to that skeeter?"

"I did."

"Want to bet me a nickel I can't do it again?"

"No." Preacher was tired of Joe's circular storytelling. Truth to tell, the only company he'd wanted along for the ride were Horse and Dog. "Your captain interests me. I'm a mite curious about him. A man's not likely to get rich in the Army."

"Nope. Nor for scoutin' for the Army, neither. Been my experience, though, a man sometimes gets stuck one place or another." Joe spat another stream of tobacco. "I spent too long at Fort Pierre Chouteau an' I knowed it. Me gettin' my walkin' papers was probably best for me. Got me back to my roots, up here in this mountain air where I belong. I still got a lot of years left to me. Ever'thin' was goin' good."

"Except for gettin' captured by the Blackfeet."

Joe was silent for a moment. "Well, I don't rightly call that gettin' captured. Not in my book. I was drunk an' asleep when they come up on me. Woulda been different had I been awake."

Preacher didn't mention his disbelief about that. The Blackfeet would have killed the man instantly. Instead, he asked, "Why'd them Blackfeet keep you alive?"

"I don't rightly know."

"Would have been easier to kill you."

"Let's just be glad they wasn't thinkin' like that."

Preacher was sure the Blackfeet had had a reason they didn't slit the man's throat or torture him to death for sport, but he had no idea what that reason might be. He filed the notion away to think on later.

Instead, Preacher asked, "So after you were let go from scoutin', you struck out for the mountains?"

"Not right away. A change comes on a man sudden like that; he wants to look over the land a little before he decides what he's gonna do next. I took a couple days thinkin' it over, but I got to admit, I was a man without definite prospects. While I was drinkin' up the last of my pay, I heard about the rendezvous an' thought I'd come up here an' try my luck catchin' on with another trapper who needs an extra set of hands. I'm good with traps and skinnin'. That's what you're doin' out here, right? Headin' over to the rendezvous?"

"I am." Preacher twisted in his saddle and checked their backtrail.

Nothing showed down the incline. No dust and no star-tled wildlife heading for safer territory. Much of the way was blocked by trees, but he could see enough of it that he was confident nobody was back there.

Something still didn't set right, though, because the hair on the back of his neck was on the edge of standing.

You got to get a handle on that kind of thinkin', old son. Don't let gettin' surprised this morning spook you. That was just a reminder that you gotta be a little more alert. Maybe some things are different since you been gone, but you ain't no tenderfoot out here. Pay attention.

CHAPTER 4

Hidden back under a stand of tall lodgepole pines, Stone Eyes, war chief of his Blackfeet warriors, hunkered down and waited for the three wagons to roll into the ambush he had set.

Forty warriors, half of them blooded in battle and half of them who would experience bloodshed for the first time today, spread out in a line on either side of him. Only eighteen of them held the new rifles, but all of them were equipped with bows because reloading the rifles would take too long once the attack started. All of them carried knives and tomahawks for when the attack closed in on the white immigrants in the wagons.

He'd chosen the area along the trail that cut through the scrub pines and tall grass. The ruts made by other wagons for the last nine winters were scars left by the white man. An animal or a Blackfoot might leave a trail through hard use, but those trails healed quickly.

The wheels on the wagons of the white men cut too deeply into the land. They didn't fade easily. When they did, they became hazards for horses and men. Either might stumble over one or into one and break a leg or sprain an ankle.

Stone Eyes had pointed out the potential danger to the younger men in his group who had not yet been blooded. He told them of his fine horse, Windracer, how he had spent days tracking her till he finally caught her. She had been a good pony, sure-footed and quick enough to outrun an arrow. Maybe the last stretched the truth a little, but his listeners didn't challenge him. He was their war chief, and no one questioned his words.

He told them of his love for Windracer and how he'd planned for her to be the mother of other swift and sure-footed mountain ponies. And he told them of the day he chased a buffalo, rode in close to put an arrow into its heart, only to have Windracer stumble and fall.

Since that time, Stone Eyes's left hip still bothered him a little during the winters. He told his warriors that, too, that it was better to be wise in all things and move in a planned fashion instead of merely reacting to something that happened.

Then he told them how he had looked into Windracer's eyes and sang to her with a hopeful heart of fields of sweet grass and brooks filled with clean water, and he cut her throat because her leg was shattered. She had died and he had taken meat from her to feed his people because losing the buffalo threatened to starve his tribe.

It was the loss of his pony he had loved so much, not the slight limp he carried, that had taught him to be a wiser hunter and warrior. And that incident had also made him hate all the more the whites who traveled through the mountains.

The familiar squeak of wagon wheels grew louder. One or more of those wheels needed bear grease or the white immigrants would have trouble farther along their journey. In truth, none of them would live long enough for that to be a concern, but it spoke to their careless ways.

Stone Eyes took a firmer grip on the rifle he carried and breathed out steadily. The unblooded braves looked to him to see how a warrior acted and he showed them because his plans required them to learn.

Forty-two winters had come and gone since he'd been birthed in his father's tipi. He was one of the oldest men in his tribe because of the wars with the white men. He stood tall and straight, with wide shoulders and narrow hips. His buckskins and moccasins fit him precisely because his wives took pride in him and would allow nothing less than that. War paint streaked the hard planes of his face. His thick black hair ran past his shoulders.

A bowshot away, the lead wagon rolled into view. Four mules pulled the heavy load.

The mules disappointed Stone Eyes. He had hoped for horses. Some of the mounts his warriors had were old and a few were nearly lame. If he wanted to attract more young warriors to his cause, he needed horses to interest them into joining him.

And he needed more rifles. The few he had gotten were good, but there were more to steal. In fact, there was a whole shipment somewhere out in the mountains. He only had to find them as he had found these.

An old man with a gray beard sat up front and guided the horses. A woman about his age sat beside him. A bonnet framed her face, but it failed to hide her age.

That was a disappointment, too. Stone Eyes had hoped for young women. Young women, and children, could be used and sold to men who purchased them to take down south. The concept of money was foreign to Stone Eyes and his warriors, but he'd learned quickly that whites put much store by it, and that gold could be traded for goods.

Two outriders rode on either side of the wagon and a little ahead. One was a boy, not even a man. The other looked as old as the man handling the wagon team.

Both riders straddled horses.

Stone Eyes's heart slowed and he mastered the anticipation within him. He wished that Silent Owl was there with him, to take part in the strike against the whites. Instead, his son was chasing the old scout, Joe Len Darby, who might know where more rifles were.

Gradually, the other two wagons rocked into view. The second and third wagons were more promising. Younger men guided the mules, and women and children flared out around the wagons to gather wild plums and berries from the surrounding bushes. Birds flitted through the trees around the wagons.

Looking to his left, Stone Eyes nodded to Bear Kills Many, who was his second in command of the war party.

Bear Kills Many took his name from the scar that swept his face in a diagonal from his left eye to his chin. When he was a babe, a black bear had attacked his mother and the other women and girls out berry hunting. Bear Kills Many's mother and older sister were slain by the predator. Five more women and children died that day. The babe, though sorely wounded, had survived. Now Bear Kills Many wore his scar with pride because it was viewed as good luck.

Rising from a seated position to a standing one, Bear Kills Many moved silently through the woods. Ten men followed him. Only three carried rifles like Bear Kills Many. Stone Eyes hadn't yet been able to provide rifles for all of his warriors, and it was something he wanted to remedy.

The whites continued along the trail and never knew death waited for them in the woods.

Stone Eyes counted time quietly in his mind in a measured cadence. He and Bear Kills Many had measured off the distance where the ambush would take place. There would be no retreat. The whites would arrive and they would die—except for those taken prisoner.

Satisfied enough time had passed, Stone Eyes lifted his rifle, took aim on the man handling the team for the first wagon. He had learned the tactic from the British military during the second war the English had fought against the Americans.

Stone Eyes had been at the fall of Fort Shelby and had been disappointed that the war there was over so quickly. He was even more disappointed when the British lost the war to the Americans. Both sides were white, but the British weren't taking land and driving Indians west.

With the sights centered on the driver, he held back for a moment so the other warriors armed with rifles could take aim, then he squeezed the trigger.

The gunshot cracked loudly, then was drowned out by the other rifle reports along the line of Blackfoot warriors.

Balls slapped into the men and the wagons. Men and women screamed and the wounded mules cried out in their distinctive voices, so like that of a donkey but different.

The man driving the wagon slumped to the side. Blood leaked from his throat. Limp, he fell over the wagon's side to the ground.

The woman screeched, but she had been wounded in the arm. It was difficult to judge which thing, the man's death or the bullet that struck her, made her cry out.

The women and children foraging in the berry bushes abandoned their buckets and ran toward the wagons. Not killing them would be difficult and some would be lost. It would have been better if they had tried to hide in the woods.

Stone Eyes turned and ran with the rifle in his hand. He was the first of his warriors who reached the ponies tied below the hill under the trees. The ponies shifted anxiously. Most of them weren't used to fighting, either, and the noise made them anxious. Stone Eyes caught up his pony, a palomino he had ridden into battle before, gripped the reins, and thrust the rifle into the sheepskin boot tied around his mount's neck.

A lithe leap took Stone Eyes to the pony's back. He settled at once and yanked the hackamore in the direction of the wagons. He jabbed his heels into the pony's sides to urge her into a gallop. Once she was pointed in the right direction, he let the hackamore reins fall to her neck and guided her with his knees.

He slid his bow from over his shoulder, reached into the quiver tied on the other side of the pony, and nocked an arrow to the sinew string. He rode toward the front wagon to cut off the mules. He didn't want the whites to scatter out. Frightened by the rifle shots and the warriors' yelled challenges, the immigrants handling the wagons froze.

On the lead wagon, the old woman grabbed the reins the old man had dropped. She flicked the reins over the mules' backs, shouted to them, and they bolted forward. A young woman stuck her head through the opening in the canvas cover.

The driver of the last wagon attempted to turn around, but he was met with balls fired from Bear Kills Many's warriors.

The second wagon jolted into motion, too.

Stone Eyes lay low across his pony and rolled with the

gallop enough that they moved as one thing. By the time he crossed the intervening distance, he was behind it. A young man, bareheaded with his hair tousled, shoved the barrel of a double-barreled shotgun through the opening at the back of the wagon and eared the hammers back.

With the pressure of his knee, Stone Eyes turned his pony slightly aside and sat up straight to aim his bow. The young man fired the shotgun too quickly and missed Stone Eyes, but the buckshot spread enough to knock the warrior to the war chief's left from his mount.

The war chief loosed his arrow. The fletched shaft sank into the young man's chest and drove him back in a stumble. Stone Eyes reached for another arrow and nocked it. The man in the back of the wagon fell back and disappeared.

Gunshots rang out in the clearing and pierced the war cries of the Blackfoot warriors, but after the initial volley, the guns fell silent.

Stone Eyes drew even with the wagon and looked at the woman. She shouted encouragement to the mules and mixed prayers and vicious oaths in with it.

The war chief raised his bow from ten feet away. He yelled, "Stop!"

"Go to Hell, you godless heathen!" the woman bellowed at him. Tears tracked her face.

The wagon jerked and jumped over the rough terrain, and it heaved side to side despite the weight of its cargo. The woman barely kept control of the mules.

Fearful the wagon would roll over and many of the goods stored aboard it would be lost, Stone Eyes took the arrow from the string and returned it to the quiver. Killing the woman would be easy enough, but dead she would be no worth to him or his plans. With his knees, he steered his pony over to the wagon. The woman pulled the mules toward him to block him.

"I'll kill you!" the woman shouted.

Wary, Stone Eyes rode away from the wagon for a moment, then dropped back a little so he was behind the seat where he wouldn't be seen by the woman. Closing in again, he caught hold of the wagon's canvas support at the front. He yanked on the thick post fastened there and judged that it would hold his weight.

He took hold of the canvas-wrapped pole and pulled himself from the pony. The wagon rattled and jerked, much different from his pony's smooth glide. He swung over to the wagon and tried to brace his foot against the side.

Patches of torn canvas and divots of wood flew from the wagon and the support post. The wood shivered in Stone Eyes's hands and the harsh cracks of two rifles came from behind him. He glanced over his shoulder as he hung on. Two men rode horses in pursuit of the wagon and put their rifles away.

His foot slid and he hung from the support post. Aware of the riders closing in on him, he struggled to pull himself up, and his foot banged against the rapidly turning wheel. If it had caught him, if he'd become entangled, he would have been pulled from the wagon and possibly run over.

The lead rider pulled a pistol from the belt slung over one of his shoulders. The other man struggled to reload his rifle while in the saddle.

Because he had no options, Stone Eyes pulled himself around to the front of the wagon. He shoved a foot into the box that framed the wagon's seat.

CHAPTER 5

The woman glanced up at Stone Eyes, cursed at him, and drew a small knife from her dress. She swung her weapon at Stone Eyes, and sunlight reflected off the blade.

Stone Eyes pulled himself back far enough to evade the knife, but the wind of its passing grazed his cheek. The *crack* of the rider's pistol, lighter than that of the rifles, echoed in the war chief's ears and the ball plucked at the loose folds of his buckskin shirt. He caught the woman's knife wrist in his hand, twisted, and pulled her up from the seat. She slapped at him with her other hand and screamed shrilly until he kicked her in the belly and propelled her from the wagon. When she hit the ground, her screaming stopped.

The first rider drew even with the wagon and raised a second pistol. Hatred blazed in his gaze as he took aim across the short distance.

Aware that remaining on the wagon seat was a death sentence, Stone Eyes hurled himself into the wagon. The pistol shot cracked and the hooped canvas blotted out sight of the white gunman. Stone Eyes didn't know where the ball went, only that he wasn't hit.

A young woman hunkered on top of clothing, furniture, and supplies in the back of the wagon. She held two small children in her embrace. The young man Stone Eyes had killed rolled like a boned fish on the crates and sacks. The arrow jutting from the dead man's chest vibrated with the rough wagon ride.

"No!" the young woman cried. "Please! Don't hurt us!"

"Stay there!" Stone Eyes commanded in the white man's tongue he had learned from the British. "If you move, I will kill you!" He ran a hand over his tomahawk meaningfully.

She tried to make herself and the children even smaller.

Hurrying because he knew he didn't have much time before the whites reached him, Stone Eyes picked up the shotgun lying beside the dead man. A powder horn lay beside a leather pouch filled with shot and wadding. The war chief adjusted for the rocking of the wagon as much as he could, poured powder from the horn into the shotgun barrels, slid the wool wadding into place to seat the powder with the ramrod, and dropped in a .60-caliber ball in each barrel. He added two more wads of wool to hold the balls securely so they wouldn't roll loose.

Poorly loaded shotguns, where the ball could separate from the load, tended to explode. A few years ago, Stone Eyes had watched a young warrior blow off his own face due to an improperly loaded shotgun.

Finished loading the weapon, he dropped the ramrod to the floor of the wagon. There wouldn't be time for reloading. If the riders outside hadn't known their people were in the wagon with Stone Eyes, they would have shot through the canvas.

The wagon jerked harshly to the left and alerted Stone

Eyes that someone had boarded. On his knees, he raised the shotgun to his shoulder and waited.

"Sue Ellen," a man called. "Are you in there?"

The young woman tried to speak. Stone Eyes glowered at her and she mewled in fear.

"Sue Ellen?" The man shoved a pistol through the opening in the canvas and followed it quickly. "You're going to be—"

Stone Eyes squeezed one of the triggers and, because he was hurriedly set, the shotgun kicked his shoulder hard enough to leave a bruise. He rolled with the recoil. The ball caught the white man in the face and blew him backward. Blood spatter coated the inside of the wagon's canvas top and more covered his features. Fire clung to his hair and beard.

Adjusting for the rocking sway of the wagon, Stone Eyes pushed himself up before the body fell. The dead man stumbled backward in front of him, went back out of the opening, and toppled over the wagon box. The corpse hung in the traces for a moment and further spooked the mules. They whinnied their peculiar *hee-haw* and ran faster to escape the stink of blood and death and spent powder.

Stone Eyes shoved the shotgun barrel through the opening and peered around for the other rider.

The dead man spilled on through the traces and took the reins with him. The leather jerked over the rapidly passing ground. One of the back wheels rolled over the dead man and jarred the wagon. Cargo rattled and clanked in the back.

The second rider drew even with the wagon, but the rider was looking over his shoulder, probably at his dead friend. Stone Eyes shot him in the back of the head before the man even knew he was there. The body tumbled from the horse, and the animal quickly veered away.

Unable to reach the reins, Stone Eyes threw down the shotgun and leaped from the wagon seat onto the back of the left mule. Once he had his balance, he leaned forward and caught the reins. He knotted his hands in the leather and pulled hard. Driven by fear and surprise, the mules finally gentled enough to come to a stop.

Stone Eyes slid over the mule's side to the ground. Thudding hoofbeats drummed toward him and he looked up at the rider bearing down on him. The war chief ducked low and threw his left arm out to make himself look bigger.

"Hyah!" he shouted to the horse. He freed his tomahawk, the metal one the British gave him from their arsenal, and he held it ready.

The horse's eyes rolled white and it jerked to the side. The sudden motion threw off its rider's aim and the ball whizzed only inches over Stone Eyes's head. The war chief stepped forward and threw the tomahawk at the rider from twelve feet away.

The tomahawk flipped once, and the heavy blade embedded in the man's chest. Stricken, the man looked down, dropped his rifle, and screamed. Before the man could finish his frightened cry, Stone Eyes drew his knife, ran to his side, and gripped the man's face. He pulled the man down and slashed his throat before he hit the ground.

Moving smoothly, Stone Eyes sheathed his bloody knife, grabbed the man's rifle, saw that its charge was spent, and placed its butt on the ground to reload. A handful of whites on horseback, some of them riding double with women and children, galloped for the woods to the south. A dozen Blackfoot warriors rode after them and whooped with excitement.

More warriors surrounded the remaining two wagons, but they hunted survivors. No shots were fired.

Bear Kills Many rode up to Stone Eyes and led the palomino by the hackamore reins. A flush of excitement darkened Bear Kills Many's face.

"It is done?" Stone Eyes asked.

"It is. All the men except those"—he nodded toward the fleeing whites—"are dead. Only the young boys remain. Three women were lost. It was unavoidable. Two fought with pistols and knew how to shoot, and one killed herself."

Stone Eyes took the reins his friend offered him. "How many do we have?"

"Twelve or thirteen. Most of them are children."

"There are three more in this wagon. A girl and two children."

Bear Kills Many smiled, and his scarred face looked misshapen. "Finding this wagon train was lucky."

"It wasn't luck," Stone Eyes replied. "We were out hunting. Hunters who know their business find what they're looking for. The whites always come in the summer. How many warriors did we lose?"

The smiled faded from Bear Kills Many's face. "Two. One is dead and the other is too badly hurt to help us in a fight."

"Who?"

"Bright Way and Singing Bird."

Both were new warriors and had no real experience in war. The losses were better than what Stone Eyes expected, and they were certainly acceptable.

The number of prisoners was good. A small group could be easily managed, and yet there were enough of them to make the trip to the Comancheros to trade for weapons and horses worth it. Tobit Moon Deer, the half-breed who dealt with the Comancheros, would take on the prisoners, and he would return with the goods he bargained for in Nuevo Mexico.

Gunshots cracked in the woods to the south.

"Send a rider out to fetch our warriors," Stone Eyes said.

"And if there are any whites left?"

"The land will kill them. They're stupid out here in the woods. They don't know enough to save themselves."

Bear Kills Many nodded.

"First, help me with my prisoners."

Stone Eyes strode to the rear of the wagon. Folds of the canvas cover closed the opening. He used the rifle's muzzle to knock the material to the side. The young woman remained in the corner of the wagon with the children. All of them wept and cried out in misery.

The young woman looked down and would not meet Stone Eyes's gaze. Her brunette hair was tied back, and her face gleamed with the same soft innocence found in a newborn fawn.

Stone Eyes wondered if she was strong enough to make the journey south to Moon Deer. Or if she would be strong enough to be a slave to his wives. All three of them had complained to him that they wanted help for the coming fur season. In addition to Silent Owl, Stone Eyes had six other children. Making clothing and feeding those hungry mouths took time.

Stone Eyes opened the wagon's rear gate and let it down.

"Get out," he ordered in the white man's tongue.

The young woman shook her head. The children cowered even closer to her.

Stone Eyes held the rifle in his right hand. With his left, he reached into the back of the wagon and grabbed the young woman by the hair. She yelped in pain and fear, released the children, and seized his hand with her own. Before she could get a solid grip on him, he dragged her out of the wagon and let her fall to the ground.

The children wailed and reached for her.

Stone Eyes shoved the first one into the second hard enough to take the boy's wind away for a moment. The two children tripped over the dead man and sprawled.

"Don't hurt them!" the young woman begged. "Please, don't hurt them!"

She tried to get up, but Stone Eyes kicked her down.

"I will only hurt them if they don't obey me," the war chief said. "Order them to do as I say and stop crying. Otherwise, I will carve their tongues from their heads."

The young woman relayed the message and the children quieted some. They held onto each other fearfully.

"Good," Stone Eyes said. "Get the children from the wagon and keep them nearby."

The young woman called the children from the wagon. It took a little while because they were so afraid.

Stone Eyes understood the fear stamped on the faces of the children. The youngest of his sons and daughters all looked the same way whenever someone brought up the whites and all the evil they did to the Blackfeet they caught unprepared and outnumbered in the mountains.

Four other warriors joined Stone Eyes. Bloodstains stood out on their clothing. Fresh, bloody scalps hung from their belts. All of them were young and eager. Their ponies shifted restlessly beneath them.

Stone Eyes pointed to two of the young men. "You take

these prisoners. Put them with the others. They are not to be harmed."

Both warriors nodded.

The young woman looked at Stone Eyes for mercy. The war chief pushed her into motion toward the braves.

"Go," he said.

Reluctantly, her face pale and filled with sickness, the young woman walked toward the mounted warriors and went with them.

Stone Eyes reached into the wagon, grabbed the dead man by the foot, and yanked him onto the ground. Squatting, he went through the dead man's pockets quickly but found nothing of any real value. No gold coins like the whites favored.

He stood and looked at the wagon. The whites had carried supplies and there looked to be a fair number of them left. The ambush had proven successful. He and his warriors could search longer for the rifles Stone Eyes was determined to find without having to hunt for food. The immigrants had carried barrels of salted beef and flour and beans.

"My son and his warriors have not returned," Stone Eyes said.

"I know."

"He should have been back by now. Tracking one old, fat white man should not take so long."

"It shouldn't," Bear Kills Many agreed. "But the white man had whiskey. Perhaps that has delayed Silent Owl."

"My orders were to come straight back with the old man and the whiskey."

"Silent Owl is young." Bear Kills Many smiled. "You and I, we were young once. You know how sometimes a young man does not listen or pay attention to the sun passing."

Anger stirred in Stone Eyes's stomach, but it was banked by a sense of unease. "Something is wrong. My ancestors are close to me at this time. I can almost reach out and touch them."

Bear Kills Many kept silent. He was never one to speak against ancestors or their ability to reach from beyond death.

Stone Eyes wanted to take his warriors and track his wayward son, but there was too much to do with the prisoners. And the supplies had to be sorted through. They couldn't take everything on packhorses. Non-perishable things, spices and furniture and tools, could be hidden and recovered later.

Once the rifles had been found.

But Stone Eyes was unwilling to simply await the return of his son and those warriors.

"Send Turtle to find Silent Owl," Stone Eyes ordered. "He is a good tracker and a strong warrior, and he has a fast pony. He will quickly find Silent Owl and bring him back."

"It will be as you say." Bear Kills Many turned his horse away and trotted back to the others to find Turtle.

Stone Eyes gazed down at the dead white man. A message was written in the cooling flesh and it spoke of the frailty of the flesh. The young man had not planned to die today. Yet he had.

Aware of something's gaze upon him, Stone Eyes looked up and spotted the large black crow perched on a tree branch twenty feet away. Its ebony feathers rippled slightly in the breeze, and it fixed a beady black eye on the war chief.

Crows delivered death messages, and this one seemed on the verge of speaking.

Angry and fearful of the bird's message, Stone Eyes picked up a dirt clod from the ground and threw it at the crow.

Spreading its black wings, the crow leaped from the branch an instant before the dirt clod shattered against the branch. Pieces of the clod rained down. The crow flapped its wings and disappeared in the tangle of trees.

Stone Eyes reminded himself that not all things he saw were omens. Some simply were events that happened. Angry at himself for being such an old woman, the war chief shook off the dark thoughts and turned his attention to the contents of the wagon.

He had sworn to get the rifles, to keep them from the Crows, who were the Blackfeet's enemies and friends to the whites. With them he would kill the Crows and drive the white men from the mountains.

These goods, and the goods he eventually got for the prisoners he was going to send south, would help him achieve that honorable goal.

CHAPTER 6

For the next three hours, Preacher and Joe Len Darby kept moving along and ascended the mountain cautiously. Knowing the Blackfeet he'd killed were a hunting or scouting party and someone would be along to find them, Preacher watched their backtrail closely.

Deciding the horses probably needed to blow because the incline up into the Gros Ventre Range had become steeper, he called a halt at an out-of-the-way place that had a small cave he'd used while on other travels through these parts.

They picketed their mounts and the pack animals under a copse of trees where the grass was plentiful. The horses could stay there and eat their fill while Preacher dressed out the pronghorn he'd shot. The animal carried a lot of good meat, and he didn't want it to go to waste.

Preacher took a moment to examine the rifles he'd taken from the Blackfeet. Like the first one, all the new ones had the distinctive mark burned into the buttstocks. It was puzzling. Only two of the rifles didn't have marks, and both were little more than trash because they hadn't been properly cared for.

He untied the pronghorn from the packhorse that had carried it and took the carcass over to a tall tree. He threw a rope over a lower branch that looked good and sturdy, then tied the rope around the pronghorn's back feet. He pulled on the other end of the rope and hauled the pronghorn up until it was clear of the ground.

The pronghorn had bled dry for the most part during the trip up higher into the mountains. Only a little blood oozed from the animal's slashed throat and dripped from the muzzle. Preacher took out his long knife and split the pronghorn's belly. He reached in and hauled out the intestines.

"Get a fire started," Preacher told Joe.

"For cookin' or for burnin'?"

"For burnin'," Preacher said. "I want to get rid of these guts. We ain't got time to cook steaks."

"We gonna light for a spell?" Joe wandered around and picked up dry branches and fallen limbs.

"Only as long as it takes to burn this. In the meantime, I don't want to draw critters that might come and look for an easy kill. Or for any that might be on our backtrail due to the blood we left gettin' here. The blood will pull predators, but smoke will make 'em think twice about closin' in."

Joe built a fire ring with loose stones, laid his gathered twigs and branches for the fire, and used a handful of leaves and flint and steel to get a flame going.

"Maybe we could cook a little while you're burnin'," Joe suggested. "If you're gonna let them horses blow an' eat an' drink, I can cook us something."

"We don't have time for steaks," Preacher said. He regretted that because his stomach rumbled, and Dog looked on hungrily.

"Not steaks," Joe agreed. "Cut me off a few small hunks of meat I can skewer an' sear over the fire. Squares. About yay big." He held his thumb and forefinger two inches apart. "By the time you finish up with the horses, I can get those bits cooked enough an' have 'em ready for us to eat in the saddle."

Preacher sliced a few chunks of meat from the pronghorn that matched the other man's request, put them on a leather wrap he'd gotten out of his panniers to wrap the harvested meat in, and carried the strips over to Joe. With eager anticipation, the old man accepted the meat. He sat back on his haunches gingerly and threaded the meat onto wooden skewers he'd carved out of green tree branches.

"Got any salt?" Joe asked.

"In the pannier right there." Preacher pointed to the nearest pannier and returned to cutting meat from the pronghorn.

Working easy and efficient, the mountain man cut steaks and flank meat that he would jerk when they bedded down that night. He also took brisket and ribs that could be used in stews. The rendezvous was at a Crow village. The Crow women could cook anything he brought in, and he was looking forward to it.

Joe helped himself to the salt, pepper, and rosemary Preacher had found growing wild. The rosemary hadn't completely cured, but it was close enough to being done to use.

"This'll do just fine." Joe returned to the campfire and seasoned the skewered meat.

The smoke coming off fire stank of offal and fresh dung. Preacher hadn't taken the time to clean the intestines because he hadn't planned on using them. Even upwind of the smoke, the stench was strong.

"That meat's gonna gather stink," Preacher said. He never cooked over a burn fire. "Won't be fit to eat."

"If it was in the smoke, maybe," Joe agreed. "Most likely. That's why I'm gonna put it on the leeward side of the fire. This here's gonna be just fine. Just you wait and see."

The nautical term brought back memories of Preacher's recent misadventures down in New Orleans and on a pirate ship. When he'd first gotten taken by the pirates, he hadn't known the difference between leeward and windward. The pirate skipper and his first mate had been harsh teachers. Preacher had learned, and he wore the scars as a reminder.

"You were a sailor," Preacher said, and kept working making meat. His blade slid easily through the muscles and fat.

"I was," Joe agreed. "For a time. Got my head bashed an' made a part of a crew on one of John Astor's ships. That first trip, only trip, I might add, I sailed all the way to China to trade furs for tea an' sandalwood. I woulda jumped ship in China, but I didn't understand the lingo an' there were far too many chances for a man to get himself killed before he knowed it. I didn't know how I was gonna get back home. So after I worked a spell over there, I sailed back to the United States an' lit a shuck as soon as we touched land. Busted a few heads gettin' that done. I made my way back out West quick as I could. I was a happy man to be back, I tell you." He glanced over at Preacher. "What you gonna do with all that meat? That's a powerful lot for us to make pemmican, an' 'sides that, we can hunt an' eat plenty right now."

"I'm not goin' into the rendezvous empty-handed," Preacher replied. "This will go fast, but it'll be there till it's gone. I'll hunt while I'm there. Same as any other trapper."

"How soon 'til we reach the rendezvous?"

"Tomorrow mornin'." Preacher paused in his work, sleeved sweat from his brow, and studied Joe.

Continuing with his fussing over the cubed meat and managing to keep the smoke away from his dinner, Joe nodded.

"Seems like knowin' how far we need to go is somethin' you should know," Preacher said. "Since you were headed that way."

"I ain't been to a rendezvous in a few years," Joe said, "but I used to go regular."

Preacher didn't know if that was true. During his time in the mountains, he'd attended nearly every rendezvous. In the beginning, back when John Colter and Jim Bridger and Hugh Glass had been regular fixtures at the meetings, Preacher had learned a lot from the older men. These days, he was often the teacher, but he fought shy of that unless he had a reason to get involved. He didn't like being bothered or being responsible for teaching others unless he chose to.

"You were a good ways south and east of Jackson's Hole," Preacher pointed out. "The tracks I found back there all came in from the north and east. You passed right on by."

"I knowed it, but I wasn't gonna tell them Blackfeet how to find the rendezvous."

"You said they caught you this morning."

Joe nodded. "They did."

"Were you runnin' from them?"

Joe tended the meat and didn't answer for a moment. "I was."

"Then they didn't come up on you accidental-like."

Joe shook his head. "Nope, I reckon they didn't. Not this mornin'."

"When?"

Joe spat tobacco juice away from the fire and turned the meat, which was sizzling pretty well and smelled good. "I figure they cut my sign a couple days ago."

"And they decided to come after you? Knowin' you were just one man?"

"'Pears so. You seen how they had me all ketched up."

"Why did they do that?"

"Well, if you'd left any of 'em alive, I reckon we could have asked. But you didn't." Joe made that inability sound like Preacher's fault. "I reckon they just seen me as easy pickin's. I'd'a stayed sober, they wouldn't have took me."

Preacher could almost believe that, but there were eleven Blackfeet chasing after one man.

"Before I signed on with the fort," Joe said, "I was good up in the mountains out here. I could find anythin' I wanted. Couldn't be touched unless I wanted to be touched. Ten years ago, they'd have never caught me. Or they'd have all been dead. I seen how close they come to catchin' me, thought I'd lost 'em last night. Had me a little celebration with Cap'n Diller's sippin' whiskey. Shore shouldn'ta done that."

"The higher up in the mountains you get," Preacher said, "the harder a strong drink will hit you."

Joe grinned. "Yep, and the captain's whiskey is plenty strong." The man nodded. "In hindsight, that was a big mistake. I coulda done without makin' that mistake. I've seen men get drunk on just the altitude. Doctor fella I knew said it was because them old boys' brains weren't gettin' enough good air. Told me oxygen gets scarce when you're up high a ways." Joe spat more tobacco juice. "Last night, I forgot how far up I was. I was drunk before I knowed it an' had the good sense to put myself to bed. Then them Injuns came a-callin'. I tell you the truth, Preacher, I wasn't lookin' forward to this mornin' after last night's drinkin' even before them Blackfeet showed up. I still ain't likin' it none now."

Preacher laid more meat onto the skins and let Joe's story settle in his mind. He didn't like it, and it stank worse than the burning offal and dung. But it was believable. Joe didn't seem like the kind of man who thought things out too far, and by his own admission he'd been out of the mountains for a long time.

What was left of the pronghorn was getting down to bone. Preacher was ready to move on. Feeling like he wasn't getting a straight story from Joe Len Darby was bothersome.

"Those Indians bein' after you don't explain how you got so far astray from the rendezvous," Preacher said. "You could have hightailed it for the rendezvous, probably got some men to stand with you against eleven Blackfeet. Those Indians probably would have backed down once they got close to the Crow village."

Joe ran knuckles over his jaw carefully and didn't make eye contact with Preacher. "I wasn't no more'n a day out," the man responded defensively. "They'd run me ragged for two days. I wasn't thinkin' straight. The whiskey didn't help none. You don't get out in these mountains regular, the landscape changes. Weather. Growth. Erosion an' the like. Changes. Don't nothin' sit still out here 'cept the mountains." He turned the meat. "Just hadn't found my way is all. I would have. Probably once I sobered up." He paused. "I'm just awful glad you showed up when you did,

Preacher. Otherwise, that woulda been all she wrote for Joe Len Darby."

That, Preacher knew, was the truth.

"I'm surprised those Blackfeet didn't kill you the minute they came up on you," Preacher said.

"Likely they was keepin' me for sport." Joe shuddered a little. "I've seen what those devils can do to someone when they're of a mind to be evil. They were just waitin' till they could take their time."

"Maybe," Preacher agreed, but he was thinking that if the Blackfoot warriors had wanted simply to torture and kill the man, they'd have already been doing it.

There was something else, something that Joe Len Darby wasn't telling. Whatever it was, it wasn't going to come easy.

"Like I said, I ain't been out to a rendezvous in a coon's age." Joe grinned and his eyes lit up. "Lookin' forward to it. Gonna be interestin' seein' how many men there know me. Seein' how many I know. I expect some of 'em will be dead by now."

Satisfied he'd gleaned all he could from the pronghorn, Preacher wrapped the last of the meat in the skins, tied a rawhide string around the package, and pushed himself to his feet. He stripped the hide from the animal and left the head and bones on the ground.

"This mornin'," Preacher said, "while you were with those Blackfeet, did they say where they got those rifles?"

Joe shook his head and ran his fingers over his bruised face. "I wasn't somebody ol' Silent Owl wanted to palaver with. I looked at him twice, I got hit. I wasn't exactly one to ask questions. I noticed them rifles, though."

He spat tobacco and looked at Preacher.

"I know you ain't got a lot of respect for me right now

on account of how I handled myself. Drinkin' an' all, I mean. If you'd seen me them two days them Indians was trackin' me, I'd'a showed you a thing or two."

"Ain't my place to fault you for what you did before this mornin'," Preacher said.

"No, it's not. I've just had me some bad luck is all. Wasn't fair, the cap'n firin' me. I did a good job for him, an' I knowed it. That's why before I left the fort an' headed south into the mountains, I liberated a few bottles of his whiskey an' took 'em with me. I drank 'em slow, just to keep myself entertained. Last night the drinkin' just plumb got ahead of me."

"It was still a foolish thing to do."

"I know."

"If you had any of that whiskey left," Preacher said, "I'd make you choose between it and ridin' on with me."

"I reckon you would."

"I'm one to drink when I've a mind to," Preacher said. "I won't try to tell you I ain't. There'll be plenty of drinkin' at the rendezvous. Those men there won't forget they're out in dangerous territory." He fixed Joe with his gaze. "Might be a good idea that you don't forget, either."

"I won't."

Preacher nodded, but he didn't much care. He'd saved Joe Len Darby, but he wasn't taking him on to raise. A man with demons like that usually ended up losing out to them. As soon as they reached Jackson's Hole and the rendezvous, Preacher planned to shake loose from the man and be glad of it.

"I'm gonna get my shovel, and I'm gonna bury these bones," Preacher said. "Won't take me long. Once I finish, we're ridin' out."

Joe frowned and looked aggrieved. "Only got another

three or four hours of daylight left. We could stay here an' rest up."

"There's six hours of daylight left," Preacher said. "Once we get on the other side of these mountains, I intend to use every one of them to put distance between ourselves and whatever trouble might come up outta that bloody mess we left behind us."

CHAPTER 7

Preacher and Horse crested the high point of the Gros Ventre Range at mid-morning. Dog loped along the crest with his nose to the ground and, in his own way, checked for those who had traveled this way. Preacher was certain Dog wouldn't find anything other than creature scents because not many came this way over the mountains.

When Preacher looked down at the valley mountain men called Jackson's Hole, he couldn't keep a smile off his face. Jackson's Hole was sandwiched between the Gros Ventre Range and the Grand Tetons, a little bit of Heaven itself, with plenty of danger for a man who didn't know his business out in the wilderness.

St. Louis and New Orleans might be interesting sights to men accustomed to living back East, and they might even think they were out on the frontier, but they didn't know what the West truly was. A man had to travel out to the mountains to find the undiscovered country. This high place among the mountains was home to several of Preacher's best memories.

Shaped by the Gros Ventres and the Grand Tetons, the valley stretched fifty-five miles long and anywhere from six to thirteen miles wide as it washed up against the foothills. A lot of the land was primitive forest and broken terrain that even seasoned mountain men and trappers thought twice about before trying to cross.

But there was plenty of hospitable land down in the valley, too, much of it fed by streams and small rivers that made good homes for beavers. Animals, furred and feathered and scaled, shared the water and hunted each other in the brush. Just as it was intended to be.

When beaver pelts were in high demand, a trapper could chop trees for firewood to dry out, settle in there for the winter, and trap the whole season long. Then, when the spring came and the land thawed a bit, a man could ride back down the mountains with his hides and sell them in St. Louis. Preacher had done that many times.

A thin streamer of smoke painted a line against the northern sky and the trees along the Snake River. The waterway came from the Tetons to the north and fed into Jackson's Lake. The broad expanse of river cut into the land and twisted back and forth between tree-lined banks. Farther south, another, smaller, river bled out of the lake's overflow. When rainfall was poor, the lower river all but dried up.

Joe Len Darby joined Preacher at the crest. He shifted in his saddle as if he were uncomfortable, and the leather creaked loudly enough to send a flock of dusky grouse sprinting through the brush. The distinctive long square tails and the dark gray feathers marked them plainly. The males had purple throats surrounded by white.

Dark bags showed under Joe's eyes, and yesterday's beating at the hands of the Blackfeet had paid off in blossoming bruises. Spending all day riding yesterday after being thrashed like that, then sleeping on the ground last night, must have made for a miserable morning.

Remembering how the man had lied by omission, Preacher found he wasn't as considerate of his road companion as maybe he should have been.

"The way that river jumps to an' fro," Joe said, "you know how David Thompson come to call it what he did when he found it."

"That's not the only name that river's carried," Preacher said. Seeing the valley again made him feel nostalgic for the old times and the stories he'd heard around campfires with men who were pleasantly drunk. "Meriwether Lewis was the first of the Corps of Discovery who saw it. He named it Lewis River. Sometimes they called it Lewis Fork or Lewis's Fork. Thompson originally named it the Shawpatin. That was as close as he could come to the Indian name for it. Later, when they came across the Shoshone tribe that lived there at the time, men learned the Shoshone called it the *Ki-moo-e-nim* or the *Yam-pah-pa*."

"Never heard it called that. What does that mean?"

Preacher knew Joe Len Darby hadn't spent as much time at rendezvouses in the past as he claimed. Or maybe those times had been long ago and he'd been drunk. Mountain men often told the same stories and lies. Some of the biggest tales were told by Jim Bridger and John Colter. Colter was dead now, and Bridger was hiring out to guide immigrants on to Oregon.

"Those were just names the Indians gave the river on account of the herbs that grew along the banks. When the Astor Expedition followed up Lewis and Clark, Wilson Price Hunt, an explorer actin' as an agent for John Jacob Astor hisownself, named it the Mad River. Only name that's truly stuck, though, is the Snake River."

Joe shaded his eyes with his hat and leaned forward in his saddle. His horse shifted beneath him. He pointed. "Yonder's smoke."

"That'll be the Crow village where the rendezvous is." Preacher had picked up information on the location while getting supplies in Santa Fe. "It'll take the rest of the mornin' to get there."

"The Crow? Thought you said the Shoshones lived here."

"They did. They will. And there are probably small tribes of them out there. A lot of Indians lived here at different times, and they rotate around even now. After the Spanish brought horses into America and the Indians learned to handle them, the tribes around here set their sights more on buffalo in Jackson's Hole and on either side of the mountains. Jackson's Hole got overhunted. Indians are successful hunters and trappers. Meat got scarce. Even the beavers are running thin in numbers these days. This season the Crows have decided to take their chances on game between the mountains rather than risk bumpin' into the Blackfeet. The Crows plan on takin' advantage of the rainy season, and they're more friendly to mountain men than most other Indians."

"Well, I'll be glad when we get there. Lookin' forward to settin' an' healin' up. I'm feelin' tuckered an' a mite aggrieved from all this ridin'."

Preacher still wanted answers about the rifles Silent Owl and his warriors had carried, so he wanted to get to the rendezvous as well. There was a good chance one of the mountain men or the Crow warriors at the rendezvous might know the answer to that mystery.

"Let's get to it then," the mountain man said.

He urged Horse down the incline and picked his way

with care. Even here, the mountains were steep enough that a fall would kill man or beast.

Once Preacher reached the river, traveling got easier. Most travelers came in over the Tetons rather than over the Gros Ventres because coming up from the southeast was generally harder. Preacher had followed that route because he'd wanted the solitude for a time before he joined the rendezvous. Over the last few months, he'd heard more than his share of yapping from people who talked just to hear themselves. He'd also wanted to see the country again. So much of the mountains had yet to be fully explored.

The Snake ran broad and deep and steady, a mite faster than it normally did at this time of the year. During the heavy rains, the river could run ragged with white water in places, and it would be dangerous. A beaver dam that looked like a narrow, prickly haystack of tree branches with leaves laid on its side in the water and cut across the river only a little farther on from where Preacher joined it. The dam was strong enough to hold back the current, and the barrier created a difference in depths from upriver to downriver that was at least the length of a man's upright hand.

Preacher took heart in that. Beavers were hard workers, but it took a lot of them to create a dam the size of the one across the river. One dam didn't mean there were enough beavers to make a man's season, though. Especially if he had competition in trapping. But he took this as a good sign.

Long, low branches created obstacles here and there along the river, but Preacher was generally able to lean down in the saddle to get under them. White wood flesh showed in several places where recent travelers had hacked offending branches out of the way.

Hoofprints chopped through pronghorn and elk tracks. Several bear prints showed in the damp soil, too, generally at wide places where a bear could easily get down in the water for some fishing. Territorial marks made by bear claws showed as white wounds on some of the trees.

Plenty of game used the river, so fresh meat and fish would be plentiful. Bird cries carried over the quiet gurgling of the river passing, and once a beaver splatted his tail against the bank to send his kinfolk scurrying for the water.

A few beaver kits swam in the river and carried twigs to the dam. Building was just their nature.

While he was watching the wildlife around them, including the bees working the brightly colored flowers, Preacher noted that Joe Len Darby didn't pay much attention to any of it.

Maybe you're a hunter and a trapper, but you ain't no mountain man. Otherwise you'd be reading the country like a deacon reading scripture.

Joe probably spent winters up in the mountains as part of a string of hunters and trappers. He was a rifle or a knife, whatever tool was needed at the moment, but he wasn't a student of the world around him.

That made Preacher wonder even more about the man's story of setting off into the wilderness on his own. Even a man with a little gumption would know such an endeavor was likely going to end badly.

Seventy yards away, a bull boat with three Indians aboard it floated around one of the turns. The tall brush hid them from view until the last minute. The bowl-shaped watercraft was purely Indian made. A stretched buffalo hide covered the frame created by willow poles. The buffalo's tail trailed in the water like an eel. The Indians sometimes tied the tails of two or more bull boats together.

"Indians," Joe warned in a low voice. He tightened his grip on his rifle and shifted it slightly.

"Don't," Preacher commanded. "Those Indians are Crow. If you offend them, they might not kill you, but I don't want to be misunderstood. With Blackfeet on the warpath, there's no tellin' what the Indians here have been dealing with."

"You sure they're Crow?" Joe demanded.

"I am."

The Crow were plainly marked by the beadwork on their buckskins and the feathers in their braided hair.

Preacher slowed Horse a little, and Joe urged his own mount at a faster pace till it plodded side by side with the other animal. The packhorses and Indian ponies followed in two separate strings behind them.

A short distance before Preacher drew even with the boat, the oldest man among the three waved at one of the younger men to put his bow away. Smiling, he called out in English.

"Preacher! Is that you?"

The Indian doing the hollering was younger than Preacher and showed no gray in his hair. His unlined face had a few scars from weapons and rough hands. He looked familiar.

"It is," Preacher replied, and took closer note of the man's beadwork on his buckskins. His wife, or wives, had a defined hand and an eye for color. Most of the beads were dark blue, and that helped the mountain man enough to identify the speaker. "It's good to see you, Blue Magpie. How's the fishin'?"

Blue Magpie reached beside the boat into the river and

hauled up a stringer of cutthroat trout that fought and wriggled.

"The fishing is good. The trout are lazy and hungry. Always a bad combination if you are the fish, but good if you are a fisherman."

The Crow warrior laughed and dropped the fish back into the river. He eyed the ponies trailing Preacher.

"You have many horses," Blue Magpie said. A hint of envy flashed in the Indian's eyes, and it was that trait that had derived his name. Blue Magpie had been born covetous, but he was a good man and treated others fairly.

"A Blackfoot war party came huntin' my scalp yesterday mornin'," Preacher explained. "Time the dust settled, they had no need for the horses, and I didn't aim to leave 'em to fend for themselves in bear country. Figured we'd sell them at the rendezvous. If we can get a good price for them."

"When I return to the rendezvous," Blue Magpie said, "if you haven't sold them all, perhaps we can talk and trade. Since I last saw you, I have a new wife and a new son. I will need another horse soon."

"You got yourself a new wife?"

Blue Magpie's boat had drawn even with Preacher. He nodded. "My brother, Smiles Like Red Fox, was slain fighting the Blackfeet last winter. I took his wife to be my wife and his son to be my son."

"Songbird agreed to that?" Preacher had good memories of Songbird. She was a strong and independent woman, and she was a good wife and mother. The last time the mountain man had visited them, she'd just had their second child.

"Songbird told me I had no choice." With the bull boat continuing downriver, Blue Magpie had to talk louder to be heard. "I had to take them. Do you know what a man who has two wives and four children does?"

"Four children? You had two. One more makes three. Unless my cipherin' is off."

Blue Magpie laughed. "It's been a while since we've seen you, Preacher. Surly Beaver and Feather Dances have a younger sister. Butterfly Whisper was born only last spring."

"With two wives and four children, I imagine there's quite a list of chores to do. You must stay busy." Preacher didn't want any form of domestic bliss for himself, and he was mostly glad he'd missed out on those hard years with his own son, Hawk That Soars. He enjoyed the relationship he had with his son now, wouldn't take anything for it. But he knew he wasn't a stay-at-home man.

"No." Blue Magpie shook his head. "They do the things that need doing. I just stay out of the way and make sure they have everything they need. I have more time for hunting and fishing. Otherwise, I'll sit in the tipi and get fat." He laughed.

Preacher laughed, too.

"Go visit Songbird when you get to the camp," Blue Magpie urged. "She'll be happy to see you. It's been a long time since she's seen you."

"I will."

"You can meet my new wife, too. Her name is Doe with Joy."

"I look forward to it."

"Tell them I'll be home soon. But not too soon. Not while the trout are hungry and I have daylight."

Preacher waved and continued upriver. His heart felt a little lighter. There would be a lot of people at the rendezvous, which wasn't something he was looking forward to, but he would enjoy seeing some of them.

CHAPTER 8

Tipis dotted the western bank of the Snake River a few miles southwest of Jackson's Lake. Thin smoke trails from cookfires danced up into the blue sky like they were trying to rope an occasional cloud. Women and small children tended to the cookfires and cooked meals. Others washed clothing along the river. Indian ponies stood picketed in the tall grass. More bull boats were moored to trees and big rocks along the riverbank. Three long canoes sat among them.

A few mountain men sat around in small groups together or talked with Indian men in front of tipis.

"We're on the wrong side of the river," Joe said.

"That happens when you come up through the Gros Ventre Range." The fact that Joe didn't know that made Preacher more suspicious of the man and what he might be hiding. "How were you expectin' to get over to the rendezvous?"

Joe frowned and shrugged. "I musta forgot. I usually come up through the Tetons. Just got on the wrong side of things back there."

That made even less sense for Joe to have gotten lost. The Snake River bent and twisted, but it stayed its course.

"That water looks mighty deep," Joe said. He frowned some more and worry lines creased his face.

"It is deep," Preacher said. "Especially right now after all the rain lately."

"You ain't gonna swim the horses across that, are you? 'Cause I'll tell you right now I ain't goin'. I can't swim."

"You can't swim?" Preacher couldn't believe that. Up in the mountains trapping and hunting, a man had to know how to swim.

"Never learned how. Went to the bottom ever' time I tried."

"You were a sailor."

"Didn't want to be one. An' when you're a sailor, you sail across the sea. You ain't supposed to leave the ship. You just go ahead an' swim on across. I'll make do on this side. We got meat, an' I can cook. An' there ain't nobody better'n me at cookin' up a mess of pan-fried fish."

"We'll leave the horses on this side while we go visitin'," Preacher said. He could shoot across the river easily in case anyone took a bad notion. The horses were in plain sight and he'd remain attentive. And there were other mountain men gathered there who wouldn't allow such nonsense. "They'll be safe enough. Someone will have a boat we can borrow to get across the river."

"Don't much care for boats, neither, but I don't want to miss out if there's a party goin' on. It looks like them fellas have already started." Joe pointed to a group of mountain men and Indians lounging in the shade of nearby trees.

The group passed a jug around and smoked pipes.

Another group of mountain men and Indian men and children had willow poles and lines out in the water. One of the mountain men reared back to set a hook, then hauled in a cutthroat trout that jumped and flopped and fought the line. A couple of the other men cheered and clapped the fisherman on the back.

Preacher spotted a good area with plenty of grass near a campsite that had been used sometime in the past. A ring of rocks stood out on a flat place where a tipi could be set up. Preacher didn't have a tipi, but he'd brought some tarpaulin he could put up against the rain. He wanted to camp away from the large group for more privacy. Farther down, more horses picketed along the riverbank grazed and swished their tails. The few campsites there had only a handful of men spread between them.

"We ain't the only ones on this side," he told Joe. "And this bunch has boats. We can probably borrow one or get a ride from one of them headed that way."

He rode Horse over to the campsite he figured on claiming and climbed down from the saddle. Without a word, Joe helped him set up on the spot. They stretched a picket line between a couple of tall oaks where the grass grew thick, and they tied the horses to it so the Indian ponies wouldn't wander off. Horse and the two pack animals Preacher had brought up from Nuevo Mexico would stay around together and not leave.

Preacher threw another rope over a tree branch high enough and thick enough to serve his needs, then he lashed the panniers and his other supplies to the rope. When he was satisfied with the knotting, he hauled on the rope and raised the panniers and supplies off the ground high enough that a bear couldn't reach them.

"What about this meat?" Joe asked. He pointed to the hide-wrapped pronghorn meat Preacher had taken from his kill yesterday. The meat sat in mostly neat bundles that were lashed together.

"We're gonna take it across to the cooks," the mountain man said. "We didn't want to show up beggin' with our hands out come supper time."

He shook out one more line and tied it to trees between the horses and the suspended supplies. He took up the tarpaulin he'd left out from his supplies, spread it over the rope, and drove stakes into the ground around it. He used pigging strings to lash the canvas in place. When he was finished, an A-frame shelter stood between the trees.

He placed his saddle inside. Joe added his own.

He checked the flintlock pistols under his belt at his back, the Patersons in their holsters at his hips, and slung his rifle over his shoulder. He added one of the rifles he'd taken from the Blackfeet and left the others covered by the tarpaulin inside the tent. Then he grabbed the meat and headed down to the river where a few bull boats were tied up. Dog followed beside Preacher.

"Stay close," the mountain man told the big cur, "so folks'll know you're with me and ain't some wolf that wandered in from somewhere to have a look-see."

Dog growled in annoyance or acceptance, but he walked at Preacher's side.

Three men sat on the riverbank and drank from a jug. Even at a distance the strong stink of the rotgut whiskey seared Preacher's nostrils, and the men were fragrant as well. From the smell of the liquor, they were men down on their luck. Or maybe they had a death wish.

"Afternoon," Preacher called out so he didn't completely surprise the men.

The three men turned around. They were big and rough,

hard men who'd gotten used to living on the dregs, or on what they could take from others. They weren't hard and fit from working in the mountains. Sometimes when the hunting and trapping got sparse, men like these took from others.

Or tried to.

Preacher had seen their kind in many places throughout his years, and he had no problem recognizing them. Before the rendezvous was over, they'd be trouble. Other mountain men who had thrown in with the Crow tribe knew it, too. That explained why these men were sitting on this side of the river. Preacher was just surprised nobody had had the gumption to run them off yet. If it didn't get tended to soon, he was of a mind to do it himself.

"It's a damn wolf!" the smallest man of the three squawked.

The speaker looked pale and sunburned and had peeling skin in places, a stark contrast to his friends. He tossed the jug, rolled to his right, and reached for the rifle lying on the ground. The other two men dove for their own weapons. The abandoned jug flew out into the shallows of the river and landed with a splash that set nearby frogs to hopping.

Knowing the men were too liquored up to listen to good reason, and not much of a mind to trouble himself by handing such advice out, Preacher dropped the bundles of meat and stepped forward. He kicked the small man in the face just as he came up and tried to aim the rifle. Preacher's kick propelled the man off his feet and sent him flying backward into the water. The rifle fired and the harsh crack of the shot pealed along the river.

Still moving because the other two men seemed dead

set on trying their luck, too, Preacher grabbed the rifle barrel of the man on his left with both hands. The mountain man kept the muzzle aimed over his shoulder into the air, and Preacher drove the metal-plated rifle butt back into the man's belly like a battering ram. The wind exploded out of him in a loud rush. Big as he was, the man couldn't remain standing with the vinegar knocked out of him.

Dog grabbed the remaining hardcase by his left shoulder and pulled him down to the ground. Panicked, the man bunched his fists and battered Dog, but the big cur knew his way around fights. Dog kept his head out of the way of the man's fists and blocked the attacks with his shoulders. He growled and shook his head. Blood threaded into the material covering the man's shoulder.

Holding onto the captured rifle, Preacher drew one of his flintlock pistols and aimed it at the big man struggling to get to his feet. The man knotted his fists.

"Go on and get to it if you got it to do," Preacher invited. He eared the pistol's hammer back with his thumb. "Normally, I wouldn't mind a scrap, but I don't want to worry none of these innocents around us. I'll put a ball right between your eyes."

The man stared at the pistol and froze. "You're lucky you caught us unprepared."

"You varmints are lucky I don't feel like diggin' any graves right now," Preacher countered. "Or like draggin' your bodies out into the woods for the bears and the wolves to get at. You stink bad enough, and dead I figure you'd foul up the air even worse."

Shaking his head, eyes full of hate and meanness, the man stayed where he was.

The man fighting with Dog squalled in pain and fear.

"Dog's just playin' with you right now," Preacher said.

"If you keep hittin' him, he's gonna chew your fists off and leave you with bloody stumps. It's best if you just lay on back before you rankle his good nature."

The man gave up and lay back. "All right, all right, but he's chewin' my shoulder off!"

"Dog," Preacher called.

The big cur released his hold, growled into the man's terrified face, and backed away a little. He didn't go so far that he couldn't flatten the man again if he needed to.

"You"—Preacher waved his pistol at the big man he covered—"fetch your friend out of the river before he drowns."

The small man lay unconscious and face down in the water. His arms were spread slackly out to his sides.

The big man caught his friend under the arms and hauled him from the water. As he stepped back out of the river with his burden, the small man regained consciousness, hacked and coughed, and swung his arms.

"Settle down, Lowell," the big man said. He never looked away from Preacher. "Fight's done over."

"I ain't done, Cotter," Lowell said through bruised lips. He held up his fists and his wet shirt sleeves fell back enough to reveal mostly healed scabs around his wrists. "I'm barely gettin' started."

Blood trickled down from his nose, which didn't set quite plumb anymore. Maybe it hadn't anyway, but it looked to be growing, too. Preacher didn't remember what the man's nose looked like before he'd kicked him and didn't much care. Lowell ran a forearm along his nose and winced in pain. Crimson streaked his forearm.

"Me an' Barney are done," Cotter said to his friend and to Preacher. The big man released Lowell and the small man stood unsteadily.

Gingerly, Barney, the man Dog had subdued, got to his feet.

On the other side of the river, several folks had gathered to see what was going on. A couple of the bull boats had put out from the riverbank and the passengers paddled cautiously across the expanse of slow but strong current. Two other men knelt in the boats with their rifles ready.

"You boys best get on out of here," Preacher said. "You threatened my dog—"

"That ain't no dog," the man with the wounded shoulder objected.

Preacher dropped the rifle he'd taken and backhanded the man across the face. Barney yelped and stumbled back a step.

"—and you've plumb used up my tolerance," Preacher continued like there had been no disturbance. "Pull up stakes and get out of here."

"Ain't no reason to drive us off," Cotter said. "We come a long ways to be here at the rendezvous. We're plannin' on meetin' up with some people."

"You're gonna go meet up with them somewhere else," Preacher said, "because if I lay eyes on you again while I'm here, I'm gonna finish what you boys started. You boys ain't no angels. Your friend there with the sunburn looks like he hasn't seen much of the out of doors lately, and he's got half-healed sores around his wrists where I'm bettin' he wore convict irons not too long ago. Unless I miss my guess, judgin' from your accents, you boys are from Missouri or Arkansas and your friend just got out of the Jefferson City penitentiary."

Preacher had seen the new prison, the first of its kind almost in the western lands. He didn't like the idea of penitentiaries coming west of the Mississippi, because lawmen clustered around such places and tended to tell other people how to handle thieves and varmints that just needed killing. Or to be run off, if a man was feeling in a more tolerable mood.

"C'mon, boys," Cotter said. "Let's go."

"We can't go," Lowell said. "We're supposed to meet—"

Cotter glared the smaller man into silence.

Lowell clamped his mouth shut and cussed under his breath for a moment. He reached for his rifle where it lay partially submerged.

"Leave it," Preacher ordered.

Dog growled and took a step forward.

"It's my rifle," Lowell said.

"I 'spect it belonged to somebody else before you got it," Preacher said.

"You can't do that," Cotter said. "An' I want my rifle back, too."

Preacher shifted his pistol to the center of Cotter's chest. "You ain't gettin' it."

"There's Blackfeet out there not so far away," Cotter protested. Desperation pulled at his features. "You can't send us out there unarmed."

"Can and am," Preacher said.

Before the argument could continue any further, a new voice yelled, "Hey, Preacher!"

CHAPTER 9

The mountain man stepped back a half-step and turned so he could sweep the river with his gaze. A bull boat reached the riverbank a short distance away. An old black man with gray shot through his hair threw a leg over the boat's side and settled his foot on the muddy ground.

"You got a problem here?" the black man asked.

He carried a rifle in one hand and wore a brace of pistols. He scowled at the three men Preacher had rousted. Despite the time that had passed since he'd last seen the man, Preacher recognized him immediately. He was a little leaner, a little grayer, but still possessed the same sharp, intelligent gaze. Humor twinkled in his dark eyes, too.

"Nothin' I can't handle," Preacher said, and smiled. "Been a good long spell since I've seen you, Lorenzo."

"It has been at that." Lorenzo looked past Preacher at the three men.

For some time, Lorenzo had hunted and trapped with Preacher, but the last time each had gone their own way, the old black man had been looking to settle down in gentler climes. Preacher had figured he'd probably seen the last of the wizened old man.

Time hadn't been easy on Lorenzo. More gray showed in his hair and whiskers, and he looked a little more stooped, but he acted as spry as ever.

"What you gonna do with these varmints?" Lorenzo asked.

"Movin' 'em on," Preacher replied.

"Some special reason? Or just on account?"

"One of 'em pulled a gun on Dog."

Lorenzo shook his head in exaggerated disbelief. "Hoo-whee. An' there they stand still drawin' air. They must be some mighty lucky men."

"Didn't want to take time to bury them and couldn't leave 'em lyin' about."

"Well, that wouldn't be no problem. Coulda just floated 'em on down the river." Lorenzo shot the three men a cold glare, and it was plain he meant every word.

"Look." Cotter directed his attention to Lorenzo and the two men who'd followed the old man from the boat. One of them was a young giant. "This fella's plumb outta his mind. He wants to take our rifles an' send us out into the mountains without a way of defendin' ourselves against Injuns."

Lorenzo frowned harshly at the man. "The three of you couldn't defend yourselves against a man an' a dog. You havin' rifles ain't gonna do you no good against a pack of Blackfeet. Now you best just go on an' git an' take care where you go till you get back to civilization."

The three men stood their ground for a moment longer. The young giant and the older man stepped out around Lorenzo to put up a front. Having no choice, the three turned and walked east, away from the Crow camp.

"Lord have mercy," Lorenzo said with a big grin when

the troublemakers had vanished into the woods, "but it has been a minute since I last laid eyes on you, Preacher."

"Last I heard, you were gonna take it easy," Preacher said. "Said you'd had your fill of huntin' and trappin' and livin' hard."

"I was. I did. An' then I got mighty bored. A man can go anywhere he wants to an' not escape boredom when it comes on him. It was on me somethin' fierce." Lorenzo gazed around at the valley. "You brought me out here for a time, Preacher, an' I fell in love with these here mountains more than I knowed I did." He rubbed a knuckle across his whiskered jaw. "I'm gettin' old, believe it or not. If I wanted to see these here mountains another time or two, an' I did, I knew I had to get on out here. So here I am."

"It's good to see you, Lorenzo." Preacher extended his hand, and the two men shook, their friendship as deep as it had ever been even though years had passed since they last saw each other.

"Mighty good to be seen." The old black man smiled. "Thought you wouldn't make it, though. Sure wasn't expectin' you. Heard you'd got yourself killed down in New Orleans over a Cajun queen or somesuch."

Preacher smiled. "That there's a story."

"Well, come on over to the main camp," Lorenzo said. "I'll introduce you around to some folks you ain't met, an' we'll visit with some we know."

"Sounds good." Preacher took a last look in the direction the three hardcases had gone.

There was no sign of them. The trees had swallowed them up whole.

"We'll keep an eye out for 'em," Lorenzo said. "Me and some o' the other fellas had just about decided to send them packin' when you showed up an' done it for us."

"Why were you going to do that?"

"Just plain good sense," Lorenzo said. "Ain't nobody I know who knows them. Me an' these other men," he jerked a thumb over his shoulder to indicate his companions, "didn't care none for the way they looked, neither."

Meeting strangers at a rendezvous wasn't uncommon, but usually men were known by other men.

"They were trouble," Preacher said. "Might yet still be."

"That meat?" Lorenzo pointed at the bundles.

"It is. Took a pronghorn yesterday."

"Well, it ain't doin' us no good on this side of the river. Let's fetch it on across." Lorenzo leaned down, patted Dog on the head, and gathered up a bundle in one hand. He straightened and looked past Preacher at Joe Len Darby. "Took on a new partner?"

"No," Preacher replied.

Joe was gathering bundles up with both hands.

"Found him bein' entertained by some Blackfeet about the time I took the pronghorn," Preacher said.

Lorenzo smiled. "Another story."

"It is. And somethin' of a mystery."

Preacher added the last of that in a quiet voice that made Lorenzo cock an eyebrow in curiosity. The old-timer didn't press him for an explanation, though.

Preacher wiped the mud from the rifle he held and spotted the small triangle burned into the stock. He compared it against the one on the rifle he'd taken from the Blackfeet who'd held Joe. They looked similar. He held the rifle out for Lorenzo's inspection.

"Have you seen that mark before?" Preacher asked.

Lorenzo studied it a moment, then shook his head. "Never have."

Preacher nodded.

"You ready to cross?" Lorenzo asked.

"I am," Preacher said. "I can smell food and pan bread cookin' from here."

"It's good," Lorenzo said. "An' there's plenty of it." He strode toward one of the bull boats.

The men surrounding the watercraft drew back fearfully.

"Preacher," the oldest of the group said, "me an' these three men were ready to back your play against them varmints, not that you needed us, but we were." He looked at Dog. "However, I ain't of a mind to ride in a boat with that . . . *dog* of yours. We get out in the middle of the river, ain't too many places to go. I hope you understand."

"You can ride with us," another man said.

A few years older than Preacher, the man stood tall and solid, wide shouldered and muscular. His skin was bronzed but held a reddish cast that showed how fair he'd been. He wore his long blond hair pulled back in a queue tied with a leather strip. His long blond beard hung to his barrel chest. Fierce blue eyes took Preacher's measure. He wore buckskins and moccasins that he looked comfortable in.

The man offered a big hand and a wide smile. "My name's Olaf Gunnarson. During my time in the mountains, I've heard many stories about you, Preacher, but we've never crossed paths."

Preacher took the man's hand and felt the strength in his grip. It was the hand of a man who worked hard. "I appreciate the use of your boat, Mr. Gunnarson."

"Just call me Olaf." Gunnarson turned slightly and nodded to the tall young man behind him. "This is my son, Bjorn. His mother's people call him Tall Dog."

The young man stepped forward. He stood at least six and a half feet tall and was skinny enough that Preacher wasn't sure he had stopped growing. His skin tone was darker than that of his father, and his hair was dark blond, cut to the skin on the sides of his head and pulled back in a long braid from the top. A scruffy beard partially covered his strong chin.

His steel-gray eyes were quick and took in everything. He carried a rifle in a big hand; a couple pistols and a tomahawk were tucked into his belt. A bow was slung over his shoulder as well as a quiver of arrows with gray goose fletchings, and a sword with a looped hilt in a scabbard over his shoulder. He looked prepared for just about anything.

The young man shook Preacher's hand. "It's good to meet you." He sounded a little like his father, but his accent was different. His grip was solid and sure, but not overpowering or prideful. "Let me help carry things."

He reached down and easily picked up two of the bundles of pronghorn meat by hooking his fingers under the ties.

Preacher followed the young giant toward the bull boat. Tall Dog placed the bundles in the center of the boat to balance it out, then stepped aboard. Preacher settled his bundles with the others, added his rifles, and called Dog into the boat. No stranger to watercraft, the big cur balanced himself and settled down next to the meat.

"I'll shove off," Preacher said.

Lorenzo, Joe, and Olaf clambered aboard the boat.

Once everyone was seated and ready, Preacher pushed the boat into the river current and followed it. The river bottom fell away quickly because the water was higher than normal. When the river was nearly up to his knees, Preacher hoisted himself over the side. The others leaned to offset his weight and he sat. He picked up one of the paddles and aided in their efforts to cut back upriver to get to the other side.

Preacher loved the clean, easy work of hauling on the paddle, of bending the river to his will. The river ran clear and deep until the bottom was lost. Despite the anticipation of joining the other mountain men and the Crow people, Preacher still looked forward to spending more time alone in the mountains hunting and trapping and doing the things he loved.

Except for the niggling problem of those rifles. He glanced at the triangle marking on the butts of the weapons lying next to the bundles of meat. The rifles weren't his problem, but he'd always been a curious man.

That would probably get him killed one day.

He just hoped that day never came while he was still wondering about something. The idea of dying without answers bothered him.

CHAPTER 10

On the other side of the river, Preacher and Tall Dog hauled the bull boat ashore. He, Joe, and the young giant grabbed the meat and headed for the center of the Crow campsite. The mountain men were welcome among the Indians as long as they provided meat and brought in trade goods. The tribe would not tolerate a freeloader or a person without something to offer.

Dog padded along at Preacher's side. The big cur's presence frightened many of the children and sent them scurrying for their mothers. Even the older boys and men stood back and watched Dog warily. Some of them knew Preacher and called out greetings, which Preacher acknowledged, but no one approached.

Lorenzo and Olaf went to join a group of mountain men throwing tomahawks at an overturned tree stump. Preacher was sure it was the jug of moonshine getting passed around that drew the men more than the sport. The solid *thunks* of the keen blades biting into the wood pierced the quiet conversations around the camp. Ribald comments came from the competitors.

"Preacher!" a woman cried out.

Recognizing the voice, Preacher stopped and turned toward the woman who had called out to him.

With a smile, Songbird walked toward the mountain man. Her buckskins were neat and clean, and her long dark hair was pulled back in braids studded with shells and pebbles. She was petite, barely five feet tall, and slim as a reed despite having children. A young child rode on her hip and gnawed on a fist. The child watched Preacher with big, dark eyes and laid her head on her mother's shoulder.

"Songbird," Preacher replied in Crow. He smiled, glad to see her just as he'd been happy to see Blue Magpie. He briefly introduced Tall Dog and Joe. "I saw your husband downriver only a short time ago."

"He was fishing?"

"He was."

Songbird grimaced, but the expression was put on for show, not a true feeling. "He always loves fishing."

"Seemed like he was doing well," Preacher said. "Gonna be plenty of fish to bring home."

"I'd rather have venison or buffalo meat. He likes fish too much. I have young children. They need red meat to grow, not fish. He needs to hunt more and fish less." Songbird blew out a breath and looked around at the nearby woods. "Except the fishing is better than the hunting. There are too many hunters here. The game has wandered farther away in the last few weeks."

Preacher raised the bundles he carried. "I've got pronghorn meat. Enough to share."

"Bring it to my tipi," Songbird said. "I can cook it up. You and your friends will be welcome to our meals."

Preacher followed her to her tipi in the middle of the other Crow homes. Joe and Tall Dog trailed after him. Preacher put down his bundles near the tipi and the other two men did the same. Songbird would see to it none of the meat would go to waste. Preacher used his small knife to carve off a sizeable chunk for Dog, tucked it into a bandanna, and tied the ends of the bandanna to his belt.

The tipi was carefully set up and stood solidly. East of the tipi, so it would catch the first light of day, a neatly tended garden of vigorous plants grew. Beans, corn, and squash occupied neat rows. When she could, when the tribe lit long enough to harvest a crop, Songbird put in a vegetable garden. Many of the other women had done the same. The gardens showed that they planned to be in the valley long enough to at least get a crop in.

Another woman sat cross-legged outside the tipi and worked on a buffalo hide with a sharp stone. She was a little more rounded than Songbird, wore her hair in braids, and was careful not to make eye contact with Preacher or the other new arrivals.

"This is Doe with Joy," Songbird said. "She is my new sister and Blue Magpie's new wife. Doe, this is Preacher."

The other woman looked up then and studied Preacher. "I have heard of you, Preacher. My old husband, Smiles Like Fox, spoke of you with respect."

"I am sorry for your loss," Preacher said. He tried to remember if he'd ever crossed paths with Smiles Like Fox and couldn't. There were a lot of people in the mountain man's past.

Doe's eyes turned misty. "He was a brave warrior, and I am told that he died well."

"You and your child are safe and with a good family," Preacher said. "That's all a man can ask for after he's gone."

The words felt stiff and awkward, but he had nothing

else to give. Living in the mountains made for a hard life, and living as an Indian made for an even harder one.

She nodded and returned her attention to the buffalo hide.

A campfire ringed by stones had been laid out in front of the tipi. A black pot hung over the low-banked coals so the contents would stay warm. The rich, herbal aroma of the stew laced with wild onions tantalized Preacher's nostrils, and his stomach rumbled.

Songbird laughed at him. "Are you hungry, Preacher?"

Preacher wasn't embarrassed a bit. Having an appetite was normal, and it was better if it could be appeased. "It's been a long time since breakfast, and that meal was eaten in the saddle. I got an early start so I could get here."

Songbird put the child on the ground. When the little girl whimpered, her mother shushed her. Immediately, the child ran to Doe with open arms and the other woman took her, pulled her close, and spoke softly to her.

"Having another wife around when there are small children is a good thing. We are all happy." Songbird stepped into the tipi and reappeared with metal bowls.

Like the kettle, the bowls had been gotten through trade with mountain men and peddlers. They were valuable things a woman would set store by.

Preacher knocked a knuckle against the metal. "Giving up the old ways of cooking?"

Songbird dipped stew out of the pot. "The old ways are fine. This is much faster, and not so much digging."

The first Crow people Preacher had known had cooked their meat in holes in the ground that were lined with raw hide from the animal being cooked. After water and meat were added, stones were heated in a fire and dropped into the water with the meat, stone after stone, until the meat was boiled.

Once the bowl was filled nearly to its brim, Birdsong handed it to Preacher.

"I have discovered I like stew. It is easy to keep and more flavorful. With so many children, stew is good to have. It lasts a long time. Their bellies are bottomless." She glanced at Joe. "Would you like some stew?"

Joe took his hat off and held it in his hands. "I don't know what you're sayin', ma'am, but if you're offerin' stew, I'd be mighty proud to have a bowlful."

"Of course," Songbird said in English.

She knew the language well, though she only used it when she needed to. Preacher had seen her dicker the dickens out of peddlers in times past. Many of those men had thought she didn't have a brain in her head at the beginning of the negotiations and had gotten snookered for their trouble.

Preacher held the warm bowl in his hands and took a sip. The broth was savory and filled with flavor. Songbird had always been a good cook, and she set a generous table for anyone welcome to it.

Joe took the bowl Songbird offered and Preacher studied the man again. How did Joe Len Darby end up all the way out here by his lonesome in the mountains and him not able to speak passable Crow? How had he planned on surviving? The questions slipped through Preacher's mind like minnows gliding through shallows.

Tall Dog took a bowl of stew as well. Songbird handed them some fry bread flavored with plums and the three men walked a short distance away to a small patch of shade. Even though the temperature was cool up in the mountains, Preacher knew the sun could still affect a man who stayed out in it too long. He set the bowl aside and took the pronghorn meat from his belt. With deft fingers, he unwrapped the bandanna and tossed the bloody chunk to Dog. Dog caught the meat in the air and gave it his full attention.

As he ate, Preacher scanned the campgrounds. The Crow village was large, probably eighty or ninety Indians. They would struggle to keep everyone fed with that many, but with the good weather and the river, they would manage. Not as many mountain men were there as he'd expected.

Their present good fortune would change with the coming of winter, but for now they were well situated.

"Is something bothering you?" Tall Dog asked.

The question drew Joe's attention and he tried to watch Preacher and the young giant without being obvious. He failed and flushed a little when Preacher caught him looking.

Preacher glanced at the younger man.

"Forgive me," Tall Dog said. "I sensed something was making you uncertain. My father warns me that sometimes I am too forward and speak often without thinking. He hopes that tendency will pass." He nodded to himself. "Your business is your own, and I shouldn't pry. I have invited myself to your meal. Perhaps I should not have done that."

The young giant made to get up from his cross-legged position.

"Stay," Preacher said. "You're welcome here."

Tall Dog nodded and sat himself again.

Preacher smiled. "If I was of a mind, I wouldn't answer any questions I didn't want to, so you ask any question you've got a mind to. You've got a keen eye, Tall Dog." He took a bite of stew meat, chewed, and swallowed. "I was just ruminatin' on a few worrisome things. Nothin' of any real consequence. More likely I'm just borrowin' trouble."

"I felt your concern. It is something I sometimes do." The young man flushed and looked embarrassed. "My father blames my mother's blood. He says some of her old ways of being sensitive to the spirits and their wanderings have wound up in me. My mother insists that I take too much after my father's Irish mother. According to my mother, my father's mother five generations back was a witch."

"A witch?" That interested Preacher. He was always one for a good story. In Indian lore, witches could be good or evil. Personally, he didn't think witches were any different than anyone else. They probably came good and bad just like most folks.

"My great-great-great grandmother was born in a place called Carrickfergus in a place called Ireland," Tall Dog said. "My father's people came there from a land known as Norway. They came to raid and wage war and steal treasure, but as sometimes happens . . . my great-great-great-grandfather found the love of his life instead. A treasure greater than gold."

"You can track five generations back?" Preacher asked. If pressed, and if he had time to think on it, he could remember his great-grandparents' names. It wasn't something that came up often, and he'd lit a shuck from his own family at an early age because he'd found the West and the West had found him.

Tall Dog nodded. "Yes. My mother has made sure I know where I come from regarding my father's people. My father carries a Bible given to him by his mother that has been kept current by all the women of that line. They each marked down the births and deaths of family members. Now my mother keeps it current."

Preacher had heard of people carrying such Bibles. Some of the women in the wagon trains he'd guided had read from those books at night around campfires, and they'd marked deaths along the journey to Oregon in the pages.

"My father was the only child his mother ever had," Tall Dog said. "So when the time came and she knew she was dying, she gave the Bible to my father. She made him promise to take care of it and to keep records of the family as each generation came along. When my mother learned of my father's Bible, she took it as her own. She learned to read in the white man's school. As a young child, barely walking, she was taken by white men to be a child to white parents who could have no children of their own. Instead, she was treated as a servant, tolerated only for the services she provided them. When she was a young woman, my father found her at one of the early trading posts along the Mississippi, fell in love with her, learned how miserable she was, and brought her back out here to the Crow. That much she remembered. During her travels with my father, she hoped to find her first family, but that did not happen. She could not remember her family, and no one recognized her. Without her true Indian name, that hope dimmed."

"Sounds like your momma has had an eventful life," Preacher said.

"She has. She hates the lack of knowing her family, of belonging to the Crow in a way more than simple blood. Only the fact that she still remembered much of the Crow tongue allowed her to stay with various tribes in the company of my father. The only true history of family she has is recorded in the Bible my father carries. That history is not hers, but it is mine. Because of that, she has adopted them as our people and taught me, and even my father, who they were."

"A witch's Bible?" Joe shook his head. "You ask me, that would be a cursed thing an' you'd best be shut of it. If I was you, I'd burn the thing an' be done with it."

For a moment, Tall Dog stilled, and dark red stained the back of his neck. Preacher set himself to interfere if the young man's anger got the best of him. Then Tall Dog let out a breath and the tension in his broad shoulders relaxed.

"Well," Joe said, seemingly oblivious to the reaction he had almost provoked, "I've et all I can. Time to see a man about a horse." He got to his feet, dusted off his breeches, and walked away. He left the bowl and spoon where he'd finished with them.

Tall Dog focused on his bowl.

"That Bible means a lot to your folks," Preacher said.

The young giant glanced at the mountain man with a measure of defensiveness.

"I'm not gonna speak against it," Preacher said. "Every man has to figure out what means something to him. For your ma, it's history and a sense of belongin'. For your pa, he loves your ma and that's enough. You're still figurin' out the things that mean somethin' to you, and that's how it's supposed to be. That's what sets a foundation in a man."

Preacher sopped up some of the stew with a piece of frybread and tossed it to Dog. The cur snapped it up in a single chomp.

"And you?" Tall Dog asked. "What holds meaning for you, Preacher?"

There was no challenge in the younger man's words,

only interest. Normally, Preacher might have ignored the question, seeing as how it was of a personal nature and he'd only just met the young man, but Tall Dog was seeking knowledge.

"That dog holds meanin' for me." Preacher nodded toward the big cur only a few feet away. "My horse. A few friends. And these mountains." He paused. "What you sensed troublin' me was me lookin' out on those mountain men yonder." He waved an arm toward the various groups of men among the Crow Indians. "There's less of them in this place than there was when I first found my way out here. Maybe it's just because some of 'em have found other places to be. I don't know. This way of life that I love, that holds so much meanin' for me, I think maybe it's goin' away. That leaves me feelin' a mite diminished sometimes when I think on it. So I try not to think on it much."

"You sound like the tribal Elders," Tall Dog said. "They worry about the same thing."

"Well, I think it's somethin' everybody who loves bein' out here in the mountains, who makes a home out here, should be worried about. The West is fillin' up, and one day it will be different from what we know now. You may live long enough to see that."

"You don't think you will?"

"Oh," Preacher said, "I think I will. I'm a stubborn cuss when it comes to dyin', and that's a fact. Livin' beyond what I know and love, that's what bothers me most of all." He grinned, but the expression held no mirth, only a trace of sadness, but he thought maybe his listener couldn't see that.

The idea of losing the mountains did bother him today. That and Joe Len Darby.

"While you are among us, I'll help you keep an eye on

him," Tall Dog said. "The old man." He nodded toward Joe, who was walking toward the men throwing tomahawks.

Surprised at how the young man had caught his thoughts, Preacher considered what he could say, couldn't rightfully put anything together, and nodded.

"All right. I'm obliged to you."

Dog lay nearby with his ears pricked and his eyes watchful. Probably he was just looking over the wilderness and thinking about white-tailed jackrabbits that might be wandering there.

Preacher fished a bit of meat from the stew, called to Dog, and, when Dog turned his attention to him, tossed the meat to the big cur. Dog opened his jaws and caught the tidbit in mid-air.

"He reminds me of a wolf from my father's stories," Tall Dog said.

"Dog?"

"Yes. In my father's stories, the wolf is called Fenrir. Have you heard of him?"

Preacher thought for a moment but couldn't call anything to mind. He shook his head.

"Fenrir was also called the Fenris wolf in the stories of the Norse. His name means fen-dweller. He was one of the children of Loki. Have you heard of him?"

That name rang a bell for Preacher. One of his best friends, a trapper named Audie, had been a professor from some university back East. Audie was just full of stories about fantastic people and far-off places, and Preacher thought he'd heard him mention the name.

"Loki was some connivin' thief or somesuch. A trick-ster like Raven in the Indian stories."

Tall Dog nodded. "That was Loki. His son, Fenrir the wolf, killed Odin, the king of the Norse gods, during a great battle called Ragnarok. Or he will kill him. The stories insist they repeat. So perhaps Fenrir will kill Odin again and again." The young giant shook his head and smiled. "The stories my father has shared of his people's beliefs are confusing."

"Sounds like," Preacher said. "I never want to meet anything I have to kill twice. And I won't have to. I make sure I do the job the first time. That's a lesson I've learned."

They ate in silence and Preacher fed Dog from his bowl and from the bread. When he was finished, he picked up the bowl and spoon Joe had abandoned and took everything back to Songbird.

She was staring to the west, and he followed her line of sight to a small group of horsemen winding through the foothills of the Tetons.

"Know them?" Preacher asked.

"Not from this distance," Songbird said. "But they're white, not Indian, and they wear white man's clothing, not buckskins like a mountain man would."

Preacher had noted those details, too. He thanked Songbird, settled his rifles over his shoulder, and headed over to the small knot of Crow warriors and mountain men gathering to meet the riders.

CHAPTER 11

Obviously cautious, the riders approached the Crow village. The eleven men spread out in two lines to present a solid front to the waiting Indians and mountain men and halted their advance. The riders carried rifles and pistols, and had more pistols holstered on either side of their saddles in the manner of cavalry soldiers. Yet they weren't clothed in the blue uniforms.

One of the men urged his horse forward a few steps and stopped again. He studied the mountain men and Crow warriors in front of him from beneath the shadow of a broad-brimmed hat. He showed no emotion, but his body was tense, ready, and he sat in the saddle straight and tall.

"My name is Arnold Diller," the man declared in a strong voice that carried.

Preacher recognized the name from Joe Len Darby's stories. This was the captain who insisted on fine sipping whiskey. Preacher glanced around for Joe, but the old man wasn't in sight.

Broad and powerful looking, Diller's chiseled face held scars from past conflicts. His right eye was partially closed because of the thick scar that bisected his eyebrow. He wore a thick black mustache that almost reached his side whiskers. Days-old stubble dotted his chin. His gloved right hand clasped the rifle canted across his saddle pommel.

"I'm seeking no trouble," Diller said. He offered a tentative smile. "Nor am I bringing any. My men and I only want to share the camp for the night."

"There's plenty of campin' spots nearby," one of the mountain men said.

Diller nodded. "That there are. As I'm sure you know, there are hostile Blackfeet in the mountains, and they're taking scalps. I thought perhaps we could enjoy the safety of numbers together for the night before my men and I ride on. Might that be possible?"

A trapper named Jess Thompkins stepped forward. He cradled his Hawken rifle over his left forearm and had his right hand on the grip, ready to ear back the hammer and let fly at the first sign of trouble. Gray hair trailed past his thin shoulders and his gray beard hung halfway down his chest. Tobacco juice stained the gray whiskers a rancid yellow-brown like a red squirrel's underbelly.

Thompkins was a formidable man among trappers and hunters. Three of his sons backed him with fierce intensity. All of them had been marked by their pa and it showed in their thin, rangy builds and big hands. Thompkins had lost just as many sons to the mountains and to the Blackfeet. He was a hard and knowledgeable man who knew and loved the wild country.

"I'm Jess Thompkins," the old man announced.

Diller nodded. "I've heard of you, Mr. Thompkins. You used to scout for Fort Pierre."

"I did," Thompkins acknowledged. "Didn't take me long to cipher out there wasn't enough money in scoutin' for the Army. Nor in soldierin'."

Diller laughed. "You're not the first man to think that. Even so, there still remains a need for good soldiers in these wild lands." The man gazed over the crowd before him. "Are you speaking for everyone, Mr. Thompkins?"

"I am unless someone decides to stand agin' it."

"Then may we share the camp?"

"Got a standing rule," Thompkins said. "Don't allow no freeloaders. You don't figure on helpin' out none, or got nothin' to contribute, best you camp on the other side of the river. The Snake's mighty big right now, but there's a place where a man can get across the shallows seven miles upriver."

Standing at the forefront among the Crow warriors, Preacher scanned the wilderness behind Diller and his men. The horses before them couldn't have been enough to raise all the dust he'd seen coming down out of the Tetons.

And there wasn't a packhorse among them. The men looked tired, like they'd been riding hard, but they didn't look half-starved. They couldn't have been living off the land. They had supplies somewhere. Probably more men, too.

"My men and I were fortunate and took down three buffalo this morning," Diller said. "Got more meat than we can eat, and there isn't any use of it going bad. I know hunting around this area has been sparse after all the time the camp has been here. Your hunters probably have to go a ways to get good meat. We would be happy to share."

Getting lucky finding meat meant Diller was looking for the camp and had wanted something to barter with, Preacher reasoned. Otherwise, a man traveling hard wouldn't have stopped to dress out big kills. Especially three of them. Diller hadn't just come across the Crows. With Blackfoot warriors restless and prickly in the mountains, Diller had to have a reason for coming out this far and for seeking out the Crow.

"The meat's temptin'," Thompkins admitted, "but we've got plenty of it."

"What about tomorrow or the day after? The meat I've got can be salted and put back for a while."

"We take care of today. Tomorrow takes care of itself. These mountains give a lot for a man who knows where to look."

Diller surveyed the mountain men. "How many of you have cut Blackfoot sign while heading up into the mountains?"

The mountain men shifted and exchanged glances.

"I did," a man said. "I was fortunate enough not to run into any of them."

"Me, too," another man said.

"I did run into them," a third man said. He touched his side where old blood showed on his buckskin shirt. "Four days back, I come up on 'em afore I knowed it. Couldn't get away fast enough. Almost didn't get away at all."

"You can camp up here for a while," Diller said. "You can hope none of those Blackfeet find their way to you, but they've been raiding small camps and attacking wagon trains. What happens should they come calling? You all are out here with not many places to go, and even less to hide." He gazed over the crowd and glanced toward the main camp. "You have women and children here, too. Those Blackfeet have got a war chief among them. A man named Stone Eyes who lives to take scalps."

Uneasiness stole over the crowd of Crow warriors and mountain men. Most of them had fought in battles. A man didn't live out in the mountains without having to fight men or beasts or weather or the mountains. They would fight if it came to it, but most of them didn't want it to come to that. No one knew for sure how a fight would go, even if it was won.

"Stone Eyes is a bad Injun," one of the Thompkins boys said. "He enjoys killin'."

Some of the other mountain men and Crow warriors quietly agreed.

Diller interrupted the rumble of conversations. "Do you have plenty of powder and shot? Because I've got extra of both. Not much, but I'm willing to wager it'll be more than what you've got right now. As far as that buffalo meat I've got goes, you can jerk it and turn it into pemmican, shore up the stores you now have in case hunting becomes dangerous while Stone Eyes is in the area." He paused. "With any luck, you won't need shot or powder or meat, but I always figure it's better to have and not need than to come up short at a bad time."

Those were good bargaining points.

Thompkins glanced over to an old Crow chieftain. They talked briefly, then the chieftain stepped forward.

"I am Finds the Balance," the chieftain said. "I speak for this camp. Should my warriors, my friends, and I come to an agreement, in exchange for meat and powder and shot, you may spend the night here. Your horses may graze here, and you may help yourselves to the water, but you will remain separate from the Crow tipis."

To Preacher, the "bargain" was too one-sided. The soldiers were giving up a lot. Of course, if they had extra powder and shot, and had just taken the buffalo, those things were just extra weight to lug around. Still, the deal made him a mite curious.

"How many men are with you, Captain Diller?" Preacher asked.

Several of the men surrounding Preacher turned their attention to him. Some whispered agreement with his question.

"There's eleven of you showin'," Preacher went on, "but there are more. If you've got extra powder and shot, you've got packhorses somewhere. They ain't out there by themselves."

Diller turned to him and smiled. "You're a cautious and attentive man, my friend. I do have more men." He jerked a thumb over his shoulder. "I've got another fifteen men back there watching over the supplies."

Twenty-six men made a sizeable force. They were all strangers, unknown to Preacher. That made him uncomfortable.

"Why ain't you in uniform?" Preacher asked.

"Because we don't want to announce ourselves as soldiers," Diller said. "I don't want Stone Eyes to know the Army's coming until we're on top of him."

"Man does have a point," Lorenzo whispered as he sidled up next to Preacher.

"I know," Preacher whispered back.

"An' myself," Lorenzo went on, "why, I wouldn't mind gettin' more powder and shot. It'll save us on gatherin' up sulfur an' lead from them places in the mountains. Would have to do some travelin' to get to those, an' that might not be safe. Especially if them Blackfeet are out there lookin' for trouble."

"They're out there. Like I told you, I ran into them myself."

"We need to get to that story soon."

"We will."

Finds the Balance looked at Preacher. Preacher knew the old chief was examining the unknown versus the known, weighing what was and what could be. The old chief had respect for Preacher. They'd met in passing a couple times.

Preacher nodded. Having the extra powder and shot would be good.

After glancing at some of the other Crow warriors and mountain men, Finds the Balance talked briefly with Thompkins, then he turned to Diller. "Bring your men into the camp. We will show you where you can stay. You will be fed."

Diller touched his hat. "I appreciate it, Chief Finds the Balance. We've been in the saddle for the last two days, and we've been living off hardtack and biscuits. We're about out of that, and some of my men are complaining. A hot meal would be most welcome. I'll send a rider to get my other men." He turned in the saddle and gave the order.

The chief summoned two of the young braves and they called to Diller and his men to follow them.

As the Army rode past, a trace of unease threaded through Preacher.

"Somethin' on your mind?" Lorenzo asked.

"Yeah," Preacher said. "There's gettin' to be too much Army in the mountains for my likin'."

"You might not think so if you're hard up against it with this Stone Eyes an' his braves."

"If you think about it a little," Preacher said, "you'll realize Stone Eyes might not be out here without bein' chased by the Army."

"Maybe so," Lorenzo allowed. Like Preacher, he watched

the soldiers, too. "Reckon that bunch of Indians you run into belonged to Stone Eyes?"

"Could be. Guess we'll see soon enough."

"Two men were with Silent Owl and his warriors here in this place."

Stone Eyes sat on his horse at the outside edge of the clearing and stared at the bodies sprawled across the ground under the thin patches of trees and clouds.

His only son lay cold upon the ground. Predators had worried at Silent Owl's body, as they had the others, and left him torn and ragged in places, but the young man remained recognizable. The pain that coursed through Stone Eyes gnawed at his shattered heart as the carrion eaters had desecrated his son's body.

But ignoring his sorrow, unwilling to let it show to his warriors, he worked on forging those pieces of his heart into hard iron with venom and rage.

"Only two men killed my son and these warriors?" Stone Eyes asked in disbelief.

Tracker Who Sees leaned on his rifle and forced himself up from a crouch. He was thin and careful. Gray mixed with his black hair and marked his advanced years. His face was long and narrow and fit his rangy frame.

He was twenty years older than Stone Eyes and no longer got around as well as he had in his youth. A fall from a cliff while pursued by soldiers a dozen years back had left him with a limp that had gotten progressively worse over time. One day soon he would no longer be able to ride with war parties, but for now the old man was the best tracker Stone Eyes had. His dark gaze moved quickly around the clearing again and he spoke softly.

"Only one man killed your son and these warriors," Tracker Who Sees announced. "Two men were here, but before the fight, one of them was a prisoner held by Silent Owl."

"How do you know that?"

Tracker Who Sees pointed to blurry impressions on the ground. "See? Here are the imprints of his knees and the toes of his boots. He was held in the place for a time." The old scout leaned down and picked up a short length of rope. "This was what bound him." He gripped the end of the rope and flicked it with his thumb. "He was cut free. There was no reason to waste good rope in country where rope might not be found so easily except to free him in a hurry."

"My son's killer fled?"

Tracker Who Sees tilted his head. "I do not think he fled. He took his time and gathered all the rifles Silent Owl and his warriors carried. After that, the two men left quickly. I found those tracks as well."

Stone Eyes took a breath. He had been so wrapped up in pain and rage that he hadn't noticed the absence of the rifles. Their disappearance raised more questions. Army men were looking for those rifles. Once the ambushed wagon train was discovered, and it would be, that pursuit would be increased.

"The man came looking for the rifles?" Stone Eyes asked. Those rifles had already caused the death of a few men.

"No." Tracker Who Sees shook his head. "Silent Owl's warriors tried to ambush their killer closer to the river. He did not know they were upon him until it was almost too late."

"He should have been dead." Stone Eyes's throat was

raw with tight rage and grief, like something with heavy claws had climbed in there and ravaged him. "Those warriors knew how to kill."

"Perhaps. But he taught them to die."

Stone Eyes stared at his dead son. "Why would a lone man come toward them? To save the man my son held prisoner? He should have run. He was outnumbered."

"It could be so, but Silent Owl and his warriors were between their intended victim and the man's horse." Tracker Who Sees pointed to the southeast. "I found the horse's tracks over there."

"You know it was his horse?"

"The man had set up camp there. I found the ash of a campfire. That horse was larger than the ponies we ride. And it was shod."

"He came back for his horse."

Tracker Who Sees shrugged. "It might be so, my chief. It could also be the captive white man called out for help."

Stone Eyes glanced around and turned to one of the warriors a short distance away. "Have you found the ponies my son and his warriors rode?"

The man shook his head.

"The man who killed your son took the horses as well," Tracker Who Sees said. "I found their tracks where he led them away."

Unable to sit still, Stone Eyes slid from his pony and dropped the reins. He fisted his rifle and strode along the area. Ruddy black blood stained the ground in puddles, and the shallow depths moved with the insects that had gone there to feast.

Bear Kills Many sat on his pony. Higher on the ridge that peered down over the river below, he had a clear field of view. The trees and brush provided cover in places, but none was enough to permit an enemy to sneak up on them. The other braves spread out to watch for any signs of trouble.

"One man could not have killed all these warriors," Stone Eyes declared. "These warriors were not babes. They'd all shed blood and taken scalps. My son would not have been taken so easily."

"Your son bravely faced the man who killed him," Tracker Who Sees said. "It is so. He stood his ground."

Stone Eyes found no solace in that. Perhaps he would later. His son was dead, and inside Stone Eyes screamed for vengeance. He looked around at the bodies. How could a lone warrior kill so many?

"One man?" Stone Eyes asked. "Are you sure about this?"

"I have walked the killer's path," Tracker Who Sees said. "I can show you his way. It was one man. On this I stake my life."

"What kind of man was he?"

"I do not rightly know. He was swift and deadly, and he made up his mind to kill his opponents quickly." Tracker Who Sees waved a thin arm over the battlefield. "All of this, all of the killing, was done in a short time. The killer was efficient and measured."

"Can you find this man?"

"The man wore moccasins that were well-worn. His horse has shod hooves that bear singular markings. I will know them if I see them again. Right now, we have a trail that leads to him."

When Stone Eyes had ridden up onto the site, he had forced himself to be still, to bank his anger and pain so that he might use those things when they were ready. He walked along the edge of the carnage and struggled to remain distant and clearheaded.

"I have never seen a man who could do this on his own," Stone Eyes said.

"The man was not alone," Tracker Who Sees said.

Stone Eyes glared at the old man. "You said it was one man."

The old scout nodded. "One man . . . and one wolf." He knelt and touched a large paw print on the ground. "This is the mark of the wolf. Some of the bodies bear wounds of a wolf's teeth and talons."

"Those marks could be from carrion feeders."

"Come." Tracker Who Sees stepped away a short distance and waved to Stone Eyes. "Let me show you." He pointed to the ground.

Although Stone Eyes was hesitant about stepping so near the violently dead because their spirits would be restless, he approached the old man. There, at Tracker Who Sees's feet, the indentation of a wolf paw stood out on the crushed grass and dried mud. When the battle had taken place, the ground had still been soft.

He knelt, brushed away some of the grass, and studied the print. It was large and deep, and black blood overlaid it.

"This was a big wolf," Tracker Who Sees said softly. He placed his hand beside the print and the wolf's mark was almost as big as the old scout's.

"And you believe the wolf came with the man?"

"It is so."

Stone Eyes glanced around at the other animal tracks on the ground. "I see prints from other wolves and from coyotes. From crows and weasels." He pointed at nearby tracks that were larger even than the wolf's. "There is even a bear who came to feast. Why do you say the wolf was with the man?"

"Because I found tracks nearer the river where the man was hunting. The wolf was with him then."

"Perhaps it was merely a wolf who came by later? One who was trailing the man?"

Tracker Who Sees shook his head. "Look at the print more closely. You must see."

Stone Eyes looked more closely. The print was large, much larger than any of those scattered elsewhere around the battleground.

"What am I to see?" Stone Eyes asked.

"Do you see the blood?" Tracker Who Sees asked.

"Yes."

"Where is it? What have I taught you? A track shows the passage of time, not just passage of a man or beast or bird."

Stone Eyes glared at the print. He was in no mood for the old man's teaching. Then he saw what the scout wanted him to see. Dried spots of blood speckled the print.

"The blood is on top of the track," Stone Eyes said.

Tracker Who Sees nodded. "It is so. The wolf was here while the killing happened. Silent Owl and his warriors were attacked and were killed. The blood from one of them covered the wolf's track."

Stone Eyes absorbed that information and sat quietly.

"Silent Owl and his braves weren't made victim to just any man," Tracker Who Sees stated. "I know of only one man who travels these mountains in the company of a wolf."

"Do not say that name," Stone Eyes growled. Old memories and stories stirred at the back of his mind. He had never met the man those things summoned, but he had heard of the Ghost Killer among the Blackfeet warriors who feared him. "I do not want my warriors to know. Not yet."

If they did know, Stone Eyes couldn't trust all of them not to leave.

"As you wish, my chief," the old scout said, "but they will know eventually."

"Once we slay the Ghost Killer, then they can know. I will not have them be afraid now. I will not have them fear him and make him more than a man. There has been enough of that. He is a man, and men can be killed. Do you know which way he went?"

"Yes. He will be easy to find. A man on his own, even in the company of a large wolf, might be hard to find, but the other man rides with him and—"

"—they took the ponies," Stone Eyes said.

Tracker Who Sees nodded. "It is so. We can find the man who killed your son easily. If that is what you wish to do."

"I will have his scalp, old man. That is a promise." Stone Eyes stood and looked to the northwest. "He took the ponies to trade. There is a Crow tribe who has camped by the river and intend to stay for the summer."

Stone Eyes had ambushed a group of peddlers three weeks ago who had traded with the Crow now camped beside the river. The peddlers had traded pots and pans for furs with the Crow. Stone Eyes had taken the furs and sent them south to be traded to the Comancheros. Tobit Moon Deer always took skins, though not as gladly as he once had.

"The Crow will be on the other side of the river,"

Tracker Who Sees said. "If he has gone there, he will be hard to get to."

"We will trail the man far enough to know this," Stone Eyes said. "Once we are certain that is where he is going, there are shallows some miles up the river where we can cross with our horses. The peddlers said there were only seventy Crow in the camp. At least half that number will be women and children. Almost half of those left will be too old or too inexperienced to fight us."

"The way will be hard," Tracker Who Sees said. "I know where the shallows are. We will not reach the crossing tonight."

Stone Eyes nodded. "Not tonight. We will care for the body of my son and the bodies of his warriors. I will not leave them to be devoured by animals."

Tracker Who Sees nodded and walked away.

Steeling himself, Stone Eyes walked over to his son's body and knelt beside it. He took in the carnage created by the gunshot to his son's chest and drew his knife. With a father's love, he dragged his fingers across the scar on Silent Owl's face. When Silent Owl had been eight, an Army soldier had tried to kill the boy. He had saved his mother from the soldier's sword but hadn't been able to save himself. Only Stone Eyes's arrival with his warriors had prevented the tribe from being wiped out.

Stone Eyes had prevented the soldier from being killed outright, then he'd spent four days killing the man. Only the man's weakness and surrender to death had kept the torture from continuing.

Holding his knife tightly, Stone Eyes gathered his long hair behind his head, and slashed through it. It hung just short of his shoulders. He would wear his grief for all to see. His would be the last face Ghost Killer ever saw.

He turned to his men and held up his fistful of hair.

"We ride to avenge my son," he declared. "Let everyone know."

Bear Kills Many drew his knife, grabbed his hair, and slashed. He threw the handful of hair to the ground. All the other warriors followed suit. Even Tracker Who Sees sawed off several inches of his hair. It was the way of the Blackfeet and many other tribes.

Stone Eyes dropped the hair to the ground and banked his grief. Ghost Killer could not escape his vengeance. If the gods were merciful, his son's killer would dance with death for days before his spirit fled his body.

CHAPTER 12

Preacher stood in the center of a group of mountain men and Crow men and boys. He poured a measure of powder into the barrel of one of the rifles he'd taken from the Indians he'd crossed paths with the day before. He patched a ball, seated it firmly, and slid the ramrod free. He shoved the ball down against the powder, remounted the ramrod, and took up the rifle.

Then he gazed at the branch he'd shoved into the soft riverbank a hundred yards away. He'd cut the branch with his big knife. The target was only as thick as two of his fingers together.

"That's too far," one of the spectators said.

"I can't even see it," another stated.

"That's because you're blind, Holcomb!" a third man taunted.

Laughter followed the comment, as did Holcomb's cursing.

"You shoulda got a bigger branch, Preacher," the first man observed.

"I got two-bits that says he don't even come close," a fourth said.

"That's Preacher," a Crow called out. "He hits what he aims at. I saw him drop a buffalo at five hundred yards a few years ago."

"Maybe so," a man said, "but a buffalo's a lot bigger than that skinny stick."

"I'll take that two-bit bet you offered," Lorenzo said. He stood to one side of Preacher and smiled confidently. "An' I'll take any bet that's against Preacher."

A dozen other men crowded up to Lorenzo to place bets. Silver coins flashed in the sunlight, and even a few Crow bracelets and trinkets were added to the pile. Lorenzo took them all into his hat, which he held in both hands before him. The whole time several of the mountain men and Indians alike heckled Lorenzo.

"If Preacher misses," one of the mountain men said, "you're gonna be walking down out of these mountains."

"Not till after he beats the dust out of the buffalo hides in my tipi," a Crow brave stated. "It will take a while. My wives are very particular about how those are done. They like them good and clean."

A chorus of laughter rang around Preacher, and he couldn't help but grin. He enjoyed the company of men in good humor at times in spite of his solitary nature. This was one of those times.

Despite the encounter with Silent Owl and the Black-feet warriors, he was calm and relaxed. Being back in the mountains with men he knew and understood was a lot better than being in St. Louis or New Orleans. Or even Texas.

The Rocky Mountains were home to him, and thank God they were big enough for a rambling man to go yondering as the mood took him.

Preacher glanced at Lorenzo. "You got your fill?"

Lorenzo shook his hat and created a soft, heavy jingling. He smiled. "I believe I do."

"Good. Now hope that this rifle shoots straight."

Lorenzo's smile melted and his eyes rounded. "Say what?"

"The rifle's new to me."

"You haven't shot it?"

"Nope."

"Well, now, Preacher," Lorenzo said, "that there seems like somethin' you should have told me."

"I didn't want to interrupt you at your gamblin'."

Lorenzo shook his head and looked unhappy. "Now it feels a whole lot more like gamblin'."

Preacher grinned, pulled the rifle to his shoulder, and locked the sights on the stick target. He slid his finger over the trigger, let out a half-breath, and squeezed.

The rifle roared, spat flame, and kicked back against Preacher's shoulder. Dark gray smoke unfurled around the rifle and created a small cloud.

Preacher automatically reached for another cartridge from his possibles bag, tore it, and spilled the powder into the rifle barrel. Hit or miss, one shot didn't prove the rifle.

"Did he hit it?" Holcomb demanded. "I can't see that far."

A hundred yards away, the stick canted to the left and a few inches off the top were gone. Splintered white wood created a prickly top where the ball had torn through.

"He hit it," a man declared solemnly. "Looks like he almost missed, though. That stick's leanin' to the left. He caught it on the right side."

"The sights are a little off," Preacher said. "I'll fix that soon enough."

"Ain't like you to let the sights get off on your rifle, Preacher," someone said.

"It ain't my rifle," Preacher replied. "This is a Hawken. Near to new. And it shoots a fifty-four-caliber ball. I'm sellin' this one to anyone who wants it. Money or trade goods. Don't matter to me."

He hauled the rifle to his shoulder again. The men around him stepped back to give him room.

"Anybody lookin' to go double or nothin'?" Lorenzo crowed happily. "Be more'n glad to take y'all's money again."

No one entered into a wager, but they all stayed to watch.

Preacher sighted again, made a slight adjustment to his aim, and squeezed the trigger. The rifle thumped his shoulder solidly and he peered through the powder smoke haze. He drew another cartridge from his possibles bag.

A hundred yards away, the stick was cocked straight back and was now missing a few more inches from the top.

Satisfaction spread through Preacher. A little bit of work on the sights would put the rifle to rights. He didn't want to trade a bad rifle to anyone for any amount of trade.

"How much you want for that rifle?" someone asked.

"We can dicker," Preacher said. He didn't plan on getting rich off confiscated rifles or ponies. They were just things he'd happened across that could be used by others. "I got five more just like this one."

"Didn't know you to be in the gun business, Preacher," another man said.

"I am today," Preacher replied.

"You say you're gonna fix the sights on that one?"

"I am."

"Me an' you can talk." A young man wearing fresh

buckskins stepped toward Preacher. The right side of his face was purple with bruising, dark with powder burns, and scabbed-over scratches. His right eye was bloodshot. "My name is Taylor. Alvin Taylor. I come out of Pennsylvania this spring an' wanted to see some of these mountains. I got outfitted in St. Louis before I headed out, an' the man who sold me my rifle must have seen me comin'. I bought a Kentucky rifle I was told was carried by Daniel Boone. Seems ol' Dan'l lived a big chunk of his life in Missouri at the end."

"Boone's been gone twenty years," Preacher said. "He was a fine man and a good woodsman, and the Kentucky rifle was a solid piece of craftsmanship."

He didn't add that it would be hard to find a rifle Boone had truly owned. When it came to the origin of weapons they bought or traded for, men often wanted to believe things they'd been told. Many men took pride in such things. Preacher never had. A weapon was a tool and only the fact that it worked when it needed to mattered.

"I'd heard that about the man an' the rifle," Taylor said. "I'm pretty sure Boone didn't own that rifle an' that it wasn't worth what I give for it. Two days ago, I took a shot at a pronghorn an' the barrel split."

"What size ball were you shootin'?"

"Fifty-four caliber. Same as that Hawken there shoots."

"Sounds like the gunsmith who sold you that rifle bored the barrel out too much," Preacher said. "A lot of the Kentucky rifles shot forty-five caliber balls, but a good many of them shot smaller. Thirty-two-caliber balls saved on lead, which could be hard to get in frontier places. East of the Mississippi, game tends to run smaller. A thirty-two-caliber ball is fine for takin' deer an' turkey an' squirrel.

I've seen some Kentucky rifles bored out to fifty-caliber, but they sometimes don't last long."

Taylor touched his face gingerly. "This one didn't last no time at all. I bet I didn't get fifty shots out of it before it exploded. Like to took my eye. I'm sure glad it didn't. If I see that man again, I'm gonna give him a whippin'."

"Who sold you the rifle?"

"Man named Elmer Wiggs."

Preacher shook his head. "Never heard of him. But I'll remember the name." He knew most of the gunsmiths in St. Louis. Next trip in, he might be persuaded to look him up.

"It ain't good to be out here without a rifle," Taylor said.

"No, sir," Preacher agreed, "it ain't." He held the rifle out to the younger man. "You step up and fire her. Let me know what you think. You should know what you're buyin'."

Taylor hesitated. "I don't have much. Don't know that I can buy that rifle."

"If you like the rifle," Preacher said, "I'm sure we can strike a deal. She's loaded."

Taylor nodded and accepted the rifle. "I'm not going to be able to hit that stick."

"That stick ain't big enough to eat anyways," one of the mountain men said. He was young, but a finger of gray hair showed in his dark beard.

The crowd roared with laughter.

"You just hold on," the man said. "I got a gallon jug here that I just emptied that's got a hairline crack. Ain't no good for nothin' but target practice. You just don't shoot me."

Taylor raised the Hawken's barrel to the sky.

"Go ahead on an' shoot him!" somebody roared. "Farris is big enough to eat!"

"Go to hell!" Farris replied good-naturedly. He trotted

toward the stick Preacher had shot, plunked down the cracked gallon jug, and loped back. "Now you shoot that, Taylor. If you can hit that, you can hit most things out here that needs shootin', an' that fifty-four-caliber ball will stop a whole lot more bear than that Kentucky rifle would have."

Taylor brought the Hawken up to his shoulder. He squinted across the sights. The barrel wavered a bit.

Preacher stood slightly to the younger man's left. "That rifle ain't gonna blow up. She's solid and she's ready. You just concentrate on hittin' the target. Breathe in, now out, and hold."

Taylor held his breath.

"Steady up," Preacher said.

The rifle stopped wavering and remained straight and true.

"Squeeze," Preacher said.

The rifle detonation cracked loudly and filled the immediate vicinity. Powder smoke wreathed the rifle and Taylor.

A hundred yards away, the gallon jug lay in pieces.

Taylor lowered the rifle and looked at the target. Then he turned and grinned at Preacher. "It's got a kick."

"A bear don't like it none, neither." Preacher smiled.

"I suppose not." An uncertain look framed Taylor's youthful face. "I want the rifle. Don't know if I can afford it."

"Keep it. We'll work somethin' out. Talk to me later, over supper." Preacher didn't like the idea of any man being out in the mountains without a way to protect himself, and he liked the way young Alvin Taylor conducted himself and stated his need. Preacher reached into his possibles bag, pulled out a fistful of .54 cartridges, and offered them to the other man.

Gratefully, Taylor accepted the cartridges and stuffed them into his own possibles bag.

"Maybe we can get some more cartridges off them Army boys," Preacher said.

"I appreciate it, Preacher."

The crowd of onlookers shifted and made room for four soldiers who approached Preacher. They were led by a broad bulldog of a man with a round, flat face that looked like it had been formed in a frying pan. A carefully groomed dark blond mustache lay like shadow under his crooked nose and reached from corner to corner across his thin-lipped mouth. Despite his wide shoulders and big belly, the man had a narrow waist. Cavalry gloves hung at his belt beside the big pistol on his hip. He carried a Hawken rifle in one hand.

He stopped a few feet in front of Preacher and looked down. The man's size hadn't been readily apparent, but a lot of bears were smaller.

"Looks like you boys are havin' yourselves a shooting competition," the soldier said.

"Just a friendly contest," Lorenzo said. "Among friends."

The big man smiled, but there was no mirth in the expression. Preacher took an immediate dislike to the man.

"Since we're sharin' the camp for the night," the man said, "maybe we can all be friends."

No one said anything.

The soldier fixed Preacher with his gaze. "I seen you were the one doin' the shootin'."

"Not just me," Preacher replied.

"Oh, I saw the young fella, too." The soldier yanked a thumb in Taylor's direction. "But you were the one everyone was watchin'."

The crowd was now watching Preacher again, and the big man who stood in front of him.

"Saw your friend was gatherin' himself up a poke," the soldier said. "Thought maybe we could see how good you really are."

The smell of liquor on the big man's breath carried to Preacher.

"I'm good enough to suit me," Preacher said. "I don't have anything to prove."

The big man grinned big enough to show his crooked, yellow teeth. "Maybe you'll want to see how good I can shoot. I'm Sergeant Walter Gordon, an' I'm the best marksman Fort Pierre has ever seen." He looked over his shoulder at the three men who had followed him. "Ain't that right?"

"That's right, Sergeant," a soldier replied. He stared around the group as if daring anyone to doubt him. "Best shot in the whole command."

"Mister," Farris said, and offered a mocking grin, "you should pull in your horns a mite. That there is Preacher, an' ain't no one a finer shot."

Gordon stared at Preacher. "I hear 'em talkin', an' you don't seem to be interested in makin' their claims true, but I got a shiny double-eagle that says I can outshoot you. What you got?"

Preacher's pride stung a little, but he was far enough down the road that he knew that was what Gordon intended. Preacher also had a handle on his pride—most of the time. There was just something about the cavalry soldier that nettled him.

Evidently Dog didn't like the way Gordon was talking. The big cur rose from where he'd been lying under a short, twisted pine. Dog's lips pulled back and revealed his big teeth.

"Easy," Preacher said quietly. He never took his gaze from Gordon.

Dog laid back down, but he remained watchful.

"That ugly beast yours?" Gordon asked.

Preacher tamped down his anger. "We travel together."

"Ugly and dumb," Gordon said. "I can see how you two get along."

Preacher stepped to the side and grabbed his rifle barrel from where it leaned against a rotted stump. "Is that double-eagle all talk?"

CHAPTER 13

Smiling, Gordon reached into his pants pocket and brought out the coin. The double-eagle flashed pure yellow gold and looked freshly minted, not like something that had been carried around in someone's pocket for long.

"I got it," Gordon said. "Where's yours?"

Preacher hesitated. Truth to tell, he didn't have much cash on him. He didn't have much use for it outside of a town. He nodded toward the stand of rifles that stood near Dog. The big cur wouldn't let anyone have them without Preacher's say-so.

"Those rifles are mine," Preacher said. "They're worth more than that gold you're so proud of."

"Sure," Gordon said. He put the gold piece back into his pocket.

"How do you want to do this?"

"A target each." Gordon reached into his pocket and pulled out a worn yellow scarf. He folded it in half and sliced it with his knife. Two rectangles of material about a foot by six inches fluttered from his fingers. He put the knife away. "Three shots. Closest to center with all three wins. Does that work?"

Preacher nodded. "That'll do."

"I'll have my friends set us up." Gordon handed the scarf pieces to the other soldiers. "Stake these out on each side. Go till I tell you to stop."

The soldiers walked forward.

A hundred yards out, Gordon said, "That's far enough."

"No, it's not," Preacher said. "You boys keep on goin'."

The soldiers looked at the sergeant.

"You declared the rules and set the targets," Preacher said. "I call the distance."

"That seems fair," Lorenzo said.

Others among the mountain men and Crow braves agreed.

"All right," Gordon said. "I was takin' it easy on you." He waved to his men. "Keep on goin'. Stop when he says to stop."

The soldiers kept walking. The crowd at Preacher's back grew more excited the farther the men walked.

When they were two hundred yards out, Preacher said, "That's far enough."

On a small rise in front of the tree line, the soldiers used knives to pierce the sides of the scarf pieces then threaded iron tent pegs through the holes. Both yellow cotton rectangles stretched taut and only belled a little with the breeze. The soldiers walked back to rejoin the group of spectators.

"You want to go first?" Gordon asked.

"You wanted this," Preacher said. "You go on ahead."

The sergeant took up his rifle, spread his feet, and steadied himself. He fired and smoke rushed out of the Hawken.

"Mason," Gordon said, and stepped back, "how did I do?"

One of the soldiers stood nearby with a spyglass to his

eye. "Almost dead center, Sergeant. About half an inch low and to the left."

Gordon nodded in satisfaction. He took a bottle of whiskey from one of the other soldiers and took a drink. He waved to Preacher with a big arm.

"Take your turn."

Preacher sighted on his target, breathed out and held it, and squeezed the trigger. He put the rifle down and reloaded.

"Well?" Gordon demanded of the soldier with the spyglass.

"Dead center," Lorenzo said beside Preacher. He held a spyglass of his own.

Gordon frowned. "I don't think you're the official spotter."

"Maybe I ain't," Lorenzo said, "but I got two good eyes, an' this here spyglass." A lazy smile twisted his lips. "If that there double-eagle in your pocket has a brother, I'm willin' to lay you a side bet that Preacher's shot is dead center. We can go on down there an' take a look if you want."

"Dead center," the soldier with the spyglass said before Gordon could reply. "Maybe a touch to the right, but it looks plumb dab in the middle."

Gordon scowled and reloaded his rifle. He pulled the weapon to his shoulder and fired.

"Center," Lorenzo said only loud enough for Preacher to hear.

A moment later, the soldier with the spyglass confirmed the shot.

Gordon smiled. "Looks like we're even up, Preacher, unless you pull off another shot like your first."

Preacher aimed, steadied, and fired. He was reloading before the powder smoke cleared.

"Dead center," Lorenzo crowed. "Sittin' just on top of the last one. They look like a number eight almost on account of them bein' so close."

The crowd of mountain men and Crow cheered. Some of the small boys standing among them howled with glee.

Gordon waited on his soldier to verify the shot. The man lowered his spyglass and nodded.

"Like he said," the soldier reported. "The number eight."

"Luck," Gordon growled. He loaded his rifle, held it to his shoulder, and, when a gust of wind blew in from the river, relaxed for a moment. He aimed again and fired.

"Low," Lorenzo said, "an' outside the center by half an inch." He lowered the spyglass. "You ain't a bad marksman, Sergeant. You can hit what you aim at, but you ain't as good as Preacher. Not by a long shot." He smiled. "An' this here's a long shot."

"It ain't over," Gordon growled, but the angry tone in his voice gave away his lack of confidence that it wasn't.

Preacher pulled his rifle to his shoulder and looked down the sights. Before he could squeeze the trigger, another gust of wind, harder than the first, ripped in from the river.

The target stretched between the tent pegs popped and snapped, then one end flew loose from the tent peg on the left. The yellow material luffed there in the breeze, stood out mostly full, then folded down on itself. It unfurled with every small gust of wind.

"Hold on," Lorenzo said. "I'll go an' pin it up again."

Preacher lowered his rifle.

"No," Gordon commanded. His voice was geared for

parade ground drills and carried over the crowd. "A deal's a deal. Preacher gets his shot just like I did. With no adjustments to the target."

"That's a load of meadow muffins," Lorenzo said. He pointed at the targets. "It was your men who placed those targets. Seems to me they cut that one side out thin, hopin' a ball might rip it free. That's cheatin'."

"The ball didn't rip the target free," Gordon countered. "That was done by the wind. Ain't nothin' but bad luck." He gazed at Preacher. "You got your shot. Take it or not. Doesn't matter to me."

"Nobody can make that shot," Alvin Taylor objected. "You could make this right, mister."

"Not me," Gordon said. "I got a double-eagle riding on this shot. I ain't gonna give my money away."

Preacher watched the fluttering yellow rectangle. The cloth moved lazily, like a live thing sunning itself or stretching out, like a fingerling sliding along underwater. Bears caught salmon leaping through the air. It was all a matter of timing.

He counted cadence silently to himself as the scarf moved out, fell down, moved out again, and fell once more. He watched the cloth through three more cycles, brought the rifle to his shoulder, counted again, and squeezed the trigger.

"Preacher hit it!" a man yelled.

"Didn't hit it," one of the soldiers said. "That was just the wind."

Without a word, Preacher reloaded his rifle.

"Ready to hand over those rifles?" Gordon asked.

"No," Preacher said. "We're going to look at those targets. Make sure of what's what."

Gordon laughed. "What's what is that you missed that last shot."

"I didn't." Preacher stepped toward the targets. He continued to count cadence and the yellow scarf moved just as it had.

"Buckalew!" Gordon bellowed.

"Yes, Sergeant," a soldier said.

"Stay with my rifles."

"Sergeant, there's a wolf by them rifles."

"Dog," Preacher called softly.

The big cur eased up, padded after Preacher, and fell into step with him. The soldier stayed back with the rifles. The rest of the spectators trailed Preacher and Gordon.

"Did you hit it?" Lorenzo asked.

Preacher smiled at his friend. "You doubtin' me?"

Lorenzo looked solemn. "Not for a minute."

One of the soldiers walked toward Preacher's target. The yellow material flipped and flopped with the wind.

"Back off that," Preacher said.

Dog trotted forward and growled.

The soldier halted five feet from the target. "Don't matter. I can see it plain from here. You missed your target clean as a whistle."

"I didn't miss," Preacher said.

He knelt, grabbed the loose end of the material, and pulled it out straight. Two holes stood out prominently.

"Told you that you missed," Gordon said.

"Look closer," Preacher advised. "On the outer most edge of the bottom hole."

"Sweet Joseph, Mary, and baby Jesus!" Farris said. "Preacher done it! He hit that target just like he said it did! Almost put that third shot through the hole made by the first one!"

The material showed where the third hole overlaid the first two and barely caught the outside edges of both holes. If Preacher had been any more on target, no one would have been able to see where the third shot had hit. He'd been lucky. He'd only hoped to hit somewhere close to the center because there had been no true accounting for the wind.

"That ain't possible!" Gordon said. He stepped forward and peered hard at the material.

"It's there!" Farris said. "That third shot gave them first two holes a belly! Time for you to pay up, Army man!"

Gordon scowled and cursed.

The crowd quickly ringed him, and all of them were on Preacher's side.

Gordon reached into his pocket, took out the gold piece, and flipped it to Preacher. The revolving gold splintered the afternoon sunlight. Effortlessly, Preacher caught the coin in his free hand without taking his eyes from Gordon. The sergeant rankled him, and there was no love lost. That showed in the big man's colorless eyes.

"Sergeant!" The soldier who had been left behind to watch the rifles Preacher intended to trade or sell came up carrying them.

"Put them back, Fiehler," Gordon said. "Turns out Preacher hit the target after all."

"There's a problem with the rifles." The soldier held one of them out and presented the stock turned so the triangle burned into the wood showed. "This."

Gordon studied the rifle. "What about the rest of them?"

"All of 'em are marked, Sergeant."

Gordon wheeled on Preacher and roared, "Where did you get them rifles?" He lifted his rifle.

Before the sergeant could get his weapon level, Preacher

stepped forward and knocked the rifle from the man's hands with his own. Despite that, Gordon grabbed hold of Preacher's buckskin shirt with both hands. Preacher stepped back and tried to raise his rifle, but the big man followed him and managed to kick his feet from under him.

Preacher fell and Gordon came down on top of him. Dog lunged forward with his teeth bared.

"No," Preacher yelled.

The big cur backed off, but he growled and paced, clearly unhappy with things.

"I knew there was something about you I didn't like!" Gordon bellowed. "Damn murderin' thief is what you are!"

Since he was unable to bring his rifle into play, and he was not yet wholly convinced he needed to kill his attacker, Preacher released the rifle. Gordon yelled gleefully and moved his hands up to Preacher's throat.

Around them, the mountain men and the Crow braves unlimbered their weapons and faced the soldiers. That confrontation was over in seconds because the soldiers weren't ready to die. They raised their hands in surrender.

Black spots swam in Preacher's vision and he couldn't breathe. Gordon was powerful, and the man wasn't holding back. Preacher raised his left arm and drove his forearm down across both of his attacker's. The sergeant's hold didn't quite break, but it loosened. Preacher rolled to his left, put as much power into his right arm as he could, and lashed out. His right fist caught Gordon full on his blunt, broad nose.

Blood exploded from the sergeant's nose and rained down on Preacher. The mountain man rolled to the left again and hammered another blow into Gordon's face.

Yowling in pain, the sergeant leaned back to avoid another blow. Preacher brought his forearm down again and knocked the man's hands free of his neck. Quickly, he slid his left hand up, reached across the soldier's body, and caught the left side of Gordon's neck and jaw in his palm. Preacher levered the hold and shoved the sergeant to his left. Off-balance, partially dazed, Gordon slid sideways. When the sergeant fought back and bulled his way back a couple inches, Preacher hit him again, this time in the left ear. He followed that with two more punches and Gordon slid sideways.

Preacher rolled away from the big man and got his feet under him. He snaked his right arm out, grabbed his rifle, and lifted it. Gordon rolled and struggled to get to his feet. Preacher eared the rifle's hammer back and pointed it at Gordon's middle.

"You have yourself a think about it," the mountain man advised coolly. His throat pained him and breathing was difficult. "I won't miss, and this fifty-four-caliber ball leaves a mighty big hole. Whatever's on your mind, you have to wonder if it's worth dying for."

Gordon stopped fighting to get to his feet. He sat back on his haunches and leaned his fists on the ground to help support himself.

"I should have cut your throat," Gordon snarled.

"If you'd tried, I'd have killed you straight out." Preacher swallowed and it was painful. The crushing pressure on his neck remained even though he knew he was free.

Gordon snorted derisively.

Hoofbeats closed on the group. The spectators drew back and made way for Captain Arnold Diller, who was narrow-eyed and stone-faced.

"What the hell's going on here, Sergeant?" Diller demanded.

Gordon pointed an accusing finger at Preacher. "This

fella is here sellin' rifles with a triangle mark on them, sir. I was havin' a word with him over how he come by 'em."

Diller halted his horse ten feet from Preacher. The Army captain's hand rested on his thigh, but it was only an eye-blink away from one of his pistols. Preacher shifted and slid the rifle a little more between Gordon and his commanding officer. In case things took an even nastier turn.

For the moment, Diller was content to sit his horse.

Gordon lurched to his feet and reached for his rifle.

"Leave it," Preacher ordered.

Dog growled menacingly and took a step forward, but he didn't try to pass Preacher.

"It's my rifle," Gordon growled, but he made no move to recover the rifle from where it lay on the ground.

"And you can't have it right now," Preacher said. "Not until I get some answers."

"I remember you from earlier," Diller said. "You were the man with all the questions."

"I wasn't the only one askin' questions." Preacher stared up at the man.

Diller's narrow eyes slitted with suspicion. "Who are you?"

"Says his name is Preacher," Gordon said. "Ask him about them rifles he's got."

"Sergeant," Diller said sharply, "you'll stay out of this."

Gordon cursed beneath his breath. "Yes, sir."

"Now, Mr. Preacher," Diller said.

"Just Preacher. Ain't no mister."

"Very well." Diller nodded. "Let's discuss those rifles."

For a moment, pure stubbornness filled Preacher, and he wasn't going to answer. The soldiers didn't have much weight to throw around at the moment. The numbers were on Preacher's side. Then he reckoned it might be more sensible to talk about the rifles. He had questions about them, too.

"I got them off some Blackfoot warriors I killed yesterday mornin'," Preacher said.

"They had the rifles?"

"Until I took them."

"Did they say where they got them?" Diller asked.

"Nope," Preacher said. "We wasn't on speakin' terms. They interrupted me huntin' for breakfast. They meant to kill me. I killed them first."

Diller looked at the rifles his soldier was holding. "That's a lot of rifles. How many Blackfeet?"

"There were a lot of Blackfeet. Not all of them had rifles."

"And you killed them?"

"I did."

"All of them?"

"Every one of them."

Diller took a moment to think over things and continued gazing at Preacher.

Finally, he said, "I expect we should talk."

"If you can do it more sensible than your sergeant here, I'd be open to it."

"I can be." Diller switched his gaze to Gordon. "Sergeant, you'll pass the word to the men that no one will needlessly bother this man anymore."

"But, sir—"

Diller raised his voice. "That will be all I will say about the matter, Sergeant. If anyone steps out of line, I'll hold you responsible. Do I make myself clear?"

"Yes, sir." Although Gordon answered the captain, his hot gaze was centered on Preacher.

"Now then," Diller said, and looked at Preacher, "perhaps you and I can find a place to talk."

"As soon as I get my rifles back," Preacher said. Those rifles had been paid for in blood. He wasn't going to just give them up.

"Of course." Diller wheeled his horse around. "Sergeant, you'll see to it those rifles are returned."

"Yes, sir." Gordon glanced at the soldier who held the rifles. "Give 'em back."

Lorenzo stepped forward and took some of the rifles. Preacher took the other three and pulled their slings over his shoulder. He never moved his rifle away from Gordon.

"What about me?" the big sergeant demanded. "Can I have my rifle now?"

"You can," Preacher said. "Just you make sure you keep it to yourself."

"This ain't over," Gordon said.

Preacher smiled at the man. "Mister, you better hope this is over. You decide it ain't, you better figure out where you'd like to be buried."

With the rifles slung over his shoulder, Preacher followed the Army captain sitting so fine on his horse. Lorenzo walked behind him, and Dog walked at his side. Every step he took, Preacher thought maybe he should just avoid talking to Diller. He couldn't see any good coming of it.

But curiosity pushed him along anyway. That horrible trait had gotten him into more trouble over the years. Of course, he'd also learned a lot of things, too.

The trick was to learn without getting killed.

CHAPTER 14

"We've been trailing Stone Eyes and his renegades for the better part of two weeks," Captain Diller said. "They've been ambushing wagon trains off and on again since last year. We've almost caught up with them a couple of times."

The Army captain sat on a stone and stared into the campfire that had burned down low between Preacher and him as they talked. The dying light held back the encroaching night and fought off the chill that came with the dark hours.

"That Indian is one wily cuss," Diller declared, "and he's got more luck than a riverboat gambler who's corralled a handful of aces. I've chased Indians in my time, and I've put plenty of them in the ground where I ran them down. I am not one to fail, and I don't intend to start now, but Stone Eyes has been most vexing."

Preacher sat with his legs crossed and favored his left side a little. Gordon hadn't landed many punches, but the ones the sergeant had connected with had carried plenty of muscle behind them.

Around them, the Crow families settled in around

cookfires, shared food, told stories and sang, and spent time with their children. The heady scent of cooked meat threaded through the branches and hung in soft gray fog in the chill air. It would get colder later, because the high mountains were always cold, but for now the evening was tolerable enough. The mountain men joined in with them or sat in their own groups tending their own meals. Still, the feeling of camaraderie persisted. Some dedicated fishermen tried their luck in the moonlit river, drank whiskey from shared jugs, and told lies.

Altogether the Crow camp was a fine place to be.

Preacher wished he was with any of them instead of talking to the Army captain. He intended to be soon enough. He hadn't traveled all this way to get involved in someone else's problems.

If he hadn't been so curious about the story behind the rifles, he would have joined Blue Magpie and his family. Songbird had promised to keep back some of the pronghorn meat she'd cooked so he could have it later. Preacher had worked up an appetite coming over the mountains.

However, he couldn't walk away from the captain's invitation yet. After a half hour of trading news, the man hadn't gotten around to asking what he intended to ask, and there was still a story to be had about those rifles.

So far Diller hadn't demanded their return, and that was something Preacher wanted nailed down. He hadn't stolen those rifles, but his possession of them was questionable. If it hadn't been for Sergeant Gordon, he might have just handed them over. Now, though, he'd fought for them, so that put a different light on them. The truth of the matter was he wanted to know where he stood.

"What put you on Stone Eyes's trail?" Preacher asked.

"Those rifles you took from the Indians," Diller stated.

"There ain't that many rifles there."

Diller held up a hand. "I misspoke. It's not just those rifles. They were just some of the rifles taken from a reinforcement detail out of St. Louis a week ago. That detail came up the Mississippi, on up the Missouri. They camped a few miles east of where the Missouri joins the Bad River, and it was there the rifles went missing."

"That stretch of the river is a bad place to be," Preacher said. "Unless things have changed."

"They haven't."

"The water's bad there. That's why the river's got that name. Shortly after the rainy season starts, which we're just on the other side of, silt's all through those waters and pushes out into the Missouri. Animals tend to give a few miles of that river a wide berth. After all the recent rain, that water'll be plenty bad right now, and it would have been two weeks ago, too. There's no good water, and no huntin', either. And only a desperate man figures he can take enough walleye and brookie from that river to live on. Personally, I'd rather eat boot leather than either of them fish."

"Agreed," Diller said.

"So why did that detail stop?"

"One of the soldiers guarding the shipment lived for a while before sepsis got him. He told me they put into the bank because they'd run out of daylight. The major in charge of the detail wanted to press their luck traveling by night. He'd figured they'd make Fort Pierre before dark."

"Only they didn't."

Diller shook his head. "They did not. They'd had a hard go of it coming up those swollen rivers, and they didn't have any trained rivermen among them who knew this part of the country. Major Roger Voight was new to the area.

According to his commanding officer, Voight put in for a transfer and came across the Mississippi to see the West."

"He didn't get to see much of it," Preacher said.

"Neither did a lot of those young boys with him. Stone Eyes and his warriors tortured them and butchered them. Left them lay where they fell." Diller swallowed. "It was a horrible thing to come up on."

Sadness touched Preacher briefly, but he made a point not to keep that feeling as a constant companion. If he had hung onto feelings like that every time he'd bumped into something disagreeable, he never would have known a time when he wasn't camping in its shadow.

Preacher considered the events. Things didn't add up.

"No one knew the shipment was going to put in for the night," the mountain man said. "Sounds like this major didn't plan on it, either."

"No."

"How did Stone Eyes find the riverboat?"

"Nobody's sure about that. Stone Eyes and his warriors might have cut the riverboat's trail and followed it for a while. Or maybe he heard about the shipment through some of those traders who don't mind playing both ends against the middle. Stone Eyes could have set up on the river with the intention of taking it and just waited for it to come along. The shipment was supposed to be a secret." Diller shrugged. "Secrets aren't always a sacred thing in the Army, and among civilians keeping a secret doesn't stand a chance. Especially not if there's a way to make a profit off it."

"Major Voight was just bringing rifles?"

"He was, and the reinforcements. The Army wanted

more men in the area to look out for wagon trains and to scout the territory."

"The Army wanted a shipment of rifles brought in?" Preacher asked. "They issue rifles to soldiers who don't have one."

"Pierre Chouteau sent for the rifles. He intended to sell them through his stores. There are more men traveling west these days, and Chouteau's business there at the fort is good. Not what it was when Astor was running the place, but Chouteau is doing well for himself."

"If those were Chouteau's rifles, why was the Army ridin' shotgun on the shipment?" Preacher asked.

"Have you ever met Chouteau?"

"Now and again, and never for long. I sold a few furs to his people, till I discovered sellin' 'em in St. Louis paid more, and there was more to do in St. Louis if I was of a mind to do it."

"Chouteau's a smart businessman. A lot of folks thought he would lose his shirt after buying the fort from Astor, but he's made out all right. As for the rifles, getting anybody up here in the mountains to ride over to St. Louis and bring back a load of rifles through hostile Indian territory would be a hard row to hoe. The pay wouldn't be much and traveling back and forth would take up a lot of a man's time. By the time a man finished riding shotgun on that, he probably wouldn't have much to show. Chouteau will squeeze a two-bit piece till it screams."

Preacher thought about that and knew he wouldn't have cottoned to the idea of guarding that shipment of weapons himself. Rifles would be hard to hide along a trail, especially a river, if someone was looking for them, and a man couldn't exactly pick them up and run off with them.

"Chouteau closed a deal with the War Department for Major Voight and his troops to deliver the rifles," Diller said. "If he could have found men to guard that shipment, they probably wouldn't have been trained, and they definitely wouldn't have been trained to work as a unit. Those boys died hard and fast."

"Why did the War Department agree to do that?"

"Logistics. They wanted to send fresh troops out here to replace some of the soldiers in the area who were helping keep an eye on things. Some of them have left the Army and gotten married or pulled out to try their luck out in Oregon Territory. Coming in with the rifles meant there was only one trip. Chouteau agreed to finance all the supplies Major Voight and his people needed. The Army didn't mind someone else paying the freight." Diller grimaced. "And I'm sure that silver crossed a few palms. That's how business with the Army gets done."

Preacher didn't comment on that, but he knew it was true. That was another reason he didn't care for working with the Army. When money was involved, and it often was because politics often ran hand in hand with greed, loyalties shifted too easily.

"It was just the soldiers and the riverboat comin' this way?" Preacher asked.

Diller nodded. "And the rifles. Maybe a few drummers and merchants trailed along when Major Voight and his detail lit out of St. Louis. Those men are like fleas on a dog. They would have seen the Army as free protection during their own journeys."

"Why did Voight allow them to come along?"

Diller shook his head. "Never got to ask him, him being dead when I found him. I suspect it was for the usual reasons. Some of those men had been out here before and had knowledge of the country the major would be taking his men through. Others might have been brought along for amusement's sake."

"What happened to the drummers and merchants?"

"As far as I know, they're all dead. My men and I found nine of them among Voight's detail."

Preacher reached over to the campfire, lifted the coffee-pot, and poured himself another cup. One thing he could say about the Army, they had fair enough coffee. He held the cup in his hands and enjoyed the warmth. But his thoughts didn't leave the ill-fated Army detail.

"So what happened after the riverboat put in for the night?" Preacher asked.

Diller shifted on his seat and kicked the dirt. His gaze was far and away. "The young private I talked to said Stone Eyes and his warriors attacked the camp about the time the men bedded down. About the time when a man lets go of the day and gets fuzzy headed. The Blackfeet came out of the woods, took out the scouts who had been posted, and flanked Major Voight and those soldiers before they knew what was what. They trapped them with their backs to the river."

"No place to go." Preacher pictured the encounter in his mind and didn't care for it. Getting jammed up like that was a bad place to be. "Voight should have taken his men farther inland so they would have had more choices if somethin' went bad. You don't want to get yourself hemmed in."

"Voight wasn't an Indian fighter, and he didn't fight in the second war with the British," Diller said. "I won't speak ill of the dead, but that's just the God's honest truth. Despite the years Voight had put in soldiering, learning to shoot and to march, to take orders and to give them, he hadn't fought in anything like what a man finds out here.

And Stone Eyes carries a lot of bad medicine with him."
He paused. "Those men never stood a chance."

"How many Blackfeet were killed?"

"Not nearly enough. They took their dead with them.
And the rifles."

Preacher scratched his chin. "How many rifles was the
major transportin'?"

Diller hesitated for a minute. When he answered,
Preacher knew what the man was leading up to.

"A hundred." Diller spoke quietly, as if the answer
carried more weight if spoken louder. "A hundred of the
best rifles Jacob and Samuel Hawken turn out in that shop
they have in St. Louis."

Preacher thought about that. "A hundred rifles is a lot."

"It is. Chouteau figures on selling most of them to travelers passing through. He plans on advertising Fort Pierre
as the last place a man can get a good rifle if he's headed
west." Diller looked at Preacher. "I have to tell you, he isn't
far wrong, and there are a lot of Indians across Montana."

"Not to mention buffalo."

"I've seen what a stampede can do to a wagon train.
There's never much left."

"No, sir," Preacher agreed. "There's not. Out here, a
man needs a good rifle."

"A lot of those homesteaders come out here with the
squirrel guns and shotguns they were raised with. They
aren't enough, and most of the time they find that out too
late. But they get smarter along the way. Chouteau won't
have any problem selling those rifles . . . if he can get them
back."

"Stone Eyes has the rifles?"

Diller nodded. "He does. The fact that you brought back
those rifles proves that."

"The rifles won't do him any good without powder and shot."

"A man can get powder and shot out here, Preacher. Indians, too. There are men like Tobit Moon Deer and other Comancheros and outlaws who will sell it to them."

That was a true fact, and it bothered Preacher.

"I didn't invite you to my campfire just to tell you all these troubles," Diller said.

"Thought it might have crossed your mind to apologize for your sergeant."

Diller shook his head. "That's not my apology to make, and Gordon looks like he's had enough apology beaten out of him."

Preacher grinned. "I'm satisfied. For now."

"Good to know." Diller locked eyes with Preacher. "I want something from you."

"You can ask. This ain't my problem. The way I see it, you're only lookin' for ninety-three rifles now instead of a hundred on account of me."

"Those rifles could be considered Chouteau's property. As a representative of the Army, I could consider it my duty to return them to him."

"That," Preacher said, "could be harder than you want to take on. I've already promised one of those rifles to a man who can use it. I'm not gonna go ask for it back, and you sure aren't gonna send Gordon to do that, either."

"I was hoping we might strike a bargain."

"I'm listenin'."

"I'd like to see where you found those rifles and the Blackfeet who had them."

"I can give you directions."

"I'd rather you took me. I'd also like to find out if we can trail them back to Stone Eyes. That killer and the main body of his warriors have to be out there somewhere. I want to find them and those rifles."

Preacher considered that. Getting a clear title to the rifles might be worth a couple days' riding to get there and back again. He wasn't looking to make money off the confiscated rifles, but he suspected there were mountain men and Crow hunters who could use them. Trading them for supplies, new buckskins and blankets, or even just for a favor to be called in later made good sense.

The rifles were a windfall, and he'd shed blood—not his own, of course—to get them.

The thought of the rifles in the hands of Blackfeet on the warpath bothered him, too. Diller and his men hadn't been able to find Stone Eyes. Preacher was pretty sure he could.

He looked at the Army captain. "Let me think on it."

Diller pursed his lips and frowned with his eyes. "All right. We'll be pulling out in the morning. My soldiers can take a night of ease and we can rest the horses in a comfortable camp. I'll need to have your answer by then."

Preacher stood and hefted his rifle. Dog got to his feet at his side. The big cur stretched and rolled his spine.

"In the mornin' then." Preacher took his leave and headed over to Blue Magpie's tipi.

As Preacher passed Gordon and a handful of soldiers gathered around another campfire, the big man scowled at him.

Preacher just smiled and kept walking.

CHAPTER 15

"Did the captain offer you tea an' cakes?" Lorenzo drawled.

"He might have," Preacher replied. "Of course, I turned him down. Saved all my empty places for Songbird's cookin'."

Songbird looked up from where she sat near the family's campfire and flashed Preacher a pleased smile.

"Your tongue is far too clever and sweet," Songbird said in Crow.

She told her children to make room by the fire and waved at Preacher to sit beside Blue Magpie.

"So what did the captain want?" Blue Magpie asked.

Preacher accepted the bowl of meat and vegetables Songbird handed him and thanked her. "He wants me to lead him to where I killed those Blackfeet."

Lorenzo picked meat off a bone and chewed it. He'd obviously nearly eaten his fill and was now taking his time filling up whatever space he could find. Preacher picked up meat chunks with his fingers and fed himself. He savored the pronghorn meat and the juices. There was nothing ever as fine as feeding himself with meat he'd taken himself.

"Are you going to do it?" Blue Magpie asked.

"I didn't give him an answer. Yet." Preacher swallowed. "But I don't reckon that I hardly have a choice."

"Passin' by trouble's something you should have learned by now, Preacher," Lorenzo said.

"Those rifles I brought in ain't the only ones Stone Eyes and his warriors got their hands on. According to the captain, there's another ninety-three of them that have fallen into Stone Eyes's hands." Preacher put down his bowl long enough to drink from his canteen. The water was cold and clean.

The children watched Preacher, and he realized maybe he shouldn't have been so plain-spoken in front of them.

"Children," Songbird said. She took the baby from Doe with Joy so the other woman could eat more freely. "You have finished your meal. You may go play with the other children, but do not go beyond sight of our campfire."

The children got to their feet in an eyeblink, promised to do as their mother said, and took off to join other children playing games and singing songs. Preacher was pretty sure none of them would get too far from the campfires. The darkness in the woods was complete and Crow stories were filled with all manner of creatures and monsters that hunted by moonlight.

"I apologize for talkin' like that in front of the children," Preacher said.

Songbird smiled at him and shrugged. "You are not used to being around children, Preacher." She glanced at the children. "They are young. Five minutes from now they will not remember this conversation."

Preacher nodded. Children were quick to move on from things. Unless it was something they were awfully interested in. Then they could be as patient as a mountain lion.

"Stone Eyes has the rifles?" Blue Magpie asked.

"I took seven of them from Silent Owl," Preacher said. "It doesn't take a heap of thinkin' to figure Stone Eyes has the others. At least some of them."

Blue Magpie resettled himself and stared into the darkness behind the light of the campfires. "Stone Eyes is a killer, and he hates the Crow people as so many of the Blackfeet do. Over the last few moons, I have buried friends and their families who were killed by Stone Eyes and his killers. And they are killers, not braves."

"I know." Preacher ate from the bowl. The food was good, but the talk put him off his feed a little. "That's why I'm gonna take those soldiers back that way in the mornin'. If I get them headed out on Stone Eyes's trail, that'll move the Blackfeet farther from you and your people. With the Army chasing him, Stone Eyes would be a fool to stay around here. And I'll stay on for a bit to help look after things."

"That would be a good thing," Blue Magpie said. He looked out over the camp. "We are too many this year to go unnoticed. I have been told that Stone Eyes has many men with him. I do not wish for them to come this way."

"Your buckskins look worn, Preacher," Songbird said.

"It's been a busy year," Preacher allowed. His buckskins were thin in places from hard use. "I've traveled a lot more than I usually do, and been through some hard times. Ain't had time to put a proper kit together."

"I spoke for one of the buffalo hides that the pony soldiers brought in with them," she said. "As is my right as one of the women leaders of this tribe. For all that you have done in the past, and for what you are doing now, I will sew you a new set of clothing and moccasins."

Preacher smiled and nodded. "That would be fine, Songbird, but I'd like to make the trade a little more even. For those things, I'll give you one of those rifles I took from the Blackfeet."

"I have no need of a rifle. Nor does my husband, the great fisherman."

"I am a fisherman," Blue Magpie asserted. "I am no hunter. When I am hunting, I will hunt with the bow as my father taught me. I prefer the old ways."

As Preacher recalled, Blue Magpie never had quite gotten the hang of marksmanship.

"You can trade the rifle for somethin' you do want," Preacher said. "A trader would take it off your hands fast enough, and you could probably get some more bowls or cookware."

"I have had my eye on an iron skillet," Songbird admitted. "I have one, but two would make cooking for growing children much easier."

Blue Magpie snorted unhappily. "You are getting too many things we do not need."

"*You* do not need them," Songbird said. "I would like them. Especially another iron frying pan. Meat can be cooked much quicker with one of those. And when we pack and move, you do not carry anything. You leave that to your wives and children. Only we will be burdened."

"I have to ride with the other warriors and make sure the way is safe. We have to chase off the bears and buffaloes and pronghorn so that the women and children and elderly may pass unscathed."

Songbird snorted. "Instead of chasing them off, it would be better if you killed them so we could eat them."

"This is true," Doe with Joy said quietly.

"I give you fish," Blue Magpie protested.

"Not even the children with their always-hungry bellies can eat as many fish as you want to feed them," Songbird said. "Plus, your other wife and I would rather have red meat."

Blue Magpie shook his head in mock sorrow and looked at Preacher. "You see what I have to put up with in these demanding women."

The complaining was good-natured, and Preacher enjoyed it. The squeals of the children warmed his heart almost as much as the campfire, but he was glad the children belonged to Blue Magpie and his wives. The mountain man preferred his solitary ways.

"If them soldiers do find Stone Eyes's trail," Lorenzo said, "they'll go on an' leave you to ride back here on your own."

"Probably," Preacher agreed.

"That would make for a lonesome trip. I'm thinkin' maybe you'd like some company."

"Company would be good."

Lorenzo grinned. "'Cause the way I see it, that blockhead sergeant is just stupid enough to go for another round with you if he thinks he can catch you unprepared."

"I'm never unprepared."

"I know, but he might think you are. I sure would hate to miss that."

"I think you're wrong about him," Preacher said. "Diller was pretty clear on the matter."

Lorenzo nodded knowingly. "An' that sergeant is plenty stupid. I guess we'll see, won't we?"

* * *

When the morning came, the eastern sky lit with purple and pink lights; Preacher sat on a fallen tree the Crow had dragged to the outer edge of camp. He cleaned his weapons. He'd brought plenty of oil to do a good job, and he took his time doing it.

Diller had roused his soldiers early and gotten them started felling trees on the west side of the Snake River. Several of the soldiers were good woodsmen. They lifted their axes and swung with strength and accuracy. A dozen oaks with trunks between a foot and a foot and a half thick toppled to the ground in quick succession. The men called out warnings each time and the trees crashed through other trees and snapped branches.

Other soldiers hooked horses to the fallen trees and dragged them into a clearing. More soldiers swung axes and lopped off branches to leave the trunks mostly clean. Young Crow boys hired on to drag the branches away were paid in sugar and coffee that Diller had authorized for use in trade.

"Givin' the beavers around here a run for their money, ain't they?" Lorenzo asked.

He approached Preacher with a tin mug cupped in each hand and a thick buffalo robe wrapped around his shoulders. Thin wisps of steam trailed up from the mugs, and the strong scent of coffee filled Preacher's nostrils.

"They are." Preacher wiped a stained linen cloth along his rifle's barrel to put a final polish on it. He opened his possibles bag and reloaded the weapon because having an empty rifle sitting around was pure foolishness.

Lorenzo handed over one of the cups.

Preacher accepted the coffee and said, "Thanks."

Lorenzo sat cross-legged on the ground, eased his rifle down, and cupped both hands around the mug. It was early, still cold enough that his breath showed only a little more faintly than the steam from the coffee.

"They buildin' a bridge to cross the river?" Lorenzo asked.

"No. They're buildin' a ferry."

"A ferry, huh?" Lorenzo sipped his coffee gingerly and smiled. "That should be fun to watch. When do you reckon Cap'n Diller realized swimmin' them horses across the river wasn't a good idea?"

"Probably last night. He had his men up early choppin' trees. Surprised you didn't hear them. Sounded like a flock of mighty big woodpeckers."

Lorenzo shrugged under his robe. "Didn't bother me none. Why, I get up in this clean mountain air among folks I trust like I do these Crow, wrap up tight in a buffalo robe made by a squaw who knows what's she's doin', an' I sleep like a baby."

"Diller's men were up at first light."

"I figure you were already up an' they didn't wake you."

"Had things to do," Preacher agreed.

"Scoutin' around?"

"I did."

"Songbird an' Doe were cuttin' up a fresh-killed pronghorn. One of yours?"

"It was."

"So you got out far enough to find game while you were checkin' on the story them soldiers told."

Preacher nodded. "I backtracked them a few miles, found the spot where they come down out of the mountains, and it was like they said. They came straight down from the northwest. Held up a short distance from the Crow camp while they looked us over. I found horse apples and enough tracks to know they spent some time there. I come across that pronghorn while I was comin' back."

"You never was the trustin' sort," Lorenzo said.

"I trust, but I like to get me a look-see at who and what I'm trustin'."

Lorenzo watched the soldiers work for a time. "Seems like this ain't the first ferry them boys built."

"Not the first for some of them," Preacher agreed.

"You reckon they're gonna get them horses across okay?"

"They'll get them across. Remains to be seen how dry they are when they get to the other side."

A team of horses dragged the ferry to the riverbank. The horses' hooves and the rough-edged timbers cut deep grooves into the earth.

"Pull, you stubborn cusses!" Sergeant Gordon roared. He pulled on the leads and kept the horses moving even though they were nearly overburdened with the load.

"You think that hunk of wood is gonna float?" Lorenzo asked.

Preacher eyed the ferry with a critical eye. The stripped timbers were lashed together and formed a rectangle that was ten feet by twelve feet. More timbers were lashed underneath to help provide more buoyancy.

"I think so," the mountain man said. "It would be better if they were using dry wood instead of green timber. It's built solid enough."

"That'll work for me." Lorenzo patted the robe and coins clinked. "Angry Beaver an' some of his friends think it'll sink afore it gets to the other side. I'm gonna go win me some more money. They're givin' better odds than I got on you shootin' an' fightin'."

"I'm glad you find me so profitable."

"I always bet on you, Preacher." Lorenzo fitted a twisted roll-your-own between his lips and winked. "I always will."

He trudged back up the small incline toward a group of Crow warriors sitting on a high spot where they could see the river and the ferry. The Army's engineering feat had drawn a crowd. Most of the Crow tribe had turned out to watch. Even children sat patient and waited. It was probably the most entertainment they'd seen all summer.

Gordon waded out into the slow-moving river and urged the team into the water with him. The horses balked as horses would in deep, moving water, but they hauled the ferry to the river's edge.

Diller sat atop his horse a short distance away and frowned.

"Don't just stand there," Gordon roared. "You men lend a hand and shove that ferry into the river."

A dozen soldiers stepped forward, none of them excited about the prospect, and pushed on the ferry.

"Put your backs into it!" Gordon ordered.

The soldiers heaved, but the water wasn't deep enough to lift the timbers yet and the mud made the going hard. They fought for every inch. Water ran over the front end of the ferry. The men struggled, but as soon as they reached the muddy riverbank, their feet couldn't get traction.

Lorenzo walked back down the hill and didn't look happy. "I do believe we not gonna find out if it'll float."

"We'll find out," Preacher said. He handed his mug back to Lorenzo, got up, and fetched his rifle. Dog got up and flanked him. Preacher looked over his shoulder and spotted Blue Magpie. "Magpie, you mind if I use your bull boat?"

Magpie waved at Preacher. "Go ahead."

Preacher walked over to Diller. "I need to borrow some rope."

"For what?" Diller growled.

"To get your ferry into the river."

"My men will—"

"They'll be plumb tuckered out after pushin' that ferry and it going nowhere," Preacher said. "If I'm going to lead you after Stone Eyes, I don't want a bunch of tired men ridin' with me."

Irritably, Diller nodded.

Preacher helped himself to three ropes from the soldiers' saddled horses. He walked down the riverbank to Blue Magpie's boat.

The Crow warriors and the mountain men talked in louder voices, excited to see something else developing.

"You are going to get wet, Preacher," Blue Magpie called and laughed.

"No, I ain't," Preacher replied.

Lorenzo bellowed, "I got two-bits that says Preacher don't get wet! Any takers?"

Men called back in quick response and took his bet.

Tall Dog fell into step beside Preacher and Dog.

"Would you like some company?" the young man asked in Crow.

"I wouldn't be against it," Preacher said. "Why are you so eager to sign on?"

"Watching the soldiers struggle getting the ferry into the river is getting boring," Tall Dog said. "You are going to help them get the ferry into the river?"

"I am."

Tall Dog smiled broadly. "Then I will help you. I would rather watch the soldiers get dumped."

Preacher grinned. "That's probably not gonna happen."

"I can be hopeful. I have seen such men as them before. They ride up into these mountains like they own them, like they know everything there is to know about this land. They do not."

"I reckon not," Preacher agreed.

CHAPTER 16

Preacher threw the ropes into Blue Magpie's bull boat and pushed the watercraft into the river. Dog leaped over the side and landed lithely in the center. Preacher heaved himself aboard. Tall Dog followed him an instant later. Both sat and took up the paddles that were aboard.

"Where do we go?" Tall Dog asked.

"The front of the ferry." Preacher dug his paddle into the river and pulled hard enough to send them on out into the water. He dug the paddle in to alter their course.

The bull boat came around and faced toward the straining horses and the grounded ferry. Tall Dog matched his rhythm and they handled the vessel like they'd been doing it together all their lives in just a few strokes.

On the riverbank, the Crow and the mountain men hooted encouragement. Some of the soldiers slacked off pushing the ferry and pointed at the bull boat.

"The Crow and the mountain men do not all expect us to succeed," Tall Dog said. "Many of them only want to watch us fall into the river."

Preacher grinned. "We'll try not to let that happen, but in case it does, do you know how to swim?"

"Like a fish," the young man answered confidently. "My father taught me when I was young."

"Good. Let's plan on staying out of the river. It's mighty cold this mornin'. On top of that, Lorenzo is likely to have bet his shirt on the outcome of this by now."

A moment later, Preacher brought the bull boat around to face Gordon. The sergeant was red-faced from exertion and anger, and he was waist-deep in the river. The horses stamped repeatedly at the water and shied at going in any farther. They didn't trust the river and their eyes rolled white.

Gordon's growled oaths filled the air. He glared at Preacher.

"What the hell are you doin'?" Gordon bawled.

"Came to help launch that ferry," Preacher said.

"I don't need any help."

"I can see that from the way it's still stuck there. I'm gonna help you anyway."

"Go away," Gordon snarled.

"Sergeant," Diller yelled in his command voice. The captain's horse stamped its feet restlessly on the riverbank, but the man sat straight and tall in the saddle. He was a good horseman and made it look effortless.

"Sir?" Gordon replied without taking his gaze from Preacher.

"When help is offered, be gracious enough to accept it," Diller said. "Or I'll get a corporal who will."

"Yes, sir," Gordon bellowed. He glared at Preacher. "All right, let's have your *help*."

Steadying himself, Preacher grabbed one of the coils of rope and hefted it. "Tie this to the front of the ferry. Not to the team. That won't do any good. Tie it tight so it don't come loose when we pull on it."

"You figure on pullin' us into the water by paddlin' your little boat?" Gordon asked.

"Nope. You just tie that rope." Holding on to one end of the rope, Preacher heaved the coil toward the sergeant.

Gordon caught the rope awkwardly, slipped in the mud, went under for a moment, and regained his footing. He reached out and caught his floating hat, which dumped water over his head.

The assembled Crow and mountain men farther up on the incline roared with laughter and the sound washed down over the river.

Taking a firm grip on the rope, ears burning and dripping, Gordon stumbled between the horses and headed for the ferry.

"Now," Preacher said to Tall Dog, "we paddle on across the river and set up on the other side. We ain't gonna try pullin' that ferry across in this boat."

The young man nodded and, at Preacher's word, dug his paddle into the river in strong strokes. Preacher pulled with him, and they made it across the river in short order.

Only a short length remained of the coil of rope by the time they neared the other riverbank. Preacher stopped paddling just short of land and took a moment to tie a second rope to the first with a reef knot, yanked on them to make sure they were tight, and helped Tall Dog paddle the bull boat onto the riverbank.

Out of the boat, Preacher strode to one of the stoutest oak trees dug into the riverbank. He set his rifle near to hand and climbed up into the tree a short distance. He located a limb nearly as big around as his thigh and tied the rope to it.

Satisfied with what he'd done, he called down to Tall

Dog to toss him the third rope. He tied a bowline knot in the third rope around the second and kept it loose enough to slide along the rope. When he was sure it was tight enough and yet remained loose enough to slide, he clambered down from the tree.

Tall Dog smiled. "I have seen something similar before. My father has helped with barn raisings and I assisted. This reduces some of the effort we have to use because we are going to use the tree's strength, as well."

"That's right," Preacher said. "And we can use our own weight, not just our strength. Used this a few times myself. It might work better with a block-and-tackle, but we ain't got a block-and-tackle like they have on cargo ships. A poor man has poor ways. We'll make do."

He looped the third rope around the tree trunk twice at shoulder height. He pulled the rope taut so it hung over the river. Water from the wet rope dripped down into the slow current.

Everything looked solid.

"You gonna pull?" Gordon bellowed. "Or are you gonna just tie ropes?"

Preacher ignored the man. He thought the rig might work, but he wasn't sure.

"Me and you," Preacher said to Tall Dog, "we're gonna set ourselves here and pull."

Tall Dog joined Preacher under the rope. The young man set his gear aside with care and took hold of the rope.

Preacher whipped the rope he'd tied the bowline knot in and sent it sailing smartly along the length tied to the ferry across the river. It came to a stop about eight feet along the wet line. Hoping the angle would be enough, Preacher took in the slack on the rope he held.

"Ready?" Preacher asked.

"Yes."

"Then pull hard as you live."

Preacher set himself. He pulled with both hands and added his body weight. Tall Dog did the same. The ropes all pulled tight. Preacher's boots skidded through the loose mud and he cursed. Tall Dog had the same problem.

"Hold up," Preacher said.

Tall Dog eased off and took in a deep breath. "It is heavy."

Preacher's back and arms burned from the effort, and for just a second, he thought maybe he'd bitten off more than he could chew. Having another man on the ropes might help, but he didn't want to have to ask.

"What's wrong, Preacher?" Gordon taunted. "Thought you was gonna show us how it's done."

Anger, bright and ugly, stormed within Preacher. Asking someone else to help was now out of the question. Pride was a hard thing for a man to carry, but it was even harder to hand off.

"We can get this," Preacher said. "Just need to get our feet set is all. Let's try over here."

Preacher led the younger man over to a tree a few feet away and pulled the rope taut again. Two of the low-hanging branches got in the way.

"Hold onto the rope," Preacher told Tall Dog. "We don't want it in the river where it'll get taken."

Tall Dog nodded. "I can climb up and clear the branches."

"Nope," Preacher said. "I took this job on and I mean to see it through."

The mountain man released the rope and grabbed hold of the lowermost branches. Dog sat at the foot of the tree. Up in the branches, Preacher settled himself in a nearby fork, took out his tomahawk, and swung.

"You like the view up there any better, Preacher," Gordon yelled across the river. "Things look any better?"

Preacher ignored the man and chopped through the two offending branches. They dropped, one after the other, into the river and floated slowly away.

As he swung around to climb down, one of the branches Preacher stood on broke. He plummeted for just an instant, then caught himself with his free hand and the head of the tomahawk. Dog stood and barked.

Across the river, the Crow and the mountain men roared with laughter. Several of them called out Preacher's name.

Grinning to himself because saving himself from falling into the river had been a near thing, Preacher clambered down to the riverbank. He smiled at Tall Dog.

"I reckon Lorenzo is gonna have to change his drawers after that mishap," Preacher said.

Tall Dog smiled back. "I thought you were going to fall."

"It was a near thing," Preacher agreed. "Now let's get that ferry into the river."

Preacher took hold of the rope again. He set himself up against the tree trunk and even clambered up a couple feet to clear space for the younger man to set his feet against it, as well.

"Ready?" Preacher asked.

Tall Dog took a fresh grip on the rope and nodded. "I am."

"Then let's get this ferry moving." Preacher raised his voice so it would carry across the river. "You men push!"

Galvanized by Preacher's command and the support that order got from Captain Diller, the soldiers, and Sergeant Gordon, resumed their struggle with the mired ferry.

Preacher pulled as fiercely as he could. The rope he'd tied onto held, but the upper branches of both trees shook. For a moment everything held and he wondered which would give first: one of the ropes, the tree, his moccasins, the ferry, or his back. It had to be one of them because he wasn't going to quit on it.

Only birdcalls and the soft passage of the river echoed around him and penetrated the bursting pressure that filled his head.

The rope came toward him a few inches, the line tied betwixt the tree and the ferry bowed, and some of the pressure inside Preacher's skull diminished.

"Got it on the run!" he yelled to Tall Dog. "Keep pullin'!"

Across the river, the ferry eased forward, then gained speed as it slid free of the riverbank. When the ferry bumped into the horses, they jumped forward and bowled Gordon over. The sergeant sank in the middle of an explosive curse. The ferry kept coming a short distance and herded the horses before it. In a few more steps, they were treading water.

The ferry floated just fine, although water pushed across the logs. Gordan surfaced at the side of the ferry and clung to it. His hat was nowhere in sight.

"That'll do it," Preacher said. He reeled in the rope to keep himself from falling, then stepped off the tree and dropped the short distance to the ground.

"We did it," Tall Dog said. The young man sounded surprised.

"We couldn't be stopped," Preacher said.

On the other side of the river, the Crow and the mountain men stood and cheered. Lorenzo was happily yelling over all of them and pointing at Preacher.

"I appreciate your help," Preacher said. He gathered up the rope because he wasn't a man to waste things. "I'll talk to Lorenzo and make it clear to him that him winnin' those bets had a lot to do with you bein' here. He'll get you cut in."

Tall Dog nodded. "I would ask a favor if I could."

"You can ask," Preacher said. "Don't mean I'll say yes."

"When you ride with the soldiers to show them where you encountered the Blackfeet, I want to go with you."

"You men secure that ferry," Captain Diller yelled. "Now that we've got it floating, I don't mean to lose it downriver. Get those horses out of the water."

Several of the soldiers waded out into the water. Most of them grabbed the ferry and hauled it back toward the riverbank. Two more men took the harnesses from the pulling team and headed them back to land as well.

"Why do you want to go?" Preacher asked.

"My father and mother intend to stay at this village for the summer," Tall Dog answered. "During my time here, I have seen most everything there is to see in this place. I have not traveled to that side of the mountain much."

The glint in the younger man's eyes was all too familiar to Preacher. On the occasions he had to peer into his own reflection, that glint still burned in his own eyes.

"Got a wanderin' spirit, do you?" Preacher asked.

"I do, and it makes my mother unhappy."

"Comes a time when a man has to blaze his own trail, Tall Dog. I figure that time may be drawin' nigh for you."

"Not yet, but soon. May I accompany you?"

"Likely be a borin' trip, and not somethin' you're gonna want to remember. Varmints have probably been at those Blackfeet."

"I have seen many bad things," Tall Dog said. "This will only be another, and I am sure there are many to come. The mountains are not a hospitable place for mild ways."

"They sure ain't," Preacher agreed. "You can ride along."

CHAPTER 17

Since the ferry was small and only three horses and riders at a time could be carried, it took the better part of two hours to accomplish the river crossing. Slowly, the soldiers formed up on the eastern side of the Snake and got their gear squared away.

Preacher took the time to attend to his own gear. He checked his powder and balls and his tack. He curried Horse and treated the big animal to some wild carrots and a handful of plums after he'd removed the stones. After the night of rest, Horse was ready to travel again. He had a wandering eye, too.

When he finished with his gear, Preacher returned to the campfire he'd set up. A few of the mountain men and Crow had joined him. All of them talked about the ferry crossings, and the story was likely to last all summer and into the winter.

Preacher gathered a few more stories about the Blackfeet while he drank coffee with his campfire guests.

"Stone Eyes is a cold-blooded killer," Peabody Mitchell stated.

He was a lanky man about Preacher's age who had

come up from Virginia. He wore his hair long and his beard was grizzled. His right hand was covered with twisted scars from a close encounter with a mountain lion when he was a young man.

"I come across two wagon trains that Stone Eyes and his band attacked. One of them was in the spring, when it was too wet and muddy to hope to get through quick enough. Even if the Blackfeet hadn't got 'em, they'd have had problems keepin' supplied. Wasn't any of them alive, an' ever'thin' they had was gone. The Blackfeet cleaned 'em out."

Mitchell spoke woodenly, the way a man did who cut himself off from emotion. Preacher listened and didn't ask questions. Peabody Mitchell wasn't a man who talked much, but when he talked a man did good to listen.

"The second wagon train I found was a month ago," Mitchell went on. "Diego Tamayo was headin' that one up. You remember Diego? Up from Juarez? Planned on gettin' into the cattle business because he thought it would be profitable because this country's still growin' an' is gettin' hungrier ever' day."

"I remember Diego," Preacher said. "He's a good man. I've run into him a few times."

"Well, you won't run into him no more, that's for sure." Mitchell tossed a twig into the campfire and watched with cold, distant eyes as the flame consumed it. "I found him tied to a tree, cut all to pieces an' just this side of death. For a minute, when I found him, I thought I glimpsed that ol' Grim Reaper a-settin' there beside him. Sent a cold shiver plumb through me."

The mood at the campfire dropped considerably. A lot of men had known Diego Tamayo.

"Ol' Diego lived another hour or two," Mitchell said.

"I spent it with him, both of us a-settin' there with all them dead people lyin' around us. I don't think he ever knowed I was there. Then he took his final breath an' cut plumb loose of all his sufferin'."

"At least he wasn't alone," Preacher said.

"No, sir, he wasn't." Mitchell blinked his wet eyes. "I made sure of that. Cut him a nice grave an' buried him deep." He took a deep breath. "It crossed my mind to try followin' Stone Eyes."

"You'd be a fool going after those Blackfeet on your own," one of the Thompkins boys said.

Like his brothers, he was tall and rangy and powerful. His chestnut-colored hair brushed his shoulders and matched the stubble on his chin. He'd come across the river to congratulate Preacher. He and his brothers and pa had laid bets of their own on Preacher's success.

"Then you can call me a fool," Mitchell said, "on account I did follow those Blackfeet. I got up all the way near to Colter's Hell before I cut loose of that trail."

"Colter's Hell ain't no place to be for damn sure," Allan Colquhoun stated. "A man would have to take leave of his senses to go up in them wild places."

Black haired and with a short-trimmed black beard, Colquhoun was thick and burly, short and powerful, and he moved like a cat in the wilderness. Like Mitchell, he didn't talk much—unless he was drunk, and then he was apt to sing old songs from his native country. He'd been born in Scotland and chased across the Atlantic Ocean by troubles he never spoke of. He'd started out in the Appalachians, but it was the Rocky Mountains that had captured his wild rover's heart.

"You ever been to Colter's Hell?" Mitchell asked.

Preacher shook his head. "Come close a time or two, but in the end, I had no need of it."

Curiosity still persisted in him, but one thing and another had turned him from making that journey in the past. Stories of John Colter's journeys after his travel with Lewis and Clark and the Corps of Discovery were still told around campfires throughout the mountains.

"They got ghosts an' creatures the like of which a man has never seen up in there," Colquhoun said. He crossed himself. "I've heard men say that not even God watches over you there. They were heathens, but, bein' somewhat Catholic despite Scotland's leanin's an' a believin' man, I still didn't want to try my luck."

"What turned you back?" Thompkins asked Mitchell.

"Good sense, I suppose," Mitchell mused. "Stone Eyes has dozens of warriors, an' there weren't but one of me." He pursed his lips. "But I heard things while I was up there. Gurglin' an' explosions, an' the air smelled so bad I was afraid I'd had me enough of it to kill me. I was days gettin' the stink of it out of my buckskins."

"You ask me," Oscar Ferrell said, "an' I'm sittin' downwind of you, you ain't got it all out."

Ferrell was a stonemason by trade who had built missions for the Franciscans in California. He was a thin man with large hands callused from handling stones. His father had been an Irish engineer and his mother was part Zapotec Indian and part Mexican. His face was a hard blade with only a few dark whiskers. He had never been able to grow a beard or more than a ghost mustache.

Mitchell smiled. "I just pulled in this mornin'. Give me time to get a bath. I'll freshen up like a daisy."

Preacher and the other men laughed because they all knew the smell of traveling and it didn't bother them.

"I'll take that bath right now, I think." Mitchell pushed himself to his feet.

"Hope it ain't on account of hurt feelin's," Ferrell said.

"Nope." Mitchell shook his head. "It ain't that. I just want to get that bath in before I head out again."

"You just got here," Thompkins said.

"I know it, but Preacher's pullin' up stakes this mornin'. All that thinkin' I done about ol' Diego, I think I'm gonna go with him." Mitchell clapped on his floppy hat and took up his rifle. He looked at Preacher. "You're gonna go show the Army a bunch of dead Blackfeet. Somehow I don't see this endin' there. If by some chance you end up findin' an interestin' trail that might lead you in the direction of Stone Eyes, I want to be ridin' with you."

Preacher didn't hesitate. Peabody Mitchell was a good man to have along if a man found himself in a tight spot.

"All right," Preacher said.

"I'll ride along, too," Thompkins said. "If that's all right. My pa's interested in what Cap'n Diller's doin' all the way out here. He wanted me to see if I could join you."

"The story of chasin' Blackfeet don't suit ol' Jess?" Colquhoun asked. "He thinks that's a bit of blarney, does he?"

"He didn't cotton to the story much, I'll say that." Thompkins looked at Preacher. "What do you say?"

Preacher had been mulling things over since Mitchell first offered to ride with him. He couldn't have the man, and Thompkins if the young man was earnest about accompanying him, riding off into more trouble than anyone was expecting.

"Stone Eyes has got rifles," Preacher said. "Likely a lot of them."

The men stared at him.

"Well, hell," Ferrell said, "if that's true, ain't none of us safe up here."

"It's true," Preacher said.

Ferrell nodded. "Got room for one more?"

"I do," Preacher said. "And I'll be glad to have you."

"You got me, too," Colquhoun said. "There's a pretty little Crow lassie I've had me eye on for a bit, an' I'll not stand for any trouble to come her way if I can help it. An' I can."

"All right," Preacher said.

"Nobody else knows this story?" Mitchell asked.

"No. Not yet. I intend to have a word with Chief Finds the Balance and Jess Thompkins before I pull out. They need to know."

"Why, I bet if you tell them mountain men over there, you'd find a bunch of 'em willin' to ride with you," Mitchell said. "Probably a lot of Crow warriors would be willin' to, as well."

"If they did," Preacher said, "there'd be fewer people here to defend the Crow women and children if anything went wrong. Besides that, I'd rather have a small group that can move fast and live off the land if it comes to it."

"Well, you ain't got that in them Army men," Thompkins said.

Out on the river, the soldiers pulled on the ropes to transfer more of the supplies they were packing. Small crates and bags of foodstuffs were lashed to the ferry and a few thick branches to keep them out of the water that overflowed the logs.

"I know that," Preacher said. "Ain't happy about it, but that's not my lookout. So we're gonna stay quiet about this and let the chief and Jess figure out when to tell everyone else. Agreed?"

The men all nodded and looked somber. The lark they'd entertained had just turned out to be dangerous.

An hour later, after his conversation with Chief Finds the Balance and Jess Thompkins, Preacher stood in the shade with Captain Diller. The Army officer wasn't happy.

"I thought it was just going to be you," Diller said. His words weren't quite a complaint, but they were close neighbors. "Maybe that black man who likes to bet on you."

Preacher looked out over the mountain men who'd asked to join him. Peabody Mitchell, freshly kitted out and bathed, smelled better than he had. The Thompkins boy turned out to be Seth, and he'd brought his younger brother Barney with him. They stood side by side, and both were outfitted with two of the rifles Preacher had brought back with him.

Oscar Ferrell sat on a stump and sipped coffee from a tin cup. Allan Colquhoun stood laughing with Lorenzo, both of them doubtlessly swapping lies. Tall Dog sat with crossed legs in front of his horse and took advantage of the shade his mount provided while the horse sunned itself. Instead of taking advantage of the ferry, Tall Dog had led his paint pony into the river without hesitation and both of them had easily swum across. Tall Dog had managed that while carrying his weapons in a bag in one hand.

"If things turn bad," Preacher said, "like they might, you'll be glad you've got those men with you. I am."

"Do you know these men?"

"We don't exchange letters, but we've kept company enough to know each other. If push comes to shove, they'll stick and be there till the bitter end."

"I don't want to waste my supplies feeding extra men."

"We've got our own grub," Preacher said. "Anything we need that we ain't carryin', we'll get as we need it."

"I still don't like it."

"Don't recall askin' you to. And I won't." Preacher returned the captain's gaze full measure. "Are your troops ready to ride?"

"Yes."

Preacher walked over to where Horse stood with Dog at his feet. He glanced at the men riding with him.

"Mount up." Preacher stepped up into the saddle with his rifle in hand.

With the Blackfeet in the area, he didn't plan on putting it down much. In the saddle, he shook out the reins and headed Horse back up into the mountains to the east.

CHAPTER 18

Tired and chafing for vengeance, Stone Eyes rode along the shallow valley that led to the Snake River crossing Tracker Who Sees knew of. A handful of his warriors rode ahead of him to scout the way. Bear Kills Many rode at Stone Eyes's side and did not speak.

Birds flitted among the branches on either side of the narrow trail that wound through boulders and trees. The air smelled crisp and clean, so the rains were over at least for a few days.

The Blackfeet had traveled all day. From what Tracker Who Sees had told him of the countryside, they would reach the crossing an hour or so before sundown. There was plenty of time to get to the other side. They could camp for the night and get an early start. That would put them at the Crow camp in the afternoon.

A lone rider, one of Tracker Who Sees's scouts, rode his pony at a gallop and reached the old man where he was among the scouts. Tracker Who Sees waved to another scout and sent him forward. The returning scout talked briefly with the old scout.

After the short conversation, Tracker Who Sees halted

his horse and waited for Stone Eyes to reach him. Saving the horse was a wise thing to do and Stone Eyes respected his old teacher for that. When he reached the old man, Tracker Who Sees took up his place on Stone Eyes's other side.

"You have news?" Stone Eyes asked.

Tracker Who Sees would think him impertinent for asking so quickly. If he were still a student, that impertinence would not be allowed and would be punished.

"We are three miles from the crossing," Tracker Who Sees said. "No one is there."

"Has anyone used the crossing recently?"

That was another impertinent question but Stone Eyes didn't care. His son was dead. The rifles were lost. He wanted vengeance and he wanted the rifles. He would allow no one to stand in his way.

"No one has been through the crossing for days," the old scout said. "It is so. Wise Turtle says he searched up and down the river on both sides. He found only coals from campfires that were at least two weeks old. He also found dead men at one of those campfires."

"What dead men? Whites?"

"The bodies were those of Blackfeet warriors. Wise Turtle believes they were hunters because they had bows and arrows. No rifles."

"Their killers could have taken their rifles."

"Perhaps, but their personal effects were left with them."

"How were they killed?"

"They were tortured." Tracker Who Sees remained impassive. His eyes took in everything.

"Whites killed them?" Though it was not often, Stone Eyes knew the whites could be just as callous and cruel as his warriors. That was one thing that made hunting them so interesting.

"Not white men." Tracker Who Sees dragged a finger over his face in a pattern Stone Eyes knew. "They were marked for ill luck in the World That Comes After."

"Some whites know those signs, as well." Even as Stone Eyes said that, though, a quiver of doubt threaded through him.

"It is so, but Wise Turtle also found this." Tracker Who Sees pulled a small totem from his robes. It fit comfortably in the old man's hand and hung over either end. "It was placed in the mouth of one of the dead men."

Stone Eyes took the totem gingerly. He believed in the power of the Old Spirits and knew they could still do good and evil in the world. He forced himself to look in the eyes of the three horrible faces carved into the wood.

"I do not know this totem," Stone Eyes admitted.

"There is still much you do not know, my chief," Tracker Who Sees said. "There still remains much I do not know, but I know this totem. The bottom face is of Bear. The second face is that of Cougar. But the top face—"

"Is Spider," Stone Eyes said. "I know that. That does not tell me who owns this totem."

"It belongs to Wind Spider."

The name sent a sharp jab of fear through Stone Eyes. The legend of Wind Spider was known among the Blackfeet, but the man was not talked of much because no one wished to call down bad luck.

"He is a legend," Stone Eyes said. "A myth."

"Yet, here is his mark."

"He would be an old man, older than you."

"There are men, men who are deadly, who are older than me," Tracker Who Sees said. "It is so."

"Wind Spider was little more than a child when his tribe was killed by the sickness brought by the whites. They were covered by the weeping sores, burned to death by fevers, and they died in agony."

"So did anyone else who got the sickness the whites brought. People knew how Wind Spider's tribe perished. When he was a child and sought succor with other tribes, they chased him away because they feared he brought the pestilence. It is said his body is covered by the scars of the weeping sickness. They mark him for everyone to know the same way they did when he was a child."

"He could not have survived on his own."

"He did, though. It is said the Spider spirit appeared to that young boy and bade him lay in the view of the sun so that the weeping sores might heal. As you know, Spider is linked to the sun, and this is why Spider's web looks like the sun in full bloom."

"I have heard that," Stone Eyes said impatiently. "I have also heard how Wind Spider took on his name because he was blown from place to place with no home."

"He had a home," Tracker Who Sees said. "He made his home wherever he wished, as does any spider."

The old scout stopped his horse, reached out for a low-hanging branch, and twisted it. Leaves twisted in the breeze and revealed the spider's web nestled between two twigs. The small insect scurried out of sight.

"Just as this one has done," Tracker Who Sees said. He gently released the branch. "Wind Spider found others like himself, men who were orphaned by disease, war, and bad luck. He called them to him and offered them new lives."

"What does the totem mean?"

"Wind Spider once lived at that crossing," the old scout

said. "Perhaps he lives there now. We shall soon see." He looked at Stone Eyes. "Unless you wish to turn back."

"No. We will not turn back."

"Wind Spider is not known for his generous ways. He takes from everyone who is not in his band because of the way he has been treated."

"I will not turn back," Stone Eyes said. "I will have my revenge."

Drumbeats filled the air around Stone Eyes and broke the words that he had spoken. He pulled up his rifle and eared the hammer back.

Ahead, the scouts stopped their horses, milled in confusion, and awaited orders.

Stone Eyes urged his horse forward and studied the trees. "I am Stone Eyes, chief of these warriors. I do not fear your drums. Come and face me instead of hiding in the shadows."

For a moment the drumming persisted and grew louder, so strong that Stone Eyes's heart sped up to beat with the rhythm. He kept his face impassive, but he was all too aware that he was exposed to an arrow, spear, or rifle ball.

But he would not fear something that was only a story.

The drumming stopped and the echoes faded in the trees.

"You are trespassing, Stone Eyes," a man warned. His voice boomed almost as loudly as the drums had. "Turn back."

"I cannot," Stone Eyes said. "I am on a mission seeking vengeance. I will not be denied."

"Then you are a fool who runs to his own death."

"Are you Wind Spider?" Stone Eyes demanded.

No answer came forth.

"Or are you only a story meant to frighten children?"

Stone Eyes raked the trees and the valley. Birds flitted and butterflies fluttered, but nothing human or animal moved in the woods.

"I am Wind Spider," the man said. "And I will not let you pass."

"Then I will kill you," Stone Eyes promised.

"You will die."

"Come kill me."

Mocking laughter rang out from the trees, but Stone Eyes did not know from where it came. The shallow valley trapped sound and sent it spinning through the trees and brush.

"Perhaps you have heard of me," Stone Eyes challenged. "Are you afraid of me?"

"I have beaten the white man's weeping sickness," Wind Spider roared. "It burned me with fever and covered my body in sores, yet I lived and became stronger because of it."

"You were made ugly by the weeping sores," Stone Eyes said. "Now you are afraid to show yourself and that vile ugliness you wish to hide."

The mocking laughter filled the valley again.

"Come," Wind Spider said. "Come to the crossing at the river and I will show you my ugliness. It will be the last thing you see."

For a moment, Stone Eyes sat on his horse and didn't move. When nothing happened, he urged his horse forward and rode on past his scouts. He didn't order them to lead the way. He chose to ride at the front to show them what a true warrior would do.

Fear lingered in their eyes, and he hated it for the weakness it was. He had strong medicine. The spirits would favor him, and he would survive this challenge. He would be avenged.

Bear Kills Many rode behind him, and the big warrior threatened all of them with death if they did not follow their chief.

Several minutes later, Stone Eyes rode out of the small valley and down onto the rocky banks of the river crossing. Wet moccasin prints gleamed on the bare rock. They could only be minutes old.

The Snake thinned here because the water had sought release through underground channels. A natural granite bridge had been created through time and erosion. Such things existed all over the mountains, especially in this area. The occurrences were worse in the Stinking Lands, what the whites called Colter's Hell.

To Stone Eyes's right, the river broadened like a beaver's tail that was at least twenty yards across. On the left, ten feet below in a chasm that cut through the mountains here, white water rushed out of the underground chambers and spilled into a large basin of what looked like still waters another forty feet below.

Trails down into the canyon below showed on both sides of the river, but the bridge was the only way across with a horse.

The granite bridge curved to encompass the lower basin. The thickness varied between six and ten feet above the lower chambers. The roar of the crashing waters drowned out all other sound.

Doubtless, the deeper waters in the basin weren't so still and probably moved swiftly. A hundred yards out, the river turned into a series of white water falls as the Snake descended toward the valley where the Crow tribe camped.

Where Preacher was. The mountain man would know where the rifles were. Stone Eyes would get that information from Preacher before he killed him.

The Blackfeet chief halted at the bridge's edge. The river was still full enough that water a couple inches deep spilled over the edge. The spillway made for treacherous footing.

On the other side of the bridge, another valley let out onto the crossing. Shadows lingered under the trees there because the sun was low in the west. Movement stood out against the darkness, and wariness filled Stone Eyes.

"Wind Spider!" Stone Eyes yelled. "I am here!"

Drumming filled the air and warred with the thunder of the crashing falls. The wind flew through the channel and whipped what was left of Stone Eyes's shorn hair into his face.

Men wearing warpaint stepped into view. Four of them beat on small drums. All of them wore wet moccasins. All of them had been in the trees watching Stone Eyes and his warriors.

"Do you fear me, Wind Spider?" Stone Eyes taunted.

"No," the deep voice called back. "I fear no man."

"If you do not let me pass, I will teach you fear."

The laughter returned, and this time it grated on Stone Eyes because it sounded insane.

"Then come teach me," Wind Spider challenged.

Stone Eyes dismounted his horse and handed the reins to Bear Kills Many.

A shadow stepped out of the other shadows and the man stood revealed in the scant light from the fading sun and that reflected from the water. He stood half a head taller than any warrior around him. His face and exposed skin were covered in scars created by the weeping sickness. He had covered all of himself with red paint so that he looked like a massive, bleeding sore. His thick, dark hair was pulled back. A necklace of fingerbones hung around his neck and more were woven into his hair.

He stripped off his buckskin shirt and revealed his massively muscled upper body. He wasn't just covered in scars created by the weeping sickness. There were scars left by knives, rifle or pistol balls, spears, and arrows. Whatever else he might be, Wind Spider was hard to kill.

"Am I not beautiful?" Wind Spider asked.

"No," Stone Eyes replied. "You are a thing of horror, something to frighten children with."

Wind Spider laughed, and the hint of madness within the sound grew louder. Despite his desire to remain calm, a chill ghosted through Stone Eyes's bones.

He pushed it away. Fear was a weakness and he had no use for weakness.

"Let me pass," Stone Eyes ordered.

"Why?"

"In return, I will let you live with your horridness."

Wind Spider laughed again, but this time it was more forced.

"You and I will battle as honorable warriors," Wind Spider said. He held up a tomahawk and a long hunting knife. "With these. Do you agree?"

"Where will we fight?"

"On the bridge. That way my men can see you run."

"I won't run."

Stone Eyes shoved his rifle into the scabbard on his saddle. He took his tomahawk and hunting knife from the sash at his waist, handed them to Bear Kills Many, and stripped off the sash and buckskin shirt. The chill wind tightened his skin, but he burned inside as he prepared for battle.

"Take off your moccasins," Tracker Who Sees said. "Your bare feet will be surer on the wet rock than the deerskin."

Stone Eyes stripped off his moccasins and tossed them aside. He once more took up the tomahawk and hunting knife. He glanced at Bear Kills Many and spoke softly.

"If Wind Spider kills me, slay him."

Bear Kills Many spoke equally softly and nodded. "He will never reach the other side of the bridge."

Holding onto his anger and his desire for vengeance, Stone Eyes turned and stepped onto the bridge. The cold water ran over his bare feet and numbed him.

CHAPTER 19

Wind Spider crossed the bridge with the sure-footedness of a silver-tailed deer who only knew its home in the mountains.

Vertigo nibbled at the edges of Stone Eyes's mind. The roaring water constantly reminded him of the long drop on one side of the granite bridge, and the still waters on the other side didn't fool him. If he fell in, the undertow would suck him down faster than *Omachk-soyis-ksiksinai*, the fearsome Horned Snake that lived in the legends of his people.

Stone Eyes had never seen a Horned Snake, but he had heard talk among the old warriors who had. Or so they claimed.

None of them had ever met Wind Spider, and that legend had been more believable. Men had seen the atrocities Wind Spider and his warriors had committed.

"Have you made peace with your ancestors?" Wind Spider taunted. He stepped confidently toward Stone Eyes, like the walk across the submerged granite bridge was an everyday occurrence. "Will they receive you with open arms and glad hearts?"

Instead of stripping away Stone Eyes's confidence as Wind Spider had intended, the questions only reinforced the war chief's desire for vengeance. Preacher would die. Stone Eyes only had to kill the disfigured madman in front of him to get there. He took two more steps on his numbed feet and imagined that he was part of the stone.

"I will not die today," Stone Eyes replied. "You would have been better served to let me pass."

Wind Spider laughed again. He stopped just out of arm's reach and locked eyes with Stone Eyes.

"Do you fear me now?" the giant asked.

"No," Stone Eyes lied.

"What do you see?"

"A monster."

"Monsters can't be killed."

"This one can," Stone Eyes said. He studied the scarred face in front of him. The man was younger than him. Older than Silent Owl was, but not nearly old enough to be the man of legend. "You are not Wind Spider."

"I am."

"You are not. You are far too young. Wind Spider should be a man in the winter of his life. An old man in his eighties."

Wind Spider thrust with the knife and followed it with a step to take away ground. He was as fast as any man Stone Eyes had seen. Even with the warning given by the slight flexing of his shoulder muscles right before the thrust, Stone Eyes was almost late in blocking the blow aside. The glancing impact was enough to knock him sideways, and he was late returning a counterstrike with his own knife.

The big, scar-faced man took another step forward and delivered an overhand chop with the tomahawk that would have split Stone Eyes's skull if it had landed. The keen edge nicked the side of Stone Eyes's right cheek to his jawline in passing, then cut another stripe along his chest.

Blistering fire lit along Stone Eyes's cheek and chest. The warmth of blood trickled down his face and body and temporarily dulled the sharp teeth of the chill wind. He stepped back without thinking and barely raised the tomahawk in time to block Wind Spirit's hunting knife. The blade screamed along the tomahawk's steel head.

Setting himself, Stone Eyes thrust with his own knife and was blocked immediately by his opponent's tomahawk.

Wind Spider cackled. "You are too slow. You are going to die."

"You will die," Stone Eyes growled.

Wind Spider swung his weapons again in a quick one-two. Barely, Stone Eyes blocked both attacks. Metal shrieked and screamed, and sparks flew. The impacts quivered through both of Stone Eyes's arms. If he lived, they would both be sore.

Silently, Wind Spider attacked again and again. Each time Stone Eyes grew a little faster, a little more aggressive.

Chest heaving, Wind Spider stepped back. "I am the strongest opponent you have ever faced." He was so angry his words carried spit with them. "I am outcast from my tribe, and I made one of my own. I took in the warriors who were driven from their tribes. I took in warriors who wanted to make war on the whites."

"And those who would make war on their own people," Stone Eyes said. His breath rasped at the back of his throat. The wind was no longer uncomfortable. Now it barely cooled him, and sweat trickled down his body to mix with blood from his original cut and two more that he couldn't remember getting.

Except for his horrific scars, Wind Spider was unmarked and looked as powerful as ever.

"My father exposed me to the weeping sickness when I was just a babe," Wind Spider said. He lashed out again and Stone Eyes turned both blades aside. "He told me if I lived, I would inherit his tribe."

"You are not the Wind Spider of legend," Stone Eyes said. "You are but a copy, an imitator who took on the mantle of another."

"I am an improvement!" Wind Spider roared. "I am more than my father ever was!"

The scar-faced giant launched another series of attacks.

Stone Eyes no longer thought about his fighting. He reacted the way he had learned through countless battles. The blades met again and again. His breath became a roaring furnace that filled his ears. Water splashed around his feet, which he could no longer feel and only trusted to be there when he needed them.

His feet moved automatically, shifted, shifted again, and his blades met those of his opponent again and again. Steel shrieked and screamed and pierced the roar of Stone Eyes's breath. For a moment, he believed his opponent was truly a monster, summoned from the dark places where malignant spirits dwelled.

Only that couldn't be true, he realized, because Wind Spider's breath roared, too. The big man sucked in air like a buffalo cow delivering a calf.

The monster was not inhuman.

Laughter spilled from Stone Eyes then. He was fighting with only the dregs left to him. Instead of reacting to Wind Spider's attacks, he beat them back and led them. Again and again, first the knife then the tomahawk then the knife over and over, Stone Eyes drove his weapons at his opponent.

Wind Spider took a step back to avoid an attack. Despite the fact that his strength was eroding, Stone Eyes pressed his advantage. He was certain that every blow would be his last. But he thought of Silent Owl and Preacher and how many people he would kill with those stolen rifles, and he found more strength.

"I am . . . going to . . . kill you!" Wind Spider yelled his promise in gasps, and Stone Eyes launched a new attack with every gasp.

Stone Eyes's lungs burned, and he couldn't get enough air. He swept his knife toward his opponent's chest. Instead of steel this time, the blade met flesh and a large gash opened along Wind Spider's stomach. Blood wept down the scarred flesh.

Wind Spider roared with rage. He tried to bull forward. Stone Eyes let the bigger man come, measured his opponent's stride, and swung his tomahawk low when the man's right leg came forward. Stone Eyes's tomahawk bit into the inside of Wind Spider's leg. When he yanked the tomahawk free, blood rushed out of the scar-faced man's leg like one of the fountains in the Stinking Land.

Blood covered Stone Eyes's tomahawk and hand, and the torrent splashed into the water running over the granite bridge.

Gasping for air, barely able to stand, Stone Eyes slashed Wind Spider's throat with his knife. The giant dropped his weapons, and they clanked against the granite bridge before they disappeared on either side into the water. He grasped his scarred throat with both hands.

"No!" Wind Spider tried to yell, but he barely had a

voice left. His face paled instantly. He stumbled forward and reached for Stone Eyes.

Stone Eyes ducked beneath his opponent's outstretched arms, lunged forward as hard as he could, and rammed his shoulder into Wind Spider's bleeding stomach. He hit hard enough to lift the bigger man from his feet.

For a moment their blood held their flesh stuck together. Then it peeled apart, and Wind Spider fell over the bridge into the basin fifty feet below. The big man didn't move before he hit the water and disappeared.

Weapons still in hand, Stone Eyes turned to his vanquished foe's warriors.

In the growing shadows, one of them lifted a rifle to his shoulder. Stone Eyes crouched, but there was nowhere to go. A dive into the water on either side of the bridge would doubtless lead to death. Instead, he rushed the man and expected to feel the impact of the ball hitting his flesh at any moment. His feet splashed through the shallow water.

A sharp *crack!* of a rifle rattled Stone Eyes's ears. The warrior who had drawn down on him froze and a trickle of blood wormed down from the hole on the left side of his forehead. His arms fell and he dropped the rifle.

Another man raised his rifle, but before he could level it, Stone Eyes was upon him. He grabbed the rifle barrel, turned it aside, and stepped into the man close enough to hold the knife to his throat and use him as a shield.

"If you want to live," Stone Eyes shouted, "throw down your weapons and take me as your chief! I want warriors who will kill anyone I order them to! Swear your loyalty to me, and I will give you mercy!"

The warriors hesitated.

"Wind Spider was our chief!" one of the men yelled.

The next instant, a heavy-caliber ball shattered his cheek and turned his head to the side.

From the corner of his eye as he held his captive, Stone Eyes caught sight of Bear Kills Many throwing aside his spent rifle and taking another from a warrior next to him. Bear Kills Many pulled the rifle to his shoulder and eared the hammer back.

"Decide!" Stone Eyes yelled. "Decide now!"

The rifles, bows, knives, and tomahawks hit the ground in rapid succession. Including the rifle held by the man Stone Eyes held with his knife.

Two hours later, and in the full dark of night, Stone Eyes sat with his back to a tree and allowed one of his young warriors to wash and care for his wounds by the light of a nearby campfire. The wounds were slight, no more than scratches. He would ache more from the fight than he would from the cuts. Still, blood poison from an untended wound would kill a warrior just as dead as a knife or a rifle ball.

When the warrior had finished, Stone Eyes sent him away and pulled his buckskin shirt back on. He draped a buffalo robe over his shoulders to blunt the freezing chill that came with the night.

He fought sleep that tried to claim him because he wanted to eat so that he could reclaim his strength. Morning would come early, and he intended to be up with it.

After the battle with Wind Spider, Stone Eyes had insisted the war party keep riding. He refused to waste any time. They were still most of a day away from the Crow tribe. He wanted to get as close as he could to the camp so there would be plenty of light for the attack.

His men shared campfires with those who had ridden with Wind Spider. They were lean and hungry. Perhaps they were good killers, but they were not so good at hunting. Some of them also had wounds they claimed to have gotten from pony soldiers a few days ago.

That battle had been one that Wind Spider had not won. Thinking back on the stories he'd heard, Stone Eyes realized that Wind Spider had been known for attacking mostly when they had the superior numbers.

The food that Stone Eyes and his warriors had taken from the wagon train only a couple of days ago dissolved any remaining feelings of distrust among the new members of his war party. Feeding warriors created loyalty. That was a basic tenet Stone Eyes had adopted.

It was an easy thing to do after the cowardly way the whites treated his people with spoiled food and diseased blankets they gave to them.

A dozen campfires fought the night's shadows and created small bubbles of golden light that trailed flickering embers into the dark sky. The smell of cooked meat filled the camp. Somewhere in the distance, wolves howled at the moon and an owl hooted.

Stone Eyes trusted the thick cedars and firs in this part of the mountain to block the firelight from any who might be searching for it. Animals would stay clear of them. He and his men had to have the campfires. Even this time of year, up in the mountains as high as they were, a man could freeze to death while he slept.

Tracker Who Sees got up from a nearby campfire and approached. He held a bowl in one hand.

"Are you hungry, my chief?" the old man asked.

"I am."

Tracker Who Sees held out the bowl and Stone Eyes

took it. Thick broth covered chunks of deer. The cooked meat made Stone Eyes's stomach growl in anticipation.

"Eat," the old scout instructed. "Be sure you drink the broth. It will help you heal and restore your strength."

"I know that."

"Because I have taught you." Tracker Who Sees used his rifle and eased himself down.

Stone Eyes ate a couple of chunks of meat. He chewed, swallowed, and wiped the back of his hand across his mouth. "Tell me again of the Crow camp."

"I know the place well," the old scout said. "I have summered there in the past when the Blackfeet ruled that land." He leaned forward and smoothed dirt in front of Stone Eyes. He sketched in the river with a pair of lines. "The river runs mostly north and south, as this does. The Crow will be on the west side of the river, which is where we now are."

Tracker Who Sees drew another line. Stone Eyes ate more meat and remembered how Silent Owl had drawn tracks of animals he had found when he was a boy. Those memories hurt now, and Stone Eyes put them away in his thoughts.

"Here," the old scout said, "the land rises. This is to the west of the Crow camp. We will come at them from this direction late tomorrow afternoon. With the sun in their eyes, they will have difficulty seeing us. If we go carefully until we are ready to attack, they will not see us at all."

"We will attack them from the north and the south as well." Stone Eyes leaned forward and added two more marks to those Tracker Who Sees had made. "They will have nowhere to run."

"No," the old scout said. "It is so."

"Have you sent out scouts to make sure we are alone?"

"I have. We are. Tomorrow we will follow the river to the Crow camp."

Stone Eyes relished the thought of that.

Bear Kills Many joined them and sat cross-legged in front of the fire.

"Our new warriors are satisfied with their arrangement?" Stone Eyes asked.

"Yes. Some of them have been with Wind Spider, this Wind Spider, for a long time. Some remember the Wind Spider before the one you killed. They did not like this one as well as the old one, but many of them were already known to travel with him and so were unable to return to their people."

"They will be no trouble?"

"I do not think so. They will be happy to have someone to follow."

"For now," Stone Eyes said. "Those warriors know no true loyalty." He picked up another piece of meat from the bowl. "It is just as well. For now, they can help us against the pony soldiers. Afterward, once we get the rifles and we ride for the Stinking Land, we can kill them."

Bear Kills Many gazed out at the campfires. "Our numbers are thin. We will need to replace those warriors we lost with Silent Owl."

"We will," Stone Eyes said. "Once we have those rifles, we can do many things. The whites and the Crow will learn to fear us even more than they do now."

CHAPTER 20

Preacher rode high up on the mountain on a path that would allow him to overlook the clearing where he'd encountered Silent Owl and his group of Blackfeet days ago. Captain Diller and the soldiers waited almost two hundred yards away. They could see Preacher, but they couldn't see the clearing. That meant if anyone was at the clearing, they wouldn't see the Army soldiers and the men who'd followed Preacher.

Preacher wanted to scout ahead and make sure there were no surprises.

Dog trotted alongside Horse, and both of his companions were steady and alert. They wove through trees and brush so they wouldn't be seen from the clearing.

It was late afternoon, right before evening set in, and the light was still good enough to see well, though it interfered some with the mountain man's view. Preacher kept track of the scents carried to him on the gentle breezes that feathered the mountainside. The arrowleaf balsamroot was in bloom, and the hills between knots of trees rolled with bright yellow flowers. The aromas of fir and spruce thickened the air, and there were other pollens Preacher knew immediately.

He didn't smell the acrid stink of spent gunpowder, which he had searched for, and he knew no one in the nearby vicinity had fired a rifle or a pistol recently.

Of course, an arrow, a knife, or a spear would kill a man damn quick if he was caught unawares.

Movement in the trees around the small clearing where he'd fought Silent Owl and his Blackfoot warriors caught his attention. Crows lit on clumps in the trees that broke the natural lines of branches and leaves. A less discerning eye wouldn't have known those rectangular shapes for what they were until he was up in the middle of them, but Preacher had halfway been expecting them.

The black birds hopped to and fro eagerly and occasionally battled each other for territory with flapping wings. Their raucous caws filled the air. If any man had been moving among the trees, his presence would have scared the crows off. However, a patient man, if he waited and made no move, could sit among the birds and not be noticed. Preacher had done that very thing a few times in the past to ambush a varmint who needed killing.

Behind a thick stand of aspen, Preacher took a fresh grip on his rifle, settled it on his saddle pommel, and slid his spyglass from his saddlebags. He pulled the instrument open, put it to his eye, and scanned the trees again.

He followed the lines of the platform suspended in the closest tree. Leaf-covered branches hid most of the platform, but he knew it was probably close to ten feet in length. That was the usual length of the scaffolding many Indians used for their dead.

"Okay, Horse," Preacher said calmly and collapsed the spyglass, "let's go have a closer look-see, and don't you go lettin' the smell of the dead bother you none. Ain't nothin' there gonna hurt us."

He slid his spyglass back into his saddlebag and put his heels to the horse's sides to urge him on toward the clearing. Disappearing from Diller's line of sight would worry the Army captain some, but Preacher trusted the man would hold up for a few minutes.

When Preacher reached the first scaffold, he rode around the clearing in counterclockwise direction so he could keep the sun to his back and not be blinded. The smell of death filled the clearing, and Preacher pushed away the instinctive reaction to shy away from it.

The smell was just dead people, men he'd killed who needed killing. He'd smelled that plenty of times everywhere he went. Death was a constant companion.

"Dog," Preacher said, "go on and have a look."

The big cur darted off and disappeared into the brush without stirring a leaf.

Preacher trusted his eyes and ears and Dog's nose to keep them out of trouble. Horse was on high alert, too, and the mountain man knew it was because the animal had gotten a whiff of the dead.

The cold temperature of the nights slowed the decomposition of the corpses, but the warm days provided enough heat to get the job done. The stink was thick and cloying here where the faint breezes were blocked by the trees and the hill he'd ridden down.

Preacher lifted his scarf and pulled it over his nose. The material cut some of the stink, but it didn't block it all. He opened his mouth to breathe so the smell wasn't so strong.

Since Captain Diller would be getting impatient on the other side of the hill, and because Preacher didn't want to miss anything of consequence, he dismounted and walked through the clearing. The arrival of Diller and his men would cover the sign that had been left. With a keen eye, Preacher read the story the horses' hooves and moccasin prints had to tell.

When he was certain he had seen everything there was to see, Preacher remounted. He returned to the outer edge of the clearing closest to Diller and the soldiers and rode up the hill to the crest.

Lorenzo and the mountain men sat apart from the soldiers and took shelter in the shade provided by nearby trees. They allowed their horses to graze and cool down while the soldiers remained mounted. The Army horses would tire faster without resting.

Preacher reached into his saddlebags and took out a square of white cloth that would stand out against the mountainside. He held it by one corner and waved it overhead to let everyone know it was safe to ride in. If there'd been trouble, a rifle shot or a pistol shot would have gotten that job done.

Once the soldiers rode toward him, Preacher climbed off Horse to let the animal rest. The ride through the mountains had been exhausting for horse and rider. He called Dog to him so Diller's men wouldn't be so apt to shoot first and find out what was in the brush second.

Lorenzo and the mountain men wouldn't do that. Preacher had introduced them to Dog and let them know the big cur was traveling with them. Most of them already knew that. While he waited, Preacher kept his gaze moving and held his rifle in his hand.

A handful of soldiers rode past Preacher to secure the area. Others fanned out on either side to establish a perimeter. They were competent men and well-trained, and they were used to working in the present terrain.

Lorenzo and the mountain men fanned out deeper into the surrounding countryside. They knew Preacher would have covered the battleground. They would find anything else that had been left. The soldiers didn't think of that.

"What did you find?" Diller asked. He reined up his horse just short of Preacher, but he didn't dismount.

Sergeant Gordon and a couple other soldiers fanned out around Diller as a security detail.

"Someone's been by," Preacher said.

"You found tracks?"

"Found them, too." Preacher smiled and nodded up at the trees. "But those scaffolds were what let me know someone had been here who was friendly with the Blackfeet."

Diller squinted at the trees. "What are those? Fortifications?"

"Burial scaffolds," Preacher answered. "The Crow, Blackfeet, and several other Indians bury their dead that way."

Diller gazed up at the trees. "Somebody buried the dead."

"Yeah," Preacher said.

"Are those dead men the Indians you killed?"

"I didn't open them up to see, but I counted 'em. The number matches up."

"So who buried them?" Diller asked.

"Ain't likely they took turns buryin' each other," Preacher said. "Whoever did it has come and gone. I found their tracks leadin' in and leadin' out."

"Don't see why anybody calls it burying," one of the young soldiers said. He was a little green and looked like he was barely old enough to be in the Army. "Not when these heathens insist on hanging their dead folks in trees like candles on a Christmas tree."

"What the hell are you goin' on about, Dwayne?" Gordon asked irritably. "What's a Christmas tree?"

"It's a new tradition here in the United States, Sergeant," Dwayne said. "It's catching on back East, especially in Boston where I'm from. Folks who want to celebrate Christmas put a tree up and decorate it with lighted candles."

"Sounds like pure-dee stupidity to me," Gordon declared. "An' a good way to burn your house down at the same time. We ain't got time to be talkin' about any kind of foolishness like Christmas trees covered in candles."

"Yes, Sergeant," Dwayne said glumly. Even though he'd obviously gone unshaved, he had little more than peach fuzz sprouting on his chin.

"I've seen a picture of a Christmas tree," Preacher said. He didn't like the way the sergeant had brow-beaten the young man and didn't mind nettling Gordon. "Ain't ever seen one, mind you, not like you probably have, but I saw one in a book by a man named Bokum."

"Hermann Bokum," Diller said. "I know that because one of the majors' wives had a copy in her library. She shared the book with the other ladies at the fort in the hopes of lifting morale one particularly hard winter."

"A travelin' peddler had the copy I saw," Preacher said. "The peddler told me the Christmas tree tradition came from Hessian soldiers locked up in a Connecticut prison house during the war with Britain."

Gordon growled a curse, but Diller shot him a stern glance and he quieted immediately.

Preacher glanced back at Dwayne. "As far as the Blackfeet hangin' their dead in trees, it's because they believe buryin' a man traps his soul underground while buryin' him in trees allow his soul to soar free the way it's supposed to. They see the soul as bein' like a bird. Don't want to go trappin' it in the dark forever."

"Yes, sir, Mr. Preacher," the young soldier said, and tipped his hat. "I thank you for your instruction."

Gordon blew out an angry breath. "Well, buryin' 'em in trees doesn't do any good, now does it? Just layin' out a feed for crows an' other carrion birds, or whatever else wants to shinny up them trees for a taste." He inhaled deeply. "That's mighty fine. Nothin' smells better'n dead Indians."

Unable to control himself, Dwayne leaned out from his horse and threw up. The vomit splashed at the hooves of Gordon's horse. The horse snorted and stepped away quickly.

"Damn it!" Gordon roared, and flailed in the saddle for a moment. "You like to covered me in that filth!"

"Sorry, Sergeant." Dwayne wiped his mouth with the back of his hand.

"A soldier ought to have better control of himself," Gordon snapped. "Get out of my sight. Go secure the perimeter."

"Yes, Sergeant." The young private turned his horse away and rode off.

"We got ourselves a damn fool for a private, Cap'n," Gordon said. "If he wasn't so good with maps, I'd send him back to the fort. I've still got a good mind to."

"Sergeant Gordon," Diller said coldly.

"Yes, sir." Despite the polite response, Gordon bristled.

"Since you enjoy the present bouquet so much, get me

an accurate count of the dead in those trees," the captain ordered.

"I can get—"

"I'd rather you did it yourself, Sergeant."

"Yes, sir." Gordon forced the reply between gritted teeth. He wheeled his mount away.

"Now, Preacher," Diller said, "tell me what you've learned here."

"Blackfeet came out and buried these dead men."

"You're sure about that?"

"Had to be them. I found hoofprints from several unshod horses."

"Indian horses."

"They're the only ones out here that I know of that are unshod," Preacher said.

"How many?"

"Thirty or forty. Maybe more. The ground's pretty chewed up and they were all unshod, so it's difficult to say. Not all of them entered the clearing, though."

"Why do you say that?"

"Ridin' in, I found two spots where groups of horses and men gathered. I'm thinkin' not all of the men were allowed in to deal with the bodies. Whoever was leadin' them, he wanted some privacy."

"Why?"

"Just like you've done with your men," Preacher waved at the soldiers spread around the clearing, "they'd want to keep lookouts watchin' over things. If it was Stone Eyes, and I believe it was, he set up a perimeter not much different than you have here."

But they'd probably been more spread out, not so

bunched up. The Army captain had a thing or two to learn—if he didn't end up dead first.

"Also, Stone Eyes wouldn't want a lot of his warriors lookin' at his dead son."

"I suppose that would be bad for morale."

"Maybe so, but that wasn't the main reason. Stone Eyes wouldn't want his men to see his grief. Grief is a powerful thing, and the Blackfeet like to keep it private. Except for the ways they choose to show it."

"What makes you think Stone Eyes was here?"

"There's hair tied to some of the scaffolds' corners. It's Blackfoot custom for a family member to cut his or her hair when one of their own dies. One of the scaffolds has more weapons and food on it, though most of that has been eaten by the crows and other varmints. Means whoever was buried there held more respect in the tribe."

"Like the son of a chief?"

"That's what I'm thinkin'."

"Silent Owl wasn't the only Blackfoot warrior you killed," Diller pointed out.

"No, he wasn't, but not every Blackfoot warrior would be able to tell the others what to do. There wouldn't have been perimeter guards set up like I saw. Stone Eyes came out here and buried his son."

Diller shifted in his saddle and gazed around. "Where did the Blackfeet go from here?"

"That's somethin' I'm gonna try to find out," Preacher said. "That's what Lorenzo and those other men are out there doin' now."

"I didn't see you assign them that task."

"Didn't have to. They know what they're doin' same as me. We came out here to find Stone Eyes and his warriors. We aim to find him."

Diller smiled. "I thought you were just joining us to show us this spot."

Preacher shook his head. "I've seen your soldiers ridin' out here for two days. You maybe got one man good enough to hold his own with these other men with me when trackin', and I'm better'n most of them. If you want to find Stone Eyes, you're gonna need me to do it."

"I'm glad to hear you say that. What about your friends?"

"I told them about the rifles. They got family and friends up in these mountains they want to protect. They'll stick till this thing is done."

Diller took a breath. "I told you about those rifles in confidence." His voice held a note of cold steel in it.

"I brought some of those rifles into the Crow camp," Preacher said. "Your secret ain't as well hid as you think it is. Joe Len Darby will probably tell others if he hasn't already. He don't seem to be a man to keep his mouth shut for long."

"Darby? You've seen Darby?" Diller's eyes narrowed with suspicion.

"He's the fella I saved from Silent Owl."

"You didn't mention him earlier."

"You didn't ask about him. You were more interested in hearin' about Silent Owl and Stone Eyes."

Diller scowled and said, "I wish I had known Darby was in that camp. I need—"

"Hey, mister!" a man squawked. "You an' your friend climb down outta that tree! An' you'd best get to it damn quick before I climb up after you an' slap a knot on your heads."

CHAPTER 21

Preacher recognized the threatening voice as that of Oscar Ferrell. That surprised Preacher because Ferrell tended to be an easygoing man. The mountain man dropped Horse's reins and turned back toward the clearing. Diller urged his horse forward, as well.

Ferrell stood beneath a tall oak tree that supported three burial scaffolds. He peered up at two soldiers hanging in the tree's lower branches.

"Mind your own business, Mex," one of the men yelled down. "If you don't, you're gonna get hurt."

Ferrell raised his rifle and pointed it at the man who had spoken. "I ain't gonna tell you again, *pendejo*."

"You got a lot of soldiers around you to be tellin' others what to do," the man said.

"You want it to go that way," Ferrell said, "you'll be the first man out. You'll never see another thing. You go ahead and call it."

Only a few of the soldiers took up their weapons. Most of them looked like they wanted to stay out of things. But the odds weren't in Ferrell's favor.

Preacher walked without hurrying, but his long strides

covered the ground quickly. A soldier stood unseen behind Ferrell and lifted his rifle to his shoulder. He was settling for a shot, or maybe to offer a threat, but Preacher kicked the soldier in the back of the knee and caused the leg to buckle. The man fought to regain his balance, but Preacher slammed his rifle butt into the soldier's forehead because he wasn't in the mood for a fight. The soldier's eyes rolled back into his head and he sprawled unconscious on the ground.

Some of the soldiers who looked like they might intervene stepped back. They weren't facing only one man any more.

Diller held a pistol in his hand and rode into the clearing ahead of Preacher. He aimed his weapon at Ferrell from a dozen feet away. "Put that rifle down."

Ferrell held onto his rifle and kept his attention focused on the two soldiers in the tree. "Order them to get down from those graves."

"I'm ordering you to take that rifle off my men," Diller growled. "Otherwise, I'll shoot you through the head."

Across the clearing, Gordon pulled his rifle to his shoulder. Silent as a shadow, Tall Dog slipped out from behind a tree and held a hunting knife to the sergeant's throat. The young warrior's face was cold and impassive. Gordon slowly lowered his rifle. Tall Dog took the rifle, settled it over the sergeant's shoulder, and covered some of the other soldiers.

"They can't desecrate those graves," Ferrell said. "God wouldn't like it, an' I won't allow it."

"He's right about desecratin' those graves, Captain Diller," Preacher said. "Ain't no call to go prowlin' through another man's remains."

"These aren't men," the man nearest the ground said. "They're Indians."

"We was gonna check to see that there wasn't any rifles buried with them," the topmost soldier said.

"You're lyin'," Ferrell accused. "You two are just thieves, an' you don't care about leavin' the dead alone. You're only after whatever you find on those bodies that you think you can sell."

"These Blackfeet are killers," the soldier yelled. "Even if you want to protect Indians, these killers don't get the same privileges as other Indians."

Diller looked across the clearing and saw his sergeant at the mercy of the young Crow warrior. The captain turned his attention to Preacher and frustration dug deep lines into the man's face. He appeared to be giving serious consideration to his next words.

"Captain," Preacher said, and seized control of the situation, "you'll have to shoot Ferrell if you want to stop him. He had a grandfather who was a religious man, a missionary in California. Ferrell won't allow those soldiers to bother those graves. Neither will I. Whichever one of those men Ferrell don't shoot, I will." He leveled his rifle on the tree. "And likely you'll lose your sergeant and any other men who might want to stand up for grave robbin'."

Dog stood tall and ready at Preacher's side. The big cur's lips ricked back and bared his teeth. A steady, low rumble came from deep in his broad chest.

For a moment, Diller held steady. Anger clouded his face and stretched his features tight.

"We got a lot of men here," Preacher said casually. "Men who will tell Chief Finds the Balance and Jess Thompkins how you treated these graves. If you allow this, and if you get by Ferrell, Tall Dog, and me, maybe more men out there who ain't here at the moment, the Crow and those mountain men down on the Snake, won't lift a finger to help you should you need it. And likely, seein' what you're up against, you'll need it. A man out here in the middle of all this wilderness needs to mind the bridges he burns. Pretty soon he'll find himself all alone at the wrong time and facin' somethin' a whole lot bigger'n him. This ain't civilized country. Even the mountains will kill you if you're ignorant about things."

Diller swallowed. "I think, if we're in this endeavor together, we should present a more unified front, Mr. Preacher."

"So do I," Preacher said. "And one thing I won't abide is trashin' a man's grave like this. A dead man's done paid his final bills in this life, and I cashed in every one of these warriors face to face."

"They're just Indians," one of the soldiers said. "These heathens have done horrible things to defenseless men an' women before you give 'em what they had comin' to 'em."

"Those Indians are through doin' those horrible things now," Ferrell said. "They deserve to make their peace any way they can in the hereafter. Now get on down from that tree."

Diller lowered his pistol and holstered it. "The two of you do as the man says. Get down from that tree."

Reluctantly, both men climbed down.

"The rest of you soldiers listen to me," Diller said. "We're out here to recover missing rifles and to put Stone Eyes in the ground. That's our mission. If any one of you interferes with these graves, or any other graves we may run across while we're out here, I will shoot you. This is the only warning I'll give on the matter."

The soldiers in the clearing nodded.

"Sergeant Gordon," Diller said, "should you find one of these men disobeying my direct order, you'll be disobeying mine if you don't immediately execute him. Is that clear?"

"That's clear, Captain," Gordon said grudgingly. "I'll tend to that as soon as I can." He cut his eyes to Tall Dog standing behind him.

"Preacher," Diller said. "Would you ask your man to let my sergeant go?"

"He's not my man. He's my friend."

"Then ask your *friend* to release my sergeant."

Preacher nodded to Tall Dog. The young warrior lowered his knife from Gordon's throat, eased the rifle down, and slipped around his former captive to give the sergeant a wide berth. He leaned Gordon's rifle against a nearby tree and walked toward Preacher.

Diller turned his horse to Preacher. "I expect you and I will be talking soon, Mr. Preacher, once we have this place behind us, if only to clarify who's in charge of this mission."

"That we will," Preacher agreed.

"There will be no other answer than me."

Preacher said nothing.

"If there's nothing more you can find of use here," Diller went on, "I suggest you discover which direction Stone Eyes and his war party went. That is what I want to know now."

"I'll do that," Preacher replied evenly.

All in all, Preacher knew that was as good a face as the captain could put on the turn of events. He'd have to forge a relationship with the man because being out here so outnumbered wasn't any kind of plan.

Not if he wanted to do something about those missing rifles.

That was something he wanted to accomplish.

Tall Dog stood beside him and spoke softly. "I have found something you should see."

Preacher nodded. "Things were gettin' a mite close here anyway." He raised his voice. "Ferrell, we're gonna go look at something. Thought maybe you'd be interested."

Ferrell shook his head. "No thanks. I'm gonna sit right here in this shade an' watch over things a bit. I got me a cool breeze an' feel comfortable. I hate the thought of cuttin' out an' missin' that."

A dozen soldiers stood under the trees, but none of them did anything more than give Ferrell hard looks.

"Might not be the best place for you to be."

Ferrell grinned, and there was no mirth in his expression. "I'll be fine. I get into any trouble, I'll shoot."

"You do that and I'll come a-runnin'." Preacher turned to Tall Dog. "All right, show me what you found."

"Where is your horse?"

"Gonna need it?"

"To get there quickly, yes."

"Are we in a hurry?" Preacher asked.

"No, but it is a distance from here." Tall Dog glanced at the clearing. "A horse would help get back here quickly if you needed to do that."

"All right." Preacher headed for Horse out past the clearing.

Diller sat ramrod straight farther up the incline. Snow-capped mountains, eternally covered even in summer, stood out along the skyline behind him. The captain watched over the countryside and only gave Preacher a passing glance.

The mountain man knew the captain was stewing over

what had happened, but it couldn't be helped. He put Diller out of his mind for the moment and stepped into the saddle.

"Where's your horse?" Preacher asked. "Or do you plan on walkin'?"

Tall Dog smiled, put his hands together in front of his lips, and created a warbling birdcall. Hoofbeats drummed the earth and his paint horse thundered out of the brush. The horse stopped beside the young giant and nuzzled his outstretched palm.

Tall Dog spoke softly to the horse in a language that Preacher didn't recognize. The horse happily shook her head and her mane.

With a lithe leap, Tall Dog vaulted onto the horse. He rode with a saddle instead of Indian fashion. He tugged lightly on the reins and the horse headed east along the outer edge of the tree line.

"What language was that?" Preacher asked in Crow.

"It is the tongue of my father's people," Tall Dog answered. "It is called Norwegian. To the north around the Great Lakes, where the sun hides and the nights grow long even in the summer, there are many people who speak the language."

"They speak German and French, too." Preacher adjusted himself in the saddle and got comfortable. "I know enough to make my needs clear in those languages, but I don't know Norwegian. Your horse does?"

"She does. I have trained her since she was a foal to understand Norwegian." Tall Dog slapped the paint's neck affectionately. "I knew not many would know the language, so it was something we could share."

"You spend much time talkin' to your horse?" Preacher swept the countryside with his gaze and wondered what the young giant had to show him.

"Do you not speak to your horse?" Tall Dog countered and looked a little embarrassed.

"I do, but not overly much. Me and Horse and Dog have kind of simplified things over the years we've been together. Ain't a lot we haven't discussed."

"Horse?" Tall Dog said it in English because Preacher had.

"That's his name. I call him Horse in the Crow tongue and he doesn't listen."

"Horse has a sense of humor. He has been around Crow people many times. I would bet he speaks Crow, too."

"I expect so. He just don't like to show off to the other horses."

"Skidbladnir is modest, as well."

Preacher ran the name through his mind again and couldn't figure it out. "What's that name again?"

Tall Dog repeated it, then said, "I took it from the name of a ship in the tales of the Norse gods. When I was a boy, my father told me many of those stories. I cannot get him to tell me now unless he has been drinking. He says I know them all. In the stories, *Skidbladnir* took the gods everywhere without fail. That is what my Skidbladnir does for me."

The filly neighed and bobbed her head like she knew she was being talked about. Tall Dog stroked her long neck.

"Mighty fine name," Preacher said. "Back there when you helped me back Ferrell's play, you got to know you likely made an enemy out of Sergeant Gordon."

Tall Dog smiled thinly. "I was already his enemy. I am Crow. He does not like Indians, not even those who help him. This way, it is all out in the open, and he knows I do not fear him."

Preacher admired the young man's straightforwardness. In a lot of ways, Tall Dog reminded the mountain man of his own son, Hawk That Soars.

The young Crow warrior turned slightly and headed into the trees. Preacher followed.

CHAPTER 22

"I trailed Blackfoot tracks back to this place." Tall Dog leaned down from his horse and pointed at unshod hoofprints in the earth.

The tracks were scattered and few, made rare by the stony earth and at least one rain that had fallen since they'd been made. Still, they were there for someone savvy enough to see them. They followed a faint game trail that only a seasoned tracker could have found. Small animals had walked over them, and birds had clawed at the dirt when it had been freshly turned.

Something had brought the Blackfeet out this way, but the reason for their interest didn't show in the tracks. From what he could see, the mountain man estimated there were six or seven riders.

Preacher ducked under low-hanging branches for a bit because the trees grew more tightly packed, then Tall Dog slipped from his paint without stopping the horse and walked like he'd flowed off his mount. Preacher halted Horse for just a moment, stepped down, and walked, as well. He carried his rifle in hand and kept his eyes moving.

Old tracks meant riders had passed this way. They

didn't mean no one was there *now*. Someone had buried those Blackfeet in the trees.

"Here are more tracks." Tall Dog pointed at additional hoofprints that showed on a spot of ground left barren beside a line of brush. "And here." He stepped over a snaking tree root and pointed to more tracks. "I think there were many riders who passed this way."

"I think so, too," Preacher said. "There's no path leadin' through here. This is an out-of-the-way place. These hoofprints are headed back to the clearin' where the Blackfeet tried to ambush me. Where'd they come from?"

"Farther north, northeast."

Tall Dog pointed to a dark patch on a tree trunk conspicuously close to the ghost trail. He placed his hand next to the patch to show that the dark stain was larger. A couple of moths were mired in the patch. One of them still fluttered weakly, but several ants tracked over it and the patch.

"Blood?" Preacher asked.

Tall Dog nodded.

"One of them was wounded."

"Perhaps," the young Crow warrior agreed. "There was violence up ahead. You will see."

Preacher studied the tracks visible ahead of them, then looked back the way they had come. "This ain't in a direct line with the clearin'. There are easier ways than gettin' through all these trees."

"From this point on, the Blackfeet rode for the clearing. That is not what they were after. They rode this way for something else. Come. You will see and understand."

Rifle in hand and his eyes and ears primed, Preacher followed Tall Dog down a small slope that led into a hollow where a narrow stream gurgled. Dog threaded through the trees on his own path and kept his nose to the ground.

If the big cur found something he didn't like, he'd let Preacher know about it. After a moment, Dog stopped and gazed ahead with watchful eyes. He looked at Preacher and flattened his ears.

"Somethin' you don't like?" Preacher asked.

Dog pricked his ears and moved more slowly. He stayed a short distance behind Tall Dog and ahead of Preacher.

A few steps later, Preacher detected what had gotten the big cur's attention. Horse smelled it, too. He shook his head and blew out a cantankerous breath.

The stink of death and old charcoal from a campfire filled Preacher's nostrils. Three more strides, well past the point where the hoofprints ended, and they would have certainly showed in the soft loam under the trees, he stood on the edge of the hollow and peered down.

"The Blackfeet rode around this place." Tall Dog waved an arm to the north where a grove of aspen grew tall and cut the hollow off from casual sight. "They came here on foot. Through those trees. I found footprints and a game trail."

The hollow stood twelve feet deep and was at least twenty feet across. It was rimmed with tree and brush roots that stuck out of the dark dirt like crooked daggers. When an errant breeze stirred the hollow's depths, the death smell and burned charcoal odor grew stronger and lifted up from the bowl-shaped depression.

What used to be two men, based on Preacher's observation that there were only two men's heads lying on the ground, although the count could have been wrong if a third head had been carried off, was scattered across the ground on both sides of the two-foot stream that trickled down the hillside. Other body parts lay in the water. They were covered in tattered clothing. White bones showed through bits of ragged flesh. Small fishes flickered and swam through the bones in the stream.

Shadows of the trees and the hillside covered the area in a shroud of darkness. A chill blew over the hollow, too, and it made Preacher wish for the buffalo robes in his saddlebags.

Varmints had been at the bodies. The dead men here hadn't been tucked away in treetops like the Blackfeet. They'd been left to lie for anything with an appetite for meat to come along and eat. Most of the meat was gone from the bones and dulled ivory gleamed in the shadows.

"If you wish to go down there," Tall Dog said, "we will have to leave the horses here."

"All right." Preacher dropped Horse's reins and took out a coil of rope from his saddlebags. "Did you go down there?"

"No." Tall Dog watched the nearby woods. "These men look to have been killed probably about the same time that you fought the Blackfeet. I believe these men are white."

"I think so, too."

"I did not want to disturb their remains before you had a chance to look at them. They wore the uniforms of the pony soldiers."

Blue cloth fluttered in the breeze and looked a lot like the blouses worn by Army soldiers.

Preacher knotted the rope to a stout pine tree covered with prickly needles. He flipped the end of the rope over the side of the hollow and it slithered down with ease amid a rush of loose soil. Twelve feet wasn't much of a jump, but the soft earth might prove difficult to climb back up even with the roots sticking out.

And he might want to come back up from the hollow in a hurry.

"What brought you over this way?" Preacher asked. He leaned over and peered down the steep embankment.

"The smell. And there were noises from carrion feeders who fought over what remains here."

Bear tracks, wolf tracks, and raccoon tracks showed in the soft dirt on either side of the stream. Beetles and maggots covered the bigger pieces of what was left of the dead men. A skull with empty eye sockets and an open mouth with missing teeth lay cocked so it stared up at the overhanging branches.

"What carrion feeders?" Preacher asked. He didn't want to be down in the hollow if bears were around.

"Crows," Tall Dog said. "They can find dead things anywhere."

"They sure can. You see anything else?"

"No. I walked along the edge of the hollow for a ways to be certain."

Footprints marked the ground to Preacher's left to indicate Tall Dog's passage. Broken leaves and small twigs on saplings and brush stood out.

Preacher slung his rifle across his back, grabbed hold of the rope, and clambered down quickly. The soft earth gave way under his moccasins and the roots stabbed him hard enough to bruise but not break skin through his buckskins.

Dog jumped and skidded down into the hollow in a scrambling rush. He reached the bottom in an avalanche of dirt before Preacher did. The big cur set himself and remained ready and watchful.

"I will stay here and keep watch," Tall Dog said from the lip of the hollow.

"Good idea. Don't need both of us down here blind to

everything that might be out in the woods." Preacher slipped his rifle from his shoulder and looked around.

The young Crow warrior crouched with his rifle across his thighs and watched the surrounding tree line.

Dog wasn't reacting to anything, so Preacher figured they were probably pretty safe for the moment. The hollow was definitely a bad place to be trapped in, and he was certain that was what had happened to the dead men lying just ahead of him. They'd died hard, scared, and alone.

With his rifle in hand once more, Preacher examined the area where the two bodies were. The hollow extended into a low cave that wasn't more than a couple feet across. Half of the available space was taken up by the stream, which looked like it was more full than usual. Some of the slowly moving water ran over grass on the shallow banks. The increased volume made sense with all the recent rain and the snow melting off farther up in the mountains.

Nothing moved inside the mouth of the cave. Preacher couldn't advance more than an arm's length inside the opening because the gathering darkness filled the space.

The firepit was an old one before the latest visitors had used it. The men who had camped there had dug out old ashes and scattered them. Rabbit bones and squirrel bones littered one side of the canyon. The two men must not have had much luck with hunting bigger game, but bringing down rabbits and squirrels proved they could shoot.

"These men were here for a couple days," Preacher said.

"They knew the Blackfeet were looking for them," Tall Dog agreed.

"Had to have. They dug in here and hoped for the best." Preacher eased around the area and read what he could of what had been left. "Don't know if they knew about this place or just stumbled across it."

"It is hard to get to, but trappers might have found it while following the stream from below."

"Water's too shallow for beaver."

"All men are curious," Tall Dog said.

"Might be a good place to hole up if you have an injury, but a man couldn't winter here. Ain't no structures to shield a man from the snows. Ain't no stumps left from trees that were cut down for firewood. I didn't see any stumps ridin' in."

"They were hunted. They were afraid, and they were in a hurry. The only way they knew about this place was if someone guided them to it."

"No sign of horses?"

"None that I have seen. I rode around the hollow. If they'd had horses here, there would have been sign."

Piles of it, Preacher thought.

"There were no shod ponies among the tracks I found."

"They didn't come out here without horses."

"No."

"So where are they?"

"Perhaps they lost them along the way," Tall Dog said. "That would explain why these men arrived here without supplies or equipment."

"Could have let the horses go in an effort to lay down a false trail for the Blackfeet, too."

"Yes."

Preacher liked the way the young Crow warrior's mind worked. And he respected the fact that Tall Dog had taken the time to get most of the story about the dead men before seeking him out.

Dog rooted around in the ashes for a moment, but he didn't find anything that captured his attention. He snuffled, sneezed, and walked farther downstream.

No weapons were in the hollow. No rifles and no knives. There was no gear and no supplies, either. Whatever the men had brought with them had been taken by whoever killed them.

Or maybe it had been abandoned in their flight from those who hunted them.

Preacher knelt and examined the bodies. He turned over what was there with a stout chunk of firewood that lay to one side of the campfire.

There were no bullet holes in the body parts, but there were hash marks on many of the bones that showed scars left by knives and tomahawks. Two broken arrows, one in the stream and one revealed when Preacher rolled over a man's torso, held Blackfoot markings. The dead men's arms and legs had been hacked off. There was no way to know if they'd been alive or dead at the time of their loss.

"They died hard," Preacher said.

He stood and backed off from the bodies. Insects scattered and ran over the bones and ragged flesh. In a few more days, only bones of the two men would remain. Not long after that, even the bones would be gone.

"Blackfeet did this," Tall Dog said. "That explains the unshod ponies and the arrows. The fletchings are Blackfoot. They trailed these men here and ambushed them."

"I think so, too, but that doesn't explain how the Blackfeet knew these men were here."

"Whites, especially pony soldiers, can be foolish up in the mountains. They forget they are not in the protected places where they normally live."

"Yeah, but these men knew they were bein' hunted. That's why they hid here. There are a lot of other places, *better* places, to camp for a night." Preacher kicked through the rabbit and squirrel bones and sent spiders and beetles scurrying for cover. "They spent a few days here, too. Probably caught small game with snares."

Eggshells showed in the bone debris.

"They were robbin' bird nests, too. That's a hard way to live when there's larger game out there for the takin'."

"They were desperate men," Tall Dog said.

"Makes you wonder what they were doin' out so far from anywhere," Preacher replied. "At least, it makes me wonder."

Downstream, blue-green glass caught light that penetrated the branches for just a moment and gleamed. Without the light hitting it, the glass faded into the color of the stream bank.

Curious, Preacher walked to the glass and peered down at it. Broken jagged pieces lay half-buried in the mud along the stream. He knelt, reached down, and pulled them from the mud. Once out in the open, it was obvious the pieces had once been a vaguely tear-shaped bottle almost ten inches tall.

Two of the bigger pieces held an embossed protrusion. Gently, careful of the sharp edges of the broken glass, Preacher flicked away the mud and pushed them together. The break had been clean and the pieces fit neatly together.

The embossed image made into the bottle depicted a plump-chested bird standing on a rocky cliff overlooking an ocean. The details were hard to make out, but Preacher had seen bottles, or flasks, like this one before. They were blown to hold a single-malt scotch blended in Ballindalloch in Scotland. He'd first tasted the whiskey while traveling the Siskiyou Trail. He'd stopped in Rancho Campo de los Franceses with some French-Canadian trappers he'd fallen in with at the time.

The bird was a Great Skua, though it was also called a

Bonxie. Though he'd never seen one of the birds, they had a reputation for stealing and plundering the nests of other seabirds. Sailors had told Preacher that the Bonxies attacked anything, including humans, who got near their nests.

The whiskey wasn't often found on shelves in taverns. The company was small and only a limited supply came over to the United States. Preacher had only ever had it the one time, but it was good enough that he remembered it—and the bird.

"Did you find something?" Tall Dog asked.

Preacher stood. "I did. Do you remember the man I arrived at the camp with?"

"Joe Len Darby."

"That's the man. When was the last time you saw him?"

"I only saw him that first day. He found a group of men who had whiskey and didn't mind sharing, and I never saw him again."

"That sounds about right."

Preacher grew irritated with himself. He should have kept a closer watch on the man, but he'd had no reason to suspect Darby of anything. On top of that, by the time Preacher had arrived at the Crow camp with the man in tow, he'd been plumb sick of his company. Joe Len Darby wasn't a man to keep his mouth shut.

But, for all his talk, Joe Len Darby was evidently a man who knew how to keep secrets.

CHAPTER 23

"Dog," Preacher called.

The big cur wheeled around fifty yards downstream where the water trickled through the hanging branches of trees that leaned in from the hollow. Shadows from the encroaching darkness filled the branches and turned the ground dark.

"Time to go." Preacher slung his rifle and reached for the dangling rope.

He was glad to be done with the dead men and their sad stories in the hollow. Knowing what he suspected of them, he didn't feel guilty about leaving what was left of them for nature to take care of. At least they'd make good eating for the varmints that lived around the hollow. Likely they hadn't been good men.

Gripping the rope, Preacher set one foot against the hollow's side and heaved himself up. Dog would be another matter. The big cur couldn't get himself up onto higher ground, but Preacher thought between the two of them they could manage. Otherwise, he'd rope onto Dog and haul him up.

"Preacher." Tall Dog spoke softly and urgently so his voice didn't carry.

The mountain man froze. "Yeah?"

"We are no longer alone in this place."

"Who's there?"

"I don't know, but I can hear them."

Only night noises reached Preacher's ears. Insects and night predators stirred in the gathering gloom of the evening.

Dog barked sharply.

Movement in Preacher's peripheral vision alerted him to the presence of someone behind him on the hollow's ridge. The man was almost lost in the shadows between the trees and brush.

Preacher released the rope and dropped to the ground in a crouch.

Dog barked again, and this time the big cur focused on the opposite wall of the hollow.

An arrow hissed through the space where Preacher had just been, embedded in the soft earthen wall, and quivered.

"Blackfeet," Preacher warned. He ran to his right and slipped his rifle from his shoulder.

Dog dropped low and vanished into the tall brush that flanked the stream on both sides.

A rifle cracked somewhere overhead, and Preacher hoped the shot had been fired by Tall Dog. Three shadows on the opposite side of the hollow hunkered down, but none of them appeared hit.

Brush popped and cracked overhead on the side where Tall Dog had waited. Footsteps closed in on the young Crow warrior's position.

With his rifle in hand, Preacher dropped to one knee and raised the weapon to his shoulder. He eared the hammer back, sighted down the barrel, and centered the rifle's front sight on one of the Blackfeet visible along the hollow's rim. The mountain man's hand slid over the trigger and he pulled the butt into his shoulder.

He squeezed the trigger, and the rifle bucked against him. The cloud of powder smoke obscured Preacher's sight, but one of the Blackfeet spun slightly to one side and fell backward.

Two more arrows thudded into the ground in front of the mountain man and stood quivering.

Preacher caught the rifle's sling in his left hand and swung the weapon over his shoulder. He was loath to leave the rifle behind, but he had to move. He drew one of the Colt Patersons in his right hand. He darted to his left and thumbed the hammer back. The recessed trigger dropped down and he curled a finger over it.

On the run, he fired at the two Blackfeet visible along the edge of the hollow as quickly as he could thumb the hammer back and squeeze the trigger. Both of the Blackfeet went backward and down into the brush and behind trees. He couldn't confirm either of them were out of the fight, but the first Blackfeet he'd shot lay still and unmoving. One arm hung over the hollow's edge.

Preacher crossed the stream in the middle of the hollow and avoided the parts of the dead men scattered there. Pinned down as he was in the hollow, he didn't stand a better chance than the men who'd lost their lives here, but he didn't intend to die.

Arrows sliced the air around him, and these came from a different angle on the same side of the hollow. More Blackfeet were hidden in the surrounding trees.

Preacher slammed into the wall on the other side from the rope he'd come down. He put the empty Paterson away and drew one of the flintlock pistols from where the pair rested behind his back. Dog tucked in against the wall a short distance from his feet. The big cur trotted along the wall and watched both sides of the hollow with keen interest.

Above Preacher, a Blackfoot warrior peered over the hollow's edge with an arrow nocked to his string.

Dog barked and leaped at the wall in an effort to get to the Blackfoot.

Aiming by instinct honed from several battles, Preacher squeezed the pistol's trigger and put a ball right up alongside the arrow into the Blackfoot's forehead.

The arrow leaped from the bow and the fletching cut Preacher's left cheek. The mountain man slipped the spent pistol through the sash at his back and stepped back from the body that toppled over the side of the hollow. Arms and legs slack, the dead man thudded against the ground in front of Preacher.

With no enemies in sight, though the mountain man was certain they were there, he reached into his possibles bag, plucked a cartridge from within, and tore it open with his teeth. He poured the powder into the barrel, patched the ball, and used the ramrod to seat it. A quick pour of the leftover powder in the cartridge primed the rifle.

Across the hollow on the other side, Tall Dog flitted between the trees and used them to stymie his attackers. Preacher counted four Blackfeet dodging through the trees and brush after Tall Dog. They tried to close on the young Crow warrior, but he was a shadow in the gathering darkness and was never where they thought he would be.

Preacher pulled his rifle to his shoulder and dropped the front sight over one of the Blackfeet in the trees there. He aimed squarely at the man's back and pulled the trigger.

The rifle's roar filled the hollow and it was now dark enough in the bowl-shaped depression that the flames of the shot were visible.

Across the stream on the other side of the hollow, the Blackfoot Preacher shot went down without a sound.

Dog barked and focused on the wall a few feet behind Preacher and to the mountain man's left.

Preacher shifted the rifle to his right hand and drew the other flintlock pistol from his back with his left hand. He leveled the pistol, rolled the hammer back, and slid his finger through the trigger guard. The Blackfoot warrior loosed his arrow, and the shaft sank into the loose ground between Preacher's feet.

The mountain man squeezed the trigger, and a second small cloud of powder smoke joined the first. Struck in the chest by the pistol ball, the Blackfoot warrior yelled in pain and toppled over the hollow's edge. Preacher slid the pistol behind his back again.

Fifteen feet away, the Blackfoot struggled to get to his feet. One of his hands grabbed the tomahawk at his side. Blood stained the right side of his buckskins.

"Dog!" Preacher yelled.

The big cur raced forward and leaped at the Blackfoot's chest just as the warrior stood straight. Driven by the dog's weight and speed, the warrior stumbled backward. His foot caught on a legbone and he went down. Dog was on the man in an instant and the Blackfoot had an instant to scream in fear. Then the big cur's fangs flashed and ripped out his opponent's throat.

Moving by instinct, Preacher dug in his possibles bag for another cartridge, tore it open, and poured the gunpowder down the rifle's barrel. He grabbed a patch and another ball, fitted them in the barrel, and ran them into place with the ramrod.

Across the hollow, Tall Dog stepped out from behind a tree and surprised one of the Blackfeet hunting him. The young Crow warrior held his sword in one hand and swept it viciously at his opponent. The Blackfoot held a knife in one hand and a tomahawk in the other. He used both weapons to block the sword, but Tall Dog's strength beat the knife and tomahawk aside. Steel screamed from the contact and sparks briefly jumped. The blade flashed in the waning sunlight an instant before it sank into the juncture of the Blackfoot's neck and shoulder.

Mortally wounded, the Blackfoot stumbled back and fell.

With his rifle reloaded, Preacher called, "Dog."

Muzzle bloody and dripping, the big cur drew back from the dead man and glanced at Preacher.

"Come on," Preacher said.

He dashed back across the hollow, reached the opposite wall, and spun around with the rifle to his shoulder. Dog ran with him and sought cover in the brush.

Two Blackfeet hid behind trees on the opposite side and loosed arrows. The fletched shafts sped through the air. One of the arrows plucked at Preacher's buckskin shirt and pinned it to the wall. The other thudded into the earth beside his face. The fletching tickled his ear.

Calmly as he could, the mountain man took aim with his rifle and fired. The bullet flew true, smashed through the bow his target held, and caught the Blackfoot in the face. Screaming in pain, the Blackfoot fell back into the shadows.

Preacher slung his rifle, took hold of the rope, and planted a foot against the wall as high as he could reach. He clambered up the rope hand-over-hand and strained to make a rapid ascent. A little over halfway up the climb, he paused and leaned back toward the ground.

"Dog, come on."

The big cur threw himself against the wall and dug his paws in frantically. Despite his best efforts, Dog couldn't maintain purchase on the loose earth and lost traction.

Preacher caught his companion by the scruff, set himself with both feet against the wall, and whipsawed his upper body to throw Dog toward the top of the hollow. Dog yelped in surprise and pain, but he scrambled to dig into the wall. Preacher's shoulder screamed in pain and he thought for a moment it was going to come apart from the strain. His attempt to throw the big cur to the top of the ridge failed to reach the mark.

For a moment he worried that Dog was going to fall back down. But the big cur managed to throw one foreleg over the top, caught jutting roots with two of his other paws, got the fourth planted, and heaved himself up.

An arrow sank into a thick ball of roots that stood out against the wall.

Further galvanized by the arrow and the two that followed, Preacher caught hold of roots with his hands and planted his moccasins on others. His feet slipped twice, but he scrambled up the side of the hollow. Roots clawed at his face and left hot scratches that bled. One of them caught his mustache, but he yanked it free even though for a moment it felt like he tore off his upper lip.

At the top, Preacher threw himself over the ridge and rolled onto safe ground. He came to a painful stop against a tree that promised bruises along his rib cage. The wind left him in a rush.

Two Blackfeet warriors wearing warpaint sprang toward him with tomahawks in their fists.

Dog growled a brief, loud warning, then launched himself at one of the Blackfeet and drove the man backward. The big cur followed his opponent's fall, crashed into the brush, and promptly disappeared.

Preacher rolled to the side and slipped his rifle from his shoulder. The Blackfoot warrior pressed his left hand against the mountain man's chest to hold him in place against the ground. He reared back and swung the tomahawk.

Twisting quickly, Preacher threw his left forearm up to catch the Blackfoot's wrist and block the tomahawk. The weapon's steel head stopped inches from splitting the mountain man's left eye. The Blackfoot cried out in pain and frustration but grimly held onto his weapon and drew back again for another strike.

The mountain man freed his rifle and grabbed it in his right hand. He raised it, caught the barrel in his left hand, and swung the weapon around to catch the Blackfoot with the butt full in the face. The Blackfoot's nose and mouth exploded into ruin, and hot blood spattered Preacher's face and chest.

Dazed, the Blackfoot reeled backward and grabbed for his injured features. Preacher rolled to his feet, took a firm grip on the rifle, and smashed the butt into his opponent's throat. The Blackfoot's windpipe shattered, and he sucked air desperately.

Three more Blackfeet warriors closed in rapidly from the woods behind Horse and Tall Dog's paint pony. Two more tried to lead the horses away, but both animals kicked and reared.

Preacher drew his second Colt Paterson and ran toward the horses. Horse wouldn't go with the Blackfeet, and Skidbladnir fought the pull of the reins. Horse set himself and reared up high enough that his flashing hooves smashed through the low-hanging tree limbs. Branches splintered and leaves fell.

The Blackfoot holding Horse's reins stumbled forward, pulled by the large animal. Too late, he realized the danger he was in and tried to get away. Horse brought both his hooves down on his attacker and smashed the Blackfoot's skull like an eggshell. The dead man dropped and sprawled loosely.

The three Blackfeet rounded the horses and came at Preacher through the trees. One bent his bow. The other two ran with their knives and tomahawks in their fists and yelled at the tops of their voices.

Preacher dodged to the left and the Blackfoot archer loosed his arrow. The shaft sang through the air from twenty feet away and the flint tip sliced the side of Preacher's neck. The fletchings caught at the mountain man's hair.

Neck burning like he'd been stung by a wasp, Preacher brought the Paterson up smoothly and shot the Blackfoot to his left in the chest twice. The man stumbled and dropped to his knees, out of control as death took him. The archer pulled another arrow back and stared at Preacher across the length of the shaft. Moonlight kissed the dark fletchings and streaked them with a blue haze.

Preacher snapped off two shots. One he was pretty sure missed the archer because the man stepped to the side. The second caught him in the chest. The Blackfoot struggled to hang onto the bow, but it slid from his nerveless hand.

With only one shot unfired in the Paterson, Preacher stepped toward the only Blackfoot still running at him and ducked beneath his opponent's tomahawk and knife low enough to plant a shoulder across the man's thighs. His opponent's momentum and Preacher's impact knocked the Blackfoot into the air. The mountain man tracked his attacker, turned, and released his rifle just long enough to grab it by the barrel. Stepping forward again, Preacher smashed the butt into the man's chest and knocked him down again.

Knowing that he'd shown his back to the Blackfoot trying to take Tall Dog's paint pony, Preacher whirled and brought up the Paterson. The Indian's tomahawk spun through the air toward the mountain man's face.

Preacher raised the rifle, swept it sideways toward the tomahawk, deflected it, and aimed at the Blackfoot's head over the paint's back. He fired and the ball caught the Indian in his right eye. The paint pony stepped forward and knocked the dying man from his feet.

The Blackfoot on the ground got up again and ran at Preacher. The mountain man blocked the tomahawk with the rifle barrel and turned aside his opponent's knife with the Paterson. Preacher raised his right leg and tried to drive his foot through the Blackfoot's chest. Preacher shoved the Paterson into its holster, but before the Indian could free his tomahawk, Dog leaped out of the dark brush and fastened his teeth around the Blackfoot's arm. The big cur whirled and dragged the Indian down.

Preacher reached into his possibles bag and took out a cartridge. He tore it open with his teeth as he strode for the sound of fighting and labored breath coming from deeper into the woods. Tall Dog had been there surrounded by Blackfeet.

Once the rifle was loaded, Preacher stepped into the trees and trotted toward the battle.

A knot of Blackfeet closed in on Tall Dog. The young Crow warrior sidestepped an Indian who rushed at him, caught him with his left arm, and spun behind him to use him as a shield.

Realizing what had happened, the Blackfoot raised his hands and opened his mouth. Before he could speak, three arrows pierced his chest.

Ten feet out from the group and so far unnoticed, Preacher raised his rifle. His trained eye took in the scene at a glance, and he stepped a little to his right to line up two of the Blackfeet. He aimed for the throat of the one in front of him and knew there wasn't enough meat there to stop a ball. If it didn't hit his spine, the ball would continue through into the Blackfoot just beyond.

Preacher squeezed the trigger. The ball launched from the rifle's barrel, tore through the first man's throat, and dug deeply into the chest of the second Blackfoot. Knowing the first man was dead and there was no time to reload, Preacher gripped his rifle in his right hand to use as a club or a shield as the moment might demand and slid his tomahawk free.

As he closed on the group of Indians, he ignored the Blackfoot with the torn throat. The man was dead even if he hadn't finished dying and wouldn't be a threat. The others now knew they weren't alone.

Tall Dog had already dropped two other Indians with blades. Their bodies lay at his feet and he stepped around. Moonlight filtered through the trees for just a moment and revealed the blood that covered his face and hands. His features were grim and impassive, but his eyes were alight with an inner fire.

He's in his element, Preacher realized. *That young man was made for battlin'.*

A Blackfoot lunged at Tall Dog with a short spear. The

young Crow warrior swung his sword and knocked the spear aside. On his return, he took a step forward and slashed his attacker's neck so hard that he almost decapitated the man. He advanced again, slammed an open palm against another Blackfoot's wrist, blocked a knife thrust in a move so fast that Preacher had trouble following it, and cleaved his attacker's head from crown to chin.

Preacher blocked a knife attack with his rifle and chopped the inside of the Blackfoot's thigh with his tomahawk. The Indian screamed in despair because he knew the blow was a mortal one. As blood fountained from his leg, he tried to swing his own tomahawk, but Preacher hit him in the center of his chest with the rifle butt, and the man went over backward. He was dead by the time he hit the ground.

Tall Dog stood in the shadows with Preacher and took a breath. Preacher did the same and smelled the coppery scent of freshly spilled blood all around them. His moccasins stuck in the gore that covered the ground where the young Crow warrior had battled.

"Is that all of them?" Tall Dog asked quietly.

He sheathed his sword over his shoulder and found his rifle where it lay nearby. He'd already fished a cartridge from his possibles bag.

"Maybe," Preacher replied. He slipped his tomahawk back in his waist sash and took a cartridge from his own bag. "Dog?"

The big cur ambled out of the brush and licked his chops.

Preacher poured gunpowder in the rifle and reached for a patch. "Hunt."

Dog took off back into the brush.

"If there's anybody out there," Preacher said, "he'll let us know soon enough."

CHAPTER 24

With the westering sun at his back and higher on the rise coming up from the lazy river winding in front of the Crow camp, Stone Eyes stood in the shadows and surveyed his enemies.

The Crow people and the mountain men gathered at the site were bedding down for the coming night. Stewpots hung over campfires, and the scents of the food carried to Stone Eyes's nostrils.

He despised the stewpots. The white men made them and sold them to Indians too lazy to hang onto the old ways. Stone Eyes's father, Wary Wolf, had told him that selling things to the tribes was the white men's way of stealing the Indian traditions. Without the traditions to keep them together and strong, the tribes would forget themselves, drift apart, and become ghosts of themselves.

That, his father had said, was the most savage thing the whites could do.

Every time Wary Wolf found a group of peddlers up in the mountains, he made a bonfire of their wares and burned them in it. When he'd been small, Stone Eyes had been saddened by his father's actions, and he hadn't truly understood them. Some of the items offered by the peddlers had caught Stone Eyes's fancy.

Once, when he'd dared take a whistle the peddler had carried, his father had caught him whistling in the woods and punished him. He still carried scars on his back and legs for that, and Wary Wolf had forced him to smash the whistle with a stone.

"The whites will take you with their shiny things," his father had warned. "You must be the man the spirits have intended you to be. They are invaders, a sickness in our lands. You see that from the diseases they carry."

Blankets made by the whites still created fear inside Stone Eyes.

Their weapons, though, Wary Wolf had allowed. The Blackfeet had no weapons that could combat the rifles the whites carried. Firearms, like horses and steel tomahawks, were taken immediately. Those things had to be taken to keep the Blackfoot tribes strong.

This evening, his warriors would descend on the Crow camp and they would kill the men where they found them. Crow warriors and half-grown sons would die. The mountain men would be killed. All of their firearms would be taken.

Especially the rifles that had been taken from Silent Owl.

Bear Kills Many stepped in quietly beside Stone Eyes.

"We are in position," the big warrior whispered.

"Swift Buck knows he must take his warriors with rifles to guard the river?" Stone Eyes asked.

"Yes. He will be there. No one will get across."

The camp was already partially split. Some of the mountain men camped on the other side of the river. They sat at their campfires and drank or told stories. Stone Eyes was counting on the effects of alcohol among his enemies to slow their reactions. He'd been encouraged by their lack of sentries. He had cut the throats of two young men himself. That had been done minutes apart without anyone knowing.

The Crow were too lax, but that was because no one was hunting them. They had a friendship with the whites and lost their instinct for self-preservation in the mountains. Tonight, that relationship with the whites was going to get them killed.

Stone Eyes dropped and moved slowly through the trees so a wayward glance couldn't catch him and set off an alarm through the camp. His shadow blended with those that grew as the sun sank behind the ridge. In only a few more minutes, they would be gone, and the camp would be in disarray. His enemies would be broken and dead behind him.

And Pierre Chouteau's rifles would be his.

He took the reins for his horse from the warrior who held them. For tonight's raid, he carried his rifle, a warclub, two pistols sheathed around his horse's neck in the manner of the pony soldiers, and his bow. He vaulted onto the horse's back, adjusted with it as it searched for its footing, and turned to Bear Kills Many.

He balanced his rifle across the horse's back, put his hands together in front of his mouth, and created the call of a nightjar. The small, nocturnal bird wouldn't be noticed under present conditions so near to the end of the day.

The call was repeated on either side of Stone Eyes as his warriors repeated it.

After a breath, Stone Eyes gripped his rifle, took up his reins, and put his heels to his horse. The animal lunged forward, broke through the brush, and raced down the gentle incline. The thunder of driving hooves filled Stone Eyes's ears as he led the charge.

When he was seventy yards distant from the camp, some of the Crow warriors and mountain men recognized the danger in front of them. They scrambled to bring their weapons to bear, but many of them were drunk or half-asleep.

Stone Eyes raised his rifle to his shoulder, sighted along the barrel toward a mountain man standing his ground, and squeezed the trigger. The rifle boomed and bucked and Stone Eyes rode out the recoil while guiding his horse with his knees. The horse dodged to the left and a ball fired by the man in front of Stone Eyes cut the air beside him.

Blood blossomed at the man's throat. He dropped his rifle, gripped his throat, and fell to his knees. He was on his back and looking up at the twilight sky with glassy eyes when Stone Eyes galloped past him.

Rifles barked along the line of Blackfeet. Bows twanged and sent arrows winging toward anyone in the camp. A woman went down transfixed through the chest by two arrows. A half-grown boy stumbled and grabbed for the arrow that pierced his leg.

Stone Eyes slung his rifle over his back and grabbed the warclub that hung from the sheaths that held his pistol. The thick barrel of the weapon was studded with bear claws and the black glass stone he'd found in the Stinking Land after it had been vomited forth from one of the land's mouths. The black glass was hard and sharp, but it could be shaped into arrowheads and knives if a warrior was patient enough.

Stone Eyes pulled back the warclub and screamed again. With his face painted, he knew he looked fearsome.

The young boy's eyes rounded in horror. He froze and

held onto his wounded leg. He was not wholly Crow. The weak white blood mixed with Indian showed in the boy's light-colored hair and pale eyes. He was dressed in Crow buckskins, but that did not make him Indian. Stone Eyes's son, Silent Owl, had been Indian, and the white mountain man had taken him away, killed him.

No mercy existed in the Blackfoot chieftain's heart.

Stone Eyes used his anger and pain of loss as fuel. The spirits moved in him then. The Serpent spirit moved within him, cooled his anger, and focused it into a weapon.

He swung the warclub and, when it connected with the boy's face, blood spurted, and chunks of the half-breed's head shot away. Stone Eyes dropped the warclub onto the sheath that held his pistols. He grabbed the pistols, one in each hand, and rolled the hammers back.

Using his knees to guide his horse, he galloped into the center of the camp and wheeled around a tent. A thick-bodied warrior stepped out of the tent with a rifle in his hands. Stone Eyes held up his horse a few feet away, aimed a pistol at the center of the Crow warrior's body, and squeezed the trigger.

In the gathering gloom now sinking into the camp, fire leaped from the pistol's muzzle and illuminated the Crow warrior's face for an instant. The ball crunched into his chest and staggered him.

Moving quickly, Stone Eyes nestled the spent pistol into the sheath and reached for the Crow warrior's rifle. He pulled hard, but the dying man wouldn't release his weapon. Stone Eyes rammed his foot into the man's face and knocked him back into the tent he'd climbed out of.

From inside the tent, a woman screamed, and children's screams joined hers.

All around Stone Eyes, warriors rode into the Crow

camp and killed people. His warriors aimed to kill the men and older boys, but their arrows and rifle balls struck women and children, too. In the confusion of battle, things did not always go as planned.

Stone Eyes pulled his stolen rifle to his shoulder, aimed at a mountain man aiming at one of his warriors, and squeezed the trigger. The rifle banged against the Blackfoot chief's shoulder, and the mountain man staggered and went down.

One of the Blackfoot warriors galloped by, leaned down from his horse, and snatched the rifle from the dead man's hands. A moment later and he sat upright on his horse with the rifle to his shoulder. He fired at a target Stone Eyes couldn't see, then jerked as he was shot. His belly wept blood, and he struggled to hang onto his horse.

Stone Eyes threw the stolen rifle at the tent, guided his horse forward and around the tent, and spotted a mountain man standing partially sheltered by a tipi. The man's feet stood out and his hands were revealed as he poured gunpowder into his rifle barrel.

Knowing the tent hides wouldn't stop a pistol ball, Stone Eyes fired where he thought the man's upper body would be. The hands froze and the paper cartridge casing fell from stiff fingers. Stone Eyes sheathed his other spent pistol and slid his bow from his shoulder. He drew an arrow fletched with turkey feathers and nocked it.

The bow couldn't shoot as far effectively as the white man's rifle, but Stone Eyes was in the middle of the battle now. As he rode through the camp, he loosed arrow after arrow at his enemies. Crow men, boys, and mountain men died in minutes.

Some of his warriors seized burning logs and branches from the campfires and threw them into tipis. Women and children poured from their burning homes and fled for the surrounding woods.

Swift Buck and his warriors took cover along the river and shot at the mountain men and Crow warriors who had camped on the other side. They would not be able to hold their positions long. Many of the mountain men were excellent shots with their rifles, and the warriors riding among the Crow tipis were within range of their projectiles.

Bow in hand and an arrow nocked, Stone Eyes slid from his horse and walked. Bear Kills Many spotted him, lifted one hand, and whistled loud and long.

Immediately, several of the Blackfeet warriors dismounted and searched the tipis.

Stone Eyes stepped into the nearest tipi and stared at the woman huddled against the back wall. She held her daughter and a young boy to her.

"Where are the rifles?" Stone Eyes demanded.

"I do not know," the woman bleated. "Some of the Crow warriors have rifles. All of the mountain men do."

"Someone has many rifles. I want them."

"I do not know what you are asking for," the woman said. "Those are the only rifles I know of."

Although Stone Eyes didn't want to ask his next question, he did anyway, but only because he had to.

"Where is Preacher?"

"He's gone."

"Where?" Fear touched Stone Eyes then because the mountain man might even now be loading up Pierre Chouteau's rifles.

"Back where he killed the Blackfeet. The pony soldier captain wanted him to take them there."

"What pony soldier?"

"The one that arrived here only a few days ago."

"Why did he come?"

"It is said he came looking for you."

"Why did they go back to that place?"

"I do not know."

That made no sense to Stone Eyes. Nothing remained back there except for his dead son and the warriors who had followed Silent Owl. He had looked everywhere in that area with Tracker Who Sees and Bear Kills Many. No one could have hidden the rifles from him.

Angry, Stone Eyes looked at the woman. She was comely and still young enough to fetch a good price from Tobit Moon Deer. The Comanchero was always in the market for slaves to sell to Mexican whorehouses. White women sold for the most, but there was an appetite for Indians as well. If not the whorehouses, she could be a slave on a large ranchero or in the towns.

"Come here," Stone Eyes commanded.

The woman shook her head. Her eyes filled with tears.

Stone Eyes aimed at the boy and loosed the arrow he'd been holding at the ready. The shaft struck the boy in the chest, sank deeply, and pinned him to the wall of the tipi.

"No!" the woman cried.

She turned to the boy to help him, but the empty look in his eyes told Stone Eyes he was already gone.

"Nooooo!"

Stone Eyes nocked another arrow. "Come here," he repeated.

She wept and held onto her dead son. Her daughter screamed and tried to hide under the bearskin on the floor.

"I am going to take your daughter," Stone Eyes said. "If you come, she will not be alone. Otherwise, she is going to watch you die tonight."

Shaking, almost unable to walk, the woman crossed the tipi and looked at Stone Eyes. "Please." Her voice cracked and she sounded hopeless. "Please let my daughter stay!"

Stone Eyes released the tension on the bowstring and held the bow with the arrow loosely nocked in his left hand. He grabbed the woman's arm and yanked her to the tent flap.

He looked back at the little girl. She would go for a good price to the Comancheros.

"Follow me," he told her, "or you will never see your mother again."

Trembling, the girl crawled out of the bearskin and walked on weak legs to her mother and Stone Eyes.

Mercilessly, Stone Eyes stepped outside the tipi and looked around the camp. Several tipis burned and the blackened bones of the tent poles stood out in the dim light of the evening.

Bear Kills Many drove his knife into the temple of a Crow warrior in front of a tipi a short distance away. He spotted Stone Eyes and cleaned his knife on the tipi.

"Signal the men," Stone Eyes said. "The rifles are not here. Preacher is not here. We must go. Tell the men to take as many women and girls as they can. We will sell them to the Comancheros for rifles."

Bear Kills Many nodded, put his knife away, and whistled again to signal the end of the raid.

Several Blackfeet lay in the open spaces between the tipis. Light from the burning tipis lit the garish scene and reflected from pools of blood. Many Blackfeet had fallen, but more Crow men and boys and mountain men lay dead.

Stone Eyes slung his bow over his shoulder and whistled for his horse. The animal came up to him instantly. He plucked a short piece of rope from the pistol harness and tied the weeping woman's hands behind her back.

On his horse now, Bear Kills Many rode to Stone Eyes, who passed up the bound woman. Bear Kills Many laid the captive over his horse's shoulders and waited while Stone Eyes clambered onto his horse with the little girl. He sat her in front of him and restrained her while she fought to get away. He put his feet to his horse's sides and galloped out of the camp.

A short time later, with the night full on him, Stone Eyes looked down on the burning Crow camp. The flames reflected on the river and wavered.

"No one pursues us," Bear Kills Many stated.

The bound woman laid still across his horse, but she looked at her daughter in Stone Eyes's arms.

"They will not," Stone Eyes said. "Too many of them have been killed. Too many have been injured. In the darkness against as many of us as we have, they know they would not have a chance."

"You said the rifles were not there."

Stone Eyes looked at his warriors. Less than half of them had taken captives, but there were at least twenty Crow women and children held prisoner.

"We will ask our prisoners," Stone Eyes said. "But I believe this woman spoke truly when she said there were no rifles. Only the mountain men and a few of the Crow warriors had rifles. If they had the rifles we are searching for, our battle there would not have been so easy."

Bear Kills Many nodded. "Where is Preacher?"

"She said he went back to the place he killed my son because a pony soldier captain asked him to."

"What pony soldier captain?"

Stone Eyes looked at the woman lying across Bear Kills Many's horse. "Do you know the name of the pony soldier captain?"

She thought for a moment, then finally said, "Diller. His name is Diller."

Bear Kills Many nodded. "We know the pony soldier captain."

"Yes. He is looking for the rifles. That explains much."

"When he is satisfied the rifles are not there, he will return to the Crow camp. He will find our trail. With so many riders, we cannot hide our passage."

"I hope that he comes to the Stinking Land to find us. That will be his last mistake."

"And Preacher?" Bear Kills Many asked.

"I hope that he comes, too. That way I can avenge my son." Stone Eyes kicked his horse into motion.

"Preacher is a dangerous man. Our people gave him the name of Ghost Killer."

"He was named by old warriors whose guts turn to water every time there is trouble. You and I are not like those old warriors. And no one knows the Stinking Land like we do." Stone Eyes smiled in satisfaction. "So let the great Ghost Killer come. I will bury him in one of the holes that open up in the ground. Let it vomit his bones up when the Stinking Land is done with him."

CHAPTER 25

Rifles ready, Preacher and Tall Dog stood behind trees and kept their gazes roving. Dog was still out in the brush and hadn't returned, but the big cur hadn't barked, either.

Once he'd finished reloading his rifle and all four of his pistols, Preacher used his large knife to put an end to the two Blackfeet who barely clung to life. They weren't going to make it, and there was no medical help available. Their suffering would only have gotten worse.

For a time, Preacher breathed quietly and listened.

"I apologize," Tall Dog said softly.

"For what?"

"I should have been more alert. Those Blackfeet nearly had us."

"If you want to blame yourself, you have to blame me, too," Preacher said. "I was right in the middle of it and didn't see or hear 'em comin'. It wasn't just you."

"My mistake could have gotten you killed."

"Wasn't a mistake," Preacher said. "Them Blackfeet were good at creepin' through the brush. We were better fighters. *Both* of us. If you hadn't held your own with them, they would have overrun me. As it was, we kept them split up and got a chance to deal with 'em." He shot the younger man a quick glance. "I ain't seen many who can fight like you. If it had been a different man out here with me, we might not have made it."

A small smile curved Tall Dog's lips. "We were lucky to have each other."

"I think so, too." Preacher peered through the darkness. "We'll want to be careful. The noise of all that gunfire had to have reached Captain Diller and his men. I ain't worried about them mountain men who followed us out of the camp, they'll look to see what they're shootin' at, but them soldier boys could be a mite skittish. I don't want to make it out of this fight and end up gettin' shot by one of them. That would be plumb embarrassin'."

Dog returned through the brush, paused, and barked softly to Preacher to let him know he was there.

"Dog's back," the mountain man said. "Ain't nothin' livin' out there that can hurt us. Let's go get our horses."

Tall Dog nodded. "You lead. I will watch our backs."

Preacher stepped out from the tree and held out a hand for Dog. The big cur stepped out of the brush and fitted his broad head under the mountain man's hand. Dog's fur was matted with blood that had grown cold and sticky.

"We're gonna need us a bath," Preacher told the big cur.

A few moments later, they reached the horses. Horse nickered and Tall Dog spoke softly in that strange tongue he used with the paint. His horse stepped over to the young Crow warrior in an easy slide of muscle and butted her head into Tall Dog's chest.

"Preacher!" That was Lorenzo's voice calling from the west, a short distance out from where Preacher stood beside Horse.

"Yeah," the mountain man replied.

"You celebratin' something?" Lorenzo asked. "Or did you run into trouble? That was a whole heap of gunshots."

"I think it was more like trouble ran into us," Preacher said. "A war party of Blackfeet tried to hooraw us."

"You all right?"

"Me and Tall Dog are still standin'."

"What about them Blackfeet?"

"All dead."

"I'm walkin' in," Lorenzo said.

"Cap'n Diller and his men with you?" Preacher asked.

"Yeah."

"You may want to let them know that."

Captain Diller spoke in his command voice. "I heard. Is that area secure, Preacher?"

"It is now."

"Sergeant Gordon, establish a perimeter with the men about a hundred yards out. I want a guard posted on every hill and in every blind spot around here."

"Yes, sir," Gordon barked.

Hoofbeats thudded softly and tack rattled.

"Bringin' a light," Lorenzo said. "Mighty dark in them woods now."

"It is that," Preacher agreed.

The light would draw the attention of anyone else who might be out in the area, but it had gotten too dark to see clearly without it. Preacher wanted to find out what he could learn from their attackers.

A moment later, a match flared in the darkness, kissed a candlewick, and dawned inside a lantern.

Lorenzo held up the lantern so the glow spilled over his dark face. "You see me?"

"I see you," Preacher said. "Come ahead."

Lorenzo walked toward the hollow.

"Peabody Mitchell," Preacher called. "You out there?"

"After all that gunfire, where else would I be?" Mitchell asked laconically. "If I'd knowed you planned on havin' yourself a little set-to, I'd've been right here with you afore now."

"You've been up in these mountains for a time this year."

"I been here since last year."

"Me and Tall Dog killed a lot of Blackfeet. I'm thinkin' maybe you might know one or two of them, what with you bein' interested in Stone Eyes."

"I'm gonna come look."

"Hurry up," Lorenzo said. "We can share a light."

"Good thing," Mitchell said. "I didn't bring one of my own."

"I got one you can borrow," Allan Colquhoun said.

Another match flared and the illumination revealed Colquhoun standing with Seth and Barney Thompkins and Oscar Ferrell. The mountain men stood apart from the soldiers. Colquhoun handed the lit lantern to Mitchell.

Mitchell hustled and stepped in beside Lorenzo. The two men kept their rifles ready.

Another match ignited with a harsh, sulfurous glow. A moment later, another light flowered and nestled inside another lantern. The illumination played over Diller's frowning features.

"I'm coming in, Preacher," the Army captain said.

"Come ahead," Preacher said.

The mountain man rummaged in his saddlebags and located a canvas bag of pemmican. He took out two pieces, kept one, and handed the other to Tall Dog. The young Crow warrior accepted the pemmican.

"Likely we ain't gonna get to supper for a bit," Preacher said.

Tall Dog nodded. "Thank you."

He bit into the pemmican and looked around at the dead bodies revealed by the light of the lantern Lorenzo carried.

"Looks like you boys done had yourself a tussle," Lorenzo commented.

"We did," Preacher agreed.

"We'd have been here sooner, but it's dark an' we wanted to know what we was fixin' to get into."

Preacher broke off half of the pemmican piece and held it out for Dog. The big cur took the meat gently and laid down with it, but his eyes remained watchful. He took small bites and chewed.

"With all of these Blackfeet around, you had to work hard to come out on top," Peabody Mitchell commented. He hunkered down beside one of the Blackfeet and studied the dead man's features.

"This ain't all of 'em," Preacher said. "Got more of 'em back in the woods there, over in that hollow ahead of us, and on the other side of it."

"How many of them did you encounter?" Captain Diller asked. He stood a short distance back and moved his lantern around to look at everything.

"Wasn't a whole lot of time for countin'," Preacher said. "It was root, hog, or die."

Diller strode across the battleground and stared at the bodies. "This wasn't just a band of hunters," the captain said. "Not if there's as many of them as you say there are."

"Reckon not," Preacher agreed. "You can tote 'em up yourself if you want."

"We heard several shots," Diller said. "That's why we came this way."

"If we could have reloaded faster, you'd have heard more. It come to hand-to-hand pretty quick."

Diller looked at Preacher. "None of these Blackfeet have firearms?"

"Nope, and if they had, this little fracas might have turned out different. Tall Dog and me only come out of it with a few scratches."

"You're lucky," Mitchell said.

"I like to think we're just that skilled," Preacher said. "Might have been different if Dog hadn't been with us, too. He tilted the odds."

The big cur growled at his name.

"How come you to be all the way out here?" Lorenzo asked. "I thought you was back yonder, till the shootin' started an' I looked around to see you wasn't there."

"Tall Dog followed a trail that led back to where them Crow were buried in the trees."

"A trail left by the Indians who attacked you just now?" Diller asked.

"No. This was an old trail. These Blackfeet didn't come this way. They were headed toward where you were."

Diller glanced at Tall Dog. "Why were you so interested in this trail?"

"Some of the ponies in Silent Owl's band left hoofprints here," Tall Dog said. "I was curious about why they came this way. The trail showed they went here and went back."

The Army captain narrowed his eyes and looked at the young Crow warrior. "You sure about that?"

Tall Dog met Diller's eyes full measure. "I am."

Diller glanced at Preacher.

"I didn't question it," the mountain man said. "Tall Dog said he found something interestin', so I came with him. Turns out he found something mighty interestin'."

"What did you find?"

Preacher took a bite of his pemmican and left the story for Tall Dog to tell. Despite the death around him, the mountain man's stomach growled. The pemmican was dry, but it took the edge of hunger off.

"I found some dead white men," Tall Dog said. "Preacher believes they were soldiers."

Diller straightened and stared at Preacher. "Why would you believe that?"

"There ain't much left of them," Preacher said. "The Blackfeet who found them, and we'll have to see if we can find sign in the mornin' when we have light to see if this is true, were probably Silent Owl and his warriors. I think that's where they found and caught Joe Len Darby. I suspect he was hidin' with them. Silent Owl chose to let Joe Len Darby live."

Why the Blackfeet leader would do that remained something of a puzzle for Preacher, but he was wrapping his head around it. He didn't quite cotton to where that particular trail was leading, though.

Diller was quiet for a moment. He worked his jaws. "Are you sure about Darby being there?"

"I found a broke flask in that hollow that once held Bonxie scotch in it. That sound familiar?"

Diller took in a deep breath through his nostrils. "It does."

"Darby told me he had a captain back at the fort who had an expensive taste in drink. He mentioned you by name. Darby said he liberated some of the scotch before he left Fort Pierre." Preacher took another bite of pemmican. "I've had me some of that scotch myself a few years back. It was good enough to remember that bird on the bottle."

"You didn't find anything else?"

Preacher chewed the pemmican, swallowed, and contemplated the Army captain. "You mean, did I find any more rifles?"

"Were there any weapons?"

Preacher accepted the counter even though he wanted to pursue his question. Now wasn't the time, though. That question might divide their forces and he didn't want that.

"No," Preacher answered, "I didn't. Like I said, varmints been at those men. There ain't much left."

Diller turned and raised his voice. "Sergeant Gordon."

"Yes, sir."

"Have you got my perimeter established?"

"Yes, sir. We're tight as a drum, sir. Ain't nobody gonna ride up on us without bein' seen."

"That's good, Sergeant. Now get a small detail together. I want to take a look at that hollow up ahead of us."

"What do you suppose Diller's lookin' for?" Lorenzo asked quietly.

"I think Diller is certain he knows who those soldiers are," Preacher said. "He's just lookin' for proof."

The mountain man stood beside his friend at the edge of the hollow and looked down where Sergeant Gordon and three soldiers searched the enclosed space. Full dark filled the hollow now, and the soldiers carried lanterns to light their way.

"He thinks those men were soldiers of his?" Lorenzo asked.

"I'd bet a brand-new hat on it."

"Why would they be all the way out here by their lonesomes?"

"Now, that I don't know." But the possibilities kept bouncing around in Preacher's head like lightning bugs. "I suspect they didn't plan on it."

"Well," Lorenzo said, and pulled his buffalo robe more tightly around him, "I'm of a mind to leave him to it. I ain't signed on for rootin' around in the bones of the dead." He glanced around at the dead Blackfeet nearby. "An' perchin' in the middle of the dead ain't somethin' I'm likely to ever cotton to. I've about had me enough of standin' around getting colder. I'm about ready to lay me a fire, cook me a piece of meat to fill my belly, an' sleep till mornin'."

"Go on then."

"I ain't leavin' you out here in the middle of this." Lorenzo yawned. "Though you don't wanna go testin' me too long on that. My goodwill only goes so far."

"Hey, Preacher," Peabody Mitchell called.

Preacher turned to face the man.

Mitchell looked tired and haggard. He held a small lantern in one hand and the light didn't reach the shadows that covered his thin face. "I found an Indian I know."

Preacher had asked Mitchell to look at the Blackfeet in the hopes he would know one of them and they could figure out more of what was going on. Preacher had looked at all the dead Indians and didn't know any of them. Neither had Tall Dog.

"Show me," the mountain man said.

Mitchell nodded, turned, and headed back into the woods where the Blackfeet had almost cornered Tall Dog.

CHAPTER 26

With Lorenzo trailing along behind him, Preacher followed Mitchell past half a dozen bodies, all of them encrusted by mosquitos and other insects that fed on blood. The winged bugs fluttered as they moved, and it gave the illusion that the corpses still held a little life.

Tall Dog stood near a body and had his arms folded over his broad chest. He held his rifle in one hand. A small lantern hung from the branch of a nearby tree and cast a cone of light onto the ground and the body Mitchell led Preacher to. Bugs flew at the lantern's hurricane glass and bounced off with audible *tings*.

Dog halted six feet from the body and laid down. His ears twitched and flipped as the voices around them changed.

Mitchell hunkered beside the dead Blackfoot. The dead man's head lay turned unnaturally because his neck had nearly been hacked in two. Moths trapped in the pool of blood beneath him flapped their wings and tried to get free.

The Indian was in his early thirties. His long dark hair was tied in two braids and had small shells and colorful rocks woven in. Although he'd been a handsome man, a rough, fingernail-sized scar showed on his cheek.

"This is Grumbling Badger," Mitchell said. "He's been ridin' renegade since last year that I know of, an' he's attacked at least three wagon trains last summer. Probably more. Grumbling Badger an' his warriors tend to be a bloodthirsty bunch an' don't leave witnesses behind. They killed a lot of setters headed for Oregon an' took everythin' they had."

"What else do you know about him?"

Mitchell shook his head. "Not much. I had a close run-in with the varmint a few months ago. Almost got caught out with no one around me. The only reason I got away was because I know this part of these mountains better than they did. I killed a couple of them an' slid on out before they could trap me."

"Around here?"

"No, that happened farther north and west. Three, four days' ride from here."

"Any idea what Grumblin' Badger's doin' here?" Preacher asked. "This place is out of the way."

"Grumbling Badger followed the tracks of Silent Owl and his warriors," Tall Dog said.

"How do you know that?" Preacher asked.

"While you talked with the pony soldier captain, I backtracked these Blackfeet and found their horses. They left them a half-mile away in a small box canyon so the neighing of their animals wouldn't alert our horses."

Preacher chided himself for not knowing the young Crow warrior had left for a time. He was usually good at keeping track of comings and goings of men around him.

"Grumblin' Badger and his warriors knew we were here," he said.

"Their tracks are very fresh," Tall Dog said. "I think they spotted the pony soldiers grouped around the place where Silent Owl and his warriors are buried. Then they saw us and decided we would be easier to take since we were on our own and away from the main body. Probably they were curious about us and what we are doing out here."

"Well," Mitchell said, and grinned, "they made a big mistake bein' curious, didn't they?"

"They did that," Lorenzo agreed with a grin of his own. "They had to have had a reason for travelin' out all this way, though."

"Me an' the others was talkin' while we were watchin' them soldiers around the Indian graves," Mitchell said. "Seth Thompkins said him an' his brothers an' pa have heard Stone Eyes has been recruitin' young braves who are spoilin' to fight the whites an' count coup. Stone Eyes has traded with some of the Blackfoot tribes that have kept to themselves. While they're there, Stone Eyes trots out his story about how he's gonna reclaim these mountains for the Blackfeet by chasin' off the whites an' the Crow people. He's tryin' to raise an army an' promising any of them Indians that will listen all manner of things. Firstly that there won't be no more whites in the mountains."

That unpleasant thought reminded Preacher of the missing rifles Pierre Chouteau had contracted the Army to bring to him. Almost a hundred rifles in the hands of the Blackfeet in the Tetons and nearby mountains would change the balance of power that currently existed in the area.

Mitchell nodded at Grumbling Badger.

"Do you see that scar on his cheeks?" Mitchell pointed a finger at the scar on the dead Blackfoot's face.

"Yeah."

"He's got one on the other side, too." Mitchell rolled the dead man's head over and exposed the other side where a similar scar was visible. Grumbling Badger's nearly severed head shifted easily and twisted at an angle that revealed the deep cut that almost severed his neck. "When he was eight years old, Grumbling Badger was shot by a soldier. A troop ambushed a small Blackfoot camp one mornin' while scoutin' for a group of renegades who burned down the homes an' barns of three families. Story goes that them soldiers got tired of lookin' for the renegades an' figured a bunch of Blackfeet women an' children in a camp was just as good as findin' the Indians they was sent to look for."

The story was a familiar one, and Preacher didn't much care for it. He believed in fighting and killing the Blackfeet who tried to kill him, but he would never make war on women and children.

"Story goes," Mitchell continued, "that Grumbling Badger's grandpa, too old an' weak to fight anymore, or even hunt, took up his bow an' challenged the soldiers. Of course, they killed him, an' Grumbling Badger took up his grandpa's bow an' shot two of them soldiers before a soldier shot him. Ball caught him in the face, passed through both sides, an' knocked out some teeth."

"Didn't appear to slow him down none," Lorenzo said.

"It didn't. Some folks around Fort Pierre lost kin to Grumbling Badger an' his warriors. They offered a reward for his scalp." Mitchell released the dead man's head and it flopped back to a rest. "His head actually. They knew about them scars an' wanted to see them before they paid out." He sat up straighter. "Who done for him?"

Preacher jerked a thumb in Tall Dog's direction.

Mitchell gazed speculatively at the young Crow warrior. "What'd you split him with?"

"This." Tall Dog reached over his shoulder and freed the sword sheathed there. He held it balanced on the forefingers of both hands.

Mitchell held up his lantern to better see the weapon. The blade was just under three feet long and had a looped handle. The sheen that covered it advertised the care it received.

"That's a big pig-sticker," Mitchell said.

"This is an *espada ancha*," Tall Dog said proudly.

"'Wide sword'?" Lorenzo asked. "That's what the Spanish translates into."

The young Crow warrior nodded. "The wide sword. Sometimes it is called a broadsword. My mother called it the *espada ancha* in her native tongue." He looked at Preacher. "As I have explained, she does not remember much of her family. One of the things she knows is that, for a time, her father rode as a *soldado de cuera*."

"A 'leather-jacket soldier,'" Preacher said. "They were called that because they wore deer-skin cloaks several layers thick that stood up against Indian arrows. I met a *soldado de cuera* standing guard at a mission in California. Mauricio Sorolla Esteban. He was quiet and well-mannered, and wasn't nobody in town who wanted to give him trouble. I saw him gut a man with a sword like that quicker than a shy girl's smile."

"Yes. These men rode for the Spanish Empire. They were fierce men who fought Indians and escorted travelers, peddlers, and cargoes from Louisiana to the Pacific Ocean.

When they weren't doing that, they guarded vast remudas from horse thieves."

"You got that sword from your grandpa?" Mitchell asked.

Sadness touched Tall Dog's steel-gray eyes. "No. I never knew him. Nor did my mother. She was taken from her family at a young age and her past was lost. While traveling in Arizona Territory with my father, she encountered an old man who had been struck down by *bandidos*. He lay dying and my mother tended to him. Before he went to join his ancestors, he gave her this sword. I was small then, but she wanted me to have something of the heritage she remembered. She kept the sword. When I was old enough, she gave it to me and bade my father find a man to teach me the ways of the sword. He honored her wishes, as he does, and I was trained. I lack in my skills, but I still learn every chance I get."

Mitchell looked around at the bodies, many of which bore wounds from the *espada ancha*. "Looks to me like you've learned right fine."

Tall Dog sheathed the sword over his shoulder.

"Cap'n Diller," one of the men called out from down in the hollow. "I found something you should see."

Preacher returned to the hollow's edge and peered down.

"What did you find?" Diller demanded.

"Milton Walsh's glass eye, looks like."

"Bring it to me."

One of the soldiers tromped across the hollow and through the stream. He held something cupped in his hand.

The Army captain stood forty yards away from Preacher beneath a lantern hanging on a branch. He was wrapped in a long coat that covered him to just beyond his boot tops. Two privates stood on either side of him and kept watch.

Preacher reached the captain's side before the private pulled himself up the side of the hollow.

"It was hard as all-get-out to find," the private said. "Even with the lanterns, it's dark down there."

Diller held out a hand. The private dropped an object into the captain's palm that rolled around a minute before it settled.

Lorenzo stepped forward till he was even with Preacher and played the light of his lantern over the object. A cocked eye about the size of the ball of the Army captain's thumb lay in Diller's hand and stared out at nothing.

"Yep," Lorenzo said, and scowled, "that there's a glass eye. It ain't the best one I've seen. The best one I saw belonged to Chauntice Delacroix. She worked at the Silk an' Steel sportin' house in New Orleans to supplement her gamblin'. She got that eye all the way from Germany an' was right proud of it. One night I seen her drop it on the table durin' a high stakes poker game."

"Did she lose her eye?" Mitchell asked.

"Nope." Lorenzo shook his head. "Other fella was cheatin' an' Miss Chauntice knew it. She popped that eye out an' laid it on the table an' told Horace Derwiler that it was gonna watch him deal the next round of cards. He got so flustered with that eye watchin' them that he dropped the pair of cards he'd been holdin' up his sleeve. Miss Chauntice pulled out her derringer she'd been hidin' up her sleeve an' shot Derwiler right through his heart an' put the second ball into the center of the gambler's forehead. He was dead before his head hit the table. An' them cards? Why they was the jack of hearts and the king of diamonds. Both of them one-eyed."

"Well, I'll swan," Mitchell said.

The story might have been true, but Preacher doubted

it. Lorenzo did like to stretch the truth a mite, but there was always a kernel of fact in there. He hadn't ever heard that particular one.

Diller ignored the conversation and picked up the glass eye between his thumb and forefinger. He rolled it around and it reflected the light on patches of the surface not crusted in mud.

"Are you sure this is Milton Walsh's eye?" the Army captain asked.

The soldier was rawboned and lanky, probably not much more than twenty. Patchy stubble covered his lantern jaw.

"As sure as I can be, Captain," the soldier said. "Milton Walsh used to like to take that eye out an' impress the new recruits an' settlers traveling through Fort Pierre. He'd shine it up on his uniform blouse in the taverns an' tell stories how he'd lost the eye fightin' Blackfeet or outlaws. Occasionally he'd tell how a snake bit him in the eye an' he pulled it out hisownself to drain the pizen. However he was of a mind to tell the story that day, that's how he would tell it. The right truth of it is he lost his eye to his pa, a mean brute if there ever was one. Left whip scars an' burns all over Walsh's back." He glanced over his shoulder. "Now he's layin' out there in pieces after them Blackfeet had at him. It's a shame is what it is."

Preacher said, "If that eye did belong to Milton Walsh—"

"It did," the soldier said stubbornly.

"—what was he doin' all the way out here?"

"I don't know," Diller said. He tossed the glass eye up and caught it. "Walsh was just another soldier who left the company."

"Like Joe Len Darby?" Preacher asked.

Diller nodded and stared out over the hollow. "Like him."

"Any idea who the other man down there was?"

The soldier shook his head. "Ain't enough of either of them to identify. If Walsh's glass eye hadn't caught the moonlight just right, why, I reckon we wouldn't know he was down there, neither."

"Thank you, private," Diller said. "Tell Sergeant Gordon to arrange a burial detail for those two men. We can at least be civilized about this."

"Yes, sir." The private saluted and climbed back down into the hollow.

Diller turned to Preacher. "My men couldn't identify the Blackfeet warriors who attacked you. Did you have any luck? I saw you four gather around one of the bodies."

"Peabody Mitchell found one known to him," Preacher said. "Grumbling Badger. Heard of him?"

The captain thought for a moment, then shook his head. "I have not. What do you know about him?"

Preacher nodded to Mitchell.

"Grumbling Badger went renegade last year," Mitchell said. "Story is he's attacked some wagon trains, killed some pilgrims, an' been a general nuisance to most folks."

"Well then," Diller said, "the world's a finer place without him in it. And all of his associates." He slipped the glass eye into his pocket. "I'm going back to the camp. You men should, too. Tomorrow's going to come early. I hope you're still interested in tracking down Stone Eyes."

"I am," Preacher said. "These Blackfeet tonight sealed the deal."

Diller smiled. "I'll see you in the morning, then."

He turned and walked away. One of the privates with him took down the lantern and led the way. The others fell in behind.

"He kept that glass eye," Lorenzo said. "What you reckon he's gonna do with it?"

Preacher shook his head. "I don't think takin' it is as important as not leavin' it behind."

"What do you mean?" Tall Dog asked.

"I don't think he wants anyone to know soldiers might be involved in the rifles that went missing."

"That's somethin' that don't make a lick of sense to me," Mitchell said. "The Army's out here lookin' for them missin' rifles Diller says Stone Eyes an' his warriors took. You took some rifles that Silent Owl an' his braves had, only they didn't have all of them. An' I know if Stone Eyes had a bunch of rifles, he wouldn't likely be runnin' from Diller an' his soldiers."

"I don't think so, either," Preacher said.

"What do you think?" Tall Dog asked.

Preacher paused a moment and wondered if he should think out loud. He only had a half-formed notion, no facts to support it, but the way he strung the facts together in his mind made sense.

"I'm wonderin' if Silent Owl and his warriors had those rifles because they took them from Joe Len Darby, Milton Walsh, and whoever that other soldier back in that hollow was."

"Silent Owl kept Joe Len Darby alive," Tall Dog said. "He might have kept him for sport to torture later."

"I don't think so," Preacher said. "Don't make any good sense. Silent Owl was out here on his pa's say-so, followin' orders he'd been given."

"Trackin' them three men they found in that hollow," Mitchell said.

"That's the only way Silent Owl would have been out here." Preacher nodded and warmed up to the theory because Mitchell and Tall Dog were following along so easily. "He was followin' the rifles."

"That means Stone Eyes did not take the rifles from the Army convoy headed upriver to Fort Pierre," Tall Dog said.

"That's what I'm thinkin'," Preacher said.

"So what is Diller doin' out here?" Mitchell asked.

"What he said he's doin'," Preacher said. "Tryin' to find those rifles. Him keepin' Milton Walsh's eyeball like that, he's probably makin' sure none of this falls back on the Army."

"What would it matter?" Lorenzo asked.

"Pierre Chouteau might be less inclined to help finance the Army out here if he finds out a group of Army deserters went into the munitions business for themselves with his merchandise. An' worse comes to worse, Chouteau might sue the Army. Either way, the War Department would get a black eye it doesn't want."

"They would rather the guilty party would be the Blackfeet," Tall Dog said.

"Yep," Preacher said. "That's how I see it."

"An' now we're mixed up in the middle of this mess," Lorenzo groused.

"You don't have to stay that way," Preacher pointed out. "You can return to the Crow camp and enjoy your summer while the days are warm."

"Now you know I ain't gonna do that an' leave you out here not knowin' who you can trust." Lorenzo adjusted his buffalo robe and pulled it tighter. "We've rode a few rivers together, me an' you. I'll see this through with you, but I'll tell you one thing I wouldn't do."

"What's that?"

"Sleep in my tent with somebody's glass eye a-lookin' at me all night, that's what."

CHAPTER 27

Preacher got up before first light the next morning, fed and watered Horse, gave Dog some pemmican to hold him over until breakfast could be arranged, and put on a pot of coffee. By the time the coffee was boiling, Tall Dog climbed up from his bedroll and put his things away. He took care of his paint horse and joined Preacher at the campfire.

Minutes later, Lorenzo, the Thompkins brothers, Peabody Mitchell, Oscar Ferrell, and Allan Colquhoun took care of their mounts and joined them. All of the men looked worse for wear, and Preacher figured he didn't look any better.

They added two more coffeepots to the fire and the smell soon filled the air.

Around them, the soldiers came to life, too, and stayed separate. Preacher didn't know if that was because they'd been ordered to stay away from the mountain men or if they just didn't feel comfortable with them. In the end, it didn't really matter to Preacher because he had other things on his mind.

Sergeant Gordon walked through and kicked the feet of

the men still sleeping under their small tarpaulins. The canvas material glistened with a coat of fresh dew and the morning was cold enough that Preacher's breath showed briefly before it was snatched away by the breeze.

Captain Diller walked over to Preacher's campfire with a tin cup of coffee in hand.

"Good morning," the Army captain greeted stiffly.

Preacher nodded. No one else at the campfire said anything.

"I wanted to make sure you're still up to the task of tracking Stone Eyes."

"We are," Preacher said. "Gonna get to it directly. The day needs a little more light to see sign better, an' we need a little coffee for the same reason."

"I have men cooking breakfast," Diller said. "You are welcome to join us."

"Me an' Oscar will be cookin' breakfast for us," Lorenzo said. "We got our own supplies. Don't want to cause you any hardship on our account. Besides that, I know how each one of these boys likes his bacon. An' ol' Oscar makes a mean flapjack."

"All right," Diller said. "I'll leave you to it. I'll have a perimeter guard stationed around this place. For the moment, until you find a trail, this will serve as a command station."

"Sounds fine," Preacher said.

Diller walked away.

"Seems a mite touchy this mornin', don't he?" Mitchell asked.

"Probably kept up all night by that glass eye," Lorenzo said. "I know I spent some time thinkin' about it."

"Then you wasted time you shoulda been sleepin',"

Barney Thompkins said with a grin. "You sound like an old woman, Lorenzo."

Of the two young mountain men, Barney was quicker than his older brother with a joke and a smile. He also had a quicker temper, and none of the Thompkins men were noted for their patience.

"You ask me," Lorenzo said, "you're almighty too dismissive of that glass eye. Just you think about it, Barney Thompkins, an' give it a long, hard think. A few days ago, that glass eye just filled a vacant hole in a man's head, but glass is a mighty attractive thing to a ghost. That's why when you look in a mirror at the right time of night you can see a glimpse of the world that lays beyond this one. That's why I don't spend much time around mirrors. Now that glass eye is probably filled with Milton Walsh's spirit, held up inside there like some genie in a lamp, or trapped like one of them ha'nts on a bottle tree down in New Orleans. An' it's just screamin' an' waitin' to get out an' get vengeance. Ghosts sometimes go mad, you know. Plumb crazy. Ain't no reasonin' with a crazed ghost. An' they've been known to attack anybody around them."

Barney laughed, but no one else did. The smile slowly dropped from the young mountain man's face as he looked around the group of men at the campfire. They all peered back at him somberly.

"That . . ." Barney said, "that can't happen. Right?"

"If you see that glass eye up an' floatin' around tonight," Lorenzo said, "you might want to run for the tall an' uncut like the hounds of Hell were on your heels. 'Cause they might well be."

Barney paled a little and looked at his brother. Seth Thompkins kept his face neutral and poured himself a cup of coffee.

"Seth?" Barney prompted. "That ain't possible, is it?

Unable to keep a straight face any longer, Lorenzo erupted into laughter and the others joined him. Preacher did, too. Despite the horror of the attack last night, Preacher joined in. He was alive, the day was bright, and he was back in the mountains among good friends who knew his ways.

He'd take that and make do with whatever else came.

Preacher searched for sign the way he'd been trained to do back when he'd first walked into the mountains. As long as whatever he was looking for had left sign behind, the method had never failed.

He and the other men had eaten breakfast in the saddle. Lorenzo and Oscar had delivered bacon wrapped in flap-jacks, then rode back to square away their pack animals and food. They knew they'd be moving on soon.

Preacher hunted sign outside the clearing where he'd killed Silent Owl and his warriors, located several sets of hoofprints that he figured were from Indian ponies, and tracked them as far as he could. Following them wasn't hard, but he wanted to make certain he followed the most recent trail. Backtracking where Stone Eyes and his band had been wouldn't do much good now. Fortunately, most of the trails in and out of the area lay in different directions.

He wished he'd thought to examine the hooves of the horses he'd brought back with him and Joe Len Darby to the Crow camp. That way he could have matched them up and eliminated them from the possibilities.

The sign he followed was fresher, most likely made after he'd rounded up Silent Owl's horses and took them along with him to the Crow camp. The recent rains had washed out some of the older tracks.

Of course, that could be misleading because the ground could have been softer from even earlier rains and allowed the tracks to go deeper and last longer. He checked the grass growth in the impression and figured out which had recovered longer.

Despite his thoroughness, and Dog's good nose, he lost the tracks a few times. Sometimes he picked up a couple of riders that branched off from the others, and he guessed they were hunters sent on ahead to find game. Piles of offal along the way confirmed that. He didn't get led off too far. By spiraling out from the last sign he'd found, it didn't take him long to pick up the trail again.

Stone Eyes and his warriors cut a wide swath through the wilderness.

Tall Dog, the Thompkins brothers, Peabody Mitchell, and Allan Colquhoun were all following similar trails. Every now and again, some of them would drop off to follow a trail, and they'd return. After a bit, they all came together and spread out around Preacher.

"Looks like they're all headed in the same direction," Preacher said. "Got a destination in mind and they ain't wastin' time gettin' there."

"I see that," Colquhoun said. "I found some sign that headed in other directions, but it looked older. I think the ones we're followin' came from another, larger group."

"They were hot on your heels right here, Preacher," Seth Thompkins said.

"They were," Preacher agreed. "I reckon they were a day or so behind me. They lost some time buryin' their dead."

"I agree," Peabody Mitchell said. "Good thing you an' that old-timer didn't decide to hang around after the party was over."

"Wasn't no reason to," Preacher said. "I knew someone would be along fairly quick when we left. Didn't take much to figure Silent Owl and his warriors were a scoutin' party, not out on their own."

"Silent Owl and his warriors come out here lookin' for them rifles," Barney Thompkins said. "Plain to see from them bodies they left in that holler that they were after those. An' from them rifles you found 'em with. That's proof right there. Likely they would have headed back to Stone Eyes if they'd had the time."

"Or gone off chasin' after the rest of them rifles," Seth said. "You reckon they knew where they was?"

That thought had nettled Preacher something vicious, but there was no way of knowing.

"I ain't sure," Preacher admitted. "By the time the killin' was done, wasn't nobody left to ask."

Except Joe Len Darby.

Preacher called himself a fool for not being more suspicious of the old man, but Darby presented himself as a hayseed really well. And there hadn't been time to consider everything that might have been going on. Preacher hadn't wanted to get caught out in the mountains by a band of Blackfeet. He had to cut and run.

"What do you reckon happened to the rest of them rifles?" Colquhoun asked.

"Don't know." Preacher kept the trail he was following in sight and rode along at a steady pace. "I'm guessin' those three runaway soldiers were plannin' on usin' those rifles to sell the rest of them. Proof that they had 'em."

"Who would they sell them to?" Mitchell asked.

"There's the Comancheros down in Nuevo Mexico. Tobit Moon Deer is always willin' to buy and sell guns north or south of the Mexican border. And if he ain't around, a man doesn't have to look far to find other Comancheros willin' to offer the same deals."

"Not to say you're wrong, Preacher," Seth Thompkins said, "on account of I would never do that, but travelin' out here haulin' them rifles would be a hard row to hoe."

Preacher ran a hand over the stubble covering his face. "That it would be."

"Already didn't work out for them soldiers who came upriver from St. Louis," Colquhoun said. "Didn't work out for them soldiers who got killed in that holler back there, neither."

"An' it for sure didn't work out for Silent Owl an' his bunch," Barney said. "Preacher seen to that."

"You might want to keep all that bad luck in mind," Peabody Mitchell said. "Because we're all out here lookin' for rifles that ain't brought nobody who's laid their hands on them nothin' but trouble."

Sobered by the observation, the men rode quiet and attentive and kept following the trail of the horses.

"These tracks have got to belong to Stone Eyes," Preacher said. "This many unshod horses has got to mean a lot of Indians."

Colquhoun leaned over from his horse and spat a blob of tobacco juice onto the ground. He wiped his mouth with the back of his hand. "A whole lot of Indians," he agreed.

An hour later, the new tracks split off from the tracks Preacher had left on the ride toward the Crow camp. The old tracks were muddied by the ones left by the Blackfeet and the group of mountain men and Army soldiers. Once the large group of horses split off, Preacher trailed the smaller group a short distance and spotted the imprints of

Horse's iron shoes. He knew his companion's hoofprints like the back of his hand.

"Those tracks belong to Horse," Preacher said.

Tall Dog rode forward and looked at the tracks for himself. "You rode on to the Crow camp. Where did Stone Eyes go? Why did the Blackfeet not follow you?"

When he considered the probable answer to those questions, a bad feeling settled in Preacher's stomach.

"I guess we'll find out if we keep on followin' them a spell," Preacher replied, and headed onto the trail of the larger group that he suspected was Stone Eyes. "Dog."

The big cur loped to Preacher and looked up.

"Hunt," Preacher said.

Dog stuck his nose to the ground, snuffed, and trotted happily along the trail. It was pretty well marked by piles of horse apples.

An hour later, Preacher reined Horse under a stand of tall spruce that offered shelter from the morning sun. Now that the day had grown older, the temperature had grown hotter.

The tracks followed a line of ragged hills that wound through stands of trees, broken rock trails between large boulders, and roundabouts that threaded through the mountains. Much of the time, but not all, the silver spine of the Snake River was somewhere in view. It would disappear soon enough, though, when the mountains grew tall enough to block sight of it. They were in high country now, and the drop-offs were sudden and steep. Riders had no choice but to follow the lay of the land.

Preacher took off his hat, poured water from one of his canteens into it, and watered Horse. The big animal drank the water greedily and lazily swished his tail at the few horseflies that pestered him.

"If this is Stone Eyes," Peabody Mitchell said, "he's usin' the river as a marker."

Mitchell took off his own hat, filled it from his canteen, and let his horse drink from it.

The other mountain men did the same.

"Where's he headed?" Mitchell asked.

"It's been a while since I've been up here," Preacher said, "but I recall there's a bridge farther up the Snake where a man can cross easily on horseback."

He might not have traveled through this stretch of mountains in a while, but he remembered the land. Out here with all the wildness and dangers around, a man didn't have time to check a map—if he could even find one. Not a lot of men made maps of this part of the mountains that made it into the hands of others.

Preacher had developed a phenomenal memory of land and men and stories that kept him mostly on course everywhere he went. He might not always know the land where he was, but he took markers from the tall mountains that towered around him. All he needed to find his way was a glimpse of the Tetons.

Horse finished drinking. The mountain man knelt and let Dog drink out of his hat, then emptied what little was left and clapped it back on his head. Water trickled down through his hair and across the back of his neck, but it felt good against the rising heat.

"That bridge is there," Peabody Mitchell said, and nodded grimly.

"Been across it a time or two myself," Colquhoun added.

"You think Stone Eyes is headin' for the Crow camp?" Seth Thompkins asked.

He was the one to say what they'd all been afraid to ask. Looking at the faces of the men around him, Preacher knew all of them had been thinking along the same lines. There was nothing else out here where a large group of Blackfeet traveling hard and fast could resupply.

"Stands to reason," Preacher said. "We all saw how these tracks followed mine at first. The intent was pretty clear then, they wanted to find them rifles, and I'll bet a dollar against a doughnut, Stone Eyes still intends on gettin' the same thing."

"Revenge," Colquhoun said.

"An' them rifles," Mitchell said. "Can't forget about them. You can bet those Blackfeet ain't."

"We gotta find out if they went there," Barney Thompkins said. "Our pa an' our brothers are there. An' we've seen sign of enough Blackfeet to be a problem. Especially with us gone an' them at the camp not expectin' trouble." He climbed back up into his saddle. "Y'all can't just be standin' around. We need to be ridin'."

"Barney's right," Preacher said. He stepped into the saddle and looked at the others. "How far do you reckon that granite bridge is from the Crow camp."

"Nineteen hours," Tall Dog said. His face was grim. "If a rider hurries his horse, he can cut a couple hours off that time."

Mitchell nodded.

"Sounds about right," Preacher said.

"These tracks are at least a couple days old," Colquhoun said. "Even addin' in nineteen hours of ridin' from the bridge, Stone Eyes an' his warriors probably hit the Crow camp last night if that's what they were aimin' on doin'. We're a day an' a half out from the camp. We ain't gonna get there in time to warn them."

"Let's hope the Crows an' those mountain men at the camp could hold their own," Mitchell said.

Preacher turned his thoughts from the bad things that could have happened, that probably *had* happened, and put his heels to Horse. The good feelings he'd enjoyed that morning evaporated.

The Army soldiers spotted Preacher and the mountain men riding in and sent word back to the canvas tent erected to provide Captain Diller a command headquarters that was out of the sun and the wind.

Preacher galloped into the camp and stepped down from Horse. Dog trotted over to his side.

Lorenzo walked over from the campfire they'd shared that morning. "Didn't expect you back so soon, Preacher. Figured you'd be gone most of the day pokin' around."

"Planned on it," Preacher said. He walked toward the command tent. "Pack up your gear. We got to get movin'. Stone Eyes foxed us. We followed his trail long enough to think he headed up to that old granite bridge crossin' farther up the Snake."

"You think he's meanin' to circle around to the Crow camp?" Worry bit into Lorenzo's features.

"I do. And he's had time to get there last night."

Lorenzo cursed and headed back to the horses.

Captain Diller stood in the shade of the tent. "Did you find out where Stone Eyes went, Preacher?"

"We think he's headed over to the Crow camp." Preacher stopped in front of the captain.

Diller frowned. "If you don't know where Stone Eyes

is, you don't know for a fact that he's headed to the Crow camp."

"He's bound on gettin' those rifles," Preacher said. "And I'm fairly certain he's gonna look for Joe Len Darby."

"Why would he do that?"

"I think Joe Len Darby knows where Pierre Chouteau's rifles are," Preacher said. "That's why Silent Owl kept him alive and killed those other two soldiers in that hollow. Maybe Darby told Silent Owl where those rifles were. He'd been handled pretty roughly."

"If he told them, why didn't they kill him?"

"Maybe they didn't believe him. Maybe they were gonna kill him after he took them to the rifles. Darby's not what I'd call a truthful man, and he'd have been playin' for his life."

"That's just a bunch of guesswork," Sergeant Gordon said.

"That may be," Preacher said, "but that's where I'm puttin' my bankroll. Me and those men who rode with me are pullin' up stakes now and headin' for the Crow camp."

Diller's eyes narrowed. "If what you say about Stone Eyes's intentions is true," the captain said, "you can't get there in time to stop him."

"That's where he went," Preacher declared. "That's where I'm goin'. You can stay here or you can try to keep up. It don't matter to me which you do. I'm ridin'."

CHAPTER 28

Preacher led the way back to the Crow camp. The frustration of riding with so many men chafed at him. They slowed Horse, Dog, and him, but the mountain men and the soldiers packed enough firepower to make a difference if they did arrive at the camp at the same time or before Stone Eyes—although the chances of that were mighty slim.

Despite the faint hope he didn't dare hold onto, Preacher accepted the fact that the Blackfeet probably had attacked the Crow camp already. Surely there had been enough Crow warriors and mountain men there to fight back and defend themselves.

They couldn't all be dead.

But whatever had been done there had been done almost two days ago.

Preacher thought of Blue Magpie and Songbird and their family. He didn't want anything to happen to them. He was passing friends with Chief Finds the Balance and Jess Thompkins. He didn't want to lose them, either. Both of those men were legends in the mountains, and the Rockies would be a poorer place without them.

Up here in these mountains, though, as much as he loved them and looked forward to returning to the wild life he lived here, . . . , it was a sad fact that no one was safe.

Just after noon of the second day, Preacher topped the ridge that allowed him to look down on the Crow camp. The blackened poles where tipis had burned offered mute testimony to how badly things had gone there.

Men and women, some of them sporting bandages, moved in the camp and tried to go about their lives. Several of them had packed up their horses and obviously intended to pull out for greener pastures.

Or places where they hadn't had to bury their dead.

Those who had been lost hung in the trees in the back of the camp, and the number that were immediately visible was a heart-breaking thing.

Guilt flirted with Preacher for just a moment, but he dismissed it and didn't let it put down roots. Guilt never did anything constructive. He had to get on with what could be done. Stone Eyes had been searching for victims in the mountains before Preacher had killed Silent Owl. The Blackfeet chief would have gotten around to the Crow camp in his own time.

"Preacher!" A man on a crude crutch limped toward the mountain man and waved his free hand.

He came out of the tree line where the mountain men on the east side of the Snake had set up. There among the trees, freshly turned mounds of dirt marked graves of mountain men who'd lost their lives.

We're a thinnin' breed, Preacher thought. *An' we done took a big loss here.*

A small group of mountain men and Crow warriors trailed after the limping man.

Preacher reined in and addressed the man. He recollected his name just before he spoke. "What happened, Dawes?"

"Stone Eyes hit us late in the evening two days ago," the man said. "We had no warnin'. He showed up out of nowhere, an' his warriors lit into us like a swarm of hornets. We held what we could, but as you can see, we lost a lot. We got all our dead sorted, but ain't nobody even started on their grievin'. Healy an' Joplin an' Morrison up an' got killed." Dawes's voice broke and he cleared his throat to get control of his emotion. "Them Blackfeet killed a lot of folks. They came here lookin' for rifles. They rode an' took women and children with 'em when they did."

"Why?"

The man shrugged. "Probably gonna sell them. The Comancheros favor that kind of trade among all the others they do. There's Mexicans down there across the border that buy slaves."

"Well, Stone Eyes ain't gonna sell the people they took from here," Preacher said. "We're gonna get them back."

And at the same time he said that, he wondered how he was going to get that done.

Blue Magpie lay on a bearskin in a borrowed tipi he shared with other wounded Crow men. His own tipi had been burned and he'd gotten an arrow in his belly. He was still fighting the infection from the wound, and he looked like he was getting on the other side of it, but his eyes still looked feverish.

"They took Songbird, Preacher," Magpie said. "They took her and Butterfly Whisper and Smiles Like Red Fox. They took my wife and children."

Preacher steeled himself to show no doubt and no fear, but knowing Songbird and those children were in the hands of Stone Eyes was a fierce blow. He breathed evenly and kept himself centered. A man who didn't think and didn't have a plan usually died all of a sudden.

The mountain man planned on killing, instead.

Doe with Joy knelt beside Magpie and pressed a wet cloth to his forehead. Fatigue showed in her eyes and trembling fingers. The other children clustered around her and the baby shared the bearskin with Magpie.

"My husband tried to go after them when few of the other men would do so," Doe with Joy said hollowly. "But, as you can see, he is not well. He almost died."

"Give me a few more hours," Magpie insisted. "I am almost done with fighting death. I will be able to ride. I can go with you."

Preacher nodded. "You rest up. We'll get to it soon enough." He looked at Doe with Joy and gave her a reassuring smile. "You take care of him."

"I will," she said.

"Do not leave without me, Preacher," Magpie bellowed. But he was weak and slipped into unconsciousness.

Preacher strode through the tipi's flap and stood outside. He took a deep breath and set his mind to what he had to do. He just didn't know how he was going to get it done.

Lorenzo sat on an empty cask a few feet away from the tipi. He held his rifle across his knees and looked fretful. Dog lay at his feet and panted. The big cur's eyes moved restlessly, like he was taking stock of the situation, too.

"You ain't waitin' to go after them Blackfeet, are you?" Lorenzo asked.

"No," Preacher answered. "I'll not let them have another minute to their advantage."

"Well, I'm ridin' with you." Lorenzo scratched Dog's ears and stood. He slung his rifle over his shoulder. "I already seen to fillin' panniers with fresh supplies an' made sure our gunpowder an' shot is full up. We're loaded for bear."

Preacher was quiet for a moment. "Ain't likely to turn out well."

"That gonna stop you?"

"No."

Lorenzo smiled. "I'll always bet on you, Preacher. You oughta know that by now."

A group of mountain men strode up to join Preacher and Lorenzo.

"You boys ain't riding alone," Seth Thompkins said. His eyes were red from crying.

"You ain't," Barney Thompkins said. "Those Blackfeet almost killed our pa, an' they did kill our little brother, Brian. Pa had to bury him. The Blackfeet are gonna pay for that."

"If Pa was able," Seth said, "he'd ride with us, but he got shot an' tomahawked. Like to killed him."

"He still seen to puttin' Brian away an' prayin' over him," Barney added.

The mountain man looked at the troops who stood before him. The Thompkins brothers were there, along with Peabody Mitchell, Oscar Ferrell, Allan Colquhoun, and five others Preacher knew by name or by sight. They were good men, straight and tall and fierce as the mountains made them.

"We got some volunteers," Mitchell said. "Men who've got some experience fightin' Indians an' know these mountains. More wanted to come, but all of 'em can't pull up an' go an' leave the Crow camp unprotected."

Preacher nodded.

"Like I was tellin' Lorenzo," Preacher said, "the chances of gettin' killed while doin' this is pretty high."

Barney looked belligerent. "You goin'?"

"I am."

"Figure on killin' all them Blackfeet by yourself?" Seth challenged.

"As many of 'em as I can," Preacher answered.

"We're ridin' with you," Seth said. "Ain't nothin' you can say that's gonna stop us from doin' that."

Preacher looked at Lorenzo. "You heard what Diller and his men are gonna do?"

Lorenzo nodded at the north end of the camp where the Army men had gathered. They were repacking gear and tending to their horses. The ferry had still been in the river and they'd gotten the horses across without incident.

"They're goin'," Lorenzo said. "I 'spect they been waiting on you. Diller an' his soldier boys ain't gonna let them rifles get away." He glanced around the Crow camp. "This here's proof of what Stone Eyes is willin' to do, an' with them rifles, he'll do a damn sight more."

Preacher resettled his hat on his head. "Well, we're not gonna let him. We're gonna stop his train here."

He walked to Horse and hauled himself into the saddle. He was tired and a little sore from all the fast riding he'd been doing the last few days, but he wasn't going to stop. That wasn't in him.

He wheeled Horse around and rode over to Diller. The Army captain sat on his horse in front of his troops.

"You ready?" Preacher asked.

"Yes," Diller said. "When we catch up to Stone Eyes—"

Whatever else the man had to say, Preacher didn't care. He put his heels to Horse and left Diller there.

The mountain men rode after him.

After a moment, Tall Dog rode up to him. The paint pony stood out against the other horses. The young Crow warrior's face was set in hard lines.

"I am going with you," Tall Dog said. "Stone Eyes's men took my mother."

Preacher nodded grimly, lowered the brim of his hat against the westering sun, and followed the churned-up tracks the Blackfeet had left.

Preacher set a hard pace, but he made sure it was no more than the weakest rider among them could maintain. Reaching the Blackfeet with men and horses tuckered out would do no good. They had to be as rested and ready as they could be.

They rode the rest of the day and a little into the night. When Preacher finally settled on a campsite atop a promontory that gave them a good view in all directions, they'd all about reached their limit. The cold had settled in, and the horses' breaths showed as gray vapor. The mountain man could see his own breath, too.

Preacher stepped down from Horse and turned to address the nearly forty men that rode with him.

"We keep a cold camp tonight," he said loudly. He knew that wasn't going to be a favorable decision because it was going to be pretty chilly this high up in the mountains.

The mountain men tended their horses and said nothing. All of them had been in similar circumstances.

"Now wait just a blamed minute," Gordon barked. He strode to the front of the soldiers. "We've all been ridin' hard all day. The least we got comin' to us is a hot meal an' a fire to warm ourselves."

Behind the sergeant, the soldiers grumbled. Diller sat on his horse and said nothing.

Dog growled until Preacher quieted him. The big cur stood to one side and glared menace at Gordon.

"You're not gettin' fires here," Preacher said. "None of us are. A fire will mark our position to anyone lookin' back this way for us. Stone Eyes will know where we are, and he can count campfires and guess how many of us there are."

"They're two days ahead of us," Gordon challenged, and walked up in front of the mountain man. "Ain't nobody can see back two days."

Preacher resisted the immediate impulse to punch the sergeant in the mouth because he didn't want to cause a division between the mountain men and the soldiers.

"The Blackfeet are ridin' with prisoners," Preacher said, and hoped he sounded like a patient man, though he probably didn't. "Likely, those prisoners will slow the Indians down. We're travelin' lighter and pushin' ourselves harder than they probably expect, so we've been catchin' up since we started out. I don't want Stone Eyes to know where we are and how many guns we have before we've got a chance to use that to our advantage."

"You're not our commandin' officer," Gordon snarled, "so you ain't gonna tell us what to do."

"Then you go and find another campsite," Preacher growled.

With a yell that telegraphed his play, Gordon lashed out with his big right hand.

Preacher wasn't in a mood to fight. He ducked under the sergeant's punch, rapped Gordon's left shin with his rifle butt and pulled the blow just enough not to break bone, and jammed the top of his head under his opponent's chin hard enough to lift the bigger man from his feet. Pain split Preacher's skull and he was dazed for a heartbeat or two. His vision cleared as his opponent fell.

Gordon spilled back loosely and lay limp on the ground.

Preacher glared at the soldiers. "I mean what I say. You don't like it, you get clear of me and these men."

The soldiers stood undecided. One or two of them might have been inclined to point their rifles, but Lorenzo, Tall Dog, Peabody Mitchell, and the other mountain men flanked Preacher on either side.

"We're gonna do this how Preacher says," Lorenzo said. "Ain't gonna be no two ways about it."

For a moment, the silence between the two groups held.

Captain Diller broke that silence. "You men heard Preacher. We'll have a cold camp here tonight. Some of you pick up Sergeant Gordon and carry him over here."

After a brief pause, four soldiers stepped forward, lifted Gordon, and carried him away.

"Well," Lorenzo stated quietly, "I reckon it's a good thing you got a hard head." He followed Preacher to a boulder and hunkered down.

"Yeah, well, Gordon's got a hard chin. Almost knocked myself out." Preacher worked his jaw.

Dog came and sat at his feet.

Mitchell joined them and sat, as well. "I don't understand it. Out here in the middle of nowhere like we are, an' especially with where we're headed, them soldiers ought to be more tolerable of things. After all, we're likely the one's gonna keep 'em alive when the goin' gets rough . . .

an' it will." He looked at Preacher. "You know where Stone Eyes is headed, don't you?"

"I suspect I do," Preacher said. "Ain't much out here. And you can already smell a trace of all that stink comin' out of that place when the wind catches it just right."

He hadn't smelled it much with dust in his nose and the strong scent of pines and aster, bluebells and paintbrush riding the wind, but it had been there.

"What you're smellin' is Colter's Hell, Preacher," Mitchell said. "That place ain't far from where we are. Maybe another day's ride, an' that stink ain't gonna do nothin' but get worse. By tomorrow noon, ain't gonna be nothin' else we can smell."

"I know."

"Them soldier boys ain't gonna cotton to that place," Lorenzo said. "Ain't gonna cotton to it at all."

"Have you ever been there?" Tall Dog asked.

The young Crow warrior had moved so quietly Preacher hadn't heard him or seen him come up. That irritated the mountain man because it was proof of how tired he was. He'd have to fix that. Tired men made mistakes and ended up dead.

"No," Preacher said. "Never had a reason to go. Not till now. But now I got it to do, and I ain't gonna quit until it's done or I'm dead."

CHAPTER 29

Preacher stared out at the harsh land ahead of him. The mountains had flattened out in places here and made room for Yellowstone Lake. Over the years, the body of water had been known by other names: Eustis Lake, named by William Clark for the then Secretary of War, as well as Sublette's Lake, named for the famous frontiersman who had co-owned the Rocky Mountain Fur Company with his brothers.

The large lake was wide and still, bluish green under the high summer sun. Behind it rose the mountains that marked the harsh lands beyond them.

Somewhere out there to the northeast, Preacher knew, were the falls mentioned in every story John Colter ever told about the area. The waterfall was hidden behind mountains and tall trees. He'd heard a lot about that place, and it was the landmark that would guide him. Those who had seen the falls had reported that they were hard to find unless a man practically rode up on them.

Evidently Stone Eyes marked his own journey by the same landmarks. The Blackfeet tracks and road apples were fresher. The spoor made figuring out which way to go a lot easier, but the mountain man made it a point to not get lulled into believing that he was safe. Any point along the way could be the location of a trap.

Preacher suspected the pursuit was only a day or so behind now. They'd made up time and narrowed the lead the Blackfeet had.

That also meant Stone Eyes probably knew they were coming.

They'd ridden around Yellowstone Lake and were almost to the northeast region where the falls were supposed to be. The falls didn't really have a definitive name because they, like Yellowstone Lake, had known different names. Eventually, Preacher knew, someone would be along to name the falls, and the moniker would stick.

Diller trotted his mount up until he could fall in beside Preacher. Sergeant Gordon kept his distance, but every now and again Preacher caught the big man staring his way.

The Army captain wore his bandanna over his lower face, but Preacher was pretty sure the thin material didn't much cut the noisome stink of sulfur that wafted on the breeze.

"What the hell is that stench?" Diller asked. He blinked shiny tears out of his eye.

"That stench," Preacher said, "means we're gettin' close to Colter's Hell. I think that's where Stone Eyes is headin'. It comes from Stinking Water River."

"Why in God's name would the Blackfeet take sanctuary there?"

"Because most folks, whites and Indians, have heard the stories about that place," Lorenzo said, "an' they don't wanna go up in there because they're afraid ol' Forktail hisownself comes up outta Hell to see who he can pick up an' carry back with him. Sometimes the Devil likes a side of fresh meat."

"I refuse to believe that," Diller snorted.

Lorenzo shrugged. "Suit yourself."

"Any man with half a brain would laugh at that."

"Ain't seein' you laugh none," Lorenzo observed. "An' if you're still carryin' that dead man's glass eye, you might want to rethink that. Ain't nothin' draws Ol' Scratch faster'n a ghost caught up in shiny glass. An' likely that's where what's left of that man killed by the Blackfeet in that holler is residin'."

Diller unconsciously touched his shirt pocket with his left hand.

Preacher had to choke back a laugh of his own. Lorenzo was like a dog with a bone when it came to that glass eye, and his words were having an effect on the Army captain.

"For your information," Diller said, "I need this glass eye for my report. I have to report Milton Walsh's death and need some kind of physical evidence to show my superiors. They expect me to be thorough."

"Well," Lorenzo said, "you shoulda brought back that man's head, too. That way you coulda showed how the eye fit into it. Woulda been more convincin'."

Diller ignored Lorenzo and focused on Preacher. "How far into Colter's Hell do you think Stone Eyes will go?"

Preacher thought about that. "Don't rightly know. That area's supposed to be about a mile to a side, but I ain't ever been there to take its measure. That's unknown territory to me. From what John Colter said—"

"How can you believe a man like that?" Diller demanded. "I've read some of the reports he turned over to the Corps of Discovery. Colter took his leave of Lewis and Clark and went off adventuring on his own."

Preacher bit back a sharp reply. He didn't much care for the way the Army captain was so quick to dismiss what he was being told.

"I've talked with men who knew John Colter," Preacher said. "By all accounts, he was a good mountain man and truthful in everything he did. He turned over reports of his exploration to William Clark. President Thomas Jefferson commended Colter on the work he did."

"What have later explorers had to say about the region?"

"Ain't nobody else mapped it out," Preacher said. "The only map of that area is still what Colter did. Like I said, nobody wants to go there on account of the earthquakes, the boilin' water, and the way the ground vomits up steam and more boilin' water dozens of feet into the air."

Diller shook his head dismissively. "Fanciful tales told by drunken men sitting around a campfire while bored. Each one of them probably tried to be more impressive than the last. Like Mr. Lorenzo's comments about the Devil springing up from the very earth to claim victims. My feeling, like yours, Preacher, is that Stone Eyes chose this place because most people would stay away from it. We are not going to do that."

"No, sir," Preacher said, "we are not."

"Don't let the tall tales turn you back from pursuing those Indians."

Preacher thought about Songbird and her children, how frightened and alone they must be. And if Stone Eyes had carried them up into Colter's Hell, like the mountain man was beginning to suspect, they had to be even more afraid.

"That ain't gonna happen," Preacher said.

Diller reined in his horse and fell back.

"Don't know about you," Lorenzo commented, "but I'm sure glad to see him go. An' I'm glad you're leadin' this little expedition."

"You stay alert," Preacher said. "We're gonna get a whole lot farther into unknown territory before we get out of it."

Two days later, they followed Stone Eyes's trail to the Stinking Water River high in the mountains. They followed the Stinking Water for another three days and constantly ate away at Stone Eyes's lead.

"That Blackfoot is one tough hombre," Peabody Mitchell said that evening. "We've been after them for almost a week an' they're still ahead of us."

"Don't discount them," Preacher said. "They're good in the mountains, and this land is all known to them. We're still learnin' the lay of the land."

"That's because of all them false trails they laid," Seth Thompkins grumbled. "There's a lot of rock out here an' it's easy to lose hoofprints. All they gotta do is carry around a sackful of road apples an' scatter 'em around. We bit on that twice before we learned better."

"But we've learned," Preacher replied. He pointed out at the Stinking Water River. "They won't fool us that way again. As long as they follow the river, we can gain on them again."

"Yeah," Allan Colquhoun groused, "but them little tricks they used cost us some hours."

"We'll get them back," Preacher said. "You gotta remember: it's always easier to be the hunter than the hunted. The hunted has already broken the trail."

* * *

The Stinking Water River whipsawed around the mountains and gradually meandered down to a fork.

Late the following morning, feeling almost rested, Preacher stood atop a promontory in the rugged country and peered down at the fork. The air was thick with sulfur but remained breathable.

"You figure out where we're at?" Lorenzo asked.

Preacher pointed toward the river fork. "Hugh Glass told me Colter's story best. He had the most detail and was always a man good with rememberin' things. Glass knew the Yellowstone area as good as any man I ever knew. These mountains lost a good man when the Arikara killed him back in thirty-three. Accordin' to Glass, we'll find the entrance to Colter's Hell about two miles on the other side of that fork."

Lorenzo took a breath. "Then we'll be there 'long about sunset."

"Yeah."

"You know what else I'm thinkin'?" Lorenzo asked.

"That sunset in that place would be a good chance for an ambush?"

Lorenzo shook his head. "Plumb scary how we sometimes think alike."

"It's mostly about the bad things." Preacher grinned. "What does that say about you?"

"That I'm a man who plans on keepin' his hair."

Preacher laughed, and it felt good to do so because he'd expected to have bad news by now. He was hopeful that they could rescue the hostages. So far, they hadn't found the bodies of any the Blackfeet had killed. That also meant the Indians viewed their prisoners as trade collateral.

He glanced back at the mountain men and soldiers taking a few minutes to rest and break their fast. It was probably going to be the last time they had a chance to do that.

Somewhere up ahead, three sharp explosions split the faint noise of the wilderness that filled the mountains. They sounded like cannons, and the thunder of them sent a shiver of fear through Preacher. The last time he'd heard something that loud, cannons had been involved.

In the distance, a smoke cloud drifted up from the treetops and rode the slight breeze. A faint quiver ran through the promontory and up Preacher's legs. Whatever had happened, it had shook the ground.

That was something to think about.

Hours later, Preacher called a halt to the expedition. Rifle in hand, he swung down off Horse. Dog came over to him and walked at his side.

"Why did we stop?" Captain Diller demanded.

"Checkin' somethin'," Preacher replied.

Behind him, Lorenzo, Tall Dog, Peabody Mitchell, and the rest of the mountain men set up with their rifles to cover Preacher as he clambered up the steep incline on his left.

All of the men were spooked. The eerie, unexplainable cannonade had continued, and the air was more foul than ever. The white clouds grew more dense and more regular, like whatever waited for them up ahead was growing excited at the prospect of them coming along.

The small creek they'd followed ran through the mountains here. Another false trail had been laid along the Stinking Water River and the one along the creek had almost been hidden. Preacher, though, hadn't fallen for the trick because he remembered the stories Hugh Glass had told him about John Colter's adventures over a glass of whiskey in Fort Kiowa shortly before the mountain man had died.

Over time, the creek had sliced down into the soil and created a channel through the mountains. It was a good hiding spot and looked foreboding. With the trees and the tall spires around them, the trail became narrow and was trapped between the hard, ridged shoulders of the mountains.

Preacher was sure there was a way around the narrow area. There always was with a river. But this was the way Stone Eyes and the Blackfeet had come.

Another couple of blistering explosions drifted back from the area ahead of them.

"What do you need to check?" Diller called up.

Preacher faced the pine tree he'd singled out because it was the tallest one around. He worked for a moment to push branches out of his way. He scanned the trunk and found what he was searching for: the letters JC, just a little taller than the width of his hand, were carved into the tree. The scars were old and weathered.

"This." Preacher pulled aside branches to reveal the letters. "John Colter carved this into the tree at the entrance to the area he warned folks about."

"Colter's Hell," Barney Thompkins said softly.

The name was picked up by the mountain men and the soldiers.

Even up near the tree, Preacher sensed the fear running through the mounted men before him. All of them had heard the stories. Even if they hadn't already known them, they'd heard them on the ride to this place. He'd heard whispered snatches of the stories around the campfires last night, and he'd caught other discussions during the past days.

"You men quieten down," Diller ordered. "Those stories are a lot of old wives' tales and nonsense."

"John Colter wasn't a man prone to old wives' tales an' nonsense," Peabody Mitchell declared. "His name is respected up here in these mountains."

"There's monsters back in there," a soldier squawked.

"Wasn't nothin' said about monsters," Allan Colquhoun stated. He stood in his stirrups and glared back in the direction of the soldiers.

"Then what do you think is back there?" Carroll Daly asked. He was a young mountain man, but he'd been to see the elephant and could handle his own against men and beasts.

Preacher released the branches and let them cover the carved letters. He stood straight and tall. "I'll tell you what's back there," he roared.

They all turned to look at him.

"Those women and children that got taken from the Crow tribes are back there. And so is Stone Eyes and his warriors. You want somethin' to worry about, you worry about whether or not you're good enough to stand up to them Blackfeet and bring those innocents home in one piece."

Preacher climbed down to level ground and they watched him. Those who were afraid weren't happy about him shaming them, but he wasn't going to back off. He needed to know right now who he could count on.

"Colter told stories about a land different than any of us have ever seen," Preacher said. "That ain't nothin' that any of us couldn't say before we got up in these mountains.

That's why we come here. To see what we could see." He looked around at the men gathered there and the swell of his own convictions filled him. "If I ever have a day come up on me where I don't want to go look at something nobody's ever seen before, well, you can just come on by and kick dirt over me, 'cause I'm a dead man. You know what I'm really afraid of?"

He stared at them, challenging them to answer him.

No one did.

"I'm afraid of livin' long enough that there ain't still somethin' new and excitin' to see." Preacher squared up his hat, took a fresh grip on his rifle, and he walked over to Horse with Dog at his heels.

They watched him in silence, and each man would have to make his own decision.

"I'm goin' in there," Preacher said, "and I ain't comin' back without those women and children. Safe and un-harmed. And I plan on puttin' Stone Eyes's head on a stick in the doin' of it."

He stepped up into the saddle and threw a leg across Horse. He rode forward, into the mouth of the entrance to Colter's Creek. After a moment, hooves thudded behind him and kept coming.

Ahead of him, cannons boomed again, white smoke filled the narrow space above the treetops, and the stench of burning Hell filled his nostrils. He kept riding.

CHAPTER 30

U p on the mountain on the south side of Little Stink
Water, Stone Eyes watched the line of riders that
came around a bend of the waterway below the cave where
he and his warriors kept the prisoners they'd taken from
the Crow camp. He watched them through the spyglass he
had gotten from Tobit Moon Deer when they'd first begun
trading in Nuevo Mexico.

Stone Eyes focused on the man leading the riders. He
had never seen Ghost Killer, but he knew this was that
man. He could be no other.

Despite the strange things going on across the wide
expanse of the Stinking Land on either side of the creek,
Ghost Killer didn't falter. He followed the trail Bear Kills
Many and others had laid down for him to find.

The trail didn't go much farther. It didn't have to. Death
waited in the caves on either side of the creek. None of the
riders would be spared.

"They're here," Bear Kills Many called up from a
ledge below.

"I know," Stone Eyes replied. "Wait until Hog Snout
speaks. When he has sounded, when the whites are con-
fused, then we will strike. Not until then."

Hog Snout was what Silent Owl had called the large hole below that spewed boiling water and mud at regular intervals. The first time Silent Owl had seen it, when Stone Eyes had discovered this place, he had been terrified. But, like any good warrior, Silent Owl had stood his ground and taken aim with his rifle.

Stone Eyes remembered his dead son well, and he hardened his heart for what would come. No white would ever live that would see mercy from him. He would kill all of those who dared come up into the mountains. When the numbers of his warriors grew large enough, he would take back the lands below the mountains.

And he would start with Ghost Killer, the man who had taken his son from him.

He put the spyglass away and looked along the line of four rifles he had set up for himself in the cave. The space was large and held him and six of his best warriors. It also held the Crow women and children tied up at the rear of the cave near the supplies he had stockpiled from ambushed wagon trains.

The roar of the spirits in the earth in this place filled the cave. It wouldn't be long before Hog Snout spewed again, and that would signal the attack. If Hog Snout didn't spew, the whites would only be allowed to travel a little farther.

They had tracked Stone Eyes for days just to come and die in this place.

The Blackfeet chieftain took up one of his rifles and knelt on the ledge in front of the cave. He remained out of sight and aimed the rifle at Ghost Killer a hundred and fifty yards away.

His finger curled around the trigger and held firm.

The ground quivered and Hog Snout growled out in the creek.

For all the strange things Preacher had ever seen, from the Pacific Ocean coastline to the Great Lakes and down to the Gulf of Mexico, he had never seen anything like Colter's Hell. Colquhoun and Peabody Mitchell compared the bubbling ground and water to stories they'd heard traveling gospel shows mention.

Mitchell had talked about a meeting he'd gone to in New York before he'd come west. Mitchell had, for a time, been apprenticed to a cobbler. While he was there, he witnessed Reverend Charles Finney bar slave owners and traders from communion. Then the fiery-tongued minister went on to paint a picture of Hell and the evils that waited there that practically scared a younger Peabody Mitchell across the Mississippi.

Even last night around the campfire, Mitchell could recount Finney's elocution almost word-for-word. At least, it had sounded that way, because the way Mitchell had put the words together certainly wasn't like the way he normally spoke.

That recitation had had a powerful effect on his listeners, too.

The men were afraid of the world they'd stepped into. Boiling water came up out of the ground and mixed with water that was like ice only a few feet upstream. Shallows held currents that were interrupted by holes that opened up in the ground and vented large bubbles of the foul, sulfurous gas that filled the air with the stink of rotten eggs and white clouds.

The acrid smoke stung Preacher's eyes, and he blinked

to clear them. His lungs burned from breathing, and he didn't favor the prospect of carrying on much farther.

Still, the trail was clearly marked ahead of him. Several unshod horses had come this way. Those hoofprints had left clear markings across the land beside Colter's Creek all the way up around the next bend.

One of the things that bothered Preacher most was the lack of life along this part of the creek. Water was a place where fish lived and where animals and birds came to slake their thirst.

He'd seen none of that in quite a while. Most of the water was far too hot for fish to live in, and neither he nor Horse nor Dog would drink the creek water.

He passed another cave on his right, on the north face of the mountains on either side of the creek. There were a whole lot of caves, but Preacher couldn't imagine anything that would live in them.

Yet this was where Stone Eyes had come. The Blackfeet chieftain was probably counting on all the stories to keep outsiders away. His thinking was clever, but taking the Crow women and children had been a mistake. So was being after those rifles.

Preacher intended to put a stop to all that.

His thoughts splintered as a dull, unearthly moan came from somewhere ahead of him. Horse flinched but kept striding forward. Dog growled irritably.

"You hear that?" Lorenzo asked. He was following the mountain man.

"I do," Preacher replied. He took a fresh grip on his rifle.

"I sure will be proud when we get shut of this place."

Preacher didn't have anything to say to that. He kept his gaze moving across the wide expanse of shallow water.

Only malformed trees and stubborn scrub brush grew in a few places.

The moan died away and the ground rumbled and moved like it had come undone. Horse slowed and lifted his hooves carefully.

Ahead and to the left, a stream of water spewed up out of the creek. A deluge of mud followed it and quickly built up a cone-shaped structure around it. The water crested thirty feet up and Preacher followed it with his gaze.

That was what saved him. Twenty feet above ground, he caught sight of a cave mouth. A handful of Blackfeet were posted there with rifles.

Moving automatically, Preacher put his heels to Horse's sides. Already tense from the spewing water, Horse bolted forward and the ball that was meant for Preacher smashed against the mountainside behind him.

"Ambush!" Preacher yelled. "Scatter and grab cover!"

He pulled his rifle to his shoulder, fought to get his bearings with the world thundering around him and hot water droplets burning his exposed hands, face, and neck. He slid the front sight over the chest of a Blackfoot and squeezed the trigger.

Struck by the ball, the Indian toppled down the mountainside twenty feet and lay half-submerged in a bubbling cauldron of hot water.

"Up on the mountain!" Preacher shouted.

He swapped hands with his rifle and drew one of the Colt Patersons. The distance for a handgun was difficult at best, chances made worse while on top of a moving horse and made even more difficult by the thick haze of smoke hanging in the air.

Several rifles cracked behind Preacher and lead smears

suddenly decorated the mountainside. Duller gray gun smoke mixed with the clean white of the spouting water.

As he took aim with the pistol and searched for a clear vantage point for the gun battle, a group of Blackfeet lined the mouth of a cave on the other side of the creek. A few of them had rifles and the rest had bows. From twenty yards out, the creek became a death ground.

"Other side!" Preacher yelled.

He aimed the Paterson at the cave and fired, rolled the hammer back and fired again and again until he'd emptied all of the revolver's chambers. It was impossible to miss hitting someone. Three Blackfeet went down with balls in their chests. Two more dropped, but Preacher couldn't see where he'd hit them. More rifles roared behind him and rounds chewed into the Blackfeet while arrows sailed across the creek.

Men yelled behind Preacher and the tones told him some of the mountain men and the soldiers were probably mortally wounded. Jammed up like this, he knew they would be hard hit. A lot of them were going to die.

Preacher slung the rifle over his shoulder and swapped out revolvers. He fired into the cave again and killed more of the Blackfeet in there. He glanced around and realized there was no escape. Going back was impossible because the path was narrow and constricted. They would only get in each other's way.

Going forward along the creek wouldn't work because they would remain exposed to enemy guns.

He sheathed the empty revolver and drew one of his double-shotted pistols. The mountain men and soldiers were scattered across the mountainside with nowhere to run.

"If you want to live, follow me!" Preacher put his heels in Horse's sides and reined the big stallion toward the cave.

He hated exposing Horse in the risky attack, but his companion was already in danger from the ambush. Horse galloped across the stream, and hot spray drenched Preacher's legs. He fired the pistol in his hand, put both balls through the head of a Blackfoot warrior in front of him, and drew his remaining pistol with his other hand. He fired again, put both spent pistols in their saddle holsters, and drew his tomahawk and big hunting knife.

Arrows sliced through Horse's wild mane and flitted by Preacher. One left a trail of fire along his right cheek and another picked his hat right off his head. Without breaking stride, Horse crashed into the Blackfoot warriors, sent them spinning, and cleared a hole in the line.

Dog vaulted up from the ground and closed his massive jaws over the face of the nearest Blackfoot. The warrior fell back, dropped his bow, and locked his fingers over Dog's teeth. The effort didn't do him any good because the big cur crunched his opponent's skull. Muzzle covered in blood not his own, Dog clamped onto the leg of the nearest Blackfoot, ran, then set himself and whipped the Indian off his feet.

Behind the Indians in the cave now, Preacher slid off Horse and faced the Blackfeet in the cave with the tomahawk and hunting knife in his hands. Before the Indians could re-establish their line, the mountain men crashed into the cave on their horses.

Chaos and confusion filled the chamber. Screams of wounded and dying men mixed with the howl of holes opening up in the land and in the creek outside. Some of the mountain men and soldiers still had unspent pistols. They fired at pointblank range. More Blackfeet fell to the rough, uneven cave floor. Blood spilled everywhere and made footing slippery.

Preacher blocked a Blackfoot's knife thrust with his tomahawk and slashed his attacker's throat. He stepped forward and claimed ground. He cleaved the skull of a Blackfoot in front of him with the tomahawk and wrenched it free of the falling body. Another Blackfoot swung a warclub overhead and Preacher crossed his weapons and caught the club in the X they formed. Even then, he barely prevented the weapon from braining him. He lifted a foot and drove it into his attacker's belly. The Blackfoot yelled in pain but never got to draw another breath because Preacher's tomahawk smashed in his temple.

The white vapor from the things outside filled the space between the mountains and rolled into the caves. The air grew hot and burned every time Preacher took a lungful. He blinked tears from his eyes and tried to clear his vision.

He drove his knife into the throat of another man and blood filled one of his eyes. He tried to sleeve the blood out so he could see. Another Blackfoot warrior came at him singing a deathsong. Preacher dodged to one side, saw Dog coming toward him, and kicked the Indian's legs out from under him.

"Dog, kill!" Preacher snarled.

The big cur leaped on the downed Blackfoot before he could recover.

Eye free of blood now, Preacher spotted Lorenzo defending himself against two Blackfeet. He stepped forward, drove his hunting knife down into the closest man's collarbone, and yanked him back. Squalling in pain, the Blackfoot tried to bring his knife around, but Preacher planted his tomahawk in the man's neck and shoved him away to die on his own.

Lorenzo slammed the butt of his rifle into his remaining opponent's groin, then lifted the weapon and hammered it down against the back of the man's skull. Bone splintered and the Blackfoot dropped limply.

"Thanks," Lorenzo gasped. His face was a mask of blood. He glanced around. "Looks like we got some breathin' space."

Glancing around the cave, Preacher saw that the tide had turned. It was difficult to see everything in the cave due to the horses milling around and the white smoke still drifting in from outside, but it was apparent that the mountain men and the soldiers held the high ground. Skirmishes were still going on, and Tall Dog stood with his sword in both hands and a pile of body pieces around him, but the Blackfeet were defeated.

Hat missing and face bloodied, Captain Diller strode over to Preacher. "Surprised you're still alive. That was one of the most courageous or most stupid things I've ever seen. I still don't know which way I'm going to call it, but I'm leaning toward lucky."

"This ain't over," Preacher said. He took his rifle from his shoulder and reached into his possibles bag for a cartridge. He reloaded his weapons as he spoke. "Stone Eyes is on the other side of the stream, and he has the hostages."

"Half of his men have been killed," Diller said. "I'd say his defeat is at hand."

Preacher shook his head. "You can't hem a fightin' man in and give him no way to win or withdraw from a situation. If you do that, you're forcin' him to defy the odds and try his luck. Same as we did when we charged the Indians in this cave." Weapons readied, he sleeved blood that was not his own, mostly, from his face. "Luck has a bad habit of turnin' against you at the wrong time if you try to depend on it."

Diller firmed his jaw. "I make my own luck. I always have."

"You're lucky that ha'nt-filled glass eye ain't killed you," Lorenzo said.

Diller ignored the comment. "The question remains, what are we going to do about Stone Eyes?"

"Ghost Killer!" a man yelled from across the creek. "Unless you want me to start killing these Crow women and children, come out and talk to me."

"Speak the devil's name," Lorenzo muttered, "an' he does appear."

CHAPTER 31

"Ghost Killer!" the man called again.

Out of choices and not wanting the hostages harmed, Preacher walked to the front of the cave and took shelter against the edge. He scanned the mountainside across the stream through the white smoke that eddied through the enclosed space. He brought his rifle to his shoulder, willed himself to be patient, and waited on a good shot to present itself. If he could kill Stone Eyes, that might break the whole standoff in their favor.

The problem was, Preacher didn't know what Stone Eyes looked like.

No Blackfeet were visible in the cave mouth twenty feet up the mountainside.

"Is that you, Stone Eyes?" Preacher asked.

"Yes, it is me."

"Show yourself."

Stone Eyes laughed. "I have heard of your sharp-shooting skills, Ghost Killer. I will not be doing that."

"All right," Preacher said. "What do you want?"

"To kill you for killing my son."

"He died well. Stood tall and intended to kill me till he couldn't do that anymore."

Silence hung over the space between the two halves of the mountain for a moment. The low moaning still echoed, and the ground shivered. Preacher wondered if that hole in the creek was going to spew water and mud again. What looked like a small pot sat in the middle of the stream and parted the water. He could dimly see the structure through the white fog. The pot looked like it was sagging, no longer fierce.

"I will give you the chance to stand tall before you die," Stone Eyes said.

"What do you mean?"

"Come and fight me."

"We can fight out here," Preacher said easily, like they were talking about the weather but not the strange events that were even now taking place around them. "Plenty of room."

"I will not do that. Your men will kill me."

"I'm pretty sure your men will kill me if I step out. I guess we're in a stalemate."

"I can kill hostages while I wait," Stone Eyes said. "What can you do?"

Preacher didn't have an answer for that. Tall Dog pushed through the others to stand at Preacher's side. All of them watched him and waited to see what he would do.

"I do not wish for my mother to die," the young Crow warrior said.

"I don't want Songbird or her children to die," Preacher said. "Hold pat and let's see what we can negotiate. This ain't over. He don't want it to be over. Maybe he has hostages, but he also can't let go of this."

"Neither can we."

"I'm not about to, but he don't know that for sure."

Reluctantly, Tall Dog nodded.

"I will make a bargain with you, Ghost Killer," Stone Eyes offered. "Agree to come to me and I will release half of the hostages. Your obedience guarantees half of them will live."

"What about the other half?"

"I will keep them."

"What's to stop us from comin' for them?" Preacher asked.

"The same thing that prevents you now. They will be dead before you reach them."

Preacher tried to figure a way out of the trap Stone Eyes had laid, but he couldn't. If they'd had more time, maybe they could have done something else. But the Blackfeet could starve them out now.

Lorenzo shook his head. "I don't like where this is headed, Preacher. Havin' them hostages cut loose like that is just gonna put them in harm's way. They'll be sittin' ducks out there."

"I know."

"That ain't like he's really releasin' them."

"I know that, too. We didn't come all this way just to give up. Besides that"—Preacher looked around the cave where the surviving members of the rescue party stood— "there's no easy way out of here for us, either."

"Maybe come night—"

Preacher shook his head. "Ain't no way he's gonna wait that long. There's still hours before dusk."

"Did you hear me, Ghost Killer?" Stone Eyes asked.

"I did," Preacher replied. "Send them out."

He watched tensely as ten Crow women and children

were herded down a series of irregular steps cut into the mountainside. They reached the bottom and stopped.

"My mother is not among them," Tall Dog said.

Preacher nodded. Songbird and her children weren't out there, either.

Lorenzo ducked out of the cave and waved to the hostages. "Y'all get on in here."

One of the older women with a baby in her arms shook her head. "We cannot. If we move from this place, we will be shot."

Preacher scanned the rifle barrels pointed out over the ledge where the cave was. The sharpshooters likely wouldn't get all ten of the released hostages, but even one getting hurt was more than he was willing to allow.

Lorenzo cursed and stepped back inside the cave. He took an angry breath and released it. "Told you we can't trust that lyin' snake."

"Ghost Killer," Stone Eyes said. "I am waiting. While I wait, I will slit the throats of those women and children I still have. Perhaps some of those before you will get away, but none of those inside this place will live."

The women and children near the stream wept. Three of them collapsed in fear. They'd been worn out over the last few days with all the traveling they'd done, in addition to their capture and the deaths of their loved ones at the Crow camp.

"I will count to ten," Stone Eyes said, "then I will slit the first throat."

"All right," Preacher said. "You don't have to count. I'm comin' out."

"If you do," Diller said hoarsely, "you're a damn fool. You won't stand a chance."

"Likely not," Preacher agreed. "But I ain't dead yet, and I know for a fact that Stone Eyes will kill those prisoners. They don't stand a chance, either."

He unbelted the holsters with the Colt Patersons and handed them to Lorenzo. Then he added his rifle and the two flintlock pistols. The tomahawk and knives followed. By the time he was finished, Lorenzo was loaded down.

"I'll be holdin' onto these for you," Lorenzo said. "You just make sure you're around to get 'em."

"I will be." Preacher shot his friend a smile and retreated into the cave.

He bent down, pressed both his hands into a pool of blood, and smeared them all along his right thigh. When he finished, he looked good and bloody.

"What you doin'?" Lorenzo asked.

"It's the best hole card I could cut for myself," Preacher said. "If I look wounded, maybe Stone Eyes won't be expectin' so much from me. This little bit of theater won't last but a minute, but maybe that'll be long enough to give me an edge." He paused. "However this turns out, make sure you get those hostages home."

"I will," Lorenzo said. "You got my word."

"Good luck, Preacher," Peabody Mitchell said. "Time comes you need us, just give a yell an' we'll come a-runnin'."

Preacher nodded.

"Ghost Killer!" Stone Eyes yelled.

"Comin'," Preacher replied.

Limping, he stepped outside the cave and held his arms out to his sides. "Ain't got any guns."

For a moment, nobody said anything.

Preacher wondered if Stone Eyes had planned on shooting him when he showed up. Now that he was unarmed and bloody, vulnerable, the Blackfoot chieftain was probably rethinking how he wanted to handle things. At the end of the day, by all accounts he'd heard, Stone Eyes liked to think he was smarter than everyone else.

At least, that's what Preacher hoped. He felt awfully naked standing there in the open without any weapons.

"Come on, Ghost Killer," Stone Eyes said. "We have our agreement. Come to me."

"I'm comin'."

Continuing to limp, Preacher made a show of crossing the heated stream and climbing the irregular steps. Knowing he was going to be facing a lot of enemy guns while empty-handed was unnerving.

At the top of the carved steps, four Blackfoot braves stood up and formed a human wall between Preacher and the interior of the cave. The mountain man stood there and expected a ball in his teeth at any moment.

One of the Blackfeet checked him for weapons with rough hands, found nothing, and stepped back. "He has no weapons," the man said.

Stone Eyes, big and fierce, stood in the middle of the cave with a pistol in his hand and three more in a sash at his waist. Behind him stood crates, barrels, and bags, all of it doubtlessly taken from the wagon trains he'd ambushed.

In the corner of the room, sixteen more prisoners sat huddled and fearful. Six warriors armed with knives and tomahawks stood guard around them.

Songbird sat with her arms around her two children. Her eyes were fierce, but they were haggard, and tears streaked her face. Neither of them spoke to the other.

Preacher knew they couldn't allow their captor to know they were special.

One of the prisoners was a man, and who he was surprised Preacher.

Joe Len Darby, bruised and battered, sat in the shadows with a bloody face and a length of crimson-stained cloth around his right hand. He grinned and showed missing teeth.

"Hello, Preacher," the man said. "I reckon this time you ain't showin' up to rescue me in time."

"Not likely," Preacher said, and that was the truth. "I found that whiskey flask where Milton Walsh and your other friend died. I know you took those rifles."

A sick grin twisted Darby's face. His eyes were fever bright. "I thought I was lucky that night Silent Owl found me. Never figured on dyin'. Didn't figure on you showin' up at all." He shook his head. "Especially not again. Guess it goes to show you just never know." He licked his split lips. "I wasn't the one who'd taken them rifles the first time, when they was took from Major Voight. I was just followin' orders when I done that."

"Silence," Stone Eyes ordered.

"I guess you found those rifles you were lookin' for," Preacher said to the Blackfoot chief.

Joe Len Darby spat blood onto the cave floor. "Not yet they ain't. Ol' Stone Eyes ain't exactly the trusting sort. I told him where to find them, but he ain't believed me. I done run outta fingers on my right hand on account of him thinkin' I was lyin'."

The man unwrapped his injured hand and revealed the stubs of his fingers. They were crusted with old blood, but bright blobs of fresh blood showed, too.

The Blackfoot warrior standing nearest Darby thumped him on the head with his knife hilt. Squalling in pain, Darby ducked down and cradled his face in his good hand.

Preacher looked at Stone Eyes. "I count sixteen prisoners over there. You let ten go. That wasn't half. You didn't bargain in good faith."

"You are white and the murderer of my only son," the Blackfoot chief said. "I owe you no good faith. I owe you only a death, and it will be a long time in coming. You will plead for me to take your life before I do."

"Ain't likely," Preacher said, and he meant that however the next few minutes went. "You'll want a bigger audience when you get around to that. We've killed over half of your warriors."

"There will be more warriors," Stone Eyes said. "The Blackfoot tribes hate the whites. Once I have those rifles this man took, I will arm more warriors and I will take more rifles to arm still yet more warriors."

"You're puttin' the cart before the horse," Preacher said. "You don't have the rifles Joe Len Darby hid yet."

"I will."

Outside, a hollow boom rang out and another cloud of white fog pushed into the cave mouth. Preacher hoped Lorenzo and the other mountain men took advantage of the confusion to save the hostages standing at the creek.

The Blackfeet in the room appeared startled and glanced at the cave mouth.

Preacher took a step toward Stone Eyes. One of the warriors guarding the mountain man pressed the muzzle of his pistol against Preacher's head.

Knowing he'd never have another chance like this, Preacher reached up quick as a snake striking and placed his hands on the pistol. Viciously, he trapped the weapon and turned it out from the man's palm. The warrior's finger snapped and came free of the pistol's trigger guard.

Luckily, he didn't fire the weapon.

Pistol in hand, Preacher turned it on the guard next to him who was trying to bring his rifle up. When he squeezed his captured pistol's trigger, Preacher put a ball up into the soft part of the man's throat. Still moving, the mountain man hefted the rifle, drove the butt into the throat of the man he'd taken the pistol from, and turned the barrel toward Stone Eyes.

The Blackfoot chief had moved and circled around behind the second warrior who was staggering and clutching his shattered throat. Unable to get a bead on Stone Eyes and knowing he had other warriors in the room going for weapons, Preacher turned the rifle on one of the men standing watch over Joe Len Darby and fired.

The ball caught the warrior in the side of the head and dropped him like a stone.

Darby had more sand in him than Preacher would have given him credit for. With a hoarse yell, the man wrapped his arms around the legs of a second warrior and yanked him from his feet.

Preacher's own troubles took up his full attention. Stone Eyes held pistols in both fists and trained them on the mountain man. Preacher seized the buckskins of the dying Blackfoot in front of him and yanked him into Stone Eyes's line of fire just as the chief fired one of the pistols.

The ball tore into the Indian's back and he stiffened in shock and pain. Preacher shoved the dead man back. Stone Eyes dodged away, dropped his spent pistol, and reached for another at his waist.

Knowing he didn't have any moves left, Preacher threw

himself at Stone Eyes and knocked the man back. He rode him to the ground and the chief fired his second pistol so close to the side of Preacher's head the powder burning off scalded his cheek and one side of his mouth.

Stone Eyes raised his body and slithered, and when the struggling was done, he came out on top of Preacher.

"I am going to kill you!" Stone Eyes shouted.

Preacher saved his breath for fighting and grappled with his opponent. He had locks on the chief's wrists, but Stone Eyes broke them again and again.

Over in the corner where the Crow prisoners sat huddled, Songbird stood and darted in behind one of the Blackfeet jockeying for position on Joe Len Darby's fight with the guard he'd tied up with. She picked up the rifle the warrior Preacher had killed had dropped and eared back the hammer. When the warrior turned around, she shot him in the face at pointblank range.

The dead man fell across Darby and the warrior he battled.

Preacher struggled, bucked, and managed to get Stone Eyes off him. They pushed themselves to their feet. The chief reached for another pistol at his waist, but he'd lost it in the mad scramble with Preacher. He wrapped a fist around the hunting knife sheathed on his side.

"Kill the hostages!" Stone Eyes roared.

"No!" Preacher shouted.

He dove for one of Stone Eyes's lost pistols, came up with it, and shot one of the warriors who turned his weapon on the Crow women and children. The ball slammed into the side of the warrior's head, and he stumbled a moment before going down.

Stone Eyes, his hunting knife clutched in his fist, ran toward Preacher. They slammed together and the chief's momentum drove Preacher into the wall at his back. The air left his lungs in a rush and black spots whirled in his vision.

For a moment he thought he'd imagined the shapes within the swirling white cloud that eddied into the cave. Then he spotted Captain Diller leading a charge and coming out of the fog. Evidently, he'd decided to take advantage of the next round of spewing and the confusion it brought.

Rifles blazed and the sharp cracks thundered against Preacher's ears. He fought Stone Eyes tooth and nail and narrowly avoided getting stabbed again and again. Pain burned along his neck, and he knew one of the attempts had come awfully close to ending things for him.

Despite the arrival of the soldiers, Stone Eyes remained fixated on killing Preacher with single-minded devotion. Preacher dodged another stabbing attempt, then smashed a hard right hand into his opponent's throat again and again.

Staggered, out of breath and unable to breathe, Stone Eyes pulled back. Preacher gave the chief no respite. He yanked the knife from Stone Eyes's hand and drove the blade through his temple. The light in the warrior's eyes dimmed. Preacher shoved the dead man away from him and gazed around the room.

Diller's soldiers had accounted for most of the Blackfoot warriors and none of them remained a threat to the Crow women and children.

"Cap'n Diller!" Joe Len Darby yelled, and stood up from the man he'd killed. He held a pistol in his good hand. "I knew you'd come on account—"

Diller raised his rifle and shot Darby. A shocked look

stretched Darby's face. He dropped the pistol and it hit so hard the ball rolled from the muzzle.

Coolly, Diller took a cartridge from his possibles bag and tore it open. He reloaded his rifle and stared at Preacher.

"Kill them all, Sergeant Gordon," Diller ordered. "We're leaving no witnesses."

Gordon stepped away from his commanding officer and raised his rifle. "You heard the captain, men. Kill them all."

Diller aimed at Preacher. "Nothing personal, Preacher. You just hit a streak of bad luck."

Another shadow stepped out of the swirling white smoke. A long blade briefly caught the light, then it swept into the first of the soldiers and cut off his arms. Two more died from two more blows.

By that time, Gordon realized there was a killer among them. He turned, bellowed a warning, and lifted his rifle. Moving on, the sword wielder thrust the blade into Gordon. The dying sergeant stumbled back and slammed into Diller.

The captain sprawled forward, almost lost his rifle, and a small round object popped out of his shirt pocket and rolled toward Preacher.

Diller scrambled up to his knees at the same time Preacher intercepted Milton Walsh's glass eye and reached out for the pistol Joe Len Darby had dropped. The ball had dropped out of the muzzle, but the load was still primed.

Stubbornly, frantically, the Army captain swung his rifle toward Preacher. The mountain man shoved the glass eye into the pistol barrel, mashed it in as far as he could, and eared the hammer back. He aimed and fired by instinct, and he knew from the first sharp crack that Diller had gotten his shot off first.

The Army captain's ball plucked at Preacher's buckskins but missed his body.

Milton Walsh's glass eye found its final resting place somewhere inside Diller's brain.

More shadows charged in through the whirling white smoke, and Lorenzo and Peabody Mitchell led the second charge. Their rifles cracked, and the few survivors of Diller's soldiers surrendered.

Nearly deaf, hurting and bloody, Preacher stood and reached into Stone Eyes's possibles bag. He reloaded his captured pistol instinctively and gazed around the room.

Songbird held her children to her. The other hostages were safe and sound.

"Preacher," Joe Len Darby whispered hoarsely.

The mountain man walked over to Darby and looked down into his panic-stricken eyes.

"I'm dyin', ain't I?" Darby asked.

"Yeah." Preacher wasn't going to shy from the truth.

"It was my fault," Darby gasped. "Diller set up the theft of the rifles from Major Voight. He figured Pierre Chouteau had plenty of money, an' Diller wanted some of it. So, he arranged to rob the cargo detail. Me an' Milton Walsh, we got some men together an' took them rifles on south. That way Diller could play his part and chase after the Blackfeet who killed Voight an' the others. None of us figured on gettin' found out by Stone Eyes. That was just bad luck."

Preacher listened, but he'd already surmised most of it. Diller's shooting of Darby had only cinched the deal. He'd known it was dangerous to ride into Colter's Hell with the Army captain and his soldiers, but he'd needed the extra firepower against Stone Eyes and the Blackfeet warriors.

"Me an' Walsh an' the others hid them rifles," Darby continued. A worm of blood escaped his mouth and bloody spittle flecked his chin whiskers. "I can tell you right where we hid them. You can find them." He gasped, blinked, and when he opened his eyes, they weren't quite as focused.

Preacher bent close and listened to Darby's directions. The man finished them right before he died.

CHAPTER 32

The Crow had relocated to an area farther downriver from where they'd been when Preacher had first found them. The spot wasn't as fine as the first one had been, but the graze was good for the horses they had, there was game, and there would be fishing.

Preacher rode at the head of the expedition returning from Colter's Hell. They'd taken their time getting back so the women and children could regain the strength they'd lost.

Not everybody who had ridden after Stone Eyes had returned. Seth Thompkins and four other mountain men had died in the battle along Colter's Creek. They were all men who were brave and fierce and had left their marks in the mountains, some of which was in the return of the hostages. Those stories would be told for years to come.

After the battle, they'd carried their dead outside of Colter's Hell because no one was comfortable with putting them in the ground there, and Oscar Ferrell scouted out a good, high spot to put them back into the clean earth they deserved.

There would be sadness in the camp to learn of the

newest losses, Preacher knew, but he was also certain the return of the women and children would outweigh that. At least, it would in time.

Blue Magpie, looking much better now, bravely limped out to meet his wife and children. Doe with Joy and his other children trailed after him.

All around Preacher, families reunited with tears and glad hearts because many of them had feared those who were taken would never return.

That night, a big feast was arranged. In addition to the supplies Preacher had brought in from what the Blackfeet had stolen, the mountain men had taken a dozen pronghorn just since that morning. The fresh meat, along with foodstuffs the Crows did not usually get, was welcome.

Later, in the dark, Preacher stepped away from the singing and dancing, from the crying and laughing, and went to take care of Horse. The big stallion had suffered a few wounds during the Battle of Colter's Creek, as Peabody Mitchell and Lorenzo were calling it, but all of those were healing well. Horse would be fighting fit soon enough.

Preacher worked the big animal with a curry comb and Horse's skin jumped and rippled in appreciation of the attention.

A shadow cast by the mostly full moon slid behind Preacher and he waited for his visitor to speak. He took a little pride in the fact that he sensed the man before he was surprised by him. The shadow of the sword over one shoulder gave away the man's identity.

"Preacher," Tall Dog said.

"Yeah?" Preacher put down the curry comb and turned to face the young Crow warrior. "Your ma all right?"

Tall Dog nodded. "She is. My father is getting healthy again, too."

"That's good."

"It is."

"Her Bible's okay?"

After they had rescued the hostages, Tall Dog's ma had been frantic to find the Bible her husband's family had made. The Blackfeet had taken it, too, because she'd been holding onto it and refused to let it go. Then, after they'd taken it from her, she'd feared the warriors had thrown it away.

"Yes." Tall Dog smiled. "She insists that Bible was the reason we were all saved."

"We had us some good luck while we were there," Preacher admitted. "It's not exactly customary for me to trust a whole lot outside of my own skin, but maybe we had someone watchin' over us."

"She says that." Tall Dog paused. "Lorenzo says you are going to go after those rifles Joe Len Darby and those men hid in the mountains."

"I am. I can't leave them out there for them to maybe fall into the wrong hands."

"What will you do with them?"

"I reckon I'll take them in to Fort Pierre," Preacher said. "That's where they belong. Pierre Chouteau can sell them to settlers headed west. With all the Blackfoot trouble along the way, and other hostiles, folks will need good weapons they can depend on. I also want to get word to the Army about what really happened to Major Voight, and let them know about the part Captain Diller played in all of it."

"Lorenzo says he may not go, that he is getting too old for the kind of trouble you get into."

Preacher smiled because he could imagine Lorenzo saying that very thing. "Yeah, he's said that before."

"I am not too old," Tall Dog said. "And I want to see more of these mountains. If you will allow it, I would like to ride with you to get those rifles."

Preacher didn't have to think about it long. The young Crow warrior had proven himself several times.

"All right," the mountain man said. "Be glad to have you along."

Later still, Preacher and Tall Dog sat in front of a campfire where the mountain men and some of the Crow warriors gathered. They shared food and some whiskey that had been in the supplies the expedition to Colter's Hell had brought back.

Although he was a modest man, Preacher didn't mind so much the stories Lorenzo told about the final battle with Diller and his men and Stone Eyes and the Blackfoot warriors. The tales were something he wouldn't have sat still for if entirely sober, but he was half-drunk, stuffed with good food, and Dog lay beside him to have his ears scratched.

"Tell it again," one of the young mountain men said. "About the way Preacher shot that captain with a glass eye."

Lorenzo threw a few more twigs into the fire. "I already told that story."

"It's a good story, Lorenzo, an' you tell it right fine."

Preacher knew it didn't take much to get his friend talking. Somebody passed Lorenzo the bottle. He took a pull and held onto it. Nobody objected. Most of them leaned in closer.

"There they was," Lorenzo said, "on their knees facin'

each other. Cap'n Diller's haulin' up his rifle. Preacher's sittin' there with a pistol load that ain't got no ball in it. Plain an' simple, it looks like it's over."

Not a sound was heard except the popping of the wood burning in the fire.

"But it ain't over," Lorenzo said, "because up jumps that ha'nted glass eye Diller's been carryin' around, against my best advice, mind you, an' it scampers across the cave, skippin' an' hoppin' like a frog in a hot skillet, right to Preacher. 'Take me,' it says. An' Preacher does. He grabs that glass eye, shoved it into that pistol, an' he fires it into Diller's forehead."

He touched a spot over his left eye and stared at the mountain men who hung on his every word.

"An' then you know what?" Lorenzo asked.

"What?" the young mountain man asked.

"Why then, that glass eye *winked* right before it nestled right there in Diller's brain," Lorenzo said.

Everyone gathered around the campfire laughed uproariously.

And that, Preacher knew, was how legends started in the wild mountains and drifted on into encroaching civilization. He wondered if the story would beat him back to St. Louis, and he figured it probably would because he wasn't going back to so-called civilization any time soon if he could help it.

TURN THE PAGE FOR AN EXCITING PREVIEW!

JOHNSTONE COUNTRY.
WHERE LEGENDS DIE HARD.

Riding shotgun, Red Ryan leads a doomed stagecoach of
the damned on the longest, deadliest journey of his life.

5 PASSENGERS. 400 MILES. 1,000 WAYS TO DIE.

According to local legend, the stagecoach known as the
Gray Ghost is either haunted, cursed, or just plain unlucky.
Each of its last three drivers came to a violent, bloody end.
And now it's Red Ryan's turn to guard five foolhardy
passengers on the stage's next—and possibly last—trip
to El Paso. The travelers are a small troupe of performers
with dark histories of their own: a song-and-dance man
with a drinking problem, a juggler with a secret,
a singer, a knife thrower with a past, and a beautiful fan
dancer who's on the run from a one-eyed, vengeance-
seeking outlaw . . .

Red's not the superstitious type. But with Apaches on
the warpath—and a one-eyed cutthroat killer on his trail—
this 400-mile journey is like something straight out of his
worst nightmare. And all the roads lead straight to hell . . .

National Bestselling Authors William W. Johnstone
and J.A. Johnstone

LAST STAGE TO EL PASO

A Red Ryan Western

On sale now, wherever Pinnacle Books are sold.

Live Free. Read Hard. www.williamjohnstone.

CHAPTER 1

In the late summer of 1889, a six-horse team brought the Abbot and Morrison mail stage safely home to San Angelo . . . with two dead men in the box.

"How many does that make?" Captain Anton Decker said.

Long John Abbot looked miserable. Stunned. His bearded face ashen. "Six," he said. He shook his head. "I can't believe Phineas Doyle and Dewey Wilcox are dead. Just like that . . . dead."

"Believe it, they're all shot to pieces," Major Lewis Kane, the 10th Cavalry doctor, said. Gray-haired with a deeply lined face, he didn't appear too old to be a doctor but was well past his prime as an army officer. He climbed down from the box, shook his head, and added, "There's nothing I can do for them. They look like they've been dead for several hours."

Captain Decker, at twenty-seven, the youngest company commander in Fort Concho, was somewhat less than sympathetic. He badly wanted a name as an Indian fighter, but the Plains tribes were subdued and there was little glamour in fighting Apaches. "I'll report the incident to Colonel

Grierson but I'm sure he'll agree that this is a civilian matter," he said.

"The army could help me round up the road agents that are responsible for my six dead," Abbot said.

"As I said, I believe it's a strictly civilian matter," Decker said. "Perhaps if your stages were carrying army payrolls we would've taken an interest, but since they were not, it's unlikely Colonel Grierson will become involved, especially after the 10th Cavalry moved out and left us so undermanned."

"I'll talk to the county sheriff," Abbot said. "But he won't do anything."

"Try him. He might round up a posse or something."

Abbot laid bleak eyes on the soldier. "He'll sit in his chair with his feet on his desk, drink coffee, and give me sympathy, not a posse."

"That's just too bad," Decker said. He saluted smartly. "Your obedient servant, Mr. Abbot. Now, see to your dead."

"Two more, Long John," said Max Brewster, a small man dressed in buckskins, dwarfed by Abbot's six foot six and maybe a little more height. "On the El Paso run like the other four."

Brewster had once been a first-rate whip until the rheumatisms in both hands done for him. Now he wore a plug hat and his stained and ragged buckskins and helped around the Abbot and Morrison stage depot. He favored a pipe that belched smoke that smelled bad.

"Phineas Doyle dead, murdered," Abbot said, shaking his head. "He was the best whip in Texas, bar none."

"And afore him, it was me," Brewster said. "Leastwise, that's what folks said."

"I ain't gonna dispute that, Max," Abbot said. He was a slightly round-shouldered man wearing a sweat-stained hat, a white collarless shirt, narrow suspenders, and black pants tucked into mule-ear boots. A man who never carried a gun, he now had a Remington tucked into his waistband, a sure sign that the death of his men had shaken him to the core.

"A gray stage," Max Brewster said after a while. He shook his head. "Now, that's unlucky. The Indians say like black, gray is no color at all and it can betoken loss and sadness. There are some Arapaho, and Utes as well, who would rather freeze to death than use a gray army blanket. It disturbs the hell out of them."

"So, what are the other drivers saying?" Abbot said.

"I just left the Alamo saloon and it's all folks are talking about," Brewster said. "They're saying three drivers and three messengers shot dead and not a bullet hole to be found anywhere in the stage is mighty strange. I reckon that's why they're calling the coach the Gray Ghost. Some say it's haunted and it was the restless spirit of Phineas Doyle that drove it back here to the depot."

"That's foolish talk," Abbot said. "It's a coach like any other."

"No, sir, it's a coach like no other," Brewster said. "It's a death trap, just ask Frank Gordon and Mack Blair, Steve Tanner and Lone Wolf Ellis Bryant, and now Phineas Doyle and Dewey Wilcox."

"They're all dead," Abbot said, irritated. "I can't ask them anything."

"And they're all dead because of the Gray Ghost," Brewster said. "Long John, it was your last stage to El Paso. You ain't never gonna find another driver or shotgun guard to work for you."

Abbot watched as the undertaker and his assistant lowered the bodies from the seat of the coach, bloody corpses with blue faces, open eyes staring into nothingness. Phineas Doyle's gray beard was stained with blood and there was a wound that looked like a blossoming rose smack in the middle of Dewey Wilcox's forehead.

The undertaker, a sprightly skeleton dressed in a broadcloth suit with narrow pants and a black top hat tied around with a wide taffeta ribbon, the ends hanging over his skinny shoulders, laid the corpses on a flat wagon and then said, his voice like a creaky gate, "Same as the other four deceased, Mr. Abbot?"

"Yeah, Silas, board coffins but clean them fellers up nice for viewing," Abbot said. "The womenfolk like that."

"I'll take care of it," Silas Woods said. His eyes moved from Long John to the stage. "Gray," he said. "Now, that's unusual, a gray stage."

"I know," Abbot said.

"Gray as graveyard mist," the undertaker said. "Why gray?"

"A canceled order," Abbot said. "I was told it was originally destined for a count in Transylvania, a country in eastern Europe somewhere. The coach is worth eighteen hundred dollars and I got it for fourteen hundred."

"You didn't get yourself a bargain," Woods said. He shook his head. "No, sir."

Abbot watched the undertaker's wagon leave, drawn by a black mule. His great beak of a nose under arched black eyebrows gave Long John the look of a perpetually surprised owl. He turned and said to Brewster, "If I can't find a driver, I'm out twelve hundred dollars and out of business." He thought for a moment and said, "What about Buttons Muldoon?"

"He's working for Abe Patterson," Brewster said. "Muldoon's messenger is a young feller by the name of Red Ryan who's right handy with a gun and they say fear doesn't enter into his thinking. But I don't think those two will switch, and even if they did, they won't come cheap."

"All I can afford is cheap, the cheaper the better," Abbot said.

Brewster gave the man a long, speculative look and then said, "By the way, Abe Patterson is in town. He's over to his depot."

"What's that to me?" Abbot said.

Brewster smiled. "Long John, Patterson is made of money. Some folks say he's so rich he's got a half interest in the whole of creation."

"Made of money, huh?" Abbot said.

"Got a big, turreted mansion house up San Angelo way and a young, high-yeller wife to go along with it. A lively-stepping filly like that costs a man plenty and ol' Abe sure spends plenty on her."

Long John brightened. "Here . . . Max . . . you've given me an idea."

"I figured as much," Brewster said.

"Sure, Patterson is made of money. Like you said, everybody knows that. Hell, I can probably unload the stage. Abe won't pass up a bargain like that."

"How much, Long John?"

"How much what?"

"How much are you willing to take for the Gray Ghost?"

"I think maybe a thousand."

"Think again," Brewster said. "How much?"

"Nine hundred?" Abbot said, his face framing a question.

"Seven hundred and fifty and let him talk you down to seven hundred," Brewster said. "Abe will dicker and he's good at it."

"That's half what I paid for it," Abbot said. A thin whine.

Brewster smiled. "As the starving man said, *Half a pie is better than no pie at all.*"

Abbot thought that through and said finally, "You think Abe will go for it?"

"Damn right he will," Brewster said. "A sharp businessman like Abe Patterson won't pass up a new Concord stage for seven hundred dollars."

"Maybe he doesn't know it's a bad luck coach," Abbot said.

"Long John, the whole town knows, and you can bet so does Abe," Brewster said. "But he ain't the superstitious type and to him a bargain, even if it's on the creepy side, is still a bargain."

"I could go into another business with seven hundred dollars," Abbot said. "I always figured I could prosper in hardware."

"There you go, Long John, selling pots and pans is just the thing for a man like you. Help you make your mark in the world."

"Right, I'll go do a little hoss trading with Abe."

"Good luck, and don't let him get you under seven hundred, mind," Brewster said.

* * *

Long John Abbot poured another splash of whiskey into Abe Patterson's glass. "Abe, seven-fifty, and I can go no lower than that without starving my wife and children," he said. "Have a cigar."

Abe Patterson took a cigar from the proffered box and said, "I hope the cigar is better than your whiskey. And that wouldn't be difficult."

"Two-cent Cubans," Abbot said. "Top-notch." He passed on commenting on the busthead that he bought by the jug.

Patterson took his time lighting his cigar and behind a curtain of blue smoke said, "I'm thinking about it, Long John. Giving it my most serious consideration."

"Red leather seating, Abe," Abbot said. "Now, that's class. I mean, that's big city."

"What about the sign on the doors?" Patterson said. "Some kind of fancy letter *D*."

"Ah, the coach was a canceled order from some count in Transylvania . . ."

"Where?"

"Transylvania. It's a country in eastern Europe. I guess the gent's name began with a *D*."

"Davy? Donny? Deacon?"

"Something like that, I guess," Abbot said. "Them foreigners have strange notions and stranger names."

"Seven hundred," Patterson said. "I will go no higher. Hard times, Long John, with the railroads expanding an' all, laying rails all over the place and taking a big chunk of my business. I just don't have as much capital to invest as I once did."

Abbot pretended to consider Abe's offer for a moment and then jumped to his feet.

"Done and done," he said. He extended his hand to

Patterson, a feisty little banty rooster a foot smaller than himself. Abe took Abbot's hand and said, "Have some of your men push or pull the thing to my depot as soon as the blood is washed off the driver's seat. Then come over yourself and I'll pay you."

"I'm glad you don't believe all that loose talk about the stage being haunted and all," Abbot said.

Abe Patterson smiled. "If I did, I'd tell you to hitch up a team and have Phineas Doyle drive it over."

CHAPTER 2

"Phineas Doyle drove the stage back to the depot even though he was as dead as mutton," Patrick "Buttons" Muldoon said, his blue eyes as round as coins. "His ghost was standing over his shot-up body, the ribbons in his hands. Ol' Max Brewster says he seen that with his own two eyes and he says the coach was almost invisible, like a gray, graveyard mist."

"I don't believe it," Abe Patterson said.

"And Max says that letter *D* on the doors stands for death," Red Ryan said. "He says it must be a stage that carried the souls of the deceased and that's why Long John Abbot got it cheap."

"I don't believe it," Abe Patterson said.

"And, boss, you got it even cheaper, mind," Buttons said. He was dressed in a blue sailor coat decorated with two rows of silver buttons that gave him his name. He and Red Ryan had just arrived at the depot after a short mail run to Abilene and were mostly dust-free. "Boss, they call the stage the Gray Ghost and they say it's cursed," Buttons continued. "It's already been the death of six men and me and Red would make it eight."

"I don't believe it," Abe Patterson said.

Red Ryan said, "Max Brewster says that over to the Alamo saloon, Lonesome Edna Vincent, she's the redhead with the big . . ."

"I know who she is, and whatever she said, I don't believe it," Abe Patterson said.

"You haven't heard what I have to say yet," Red said. "Well, anyway, Max says that Edna says that she was asleep in her cot the very night the stage was delivered to Long John Abbot's depot. Then, when all the clocks in town chimed at the same time, saying that it was two in the morning, a loud and terrible scream woke her."

"I don't believe it," Abe Patterson said.

"Then Max says that Edna says she got up and looked out the window and then she heard the howls and wails of the damned coming from a gray coach. Max says that Edna says that the stage was rocking back and forth and seemed to be covered by an unholy blue fire. Max says that Edna says she got the fear of God in her and didn't get another wink of sleep all night."

Buttons said, arranging his features into an expression that passed for sincerity, "So, boss, after all them scary ha'ants you can savvy why me and Red can't drive the Gray Ghost. And now let us both thankee most whole-heartedly for your kindness, consideration, and under-standing."

"I don't believe it," Abe Patterson said. "I don't believe that two grown men would set store by such nonsense. Road agents and maybe Apaches done for Long John's men, not a curse."

"But, boss . . ." Buttons said.

Patterson held up a silencing hand. "No buts. Here's the situation. You already know, or maybe you don't, that the Apaches are out, a dozen renegades riding with the four half-breed Griffin brothers."

"I heard them Griffin breeds were hung by vigilantes up in the New Mexico Territory," Buttons said. "Didn't you hear that, Red?"

Red shook his head. "No, I can't say as I did. But folks don't tell me much."

"Seems that you heard wrong, Mr. Muldoon," Abe said. "A Texas Ranger by the name of Tom Wilson told me that five days ago the Griffins and the Apaches with them attacked a ranch house to the east of here, killed three men, and ran off with a couple of women. Wilson said he doubts that the women are still alive, but if they are, by now they'll be wishing they wasn't." Abe consulted his gold watch, snapped it shut, and said, "Ranger Wilson had more to tell. He told me no later than this morning that Powell left Fort Worth four days ago. Remember him? The local lawman wired that Powell has took to wearing an eye patch, and he swears that him and his boys are headed south."

"Or so the lawman says. Nobody's heard of Luke Powell in years," Red said.

Buttons said, "Who is he? I never heard of him until now. Maybe I was at sea at that time."

Red said, "It was before my time as a messenger, when I was still cowboying for Charlie Goodnight's JA Ranch up in the Panhandle, that Powell worked his protection racket, guaranteeing owners that their stages wouldn't be robbed if they paid up. He made some good money at it, too. But the last I heard he was an expensive hired assassin who squeezed cash or property from the marks to spare their lives. That way he got paid at both ends. But he suddenly dropped out of sight two or three years ago. Some say he fled abroad to escape the law, some say he found religion, so who knows what happened to him."

Abe waved his cigar and blue smoke curled in the air. "Maybe Luke Powell has returned to his old ways and he and his boys killed Doyle and Wilcox last night or this morning . . . or the Apaches did. The Apaches would do it for fun and Powell out of spite because the Abbot stage carries mail and never a strongbox. Well, I should say that it did carry mail. Long John told me he's quit the business and he's transferring the mail and his passengers to me."

"Powell was never known to be a road agent," Red said. "It's not his style."

Buttons snorted his disbelief. "Of course it wasn't Powell or Indians or anybody else. Everybody knows it was the Gray Ghost its own self that done for them six fellers."

"Mr. Muldoon, I don't wish to hear that again," Patterson said, frowning. "The coach is now with the Abe Patterson and Son Stage and Express Company and you will kindly refer to it as Number Seven. Do I make myself clear?"

"Why us?" Red Ryan said. "Boss, you've got other drivers and messengers."

"None of them as reliable as you and Mr. Muldoon," Patterson said. "That's the fact of the matter."

"And suppose we refuse?" Buttons said. His chin was set and stubborn and the buttons on his coat shone like newly minted silver dollars.

"Ah, if you refuse to work?" Abe rubbed his chin. Suddenly his eyes had all the warmth of shotgun muzzles. "Hmm . . . well, in that case, you'll be dismissed instanter. And you'll never work for an employer more caring of his men than me. That is, if you can find another situation in these hard times."

Abe Patterson saw Buttons's crestfallen look and his face softened a little. "Here, have a drink." He opened a desk drawer and produced a bottle of Old Crow and three glasses. He poured the whiskey and said, "I know how you men feel, and I don't have a heart of stone. Your maidenly fears have not gone unheeded, and that's why I've chosen an easy run just for you . . . five theater performers to Houston, passengers as genteel and gracious as they come. Drink up, boys."

"I'll be driving the Gray . . ."

"Careful, Mr. Muldoon. I don't want to hear that name ever again, remember?"

"Driving ol' Number Seven," Buttons said, his face glum.

"Yes, and she's a beauty, ain't she?" Patterson said, beaming. "Red leather upholstery and curtains, special-order thoroughbraces so it feels like you're riding on a cloud. She's a work of art, by God, and once you get used to her ways, you lucky boys will love her."

Despite the warm caress of the whiskey, Buttons was still in a funk. "Three hundred and fifty miles of nothing but grass," he said, "on a route I've traveled only a couple of times afore, plus Apaches, the Griffin brothers, and road agents takes a heap of loving."

"And that's exactly why I kept the Houston run for you and Mr. Ryan," Patterson said. "The Apaches and the Griffin boys are raising hell to the west of us so you'll be well away from those savages. And Luke Powell need not concern us. The Ranger said he stays close to towns, especially Fort Smith and New Orleans, where there's whiskey and whores and pilgrims to be fleeced. I can't see him crossing an empty prairie, even to get his revenge on Miss Erica Hall." Abe spread his hands. "I'll tell you about her later. Now, Mr. Muldoon, don't complain. It will be an easy run. The way is smooth and the weather is fair. It will be like taking a bunch of flowers to your favorite maiden aunt for her birthday." He smiled. "And you boys can see paddle steamers in the Houston canal. Now, that's worth the trip, don't you think?"

"If we get there alive," Buttons said. "If ol' Number Seven doesn't decide to do for us like it did to them others."

"Well"—Abe's smile was as sincere as the grin on a Louisiana alligator—"it's come down to this . . . You boys have a choice to make and I can only hope it's the right one."

"And that is?" Buttons said.

"Get on the stage or get fired. Think it over."

"We've thought it over," Red Ryan said.

"And?" Patterson said.

"We'll ride the stage," Red said.

Buttons looked at him aghast. "Are you out of your mind?" he said.

"Study on it," Red said. "Summer's almost over and winter will come down fast. We got a cozy enough berth here in San Angelo and don't need to be spending December with empty bellies riding the grub line."

"And here's a kicker, a real humdinger as they say up Montana way. A twenty-dollar bonus for each of you after you deliver your passengers safely to the Diamond music hall in Houston, where they expect to be hired in a heartbeat, and I reckon they will," Abe said. "So there it is, gentlemen, an extra double eagle each for a nice, easy drive in the late summer sun. Even if you were my own sons, my own flesh and blood, I couldn't say any fairer than that."

"We'll take it," Red said. "When do we start?"

Abe glared at Buttons. "You don't look too sure, Mr. Muldoon."

"All right, I'll drive the gray stage," Buttons said. "I'm not one to believe in ghosts and ha'ants an' stuff, but the first time it comes up with something spooky, I'll mount the passengers on the backs of the team and leave Number Seven right where it's at."

"It won't come to that pass," Abe said. "Trust me, you'll have a safe journey, I guarantee it. Now, let me read you the passenger list I got from Long John Abbot. Remember, these are all theater performers, what they call vaudeville artistes, so needless to say there will be no cussing, tobacco spitting, or crude jokes when you're around those nice people. Do I make myself clear?"

Red nodded, and Abe took that as a yes from both of the men. He balanced a pair of pince-nez spectacles at the end of his nose and read from a scrap of paper.

"As I said, all this is from Long John," Abe said. "He said the artistes came from Fort Worth to San Angelo on two different C. Bain and Company stages, and that Erica Hall is the main attraction. She's a fan dancer from England and by all accounts is a lovely lass."

"What's a fan dancer?" Buttons said. He was surly. He guessed fan dancing was another of those fancy, big-city notions that were steadily eating away at the already shaky foundations of the western frontier.

"According to Long John, Miss Hall dances naked around the stage with two Chinese fans, but she uses the fans to cleverly cover up her lady bits so nobody ever gets a glimpse," Abe said. He saw the puzzled expressions on

Buttons's and Red's faces, shrugged, and said, "That's what Long John told me. I've more to say about her, but I'll leave that till later. The other woman is a singer, goes by the name of Rosie Lee. Then there's the Great Stefano, a knife thrower, Paul Bone, a song and dance man, and Dean Rice, a juggler." Abe took off his spectacles and laid them on his desk. "All in all, an interesting group of people."

"Boss, you said there's more to tell about the dancer gal," Buttons said. "Does she ever drop them fans?"

"I don't know," Abe said. "Maybe at the end of her turn."

"I'd sure like to see that," Buttons said. "I reckon I've never seen the like before."

"Maybe she'll dance for you on the trail," Abe said. "Stranger things have happened."

"Hee-haw! Now, wouldn't that be something," Buttons said.

"Boss, what else were you aiming to tell us about her?" Red said. Something deep inside of him feared that this was news he really didn't want to hear. And he was right.

Abe Patterson thought for a while and then said, "All right, you boys are boogered enough and I figured I wouldn't tell you, but now I've studied on the right and wrong of the thing, my conscience won't allow it. One thing about Abe Patterson, he's always fair."

"Now you got me worried, boss," Red said. "Wring it out. Tell it slow and easy so we understand. Me and Buttons don't want any head scratching."

"Well, see, this is how it is, plain and simple," Abe said. "You know I told you that Luke Powell left Fort Worth with just one eye."

"Yeah, we know," Red said. "He's got a patch over it."

"Well, it seems that Miss Erica Hall made him that way," Abe said.

"What way?" Buttons said.

"The one-eyed way," Abe said. "Rosie Lee told Long John Abbot that Miss Hall took out one of Luke's eyes in Fort Smith with a hot curling iron. It was a quarrel over Luke cheating her out of some money and it turned violent. Rosie said it was Luke's shooting eye that got poked and he ran out of the hotel screaming in search of a doctor. Well, sir, Miss Hall packed a bag and wisely skedaddled on a C. Bain and Company stage that was just pulling out of town headed for San Angelo. Later Powell came back looking for her with a knife in his hand and only one eye in his head only to find that the bird had flown. Four days afterward, the other artistes talked with a driver who remembered the beautiful lady who boarded his stage at the last minute and the next day they fled in another C. Bain stage to San Angelo with all the luggage, most of it Miss Hall's."

"Luggage? Seems to me all she needed to pack was two fans," Buttons said. "Me and Red ain't boogered none by that story. It don't scare Red and me any."

"You ain't boogered because that ain't the scary part," Abe said. "The scary part is that chances are Luke Powell also talked to the same stage driver and by now he could know where Miss Hall is at. He's left Fort Worth, and Rosie Lee says he vowed to take both Miss Hall's eyes and kill all he finds with her."

"All he finds with her . . . You mean, like me and Buttons?" Red said.

"That's what he means, all right," Buttons said. "And kill all he finds with her . . . It ain't a friendly thing to say."

"I told you, and now I'll tell you again," Abe Patterson said, "Powell will stay close to settlements. You won't see hide nor hair of him between here and Houston, trust me on that. And besides, Houston has an excellent police force. I'm told twenty-two stalwart officers stand ready to uphold the law and protect the innocent." Abe sighed and rose to his feet. "See, you boys got nothing to worry about. Now, if you will excuse me, I got to talk to the bank about a business loan." He shook his head. "Hard times coming down, boys, hard times."